# FALLING SUNS

# FALLING SUNS

## A Psychological Thriller

### J.A. Corrigan

Published by Accent Press Ltd 2016

Paperback ISBN: 9781786152497
Ebook ISBN: 9781786152480

To Steve and Rhiannon, my little clan

There is no pain so great as the memory of joy in present grief.

Aeschylus

# CHAPTER ONE

*March 11th 2000*
*Sutton Coldfield, UK*

From the kitchen window I watched blond hair and a sliver of petrol-blue fabric move inside the garden studio. 'Joe,' I whispered.

The distinctive colour shifted again and I strained to see the Doctor Who motif embroidered on both of its ends.

But it wasn't Joe; it was Liam wearing our son's scarf.

'Big seller with the young'uns,' the shop assistant had said as she placed it in a bag. I knew Joe would use the scarf only occasionally, to please me. He hated things wrapped around his neck. It had become a joke between the three of us that Liam took to wearing the Doctor's scarf, 'waiting for Joe to get over his phobia'. I'd purchased it on a whim, and only because the colour perfectly matched the jumper I'd bought Joe three months before. For his seventh birthday.

The same jumper my son wore the last day I saw him.

And then the deluge of emptiness swallowed me again. Was Joe scared? Was he lonely? Missing his mum? And the other question, clawing its way to the surface, despite all my efforts to keep it buried: was he still alive? For long seconds paralysis settled and only noise from the landline brought me back. The caller was persistent, and, stirring myself, I picked up.

'Rachel?'

I recognised the voice and relaxed. 'Hello, Charlotte.'

'How are you, lovely? And Liam?'

'We're not good.'

'I know – is he there?'

'In the den … studio. Avoiding me.'

Charlotte cleared her throat. 'Have you heard anything?'

'Some news. We'll know later today, hopefully. I'll call you when we find out.'

'You two need to carry on talking. I know what you're like, known you long enough. You have to open up. You can't hold it all in.' She paused. 'Are you sure it's not you avoiding Liam?'

I remained silent. I was avoiding him as much as I could.

'Is there something else?' she probed, anxiety in her voice.

'Christ, what else could there be?'

'Sorry. Nothing else.'

'It's OK.' I circled the kitchen three times with the phone lodged between my chin and neck, ending up back next to the sink and gazing into the garden. 'He thinks we'll find Joe.'

'You will find Joe.'

'I know the scenario. It was my job, remember?'

'Look, I'll come over tomorrow. Sort you both out.' Her laugh was brittle.

'Don't worry about me, I'll be fine.'

Charlotte didn't answer immediately. And I knew, or I thought I knew, what she was thinking. You are so not fine. I would tell her about Liam when I saw her.

2

I had to tell someone.

'Get out of the house, if only for a few hours,' she said finally.

Looking through the window, I watched him closing the door of the den. 'I've got to go, Liam's on his way up the garden.'

'Good. Talk to each other.'

I watched Liam's careful movements as he negotiated the slippery decking. We hadn't spoken properly for weeks, since long before Joe had gone missing: only argued. Rather than come inside he began sweeping the wooden floor of the patio. Staring past him I watched the Judas tree sway in the wind, its buds ready to open.

Liam went about his task vigorously. It was the way he was dealing with this. Keeping busy.

Many times in my former job I saw how people reacted so differently in tragic situations. Liam's grief manifested itself in putting rubbish out for the refuse collectors, opening blinds to welcome another horrendous morning, sweeping the decking. In a few terrible days we'd managed a complete role reversal. To deal with Joe's disappearance, my husband became tormented with the details of a domestic life in which previously he'd been utterly uninterested. My suspicions about him seeing another woman had become inconsequential.

Waiting for Liam to come inside I sat down and pretended to read a magazine, rubbing the inflamed skin on my hand. It always bothered me more when agitated. Old scald scars were the worst; the GP had said long ago. Today mine were scarlet, and painful.

My eyes drifted away towards the fridge, and, like every other family's fridge in the western world, it was covered in a child's paintings. Joe's paintings. The last one he'd brought home took centre stage. It was a bright red and orange sunset. Or, I should say, 'sunsets'. Three suns of differing sizes were painted cleverly, seeping into Joe's horizon. Liam had said it was a mini masterpiece, proud that his son was showing the same artistic leanings as himself. Joe's teacher had given him three house points for the 'unusual' picture. I'd given Joe a big cuddle and a promise to visit the nearest theme park. I bought the tickets the same day. My eyes settled on the calendar hooked onto the right side of the same fridge. Today was supposed to be our day at the theme park, and the disbelief at what was happening pooled around me like uncontained mercury.

Would I ever go to a theme park again? Would we add more paintings to the fridge? I searched for hope, for understanding, for an answer.

Last night my old boss, Tom Gillespie, who was leading Joe's case, had attempted to skew the statistics. As if giving a different slant on a list of numbers could give me hope. He'd tried hard to say something positive, as he would have done easily with any other victim's mother, but I wasn't convinced, and neither was he. I saw it in his eyes.

'Are you staying home today?' Liam's voice was tight and weary.

I hadn't heard him come through the patio door. His honey-coloured hair was uncharacteristically unkempt and tufts jutted out from the top his head. His deep blue eyes seemed sunken and the skin taut over high, triangular cheekbones. He'd been nowhere the past week, only to see Tom. I knew he hadn't seen *her*, whoever she was. Now, I didn't care about her and I suspected Liam didn't either.

'I guess so,' I said, noticing the stubble that was growing into a beard. It had taken six days to transform

4

him. He wasn't wearing Joe's scarf, and had probably left it in the den. 'Still reporters camped out at the bottom of the street. Tom managed to move them from the front of the house.'

'I know. That's good,' Liam said.

'I wish they'd piss off.'

He stood behind me and rubbed what felt like tangled metal wires in my shoulder muscles. 'They're just doing a job.'

I pushed his hand away. 'I know.' Turning my head, I looked up at him. 'How's the new painting going?'

'It's not.'

'You shouldn't be working.' I said it automatically; Liam would work and paint through a nuclear holocaust.

'We have to talk,' Liam said.

'About Joe?' I watched the face of a man I'd loved since my twentieth birthday and forgot, for a moment, the other woman inside our marriage.

'Of course about Joe. We'll find our son. You have to believe it.'

He pulled me towards him and I resisted.

'I know that's what you want to believe. But we have to face the truth,' I said.

He let go of me. 'You deal with it your way, and I have to deal with it in mine.'

'Liam ...' We did have to talk, and not about Joe.

He was already heading towards the patio door. I wanted to tell him I still loved him, but could not. It would help him. But not me.

'I love you,' he said.

Liam returned to his den.

As I spooned coffee into the filter machine, my breathing became shallow and too quick. I listened to the grumbling of my empty stomach. How could I be hungry?

My son was God knows where and my body told me it needed food. I pushed my fist into the flesh beneath my protruding ribs, pressing hard until it hurt. I stood doing nothing for long minutes, not wanting to feel the sickening hunger. I wanted to feel nothing.

I picked up the jug of freshly brewed coffee and threw it onto the floor. Liquid and shards of glass covered the kitchen and, as a strong smell of Arabica diffused through the room, I finally felt some sort of relief. But it was short-lived. I sank onto the cold tiles, into the pool of coffee, and watched as Joe's picture fell downwards, like a leaf floating from an autumn tree. I wanted to catch it, save it, save Joe, but I could do nothing.

Only watch the falling suns.

# CHAPTER TWO

I'd finally moved from the floor, cleaned up and carefully attached the picture back from where it had fallen. I'd even managed to sleep for a couple of hours on the sofa.

My eyes moved towards the calendar, noticing the 5 p.m. slot I'd ringed in red to remind me of Jonathan's visit.

Liam had gone out, but must have checked on me before leaving: he'd placed a blanket over my legs, knowing they got cold when I slept, no matter what the temperature was. It wasn't something he would normally think of doing, although Joe would, and had done often, when I nodded off while watching CBeebies with him.

A pain that was never far away crept back into my body masquerading as hunger. It was hunger. Hunger for my son. I got up, and hoped movement would stop the grotesque pain. My stomach continued to rumble. I went into the kitchen and pulled out a packet of Doritos from the cupboard. I never ate them; they were Joe's weekend treat. I put them back. For when he came home.

The jovial-sounding doorbell chimed and my heart wavered. I ran to the lounge and looked through the window, dreading the sight of Tom Gillespie with a female officer. Tom alone was safe. It meant I could still hope for Joe's case to be different, for him to be alive somewhere.

It wasn't Tom with a female PC, or Tom alone. It was Jonathan. I glanced at the clock; it was later than I'd thought. Exactly five. Always on time. Always reliable. He was one of the journalists covering our story, but I trusted him. He'd shown his loyalty and integrity on many occasions, including with the 'Asian Bride' story: a case that seemed a lifetime ago. My feelings for Jonathan went further than merely professional, and I found myself wanting to talk to him in a way I knew I couldn't talk to Liam.

Liam: how long could we remain living under the same roof? Unable to speak to each other; unable to look each other in the eye. Our unspoken dialogue found its roots in the unspeakable future I saw but Liam denied.

I ran fingers through my greasy ponytail and answered the door.

'Hello, Rachel.' I watched Jonathan scrutinising my hair, my face. His concern travelled much deeper than that of a colleague. 'Is it OK for today? I can leave, come back tomorrow – if that suits you better?'

His look of disquiet made the hunger worse. He was a natural optimist, and any sign of his muted pessimism would send me hurtling to the place I was trying to avoid. I continued looking at his features, attempting to read them. Did I see pity? Worse than pessimism was pity.

'No, it's fine. I've just woken up.'

He nodded. 'Sleep's good.'

'Come in.' I stepped away from the door, but not before peering down the street.

'They won't bother you,' he said.

'I know. It's too fucking sad, isn't it? Even for hardened journos.'

'Thanks for agreeing to see me.' He touched the hotness on my scarred hand.

'You're my friend.'

'Shall we go and sit down?' he said, raising one thick eyebrow, a gesture I'd come to know as his preamble to journalistic questioning.

'Let's go in the garden. Leave your coat on. It's chilly.'

I observed as he buttoned up his insubstantial jacket then pulled at its hem to straighten it up. A coat totally unsuitable for the temperature, but it was 'designer'.

'Coat looks good.' I nearly smiled.

He half-grinned.

'Coffee?' I asked. 'I only have instant though: I dropped the cafetière.'

'Be good.'

We picked up the drinks and made our way outside through the kitchen. I gave Jonathan my mug and mopped up the film of last night's rain from two chairs.

Jonathan looked towards the bottom of the garden. 'Is Liam here?'

'No, he's gone out.' I moved closer and took one of the mugs from him. 'How's Michelle?'

He put his mug down and pulled his jacket tighter around his body, raking a hand through thick, wavy black hair. 'She's OK. Our relationship's not that great, but that's another story.'

'I'm sorry.'

'It's fine. Marriages have ups and they have downs.'

He touched my arm, his eyes expressive, kind and enquiring. 'Do you want to talk?'

'About Joe?'

'I've come to see you as a friend.'

'I know you have.'

'You look terrible.'

'I know that, too.'

'Are you and Liam OK?'

'No, not really.'

'Does Gillespie have any real leads?'

'No, not really.' For a moment I allowed something to give. 'What am I going to do?'

What was I going to do? I couldn't live without Joe, couldn't function without him. I wanted to smell my son. I wanted to put my nose in his hair and smell his cleanness, the toffee popcorn.

'They'll find Joe,' Jonathan said quietly. 'I know they will. Not all cases end badly.' He looked at me hard. 'Not all yours ended the way you were anticipating. What's happened to positive Rachel, the woman who doesn't give up? You shouldn't be here, alone. What about your family … your mum, your dad?'

I laughed at that one. My mother, my dad had told me –as gently as he could – wasn't coping very well. She wasn't coping very well walled up in her pristinely clean semi-detached house.

I could see her. Hair coiffured and backcombed into a high bun. Lipstick perfectly pencilled onto thinning lips. One of her regulation plain white blouses buttoned high towards her ageing neck, getting ready to go to church. Not worrying about me, or indeed her grandson, but about how all this would affect her standing in a community that she shunned as not being good enough for her.

My mother, even now, resented what I'd chosen to do as a career, and she was ashamed that an ex-police officer could be stupid enough to 'lose' her child. She was disconnected from the reality of life, and this detachment had always been left unchecked by my father's emotional weakness.

Joe's disappearance was an inconvenience for my mother. She blamed me. And it was the only time in my entire life that I admitted she was right.

I thought back to a conversation I'd had with my dad, just before Joe's disappearance. It had been after I'd left Joe with my parents for the day, which, in itself, was an unusual occurrence. I'd never leave Joe alone with my mother, and so it had to be a weekend when Dad wasn't working. I'd left Joe on a Saturday. When I'd picked him up, later that evening, Dad had mumbled something about a visitor who'd upset my mother. I was only vaguely interested in who the visitor had been, and cross that my dad was still worried about how the world, and people in the world, might upset Margaret. He'd tried to tell me more, and I'd cut him short.

But it was always like that in conversations about my mother with Dad. Things half said; things never said. Secrets hiding in every corner of our house. The three of us talking but not really talking; all of us pretending we were a normal family. But we weren't a normal family; I knew that when I visited my friends. I knew there was something wrong.

'You know how I feel about my mother,' I said finally.

Jonathan nodded. 'And your dad?'

'He's looking after her. That's the way it's always been.'

'Being alone isn't good.' His eyes wandered towards the end of the garden. 'You're acting… '

'Out of character? I have no character now. Whoever I was has gone, and she'll only return if Joe does.'

'When Joe returns. It's not over until…'

Again, I searched his face looking for optimism, but despite what he was saying, it was hard to find. 'Until what? Until they find Joe's body?'

Satisfaction at seeing another's discomfort soothed my guilty soul for a few seconds. It was my fault for arguing with Liam in front of Joe; my fault for wanting to go back to work. My fault that Joe had run away.

'There's something else, isn't there?' he said.

I picked up my coffee and sipped, burning my tongue. Pain from the blister that was already forming inside my mouth gave me comfort. Perhaps if I felt pain, Joe would be safe. 'How do you know so much?'

'I don't, I'm guessing. I've spoken with some of the PCs who are involved with Joe's case. They're surprised.'

'Surprised?'

'That you've been ... "meek".'

'For Christ's sake. I stopped being a detective seven years ago. Joe is my son. Tom and his team are doing all they can.'

Jonathan leaned towards me. 'I know, but your reaction to the investigation is out of character.'

I pulled my knees towards my chin and held them tight, resting my heels on the edge of the seat. My wedding ring glinted in the last strand of sun. 'I want to tell you something. I have to tell someone.' He moved his chair nearer. 'This is off the record, right?'

'You know.'

'The day Joe went missing he was at his friend's house. Melanie, Ben's mother, we take ... took it in turns on Wednesdays, you know, reciprocal.'

'But I know all this, Rachel.'

'Stay with me, please. Mel picks Ben and Joe up from school and takes them to hers for tea. Joe walks home alone afterwards – gives him independence, you know? I was always so worried that because of the job I'd done, I'd be too protective with Joe – a boy. He's ... was ... sensitive. Liam's sensitive. I wanted Joe to be independent ... stronger.'

'Stop using the past tense.'

My shoulders slumped forwards, and I nodded forlornly.

'That Wednesday, I had a meeting with Tom Gillespie, to talk about me going back to work. I forgot to remind Liam I'd be back late. He didn't know I was meeting Tom. He would've been angry: perhaps that's why I forgot to remind him. I'd told him the day before though, that I'd be late, but he's got a terrible memory when he's painting, working. Liam's car was here; Joe would have thought Liam was home.'

'He would have thought that.'

'As you know, that day Joe didn't walk home alone. Melanie walked with him. Chloe, her youngest, had swallowed one of Ben's toy soldiers, well, the soldier's hat actually.' I smiled sadly at the detail. 'Chloe was OK, but Melanie wanted to take her to the doctor – just to make sure. She walked with the boys and Chloe, dropping Joe on the way. I'm guessing that when Joe found no one was home, he didn't tell Melanie: he wouldn't have wanted to trudge to the doctors with her. Besides, Melanie would've been distracted; she was distracted. She told the police ... Tom ... that she hurried on to the surgery as soon as Joe reached the door. She didn't actually see him go in. She feels so bad about it.'

I glanced at him, carrying on, 'Joe knows where Liam keeps the key to his den, underneath an old plant pot.' My eyes wandered to the bottom of the garden. 'You know what boys are like with "dens". And Joe loved ... loves his dad's.' I rotated my wedding ring around my finger, making the skin a furious red, matching the vermilion colour of the scar that was now on fire. 'Joe was upset when I dropped him at school that morning. I should have come home on time. I should have remembered to remind Liam. I'm so stupid.'

'Nothing's been said about Joe being upset; that's one of the reasons why his disappearance is such a mystery. Gillespie's assuming Joe went off for a walk, waiting for his mum and dad to come home. Joe would have known you wouldn't be long in arriving, he's a sensible boy.' Jonathan touched my knee lightly. 'Why do you think Joe was upset?' He asked the question quietly; the journalist in him knowing instinctively that important information was coming.

'Liam and I have been arguing a lot. About a lot of things. He didn't want me to go back to the force in the same capacity, he wanted me to carry on staying at home, be a proper mum. He couldn't understand why I wanted to go back to work. You know what Liam's like, obstinate when he thinks he's right.'

'I do know what Liam's like.'

When we'd worked together in the past, I'd made a point of not talking too much about Liam to Jonathan, but he'd never liked the sound of my husband, and after meeting him, liked him even less. I knew Jonathan's feelings for me went deeper than they should. And my feelings for him were ones I had always buried. I was married. I had a child.

'There's something I need to get out, tell someone,' I said.

He moved closer. 'Go on.'

'I think Liam's having an affair.'

'Christ, Rachel…'

'I think that's where he was the day he should have been here.' I faltered, 'But he didn't know he had to be here for when Joe returned … because I forgot to tell him.'

'This is not your fault. Liam forgot.'

'I should have been here. He categorically denies

having an affair, even though it's obvious he is. But as well as arguing about that, we were also having words about me going back to work. Joe had been listening to us at each other's throats for weeks. And that morning's argument was particularly intense. When Joe came home that day I think he was still upset.'

'Do you have any evidence that Liam's playing away?' Jonathan wavered. 'And who with?'

'No hard evidence. But I'm certain that's where he was that day. With her. And no, I don't know who it is.'

'You know how these cases work. The more the police know about the emotional background of the missing child, the better.' He smiled dimly. 'And you might have the wrong idea regarding Liam?'

'It doesn't matter now.' For the thousandth time I ran through the events of the day Joe disappeared. 'I got home soon after Liam had returned from the walk he said he'd been for. He said he was struggling with the painting he was working on, needed air. He'd thought Joe was still with Melanie. Melanie had popped into ours on her way back from the doctors. And that was when I stepped through the front door. When my life fell apart. Melanie told us Joe had come home, that she thought Liam was in the house. I'd thought then that Liam would be angry with me for not reminding him to stay home, but he wasn't, he seemed distracted. Of course he was distracted. Our son had disappeared. Off the face of the earth.'

'You've said nothing to Gillespie about Liam?' Jonathan's brow was tight.

'No. My head was all over the place. All I could think about was Joe: where he was, and how guilty I felt for both Liam and I. What appalling parents we are … were.' I looked towards the Judas tree. 'I thought we'd find Joe. I thought Tom would find him, Jonathan.' I rubbed my stomach, remembering Joe had once lain there.

His brow puckered. 'Do you think Joe went to the den after Melanie dropped him off?'

'Liam said no. The key hadn't been used. He always knows. But Tom's gone through all this. He just doesn't know about the arguing, me suspecting Liam's having an affair.'

'It's irrelevant whether Liam's having an affair or not; what's important is that Gillespie and his team know that Joe was in a fragile state of mind.'

The hunger that had been gathering inside my body while telling Jonathan the facts was now unprecedented – like a thousand knives stabbing. I felt the roaring of grief and guilt, a real sound inside my head. I felt my breathing becoming faster; I choked for air, and, bending forwards, I thought that maybe in the garden, near to the Judas tree, in front of Jonathan, I would die.

Jonathan moved towards me, gently guiding my head downwards to my knees and, slowly, my breathing calmed.

'Thank you,' I said. 'I needed to talk it through.'

'I wish you'd told me before – but now – we have to move forwards. Promise me you and Liam will tell Gillespie?'

I nodded. For the first time in six days a tiny fragment of direction settled within me. 'Have you interviewed any of my family yet?'

'I saw your mum and dad a couple of days ago.' He smiled. 'I think I can see why you don't get on with your mother. Our conversation was short. Surprised she let me in the house.' He pulled at his jacket. 'Your dad could hardly speak.'

'He loved Joe.'

'He loves Joe.'

'Yes,' I said, watching him.

If Jonathan thought there was a chance for Joe; if Liam thought there was chance for Joe, then why couldn't I have this thought? Were both men deluding themselves, and me? I searched his face looking for signs of an untruth, and saw none. He believed what he said. And I tried to believe him.

'I visited Sam and Bridget, too.'

'How were they?'

'Upset, distressed.' He looked at me. 'I asked about their son, Michael. I remember you mentioning him. Lives up north now, Chester? Bridget says she hasn't seen him for more than two years.'

'She wasn't the best mother, difficult for her, I'd imagine.' I did remember telling Jonathan about Michael Hemmings. I'd probably told him more than anyone about my cousin and my childhood, including Liam. Jonathan had always been someone I could confide in and trust. Someone I felt comfortable with.

'Yes, from what you said, he was an oddball,' he said.

'I like Sam and Bridget, though. I paused. 'But Michael ...'

Snatches of memory – me coming home from school and Michael Hemmings getting ready to leave. Mad Michael, I'd called him. His visits always happened when Dad was away, or so it seemed to me, and when I was out the house. I didn't like him, never had. I tried to tell Dad about the visits, but that was another of those half-spoken conversations, going nowhere.

Jonathan and I spent another half hour recounting the facts that we knew about the case, both deciding that something had to happen soon. He was back to being a journalist and, briefly, I became the person I had once been: a police officer. As we talked about leads, the media and investigative techniques for a few moments, I stopped feeling the savage hunger that had begun the day Joe disappeared.

Jonathan made to leave, and a sense of something grabbed at me. It was the look of concern that covered his features, a look that travelled beyond friendship and professional camaraderie.

I watched him walk to the other end of the street, towards the alley that led to open fields, and I knew he would soon go back to being a reporter, getting a feel for the scene.

Police were still combing the expanse of land.

Although I'd told Jonathan everything about what had happened the day Joe went missing, I hadn't told him what Tom had told Liam and I the previous night. I didn't want to jinx any news, any developments.

Tom and his officers had found numerous cigarette butts in the nearby fields. It was a known place for men to meet up and, sometimes, women too. I'd heard this when I attended the neighbourhood meetings. They were petitioning for lighting and patrols along the land that had been attracting 'unwanted, indecent behaviour'. The more recent butts had been taken away for analysis and the DNA was being matched up against offenders in the area.

Suddenly I realised where Liam had gone; the prescribed drugs were taking their toll on my reasoning. Liam and I had arranged to go to the station to see Tom, who'd said the results from the DNA tests would be available later in the day. Liam had gone early.

Re-scraping my hair into a ponytail, I called the PC who'd been assigned to me, asking him if he would take me to the station to see Tom Gillespie.

I was there in half an hour.

# CHAPTER THREE

It had been a long while since I'd sat in Tom Gillespie's office. The last time I'd seen him, on the day Joe went missing, we'd met informally in the pub to talk about me returning to work. In the years since giving up my job, after having Joe, we nearly always met in this pub, near to the police station, or sometimes at his home where Rosie Gillespie cooked Liam, Joe and I the most amazing Sunday roasts.

Liam was sitting on the corner of Tom's desk. Tom sat behind, perched on the edge of his chair. Liam had combed his hair but looked tired and agonised.

I walked towards Liam and he held his arms out like a blue-eyed bear. It was the first proper embrace we'd shared for weeks.

'You should have called me,' I said.

'I wanted you to sleep,' Liam replied.

'How are you?' Tom said.

'Crap,' I said.

'I'm sorry, Rachel, but I haven't got the results back from the lab yet. They're still working on it. I think that we'll find something, though,' Tom said.

'Something I don't know about?'

'Yes – only came to light this afternoon.' Tom threw a look towards Liam.

'You can tell me, you know, I am Joe's mother.'

'Calm down,' Tom said, 'I am going to tell you. Sit

down.' He chewed his thumbnail. Rosie was always telling him off about it. Liam and I used to laugh at her scolding. 'Someone's come forwards.'

'Who?'

'The day Joe disappeared, Rachel, was he upset? We've spoken to Melanie on three occasions and she said Joe was fine when she dropped him at home.'

'We've been arguing a lot recently,' Liam said, looking at me. 'Joe heard. He could have been upset.' Liam's eyes dropped downwards towards the carpet.

I looked at Tom pleadingly. 'Liam and I are … were having a few problems. Tell me what you know about Joe. Please.'

'The man who's come forwards, he's a regular "punter" on the field near your house. There most weekends, trawling for sex. He didn't come forwards before, for obvious reasons. But, in fairness, he's been out of the country since this all broke – got back yesterday. He's a businessman.' Tom allowed himself a skinny smile. 'He had a positive sighting of Joe. Described what he was wearing, everything. Petrol blue jumper, jeans, black trainers. He said the boy was upset. The man, Gareth Summers, isn't normally on the field, or, should I say, in the bushes, on a weekday. But that Wednesday he'd arranged to meet a "newie" in the area. He met the "newie" and they did have sex.'

'Did Summers speak to Joe? See anyone with Joe?'

'Yes, as weird as it seems, Summers, our only witness, asked Joe if he was all right. Apparently, so Summers tells us, Joe wasn't crying then, but it was obvious that he had been. Summers told Joe to go home … Joe didn't, and carried on across the field; it would have been getting dark at that time of day. Summers began to follow Joe, to encourage him to go home, but then he saw someone in

20

the distance, and Joe run towards that someone. Joe seemed OK to go with the someone.' Tom paused. 'Summers later said the someone was the same man he'd had sex with earlier in the evening.'

'Do we know the name of the man Summers had sex with?'

Tom nodded. Liam was watching me closely.

'The guy told Summers, after the sex, that he lives up north. Chester.'

And then my heart plunged downwards.

'Michael Hemmings?' I said quietly.

Tom nodded.

'Have you sent anyone up there?' The strange hunger returned. Tom knew about my cousin, Michael Hemmings, and his criminal record.

'Yes, I have.' Tom put his arm around my shoulder. 'He's not at his flat in Chester, hasn't been seen for over two weeks.'

I tasted sick in the back of my mouth, and felt contractions inside my stomach. I rushed over to where Tom kept his wastepaper bin and emptied the small amount of food that was in my gut into it; and then felt Liam's hand on my back.

An hour later, and still cocooned inside Tom's office, the results for the DNA analysis came through.

The evidence was conclusive, placing Hemmings on the field where Joe was last seen.

I didn't sleep that night. Distorted images travelled in infinite circles inside my head. Mostly, the images were of Michael Hemmings: mosaic, kaleidoscopic-flash depictions of him in our house, always about to leave, when I got home from school.

Sweat saturated my side of the bed. I'd put a T-shirt on

to sleep in; it had been freezing in the night. The drop in temperature mirrored the feeling inside my body. Nothing mattered anymore. Only Joe.

When I got up and made my way to the bathroom I saw a razor blade sitting awkwardly on the sink. It would be so easy. I thought about taking the pills that were nestled in the bathroom cabinet, knowing that swallowing the whole packet would stop my breathing. Yet the part of me who was Rachel, the mother, Rachel, the police officer, realised that suicide wasn't an option. Not yet.

Standing in the cold bathroom, I knew. I felt it. A visceral knowledge to which only a mother has access.

It was the first time I'd smelt toffee popcorn since my son had gone. And I knew Joe was dead.

As I opened the cabinet, a silent scream came from my lips; I emptied several of the pills into the palm of my hand, hoping they would quieten the deadened howl that would not leave me.

*The day after: 7.30 a.m.*

I saw the tall form of Tom Gillespie passing my kitchen window. A female PC followed closely behind. I heard the quiet knock on the door, and like the falling suns from the fridge my heart fell in my chest as if it was escaping my body. My throat constricted and, for too long, I didn't take a breath.

'Rachel…'

Liam's haggard face hovered centimetres from mine. Tom's haunted countenance wasn't far away.

'I don't want to know,' I said. Although I already knew.

'I'll call the doctor. She needs something to calm her

down.' I heard the policewoman whisper.

I closed my eyes. They thought I couldn't cope with the news, and I could not. Only the thought of a far-off retribution stopped me from trying to join my son and take care of him at his last destination. Be with him through the end.

Tom Gillespie told me about my beautiful Joe, how he died. I didn't want to hear, but I had to know. And I listened.

*13th March 2000*

What could I have done to change Joe's destiny? My eyes were closed, but that did nothing to shut off the voices that rattled ceaselessly inside my head. What if Liam and I had told Tom immediately about our violent arguments and their effects on our son? This was my driving thought, but then other variables came to mind – like the very real and disturbed history of my cousin, Michael Hemmings. I'd done everything possible to ensure Joe had little contact with him.

When Michael Hemmings moved away to Chester, I'd been relieved. The only time I'd set eyes on him since then was more than three years ago, on a visit to see my uncle Sam and aunt Bridget. If I'd known Hemmings would be there I'd have stayed away. In the end Joe and I stayed less than an hour.

My mind made its way down the narrow and convoluted lanes of memory, trying to work out if anything had happened that I might have missed during that visit. Nothing came to mind. Hemmings had practically ignored Joe.

I heard the shower start upstairs and then heavy

footsteps as Liam moved around the bathroom. I don't think he had slept either, but I wasn't sure as I'd given up pretending to sleep and made my prison on the sofa.

Tom was picking us up at eight-thirty. I looked at Joe's suns. He should be sitting here with me, discussing his favourite ride. Gently, I took the painting down and began rolling it up.

'That's quick.'

I hadn't heard Liam. His deep voice held a new edge.

'For now, Liam. I have to.'

He nodded and pulled the towel tighter across his hips.

'You don't have to come. Why don't you let me go ... alone?' He moved closer and took the rolled-up painting from hands that would not stop shaking. 'It would be better.'

'I have to go.'

He stared at me. 'I know.'

So, instead of sitting at the kitchen table and talking to Joe about our trip to the theme park, at nine-fifteen, surrounded by too many policemen, I stood outside the room that held Joe.

I still didn't believe it. The body lying inside couldn't be Joe's. But I was lying to myself. I knew, and this knowledge took away my breath, seemed to take away my senses. I didn't feel the coolness of the wind, I didn't smell the antiseptic aroma that lurked outside the building; I didn't register the pitying expressions of those around me. I took my hand from my pocket and wasn't surprised at the blood on my palm, smearing onto the lining of my coat. My nails were pressing so hard into numb skin.

How many times in the faraway past had I stood in this same spot with a distraught and desolate parent? Dreading their reactions, watching their faces as they entered the disinfectant-smelling room to identify the body of their loved one, sometimes a child; the reality hit so hard they would freeze, unable to utter a word. I was the officer who accompanied those relatives and my empathy, I'd thought, was real and strong. I'd told myself that I understood their pain; the corkscrew of grief as it burrowed deep beneath their skin, unasked for and unwanted.

I realised now that I had not. And if I had, the job I'd once done would have been impossible.

As Liam and I waited for the mortuary assistant to pull away the plastic, I realised how worthless the empathy I'd tried to show had been. The assistant revealed Joe's face. His skin was pale and white like Pentelic marble. As I looked at my son, Joe, my angel, my beautiful boy, I acknowledged of all those past parents: I had understood nothing.

What had they done to make Joe look so peaceful?

Then again, I didn't know what the rest of Joe's body looked like.

As I kissed my dead son my own torment was raw, yet outside the morgue I could feel the grief of all those other parents. It multiplied and overtook me. I felt my insides contracting, as if my gut were desiccating.

I was engulfed in grief, inhabiting my own personal purgatory.

# CHAPTER FOUR

The trial began at the beginning of December. There was no question that Michael Hemmings would be put away.

After locating Joe's body, the police had received a call from Hemmings. Tom and his team found Michael, in a pool of blood, in the squat he'd been staying in since returning to Sutton Coldfield. He had a mobile next to him. Hemmings had made a half-hearted cut to his right femoral artery. Later, in hospital, he'd admitted to Joe's murder.

He wanted to be found, didn't want to die; I knew that, but the defending barrister managed to twist the facts and walk all over Tom. I'd never seen my old boss get truly angry, but he did the day Hemmings' barrister questioned him.

Afterwards, Tom's chewed thumb bled and I saw that his heart was breaking in sympathy with my own. I knew, as did Tom, that Hemmings' attempted suicide was all part of a plan: to be diagnosed with a psychiatric disorder. His barrister was aiming for 'diminished responsibility', and a diagnosis that the disorder was treatable, hoping for a conviction of manslaughter. And, if Michael Hemmings was deemed treatable, he would be admitted into a secure psychiatric hospital.

That was my worst-case scenario. And Hemmings' best. The prosecution fought hard on a charge of premeditated murder, to see him sent to a Category-A prison, arguing that Hemmings had known exactly what he was doing when he abducted and then killed my son with a frenzied knife wound across Joe's throat.

I thought of the scarf and Joe's terror of having things wrapped around his neck, and tried to stop myself from crying in front of Hemmings. I wouldn't give him that satisfaction. Although I did cry, silently, inside.

I'd always known what sort of person my cousin was. What I hadn't known was that two years previously he'd been admitted to a mental health ward in Chester. It came out in court that a leading psychiatrist in Chester had recommended that Michael Hemmings be detained for longer for further assessment. However, this psychiatrist was taken ill, his recommendation lost or ignored, and Michael Hemmings was allowed to leave.

The judge adjourned the court soon after this revelation, at the request of Hemmings' barrister. Later our barrister would argue that when Hemmings' mental state was questioned two years previously he had fought against being sectioned, so it was curious to find him now embracing detention within a psychiatric institution. Our barrister argued that the defendant was entirely aware of the advantage of being sent to a psychiatric institution now that he was on trial for murder.

Hemmings' barrister argued against us effectively and, to her credit, she was good.

We were into day ten of the trial. Liam and I were sitting in the small room we'd managed to find, away from the prying eyes of the public, surrounded by much of the cleaning stuff for the courtroom. A stale smell of cigarettes hung in the air. We'd been in there a few times and I felt oddly safe inside its dirty walls. It seemed like a place that shouldn't exist within the court building. That was why I liked it. We perched on the two available chairs and drank watery coffee; the silence between us like white noise. That's how it had been for months, in between the arguments.

'I have to go to the Ladies,' I said.

Liam nodded, sipped his coffee, put the Styrofoam cup on the grubby floor, and then placed his head between his knees.

'Won't be long,' I said. He didn't reply.

My uncle, Sam Hemmings, was sitting on the bench outside the courtroom, in exactly the same position in which I'd left Liam. I hovered and he looked up. I wasn't sure if his face registered surprise or relief that I had stopped in front of him. We hadn't spoken since the beginning of the trial.

'Hi Sam,' I said.

'Hullo, Rachel.' He straightened up on the uncomfortable-looking bench. 'I'm so sorry.'

'It's not your fault … what your son is.'

'It is though, isn't it? Mine and Bridget's.'

'It's not your fault,' I repeated.

'She won't come.'

I bent forwards; I could hardly hear him.

'Bridget, she won't come to court, says it's too much for her.' He wiped a droplet of sweat from his temple. 'Too much…'

I wanted to reach out to him, but I couldn't. There was nothing left inside. I went to touch his shoulder but stopped short. Sam held out an arthritic hand that had kneaded too much dough in the bakery he owned. Automatically, I flinched.

He looked up at me. 'So sorry.'

Any reply lodged resolutely in my throat and I made my way to the Ladies.

—

As I returned, the court usher called us back in. Liam had emerged from our room and was talking to Sam. Holding back for a few seconds, I leaned against the wall. What were my thoughts about Sam and Bridget? They'd abandoned their son long ago: Bridget, because he was too much hard work, Sam, because he was so bitterly disappointed in him. They had given up trying to make a difference and I doubted that either of them knew very much about him.

Sam had been sitting in the public gallery most days, while Bridget's only appearance at the court was in the witness box where she gave her version of events in the weeks prior to Joe's disappearance, as had Sam. Neither had any idea that their son had left Chester and was staying in a squat in Sutton Coldfield. They had not laid eyes on him for eighteen months. The old detective in me thought Bridget didn't tell the complete truth under oath.

Now, I watched Sam with Liam and I tried to feel something for my uncle. I really did try, but could not. My compassion had been sucked away. I was quietly disappearing into my own world.

Then I saw my dad. He was doing one day on, one day off, and avoided sitting anywhere near Sam. They were brothers, but I didn't think their relationship would ever recover. My mother had stayed at home, which was, at least, something I could be pleased about.

Most of the time in the courtroom I felt as if I wasn't really there. Occasionally, when it was quiet, in between witnesses, or sometimes when the gruff-faced judge allowed the jury to contemplate a new piece of evidence, a new fact, I smelt toffee popcorn. There was a small mezzanine gallery at the back of the courtroom that remained empty for the entire trial. Liam told me it was because it was having work done, had been deemed unsafe. I would look up towards it and see a haze of petrol blue. I had to take off my reading glasses to peer up into the gallery. I couldn't see Joe's face, and wondered why I could smell the popcorn when he was so far away.

Liam had noticed me looking upwards.

'Can't you see him?' I'd asked.

'Who?' he replied.

'Joe. He's watching.'

Liam had rubbed my leg awkwardly, and looked up, and as soon as he did Joe disappeared, if he'd ever been there. Apprehensively, Liam looked at our barrister.

I didn't mention seeing Joe again. As the emptiness of our lives swelled through me I was moving away from Liam.

—

We all returned to the courtroom. I glanced at Hemmings, who stood tall and erect. The last time I'd seen him at Bridget and Sam's a few years before he'd worn a wig, but today he did not.

Often Hemmings looked bemused, acting towards the judge as though he wasn't all there. But I could see the rationality behind his features, and saw it more when he looked downwards towards me, which he was doing now.

Determined not to shy away from his stare, I stared back. I placed my hand on Liam's knee as if already saying goodbye, and shifted my chair backwards a little so I could slump forwards. Finally taking my eyes away from those of Michael Hemmings, I thought about Joe and Christmas, in happier times, and a long time before I'd ever smelt someone else's sweat on my husband's underwear.

—

31

Liam had decided to buy two-year-old Joe a swing. Not a plastic primary-coloured one, but a proper timber-framed construction, complete with tyre, bucket seat, and a slide attached at the side. The company supplying it had delivered late, not giving Liam enough time to put it up on Christmas Eve. So we placed all the timber, the tyre and the bucket seat in a big, neat pile. We commandeered thick blue ribbon from our friendly car dealer (apparently they used it when people bought their partner a car as a present) and painstakingly wrapped the skeleton of the swing in the azure-blue braid. Liam attached blue string to a picture of the finished product and placed it under the Christmas tree. The string wound through the house, under the patio door in the kitchen, down the garden, ending spectacularly at Santa's present. Liam was drunk as he pulled the string down the garden. I sprinkled glitter. I'd been wobbly too, but ensured Rudolph's footprints were obvious on the hard December grass. Liam promised to construct it all on Boxing Day. We always stayed home Boxing Day. Remnants of memory from another day after Christmas long ago had made me superstitious.

—

The worst part of the trial, for me, was my time in the witness box. I could feel Hemmings' eyes all over me, and although I tried avoiding his stare, sometimes it was impossible. Liam handled it better; or seemed to. He managed to distance himself. And making that day worse was the evidence that came later in the afternoon – the photos of Joe's body. I was spared having to look but I watched the reactions of the jury as they were shown them.

Our barrister placed one image, carefully and deliberately, in front of each juror; their faces, all twelve of them, told me everything. But the barrister's gamble didn't pay off. Yes, the jury were sickened, as was the judge, but it reinforced (to all but me) that Hemmings did have a psychiatric disorder. Of course, it wasn't only the photos; there was more evidence that pointed towards Hemmings' madness: the testimonies from old girlfriends and boyfriends, including Gareth Summers, the man from the field.

On the final day of the trial, in the second week of January 2001, before Hemmings could sabotage the first glance, I studied him. There should have been some courtroom etiquette disallowing him from wearing his wig in court. Fraudulent blond locks cascaded down his back. They looked quite real, but the hair was as fake as his insanity. I glanced across at the defending QC. She was about my age and, I'd heard, had four children and a househusband. She was one of the most successful defence barristers in the country. I wondered how she could live with herself.

Only minutes before the judge began his closing speech, my mother shuffled quietly into the courtroom with Dad, who was probably thinking he was doing the right thing. The usher sat them as near to Liam and I as was possible. I smelt the waft of lavender as Margaret sat down and I glanced at her quickly. The white blouse was buttoned high. She hung on to Dad's arm as if she were an invalid, which she wasn't.

Hemmings was gazing at my mother; it was the first time during the trial that he lost his nonchalant look. He never took his eyes away from her, even when the judge began his low baritone monologue. I thought of a black and purple room, of Michael and my mother.

The judge read out quotes from psychiatric reports, details of when Tom and his team had found Joe's body, and details of Hemmings' confession.

The defence had not disputed the factual evidence. The substantial evidence against Hemmings came from the prosecution psychiatrists, who argued there was no proof of a mental disorder severe enough to reduce the defendant's responsibility for his actions. The defence argued that there was.

The judge talked about what Hemmings had done to my son's body; the only thankful thing was that he had done it after Joe had died. As the judge spoke clearly, but now with emotion, every one of the jurors nodded their head in sadness and in relief that their own children were safe at home.

I felt myself subside; I heard a moan from afar and realised it came from my mouth. Liam's hand was clamped on my knee; I felt its sweatiness through the thick wool of my tights. I thought my eyes were open yet I saw nothing, only ebony blackness. The courtroom and everyone in it disappeared. I flailed around as if in a deep ocean where there is no up, no down, just a void of empty, meaningless, cold black space. Into the chasm walked Joe. I reached out towards him. He was inside the courtroom; he wasn't dead. This had all been a terrible misunderstanding. I inhaled his toffee popcorn aroma; I held him.

When I opened my eyes I stared at oak panelling. Liam and Sean, our barrister from the Crown Prosecution Service, , were leaning over me.

'She's passed out, m'lord,' I heard the barrister say.

'Take an hour for Mrs Dune to recover, we will reconvene at three and complete the summing up of this case.'

It only took the jury a morning to come to a decision.

The judge addressed the foreman of the jury, 'Are you

agreed upon your verdict?'

'Yes, Your Honour.'

Clerk: 'Do you find the defendant guilty or not guilty of murder?'

The foreman's reply seemed to take forever. Liam squeezed my hand. Our barrister fidgeted in his chair.

Foreman: 'Not guilty.'

I felt a feral yelp inside my throat but no noise came. Liam let go of my hand that burned like fire.

Clerk: 'Do you find the defendant guilty or not guilty of manslaughter on the grounds of diminished responsibility?'

Foreman: 'Guilty.'

Judge: 'My thanks to all the jury members. This has been a difficult case.' He addressed the defence team. 'A hospital order is made under Section 37 of the Mental Health Act 1983, together with an order under Section 41, restricting Michael Hemmings' discharge without limit of time to a maximum security hospital.'

Michael Hemmings was to be detained at Littleworth, a high-security psychiatric hospital just outside Liverpool.

The judge looked at me as he finished and his face softened. He had been a severe but fair arbitrator throughout and now I detected his relief.

As Michael Hemmings was led away, still with his eyes on my mother under the harsh lighting of the courtroom, I watched again the strange reciprocity between my mother and my cousin, and a clear playback from my childhood began.

—

It was the day after Christmas 1971, and the usual family gathering. We always went to Uncle Sam's on Boxing Day. Sam and Bridget had the biggest house. Mum never wanted to go and I couldn't understand why, seeing as

Michael often came to ours. It's funny how as a child there are some things you know you can't mention, and one of those things was Michael's visits. I didn't want to go to Uncle Sam's, either, although I did look forwards to the great cakes that were always on offer in the Hemmings' household, and that made up for Michael's presence there. Also, I really liked Sam and Bridget even though I didn't like their son.

A mop of blond hair flopped over my cousin's small eyes, masking their brown emptiness. I peered at him. It was his eyes that made me feel uneasy. And his posture: considered, like a tiger ready to pounce. I knew he'd homed in on me and I gauged my choices. More boredom with my older relatives, or take a chance with weird Michael.

'Do you want to come up to my bedroom?' he said. His eyes bored into my forehead. I shrugged. Glancing towards him, I made a difficult decision. 'Better than staying down here,' he carried on.

'I was going to watch Doctor Who,' I lied. It wasn't on for another two hours.

'That's for kids. Got something to show you in my bedroom.'

The gauntlet was thrown down, and in the background I heard the adult conversation moving towards supermarkets and their muscling into Bridget and Sam's small bakery trade.

'OK,' I said, already following him into the hallway and towards the stairs.

'Margaret tells me you're learning to play the guitar?' he said, pushing open the bedroom door with his foot.

'My mum likes you, doesn't she?' I said.

He didn't answer, but held the door for me to enter. I'd never been inside his lair. Two walls painted ebony black, two walls purple. If I had to imagine the preliminary room to hell, that room would have been it.

I didn't know what to say and spotted a guitar leaning up against the unmade bed. I mumbled, 'I've had four guitar lessons ... at school.'

'School, pah! You need someone like me to teach you.'

'I like my guitar teacher.' I looked him straight in the eye, 'He's kind and patient.'

He concentrated his gaze around my navel. 'Come on, sweet Rachel – I'll show you how to play the guitar.' My eyes fluttered erratically around the room. 'I'm not going to eat you, Rach,' he finished.

The room smelt of stale sweat, an old aroma of fried bacon and something else, like animal, an animal that hadn't been cleaned properly. I wondered if Bridget ever cleaned. My own mother cleaned all the time, as if by having a clean house she would make her family clean, herself clean. I loved my dad, but our family was grey; our emotional home life grimy.

I started at the rustling movement from the far end of the room. In the corner sat a hutch with a brown and white rabbit inside. I remembered his rabbit Ruby from last Christmas; only then she'd lived outside the back door. He saw me looking towards the hutch.

'My idea to bring old Ruby indoors for the winter. Sorry about the smell.'

I wandered towards the hutch and peered at Ruby. The last time I'd seen the rabbit she'd been chubby and lively. She sat looking out from behind the bars; eyes dull, fur mangled and dirty. 'She doesn't look that healthy.'

His flat eyes studied the purple wall behind me. 'She's a rabbit, Rach, not a human.'

'My mum doesn't like people calling me Rach.'

'Fuck your mum.' He laughed almost hysterically. 'Yep, fuck your mum, Rach, and fuck the rabbit.' He kicked the hutch violently.

Ruby cowered in the corner. I opened the door of the hutch; my overwhelming desire to cuddle Ruby was overriding the fear.

He smiled, 'Yes, get Ruby out, let's have some fun.'

The fine hairs on my clammy skin stood up.

'You going to show me how to play the guitar, then?' I said, attempting to deflect him.

He pushed me to one side and grabbed Ruby by the scruff of her neck, 'D'ya want to see something really funny?'

I didn't. I said nothing.

He took the hapless rabbit towards the bed, and sat down with her on his knee. He held Ruby with one wiry arm, while with the other he lit a cigarette.

'Does your mum know you smoke?' I said quietly, thinking that Bridget almost certainly didn't.

'It's none of her fucking business. Fucking women. Watch this.'

Anticipating its fate, the poor animal peed over her tormentor's trousers and the bed. He threw Ruby on the floor and then crouched down beside her, roughly pinning her down as best he could. She stared at me; she was docile through maltreatment and not even attempting to wriggle away.

'Fucking animal!' He took the cigarette, which had been hanging from his cracked, dry lips, and pushed it into Ruby's face. She screeched, as did I. Defying all the odds, Ruby managed to break free from her tormentor and ran towards the pseudo safety of her cage.

'So,' he pulled the guitar from beside his bed, 'let's have a practice, shall we?'

'Will Ruby be all right?' She sat in the furthest corner of her cage. Completely still.

'Fuck knows. I'm bored with it. Do you want it?'

I knew my mother wouldn't let me have Ruby, but I wanted to save her.

'Yes.'

'And no friggin' rattin' on me about the rabbit, OK? Or who knows what'll happen.' He peered at me. 'You should see what she does when I do other things to her. Fuck, Rach ... maybe I'll show you now.' He'd risen from the floor and was making his way to Ruby's cage. Then he stopped and turned towards me. 'Or maybe, sweet Rachel, instead of Ruby, I'll do it to you?'

Ruby was frozen inside her cage; the dull light of the room seemed to flicker. I heard the low tone of the resting record player.

And then there was a loud knock on the door and I sighed with relief at hearing my mum's voice.

'No ratting,' he mumbled. The bulge in the crotch of his trousers was too noticeable, as was the heightened colour in his face. He was still looking at Ruby in the cage.

My mum opened the door before he replied to her knock. I watched something very near to fear cross his face as she entered the room.

She didn't look at me, and stood like a tower of grown-up normality in the black and purple room. Out of place in her signature buttoned-up blouse, pale blue for Boxing Day instead of her trademark white, both hands placed on her large hips. The blouse ballooned around her small chest. Michael looked directly into her icy blue eyes, seemingly unable to pull himself free from the gaze.

'Are you being a naughty boy?' she said. Her eyes

travelled to his crotch. She smiled but said nothing. Emptiness engulfed me as I realised that my mother had not come to save me. That she had come to see Michael.

I expected a swear word. At the very least, a rude retort. But Michael shrank backwards away from the door and my mother. As submissive as Ruby.

'No – I'm not being a naughty boy,' he said, both hands moving towards his mouth.

His hands stayed in the same position for at least an hour after we left his bedroom. He ate none of the Boxing Day tea; it would have been difficult getting food past both of his wiry hands. Bridget had lost patience with her son soon after we had all sat down at the table; ignoring him and then taking his plate away.

As I knew she would, my mother said no to the idea of taking Ruby home with us.

We stayed at Sam and Bridget's that night, but it was to be the last night we ever stayed there. The next morning I was the first up, apart from Bridget. She looked dishevelled and sad.

'What's the matter, Aunt Bridget?' I asked.

She nodded over to the other end of the kitchen. Ruby's hutch sat in the corner.

'Is Ruby all right?' I could tell she wasn't.

'No she's not, Rachel. She died.'

'Did you bring her hutch down to the kitchen last night?'

She sighed heavily. 'No, she was up in Michael's room. I've just brought it down.'

'What happened?'

'She just died, Rachel.' I walked over to the cage. Bridget moved towards me. 'It's a dead animal, Rachel. Leave it. Sam and I will bury her later in the garden.'

I looked inside the cage anyway. Ruby lay on her back, her neck at a distressing angle. I knew it had been broken. I said nothing, only opened the cage and stroked her cold fur.

'You go and get ready. Your mother will be wanting to leave after breakfast.'

'All right, Aunt Bridget.' I looked at her, about to say something, to ask her if Michael had done it. I knew he had.

'Go on,' she said. 'Now, love.'

Tears covered my face. 'You'll bury her properly, not let Michael do it?'

'It'll be Sam and I. Michael's still asleep. He'll be in bed until the afternoon, so don't worry.'

No one ever mentioned Ruby again.

—

Liam and I found ourselves outside the court building, greeted by a muddy sky that was still visible in the wispy fog of the late afternoon. It had rained continuously for the last forty-eight hours, but as we caught sight of the insatiable media the downpour was the least of our problems.

I pulled my wool beret over courtroom-warmed ears and looked down towards the slippery wet ground. Our barrister had told us to say nothing, which was physically easy, as I felt I would never speak again. For the past seven weeks the dry atmosphere of the courtroom had robbed me of a proper voice, as Hemmings' act had robbed me of a proper life. Tom Gillespie caught Liam's arm, whispering things that I didn't even try to catch. My existence seemed to be disappearing into a void; the small bit of life that Hemmings had left for me plucked away during the trial.

I loitered in the entrance of the court building, thinking that I would smell Joe. I did not. Coolness ran through me, a purl of motion in between the crevices of my spine.

Joe wasn't with me.

—

As we left, Tom squeezed my arm lightly but didn't attempt to give me a familiar kiss on the cheek. Liam and I had slowed down his investigation by holding back information about Joe's state of mind the day he had gone, and in so doing we had compromised our relationship with him. In my previous life, I'd been talking to Tom about going back to work. Once upon a time that thought had excited me.

Tom walked quickly to a waiting car. He slipped into the driver's seat and glanced towards me, nodding slightly. He wanted to get away.

I felt a gentle jab in my back. It was Jonathan. I'd hardly spoken to him throughout the trial. I turned towards him, and so did Liam, his face sullen.

'You need to get away from here as quickly as possible.' Jonathan smiled thinly. 'Can't take away the nature of the vulture. I should know.'

'We're fine, Jonathan. Rachel knows how to handle this stuff,' Liam said.

'Does she, Liam?' Jonathan said quietly.

Very obviously Liam elbowed past him, only to move a few inches nearer to the street.

'We're just about to leave, Jonathan,' I said. 'Are you free to come over? I've hardly seen you …' I didn't care what Liam thought. Not anymore.

At that moment in my peripheral vision I caught sight of my dad and mother leaving too. Dad saw me and moved his head towards the car park, indicating that he'd accompany Margaret to the car and then return. I couldn't face her and the silent accusation that this was all my fault.

Joe's murder was somehow my fault.

I looked at Jonathan. 'Come over, please?' To Liam I said, 'Can we wait for Dad?'

'The place is crawling with press.' Liam said. 'We need to go.' He cast his eyes around. 'Too late.'

Already, journalists had surrounded us. I recognised a few from the local papers, the nationals, too. Flashes and tussling ensued as our barrister made his way forwards. Sean Skerrit, QC for the Crown Prosecution Service, was older than he looked; something that I think went against him in court. I'd always felt the jury resented a young prosecution, especially if the jury was mature, which this one had been.

Sean directed his speech towards Liam, and I felt invisible, useless, but too tired to complain. 'I intend to give a statement.' Sean said to Liam. 'You and Rachel go home. I'll call later. Better I do this alone.'

'This means a life sentence?' I asked Sean, hope in my voice.

He grimaced. 'A do-good mental health tribunal could well decide to let him out within five years, if he plays the game.' He caught my eye. 'But hopefully that won't be the case.'

'But it could be the case ... couldn't it?'

'I hope not, Rachel,' Sean said, with leaden heaviness in his voice. I'd got the distinct impression that Sean Skerrit QC didn't like to lose, and had taken Hemmings' sentence as a direct affront to his professional agility.

Did I think of revenge then? Deep inside I think I did.

Sean ran slender and well-manicured fingers through his mane. Not one grey hair in his boot-polish black hair. He turned slightly to accommodate a photographer and,

43

looking at the lens, said to me, 'We'll talk later.'

'I'll come over, Rachel,' Jonathan said, 'just for a short time. I have to be back in London.' He was already moving away.

'Good,' I said to Jonathan's back.

My dad had made his way over. He wavered and I recognised the vacillation with which I'd grown up. I guessed my mother wanted to talk to me, but I had no intention of going to my childhood home today to argue with her. Not today.

'Your mum wants to talk to you,' Dad said.

I sighed. 'I'll come over tomorrow. I promise, I will.'

'She's asked me to bring her over to yours ... now. She's waiting in the car.' He pulled at the sleeve of his jacket.

'Charlotte's made food, Alan. Both of you come and eat at ours,' Liam said to Dad, avoiding looking at me, knowing there was no way I'd want my mother anywhere near me.

Liam was functioning on automatic, something he'd seemed to be doing since Joe had gone. He felt as guilty as me; sometimes I thought more so. We still hadn't talked about the affair, not properly, not directly. Although Liam was aware I knew something.

I watched my father. A patient man, a kind man. How could he love my mother? How could anyone love my mother? Joe hadn't loved her. But he had tried.

'We'll drive over now,' my dad said. He turned to return to his wife.

Liam pushed me gently into our waiting car. A PC whom I recognised sat ready in the driving seat. From the back seat, I saw his forced and sad smile in the rear-view mirror. The pity, again.

We drove southwards towards home, passing the local

park on the way. It had been built around the time Joe had been born, overlooking the main road, on elevated ground. The council's thinking: where the kids could be seen.

Liam broke the short silence. 'I'd rather Jonathan Waters didn't turn up today.'

'He's my friend.' I stared through the window. 'You can't have an opinion on this. He's been good to me.'

Liam didn't answer.

# CHAPTER FIVE

Jonathan watched as Rachel and Liam were driven away, and the profound feeling of sadness that hit him made him catch his breath. He scanned the street and the entrance to the court buildings; the place was still crawling. This case had caught the attention of the whole country. He felt his forehead crease into a frown. Give it a few days and everyone would have forgotten. Everyone but those directly involved.

'Waters! Jonathan!'

He turned, immediately identifying the voice. Barry Haslop. He'd recognise it anywhere. Low, rasping and authoritative. A journalist who Jonathan not only admired, but liked.

'Baz, I didn't know you were here … you haven't been covering this story?'

'Editor sent me for the sentencing. Wants me to write a special piece on the case.' The older man wiped his brow. Despite the cold Barry was sweating. He wasn't the healthiest journo. 'Not a big surprise, the sentence, but bad for the parents.' Barry cocked his chin upwards. 'You know anything? You know the mother well…'

'Know as much as you, mate,' Jonathan replied.

'Yeah, right.' Barry smiled, good-naturedly. 'How's that wife of yours?'

'Michelle's OK.'

'You know where I am if you ever need a bloke chat.' Barry grinned sympathetically. He was on his fourth wife.

'Might take you up on that.' Jonathan sighed. 'It's not as good as it could be.'

'It never is, mate.' Barry's shoulders lifted upwards in sympathy.

They were standing on the kerbside. Hooking up with Barry was always fruitful; what the old hack didn't know wasn't worth knowing. He'd helped Jonathan out on more than one occasion with research. Jonathan had realised early on that Barry Haslop could uncover just about anything. He'd learnt a lot from Baz; most of his own hacking skills were due to the old reporter's input.

He thought that he'd also like to talk about Michelle. Perhaps a pint together sometime soon would be good.

Suddenly, loud scuffles were heard coming from the court steps. Both men looked up. It was Barry who spoke.

'Looks like Hemmings' parents are about to leave.'

Bridget and Sam Hemmings were surrounded. Michael Hemmings' barrister was nowhere to be seen. She was probably already sitting in a pub somewhere, celebrating.

Jonathan watched. The journos surrounding the couple were well out of order, jostling, shoving. Sam Hemmings looked knackered and Bridget looked terrified. He'd met the couple a few times and liked them both, but it had been Sam he'd warmed to. There was something about Bridget that … well. But, looking at the two of them now, Bridget's coat wrapped tightly around her barrel-shaped body, the fear on her face, the look of desolation on Sam's, he felt he had to intervene.

'Wolves,' he said to Barry, but not looking at him. 'Wait here.'

Barry chuckled. 'Always the knight, eh, Jon?'

Jonathan was already moving towards Sam and

Bridget, shoving his way through the journalist pack and recognising a few of them.

'Come on, people, give them some space!' A few moved sideways. Jonathan grabbed Bridget's arm. 'This way.' He pulled Sam, too. 'My car's parked illegally at the back of the building. I'll give you both a lift home.' Jonathan motioned to Barry, who'd followed him. Probably hoping for some story. Jonathan didn't mind; it was his job, both their jobs.

With Barry's help he got Bridget and Sam to his car, Bridget panting by the time they got there. Sam looked greyer than the canopy of sky that spread over Birmingham.

He ushered Bridget into the back seat. Sam sat in the front. With them safely inside, Jonathan nodded towards Barry. 'Thanks, mate, I owe you one.'

'You do. A line or two about Rachel and Liam Dune's state of mind? Are they intending to appeal?'

'I hope they are, Barry,' Jonathan said.

'More?'

'Rachel's devastated. She doesn't believe Michael Hemmings has a mental disorder.'

'And Liam?'

'I know fuck all what Liam thinks.'

'Enough said, mate.' Barry was quiet for a few seconds. 'All not well between them?'

'I'd say probably not. But who would be well after this?'

'Point taken.'

Jonathan was getting into the driver's seat. 'I'll call you soon, Baz, OK?'

The old hack smiled. 'Look forwards.'

Spotting a few reporters making their way over, he slammed his door, turned on the ignition and sped away.

Feeling like a character from a movie, he smiled.

Bridget leaned forwards from the back seat and tapped him on the shoulder. 'Thank you, Jonathan.'

He turned. 'My pleasure. We're not the nicest people when hunting for a story.' He glanced at Sam, who was staring straight ahead, silent, before looking back to Bridget in the rear-view mirror. 'It's good you came for the sentencing, Bridget.' Now she didn't look terrified, only worried, preoccupied. But what mother wouldn't be? Your only son convicted of the brutal murder of your seven-year-old great-nephew.

She slumped back into the seat. 'This is a nightmare.'

Sam, still gazing straight ahead, said, 'It is.'

Jonathan peered at Bridget in the mirror again. He liked her, but, as he'd always felt, something was definitely amiss.

# CHAPTER SIX

It was a Tuesday during the school term when the judge decided that my son's killer was not a murderer and could be rehabilitated.

The park we were driving by was empty. The car slowed as an old lady crossed the road. I peered from the window; my eyes lingered on Joe's favourite game, the zip wire. The petrol blue flickered for seconds. A strong smell of the toffee popcorn. I felt as if Joe had slipped inside the car.

'I'm fine.' I thought he said. 'No, this is not fine, Joe,' I replied, unsure if I'd said it out loud. I love you Joe, more than the universe, more than infinity. I used to say that to Joe when he was feeling low. It always made him happy.

Liam looked at me. 'What did you say?'

'Nothing, I didn't say anything,' still staring at the park, the petrol blue gone. 'I don't want to see Margaret.'

'You have to. She's your mother.'

Yes, she was my mother. So much unsaid, so much I had never told Liam – not because I hadn't wanted to – I had, especially after I knew I was pregnant with Joe. But something always stopped me, and I halted myself from questioning exactly why. Now I sighed and remained silent. Perhaps the problem in our marriage was me.

Charlotte was standing outside our front door when we pulled up. Petite and pretty in a sea of winter-grey. The hem of her long red dress flipped in the tight wind. She'd declined to come to court, saying it was better if she stayed and got some food ready. She'd filled the hanging basket outside our front door with winter pansies. It had been empty since Joe. She'd kept herself busy. Spotting the batch of reporters waiting, our driver accompanied us to the front door. Liam and I mumbled 'no comment' as we made our way up the driveway.

We went inside. Charlotte had made what looked like a celebration feast. That's what she did when anxious: cook and fill hanging baskets. She had a superb kitchen in her own rambling house on the edges of Sutton Park in Birmingham: a prime location. The house was courtesy of her son Jacob's burgeoning success within the British film industry. A twenty-year-old Jacob had bought her a very nice holiday home in Venice Beach, California, too.

I wondered what Joe would have looked like at twenty.

Charlotte was a determined optimist. She had been when we first found out about Joe's disappearance, and later, on the likelihood that Hemmings would spend the rest of his life in a mainstream prison. And she was about Liam's suspected affair, too. Charlotte refused to believe that he was having one. In fact, she refused even to contemplate the possibility, which had made it difficult to discuss with her.

Charlotte seemed to exist in a bubble where only good things happened. Jacob had come along soon after we'd left university; she'd had no intention of marrying his father. Everyone told her to have an abortion – apart from me. Her early life was hard, yet she'd managed well, and with good humour. Liam and I had been transferring money into her account for years to help put Jacob through theatre school. His success allowed her to pay us back every penny with interest. Sometimes I thought Liam loved Charlotte as much as I did.

When we were safely inside I hugged her. 'Have they been here all day?' I asked, peering through the window at the gaggle of journalists.

She nodded. 'I made tea for them.'

'Charl?' I tried to smile. 'Have you made masses of food?'

'I thought Tom would be coming with you ... Jonathan?'

'Just us, and yes, hopefully Jonathan will come ... and Dad, Margaret.' Calling her mother had become even more difficult since Joe's death.

'Oh, OK. Fine, your mum ...' she faltered.

'Sorry – '

Her caramel-coloured eyes flickered with amusement. 'She's your mum.'

My mother didn't like Charlotte. Because Jacob had never known his father. Because Charlotte was black. Because she lived in a fuck-off house and my mother didn't. The feeling, I knew, was mutual.

'I know. Never mind.' I looked at the kitchen table, heaving with quiches and salad. Two cakes. Charlotte must have made those at home. Beautifully decorated, they would have taken her hours. The chocolate cake was missing a half. I hovered by it.

She smiled. 'Cake with the tea for the journos.'

'Did you speak with them?'

'About the trial? Course not. I talked about Jacob, gave them a few titbits, kept them happy.'

Again, I attempted to smile.

Liam had opened a bottle of wine, and poured himself a large glass. 'Good tactic, Charl.' A mild guilt crossed his features. 'I'm going down to the den. Give me a shout if you need me.' He was already opening the patio door. The guilt, I thought, because he was hiding.

'He's going so he avoids Margaret,' I said, watching his slim form disappearing down the garden. 'Or more precisely, avoiding me with Margaret.'

'It's been hard on him,' Charlotte said. She'd always had a soft spot for Liam. 'For you both. You look terrible.' She turned her head slightly. 'Someone at the door?'

'Dad and Margaret, probably,' I said. 'Can you let them in?' I took a glass from the draining board and poured myself a large glass of wine, too, keeping it near me so that Margaret would know it was mine. Margaret hated people drinking alcohol. I waited.

Everyone around me, including my dad, had diminished in the last months. The ageing process was speeding up for all of us. Even the perennially youthful Charlotte looked older, more drawn, the translucency of her skin dulled.

This was not so for my mother. As she walked into the kitchen, she appeared rested and serene; cold and detached, too, but even in my exhausted state I questioned if it was only I who saw that; that my aversion to Margaret distorted my view of how everyone else saw her.

The doorbell rang again. I hoped it would be Jonathan and, moving quickly past my mother, I made my way towards the door, anything to remove myself from her. It was Jonathan.

'I'm glad you came,' I said.

'Everything OK?' He pushed dark curls from his forehead and reddened. 'As OK as it can be … I mean.'

'I know what you mean,' I smiled minutely. 'My

mother's here.'

He grimaced.

'But Liam's disappeared to the den, so not all bad.'

'Rachel, I'm so sorry about the sentence.'

'It's OK. I half expected it. Come in.'

Jonathan and I walked into the kitchen. The smell of lavender hit me hard; the same perfume she'd worn for years. The smell mixed inside my mind with the image of Hemmings. Lavender and Hemmings together in the courtroom had disorientated me.

'Hi Jonathan,' Charlotte said. 'Would you like a drink? And you Margaret, would you like one?'

'I'm fine … thank you.' Her glance moved straight to the wine that I was now sipping.

The acid taste made me feel sick. I gulped it back.

Jonathan watched me and answered Charlotte. 'Beer's good, thanks.' He turned to Margaret and my dad. 'Good to see you both again. I saw Bridget and Sam at the court, about to be mauled. I took them home.'

Margaret pulled out a chair but didn't sit down. 'That was kind of you. I'm sure Bridget wouldn't thank you for it.'

'She did actually, Mrs Hemmings.'

Margaret touched her hair and then fingered the top button of her blouse, making sure it was done up right to the collar, but she didn't answer Jonathan.

My dad hovered, looking more ill as each second passed, but managed a smile aimed at Jonathan. Then he looked at me. 'Your mum has something to tell you, love.'

'I am more than capable of speaking for myself,' Margaret said, addressing the table, then peering at Jonathan and Charlotte.

Charlotte took two beers from the fridge, giving one to

Dad and one to Jonathan.

'What is it?' I asked, trying to soften my voice.

'Perhaps Charlotte and Mr Waters could leave?' Margaret said.

'No, they can't leave,' I said. 'Couldn't it have waited? The trial only ended today.' I tried to like my mother. She had lost a grandson.

'Drinking wine won't make this situation any better,' Margaret said.

With anyone else in the world that statement would be valid, caring. I watched the muscles in her neck tighten, pushing violently against the fabric of her blouse. I lost myself, and didn't answer.

'... Will it?' she carried on, a softer tone detectable in her voice.

'Would you like a piece of Charlotte's cake?' I asked.

'No, I would not.' She took in the table, the food. 'This isn't a celebration.' She paused. 'Where's Liam?'

'In the den.'

She nodded.

'What do you want to say, Mu ...?' The word puckered in my mouth.

Finally she sat down, her bottom perched on the edge of the chair; she was ready to go at a moment's notice. She skimmed a look at Jonathan and Charlotte before turning back to me. 'Do you remember when Joe came to stay? You should remember, because you didn't allow him to come very often.'

I wondered where this was going. I took a long breath. 'That's because you weren't the best grandmother.'

'I'll ignore that. Why are you always so aggressive?' She faced me. 'Your dad had to go out that day.' For the first time since entering the kitchen she looked uncomfortable.

'Go on,' I said quietly.

'While your father was out, Michael Hemmings came to see me.'

The wine lacerated my throat. I fixed my eyes on her. 'Why did he come to see you?'

'I have no idea,' she said, touching her neck.

I looked at Dad. 'You never told me. You were there?'

'I had to go into work that day.' He hesitated. 'I did try to tell you, but you didn't want to listen when you picked Joe up.

'Joe was alone with Mum?' It came out without thought.

'Yes,' my mother answered. 'Alone with his grandma, Rachel.'

'Why are you telling me now?'

'Because it might be why Joe was happy to go with Michael that day on the field.' She crossed one thick thigh over the other. 'Why did Joe run to the field, Rachel?'

I placed my empty glass back on the table and stood. I heard the higher pitch of my voice. 'Why have you said nothing about this to the police?'

She uncrossed her legs. 'There was no reason to.' She gently touched my scarred left hand, and a rush of something cold flooded through me. Again, she asked, 'Rachel, why was Joe on the field?'

I pulled my hand away. 'How long did Hemmings stay?' I asked. 'I don't know why Joe went to the field.' Hysteria in a voice that didn't seem to belong to me.

'He stayed most of the day. He played with Joe. I couldn't see what harm it would do.' Her face fell. 'I wasn't to know then, was I?'

I looked across at my dad and asked again. 'You knew?' The same discomfort crossed his face as I had seen many times as a child, when he had attempted to

57

protect me from my mother's coldness, while at the same time trying not to upset her. 'Is this the day you told me about, just before Joe disappeared, that someone had upset Mum?'

He nodded.

'Why didn't you tell me, then?'

'You didn't want to know, if you remember? It was you who cut the conversation short, love. Anyway, I thought Joe would tell you to be honest.' Joe hadn't said a word and I could only think it was because Margaret had told him not to.

'I can't believe this.' I looked at my dad. 'You should have told me before today. You should have told the barrister; you should have told Tom.'

'Your mum ...' he stuttered.

'Don't speak for me, Alan,' she said, interrupting. 'It was irrelevant.'

'Then why are you telling me now?' I said.

'I could hardly turn him away, could I?' She said coolly, calmly. 'I thought you should know. That's all. Thought it might help you.' Her face crumpled into something. Was it real grief? I was unsure.

I paced towards the sink, the window. 'If that's it, then you can go.'

'Aw, love,' Dad said.

'You both should have told the police. So,' I looked at Margaret, 'the only reason you're telling me now is because Dad said he would tell me anyway, am I right?'

'Your mum's only trying to help, love,' Dad said.

'Am I right?' I asked again.

'Yes, you are right,' Margaret answered quietly, getting up from the chair. 'Clearly Joe was upset the day Michael found him on the field. Something happened that I think you,' she looked at me with a mild smile, 'and

58

Liam are holding back. Such a secretive child, you always were. I only want to help.'

'Just go,' I glanced at my dad, 'both of you.'

And they did, leaving me with the strong smell of Margaret's perfume.

Charlotte sat on the floor, crossing her legs. 'Christ.'

I leant over the sink, trying to catch my breath. Trying to understand why I felt such guilt.

Liam returned from his den. Jonathan quickly finished his beer. 'I think I should go, Rachel.' He went to touch my hand but stopped midway. 'You've got my number.'

'Thanks for looking after Sam and Bridget,' I said.

'No problem.' He made his own way out.

# CHAPTER SEVEN

*Five days later*

Charlotte had left for California on a two-week holiday, staying at her house in Venice Beach, and catching up with Jacob who was filming in the States. Liam had taken her to the airport the day before; they had both said I should stay home and rest.

Jonathan had called me earlier in the morning asking if he could come and visit. I'd said yes easily. Liam was going on to visit his parents from the airport.

I could not rest.

The house was desolate and empty and I was spending too much time in Joe's room. Waiting for the toffee popcorn, waiting to glimpse the petrol blue, but seeing and sensing barely anything; only hearing the ticking of the Doctor Who clock on the wall, the ruffling of the matching Doctor Who curtains, feeling the cold breeze that floated through the open window. No Joe.

I sat in the rocking chair. Liam had bought it for breastfeeding, which, to my distress, I'd been unable to achieve. I'd done all the right things: I'd loved my baby, but the milk didn't flow. As Joe grew, I blamed myself for his propensity for sore throats and bad colds, and had convinced myself they were due to the lack of mother's milk.

As I thought of my inability to feed Joe, cool air from

the window blew into a mini gale giving me goosebumps, but it was good to feel cold, good to feel anything. I rubbed at my breasts roughly and from nowhere the image of a young Michael Hemmings' face intruded. I squeezed my eyes shut as if this would erase the impression, and gradually it did fade.

A plate with one lone muffin and a knife sat on the floor. I slipped downwards onto the carpet and cut it into equal halves, as I'd always done.

One half for me, one for Joe.

I ate my half and it tasted of nothing. I placed the plate with the remaining muffin on Joe's bed, in the middle of the blue Tardis image that filled the duvet cover, thinking back to the last day of the trial. Of Margaret and Dad's confession. It explained why my son had gone easily with Hemmings.

I lay on top of Joe's Doctor Who rug and stared at the ceiling. I'm sorry, Joe.

Eventually the chime from the door roused me. It was exactly one and I smiled at Jonathan's familiar punctuality. But it wasn't Jonathan; it was my dad, his face more gaunt than the last time I'd seen him and any anger I held slipped away.

'Hi Dad, come in.' I stepped sideways.

He held a package wrapped in brown paper and offered it to me. 'Hope I'm doing the right thing.'

I took it from him. 'What is it?'

'The day Joe stayed at our house ...'

'I don't want to talk about it. Really, I don't.'

'Joe did some paintings,' he pointed to the package, 'I thought you and Liam would like to have them.'

I placed the package on the hall table. 'I can't look. I can't.'

'When you're ready, love.'

'How are you? And Margaret?'

'We're all right. I want to talk to you.'

'Come through.' We sat down. 'You should have told me.'

I did want to talk about it.

'I know.' He leant onto the table, wedged his elbows on its edge. 'There's something I do need to tell you.'

I waited.

'You wanted to know why Michael came that day, to see Margaret? Because he did go only to see Margaret. There's something your mum and I have never shared with you. There was no point. It wasn't relevant. But you should know. Margaret looked after Michael when he was very young. Full-time. Sam and Bridget were building their business, your mum had left her job as a teacher to have her own children ... but she didn't fall pregnant. So she looked after Michael.'

'What?' Was I really surprised?

'Then you were born and she stopped. Caused a lot of aggravation between your mum and Bridget. Truth was, Bridget didn't like having a kid, it suited her to palm Michael off onto Margaret, then Margaret having a baby – you – inconvenienced her.'

'Margaret looked after Michael?'

'As I said, often. He stayed over, it worked. I travelled a lot, then, with my job.'

'Michael came over to our house when I was growing up. I used to tell you but you chose not to listen.' I looked up at him. 'Not often, but he came.' I turned my eyes away towards the window. 'Did you know he came, Dad, to visit?'

He shuffled in his chair. 'Of course, I knew he came occasionally. But there's nothing alarming in that, is there?'

I shrugged.

'Well … as I said, your mother did look after him, so I don't think it's that strange.' He exhaled loudly. 'Soon after she stopped taking care of him he got meningitis. It changed him, even after he recovered. He became odd. That's what we all put it down to, the meningitis. Sam did as much as he could, but Bridget wasn't the best mum. Not unkind, just not cut out to be a mother. It was Sam who wanted a child, not Bridget. That was why they only had one.'

'Margaret hasn't been the best mum, either.'

'She's tried. She wanted you, was desperate for a child.' He placed a clammy hand on top of mine. 'You two clashed from the minute you were born.'

I knew there was a part of that statement that was true. We clashed from the minute I could question her.

'Why did she give up teaching?' I remembered why I'd been so upset the day Joe disappeared, and it wasn't just about Liam's suspected affair, it was more about not being able to work. But the two were connected. I'd felt he could do whatever he liked, and I could not. 'Maybe if she'd carried on with her job … she wouldn't be the way she is.'

'Maybe.' He wriggled in his chair. 'Michael has always had a sort of love/hate relationship with your mum. I think he missed her.' He looked up at me. 'He became aggressive towards her on the one hand, but wanted her, loved her, if you like, on the other. I kept out of it. The day he visited, after you'd dropped Joe, I was called on to do something unexpectedly for work. I knew you wanted me around when you left Joe with us … I knew that, so I didn't tell you I'd been out all day when you picked him up later that evening.' Guilt passed over his features as it did mine, I was sure. 'Michael had taken the coach down from Chester for the day, that's what he told us.'

'You should have told me when I picked Joe up. And you should have told Tom about this.'

'There's no point telling them anything now, Rachel. It's over. Michael came to see Margaret, that's all. Nothing sinister.' He watched me. 'Just as it wasn't sinister if Michael came over occasionally when he was growing up. No matter what we know now, he was my nephew. Someone who'd spent the first part of his life with us. I'd always felt a bit sorry for him, despite his history with the police, but now … the guilt eats at me every day.'

'Dad, he spent the whole day with Joe.'

He seemed to tuck into himself and then stood, tears forming in his eyes. 'Your mother was trying to be nice; she knew he had no relationship with Bridget, that Sam found his son difficult.'

'Margaret trying to be nice?' I rubbed my finger in a small well of water left on the table. 'I find that hard to believe.'

Margaret wasn't nice. That would never be a word I'd use to describe her, although I accepted that she portrayed that image to many people. She was active within the church, did a fair amount of voluntary work. People didn't love her, but our small community held her in respect.

She was different outside the four walls of her home. I knew it, and my dad knew it too. I touched my scar and a memory floated to the surface.

I think it was the summer after the auspicious Boxing Day when I went on my first school trip. Two nights in the Peak District, camping. The highlight of the trip, apart from frying bacon every morning around a campfire, was visiting the Blue John Caverns. I'd missed my dad but loved being away from home and my mother. The school bus was due back into Birmingham and the car park of our school at 6 p.m. It was a Thursday, I think. The teacher had made a call from the service station to the lead parent (no one had mobiles then) saying we would be on time. We arrived back at 6.10 p.m. Margaret was picking me up. My dad was away with his job. My teacher and I were still waiting at 7.30 p.m. No Margaret, and no answer on our phone at home. We waited. Still no Margaret at 8.30 p.m. Everyone had gone; it was just the teacher and I left. Eventually, he took me home. Margaret answered the door in her dressing gown, a copy of *Madame Bovary* in her hand. I don't remember what she said to my teacher; not a lot I'd guess. My teacher didn't know what to say. I think he mumbled an apology for disturbing her – she had that effect on people – and he left as quickly as he could. She didn't say a word to me, only looked at the heap of my rucksack and the plastic bag that held wet and dirty clothes. I took everything up to my room trying desperately not to cry. I pulled out the Blue John brooch that I'd bought her from the gift shop and put it in my bin. I felt so stupid.

When, finally, I went back downstairs to the quietness of a house that always felt so empty without my dad around, I realised my mother had gone to bed.

So I did, too. Hungry, sad and still cold.

Now I watched my dad making his way to the kitchen door and away from me, if he'd ever been with me. Without Joe, whatever we shared had come to a full stop. In that moment loneliness engulfed me completely.

'This is all too much for me, love,' he said. 'We can't change what happened.'

'Why do you love her, Dad? How can you love her?'

'She is who she is. I've always stood by her, through everything.'

'She doesn't love me; she didn't love Joe. I don't understand.'

He didn't even try to contradict me. 'Some people, people like your mother, are difficult to understand, but it doesn't stop me from loving her. And she did love Joe, in her way.' He stopped, looked defeated. 'And I love you.'

'Did she love Michael?'

He peered through the kitchen window. 'I think she did.'

A sharp pain stabbed at my stomach. 'I can't see her again, any time soon.'

'I understand. Look, I'll come around again next week, to see you and Liam.'

I nodded, followed him through to the hall and watched him amble down the driveway. As I closed the front door, I noticed the package on the hall table and picked it up. Walking towards the cupboard under the stairs, I opened the door and placed it at the back unopened.

I made my way to the kitchen and sat at the table. Loneliness was becoming a part of me but perhaps that was a good thing.

Twenty minutes later the doorbell rang again. Jonathan. I was looking forwards to talking to him – seeing as Liam and I were hardly speaking. Charlotte had said it would take time, but I knew no amount of time would heal what was between us. The strange hunger I'd felt throughout Joe's disappearance, which abated during the trial, had returned. The thought of the closeness between my mother and Hemmings had unsettled me. Should I tell Tom Gillespie about my mother and Hemmings? But what good would it do? That part was over.

I walked back towards the front door, let it off the latch and opened it.

'Hi, Rachel.'

'Jonathan, good to see you, come in.'

He looked over his shoulder. 'Just seen your dad, sitting in the car, down the road. Has he just been?'

'Left about twenty minutes ago.'

'He looked upset.' He caught hold of my hand. 'You look upset.' He followed me into the kitchen. 'I think he was crying. He didn't see me.'

'My dad's always been the one person I could trust, but I just don't know anymore.'

'It's only been a few days since the end of the trial; it'll take months for things to settle. Give yourself, everyone, time. Has Charlotte gone to California?'

'Yes, yesterday.'

'Perhaps you should have gone with her?'

'Perhaps.' I flicked on the kettle. 'Coffee?'

'Would prefer tea.'

I pulled out a dusty teapot from the back of the cupboard. It was never used; neither Liam nor I liked tea. 'I'm not sure what's happening, Jonathan, I'm totally confused.'

'What's going down with your dad?'

'He told me that Margaret looked after Michael for Bridget when he was young. He practically lived with Margaret and Dad before I was born. I'd no idea. But it explains …' I faltered.

'I suppose it explains Hemmings' visit to your parents the day you dropped Joe there?'

'Yes, I suppose it does. It explains a lot …'

'You could speak to Tom Gillespie about this.'

'It won't change anything,' I said, rubbing my scar.

Jonathan leaned against the sink. 'I know your family had little to do with Bridget and Sam in recent years, but surely if your parents had looked after Hemmings as a child, there was some bond there? I mean, did he ever visit, independent of his parents?'

I slithered onto the floor, tucked my knees underneath my chin, and looked at Jonathan. 'That's the thing; Michael Hemmings did visit my mother occasionally.'

'That sounds normal.'

'It does, doesn't it?'

'Considering that she looked after him as a kid, I think so. Did you have much to do with him … when he came?'

I froze. Unable to say anything.

'Rachel…?'

'No, I didn't. I never liked him. I was glad when he stopped coming.' I twisted and fingered my ponytail.

It took him a while to answer. He moved and sat with me on the floor. 'If you plan to say nothing about Hemmings visiting Margaret, then let all this go. If you rake this up it'll achieve nothing.'

'You mean it won't help Joe, don't you?'

'Of course it won't help Joe.'

'It feels as if my life is over. It might as well be over.'

'I know, I think, how you feel. Michelle felt the same way when Daniel died. She still felt that way when I met her, and for a long time after her son's death. I thought I could help,' he ruminated.

'I'm so selfish. How are you and Michelle?'

'Still together, just.'

'It's good of you to come over to see me.'

'Glad I did, sounds like you could use some company. Got any biscuits?' I smiled and got up, got a packet from the cupboard and handed it to him. 'Leave what Margaret and your dad have told you. You and Liam have to stay afloat. This is the hardest time, you know that.' He flattened perfectly ironed jeans. 'Have you talked to Liam about what you suspected?'

I shook my head. 'I'm sorry about you and Michelle,' I said instead.

'We'll be OK.'

Michelle was older than Jonathan by five years, a similar age to me. Jonathan was her second husband. She'd got divorced soon after the tragic death of her son, Daniel. I'd known Jonathan since before he'd met Michelle, and I knew that part of the reason they'd got together was through a sense of shared grief. Michelle's because of Daniel and her divorce, Jonathan's because of a past that continued to haunt him.

Jonathan and I had become friends when I'd investigated 'The Asian Bride' case during the late 1980s. I thought back fondly of Marek Gorski, the talented cosmetic surgeon who had treated the tragic bride. She was still a girl and engaged to be married to her cousin, who was at least twenty years older than her. He had flown in from Pakistan only three weeks before the wedding date. At the end of the second day of 'marriage celebrations' the teenager went outside the mosque and talked to a male guest, taking a drag of the cigarette he'd offered her. When the new bride and groom returned to their flat in Northampton, the groom retrieved battery acid from underneath the sink, held down the seven-stone girl and poured it over her face. Over the next two years, I observed as Marek Gorski miraculously transformed Sorojini Jain's pitifully burned features. Jonathan, with her approval, ran a series of articles on her, and others like her. I'd carried on visiting Sorojini long after my official role was over.

During a visit to a pub near the London hospital where

Sorojini was being treated for horrific acid burns to her face and upper body, Jonathan and I had swapped life stories.

Jonathan's quiet voice brought me back to the present.

'When Daniel died Michelle wanted to disappear, go home, shut the door, not be with anyone. He'd been ill for so long, in hospital for the last year of his life, she just wanted to be alone. She wanted revenge, but there was no one to take revenge on. Only God. It's why she split from her husband.' He paused. 'Essentially, it's why we're having problems now. Because of her grief. You love Liam, don't you? Despite what might have happened before Joe went missing?'

'There was no one to blame for Daniel's death,' I said quietly, sitting back down on the floor. 'It was, and still is, a terrible place for Michelle to be. I don't love Liam anymore, Jonathan.'

'I'm sorry. Have you heard anything about an appeal?' he asked, changing from one uncomfortable subject to another.

'Our barrister says it's pointless pursuing it, and I have to agree, looking at the judge's previous sentencing, other cases, the psychiatric reports. Hemmings has a mental disorder, and theoretically it is treatable.' I looked at him. 'And Liam has no wish to pursue it.'

He nodded his head. 'I'm sure it's crossed your mind that maybe all the reports are right. That Hemmings does have a mental problem ...' He stopped mid-sentence, then carried on. 'What Hemmings did, all that he did, were not the actions of a sane man.'

'Or just the actions of a very bad and evil man?'

'It sounds as if Hemmings was always a weird bastard, maybe Margaret just didn't want to admit to being so close to him when he was a kid. Maybe she wants no blame for the way he's turned out.'

The bright light of the day that had been beaming through into the kitchen dimmed for a moment, and again, as it had so often done since Joe's disappearance, the memory of something long ago flickered, like an old film, through my mind.

'And the day Hemmings spent at Margaret's with Joe?' I said.

Jonathan sighed. 'It was unfortunate Joe was there that day.'

'Unfortunate?'

He pulled me towards him, almost hugging me. I didn't stop him, and a heat of something folded over me, and then as quickly as the warmth appeared it dissipated, and the guilt came again. Guilt that I was having any feelings at all other than grief or anger. Sensing my thoughts, he moved away and stood up.

'Joe had met Hemmings before, you told me that. You're focusing on this and you don't need to.'

'No, I don't need to,' I said, getting up too.

'Maybe you should think about going back to work in the force, not yet but in the near future. You were good at your job.' His face softened. 'You were good with the victims, and the perpetrators. People tell you things. You're insightful; I think that's the right word.' He paused, smiled. 'You should have been a journo.'

'I don't know about that – people telling me things, about being insightful,' I said ironically.

'You helped me when I spilled my guts to you.'

I thought back to our conversation in the pub near the hospital, all that time ago, when he'd told me about the death of his parents.

He began to fidget and carried on, as if knowing what I was thinking about. 'Did you keep in touch with Marek

Gorski? Has he been in contact, since Joe?'

I had heard from Marek, soon after the trial. He'd sent me a beautiful handwritten letter.

'Yes, he wrote to me. He's set up a clinic in Warsaw, specialising in facial cosmetic surgery. His plan was to help people who have been victims of violence, to charge as little as possible, but he's taking proper paid work too, to cover the costs of the people who can't pay.'

'A good bloke.'

'He is.' I smiled at him. 'I appreciate you coming.'

'Anytime you want to talk.' A hint of scarlet flushed his cheeks. He placed his mug symmetrically between the grainy lines of the wooden table, ready to leave.

I walked him to the door, feeling, on the one hand, I didn't want him to go, but on the other, that it was better if he did. I watched him walk down the path. He faltered at the painted red gate and turned. 'So promise you'll think about work – in the future? I'll call you soon.'

'I will, and yes, do.'

Again he paused, about to say something else, I thought. But then he moved on.

I closed the door firmly, and thought of Jonathan's wife, Michelle. Even now, all these years after Daniel's death, she only wanted to be alone with her son, as I wanted to be alone with Joe. Although he'd tried, Jonathan couldn't fill the gap for Michelle. Would someone like Jonathan fill the gap for me? Because I knew Liam never would.

The door of the airing cupboard under the stairs had cracked open. Hesitating briefly, I walked towards it and peered inside. Dad's package leant against the side sloping wall. I pulled it out, the paper warm from sitting next to the boiler.

Back in the kitchen I sat down and placed it on the

table. Slowly I opened it. I expected more sunsets: they'd been a theme for months before Joe's death. Thick pieces of paper stared up at me and I allowed a smile: yes, the sunsets again. These though, instead of bright oranges and reds, were painted in greys and silvers, almost like 'moonsets'. I leafed through, and then faltered. The last two were stuck together, put away before the paint had dried. I sat back in my chair. If I pulled them, both pictures would rip, be destroyed forever. I rose and went over to the kettle, switched it on and waited for it to boil. The skin around my scar itched, a memory jabbed, and I pushed it away.

I used the steam to pry the pictures gently apart, the laborious task somehow pleasing. After ten minutes of patience, the paintings slipped away from each other like Siamese twins after long and painful surgery.

From one piece of paper an image of a bald man stared at me. Liam would love the proportions; it was a perfect study of pain – the head too big for the body, but so big I knew Joe had meant it. So big that Joe could etch the grief and torture on the face's features. Joe had caught the likeness of Michael Hemmings so well, and suddenly the gnawing hunger pain returned. My eyes travelled to the top right-hand corner of the paper, at the other image, the other person. It was undoubtedly my mother. The white blouse, the small waist, the large and caricature-like hips. Her face, captured so well, unsmiling. The deep lines that travelled from nose to mouth were pencilled in, shaded to give them depth. Joe had managed to paint the anger in her expression; it was an anger that she hid so well from the outside world, but it was obvious that Joe had known she was full of the vitriol and astringency that I'd grown up with. Why did I leave Joe with Margaret that day? I'd thought my dad was there with Joe. I didn't like my mother and I knew Joe had struggled with her, and I had left my son so that I could go shopping with Charlotte. It was more guilt I packed away.

There in Joe's picture was Hemmings' sadness and my mother's anger; anger seemingly directed at Hemmings. What had Joe seen? What had Joe heard? But it was clear that Joe had felt sympathy for his would-be murderer. There was no question that he would have felt safe to go with him that day on the field.

The other piece of paper showed a picture of me, my body blurry where it had been stuck to the back of the image of Hemmings and Margaret. I stared at it; I was smiling. I debated with myself whether to show the pictures to Liam.

I took out the one with Margaret and Hemmings, placing the 'moonsets' and my image to one side.

Those Liam would see.

# CHAPTER EIGHT

*Eight months later*
*September 2001*

It took me eight months to find the strength to go and see Margaret. In that eight months my marriage to Liam was over in all but name. At Jonathan's suggestion I had gone to talk with Michelle. He'd thought it would be good for me to share my grief with another and he was right.

We'd had lunch in London and I'd come away from our meeting feeling a little more settled in one way, but less so in another. From speaking with Michelle I knew that her and Jonathan's marriage wasn't good, and this made me sad, but I also knew that if they did ever split, and I hoped they wouldn't, it would be amicable. When Liam and I finally got around to a divorce, ours wouldn't be. He'd never fully denied having an affair, and had managed to evade the subject cleverly. Liam was good at that. This avoidance on Liam's part – to acknowledge anything – made my grief and anger at Joe's death even harder to bear.

I had told Liam about Margaret looking after Michael Hemmings as a child, and about the day Joe stayed with his grandmother when Hemmings had visited. Liam had said very little, but his body language suggested that somehow I was to blame. Liam's unsaid thoughts – that it was my fault about Joe – resonated, and sent me further into the ocean of dark blue grief from which I seemed unable to climb out.

Although I had to confront Margaret about Michael Hemmings' contact with Joe, there was also a part of me that wished to make some semblance of peace with her.

Perhaps my dad was right. *You find it so easy to vilify her, love, it's always been a problem;* he'd said only recently.

As a child I'd loved my dad to distraction. He had been a good father, done all the things a dad should do: ferried me around as a teenager, took me to secondary school sporting events without fail, helped me move digs numerous times as a student at university. What I couldn't work out was why I'd felt less sure of our relationship since Joe's birth.

He'd worked for himself and so was often able to pick me up from school, and then there would be only the two of us. One of those days remained with me as clear as spring water.

'Dad, I got three stars for my science,' I'd said.

'That's great love,' he replied. 'Make sure you tell your mum when we get home.'

'She's not bothered.' My excitement at my three stars already shrivelling.

'Don't talk about your mother like that.' He'd turned his gaze away from the road and said slowly, 'You have to be more considerate, Rachel.' His eyes travelled back to the traffic ahead. 'It's your attitude that riles. It's not just about you, love. Do you ever ask her about her day? Help her out at home? You can be a bit selfish.' He paused. 'And she doesn't like it when you make things up about her.'

'I don't make things up…'

78

'Your mum says you do,' he said. 'The door thing?'

'I didn't make that up. She knew my hand was there, and she slammed it.'

'I don't think you even know you're doing it sometimes.' He sighed heavily. 'Your mother gave up a lot for you.'

As was usual during these conversations with Dad I ended up confused and disconcerted. It was only since having Joe that I'd noticed his adeptness at putting a spin on anything my mother did.

And so. And so. lispI went to see Margaret. And on that day, just before I left and for the first time in months, I smelt the toffee popcorn.

# CHAPTER NINE

I stood outside the familiar door of my parents' house and tried to calm myself, digging deep to find the policewoman within me.

Swallowing, I pressed the doorbell.

As if she had been standing on the other side waiting, Margaret opened the door immediately. She wore a high-necked blouse, lavender in colour, matching the flowers that were used to make her perfume, a calf-length skirt that hid her thick thighs and an apron. She greeted me with no smile. I was reminded of the days I came home from school, when, whatever tale I had to tell, whatever I'd achieved – if I chose to tell her at all – there was never a welcome ready on my mother's face. My homecoming always felt like an intrusion.

'I'm not early, am I?' I asked.

'Come through, Rachel. No, you're not.'

We passed the sitting room and I noticed that the walls had changed colour. 'Been decorating?' I asked.

'Life goes on,' she said in her considered monotone.

My stomach rebelled at the waft of cooking smells coming from the kitchen. She was making bolognese sauce. I took a deep breath and gulped down my burgeoning distress. As a child my dad was always telling me to stop exaggerating, being dramatic.

Why had I come? I had come to try to stop the dreams

that were making me wake every night in a sweat-drenched bed. I knew you weren't supposed to smell in dreams. I'm sure some psych who'd worked in the force had told me that. But I did. Bolognese sauce, Margaret's lavender perfume. I saw and heard, too. Tomatoes, a kettle, its whistle cutting through my sleep.

Impatiently, she ushered me through to the kitchen and I followed dutifully. As I had done as a child. Obedient. So aware of the quiet rages that were always stewing below my mother's epidermis, but always wanting to please her. Never wanting to upset her, say the wrong thing, or be there at the wrong time.

Like the day I came home from Sunday school too early.

She moved towards the sink. 'Your father tells me you're thinking of going back to work?'

'Haven't made up my mind.'

'You need to do something.'

'You gave up work to look after your family…'

'That's as it should be.'

'And that's what I did.'

She shrugged, not saying the obvious: that now I didn't have a family.

'You gave up work before having me, didn't you?'

A hint of anxiety passed over her features. 'I did, yes.'

'I want things to be better between us: that's what I would like. Dad's told me about you looking after Michael Hemmings when he was young … to help out Bridget and Sam.' I watched her. 'You helped Bridget out.' I paused for effect. 'That's nice.'

Her face relaxed a fraction. 'That was a long time ago. Your father shouldn't have mentioned it. It's irrelevant.'

'I don't think it was irrelevant, you helping Bridget.'

She liked that. I took courage, delved deeper. 'I think you should have mentioned to me at some point that Michael stayed with you and Dad when he was little.' I said it as gently as I could, attempting to empty my voice of malice.

She watched me. 'Do you, Rachel?'

'I do.' I paused. 'And you should have said something before the day of Hemmings' sentencing about him spending the day with you ... and Joe.' I waited, then carried on quietly. 'Don't you think that maybe you should?'

'I need to carry on making the bolognese sauce,' she said, ignoring my last question.

Margaret flicked on the kettle. Not speaking, we watched it boil. Simultaneously I felt the heat rising upwards from my toes, reaching my stomach, finding its way towards my neck, and lastly my hand. Unlike the kettle with which I grew up, this one had no whistle. It grumbled with steam and finally, violently, flicked itself off.

She picked up a bowl of fresh tomatoes from the counter top, placing it in the sink. 'I didn't skin enough of them,' she said.

Grasping the kettle she poured the hot water over the red fruits, and I shivered in the oppressive heat of the room, itching with venom the scar on my hand.

Looking up, she moved an imaginary strand of hair away from her eyes and smoothed down the bun she'd been styling her hair into for the last three decades. She glanced fleetingly at my hand, her expression never changing.

'You make too much of things,' she said. 'You always have. Things happen, accidents happen. You always centre everything on yourself.' She poured the tomatoes into a colander. 'You are selfish, and can sometimes be cruel.'

I erupted. Not visibly, but inside. I didn't want her to see my desperate rage. I rubbed the imperfect skin around the palm of my thumb.

'Me, selfish?' I said, as controlled as I was able. 'Me, cruel?'

She looked at my hand, she looked at my forehead and I thought of Michael Hemmings. 'Accidents happen.'

'I didn't come here to argue, I came to try and smooth things over.'

'It doesn't seem like that to me.'

'I'd just like a few answers, if that's possible.'

'I'm really not sure that I wish to be interrogated by my unbalanced daughter.'

'Fuck, Margaret ...' I wanted to bite my tongue.

'I'm not having this, I'm really not having it.'

'Look, I'm sorry,' apologising, as I'd seemed to have done all my life to Margaret. 'But I do remember Michael coming to ours...'

And I remembered my dad cutting me short the several times I'd mentioned it as a child, learning by reflex not to touch on the subject again.

'He came to see me a handful of times, that's all.' She watched me. 'Michael liked me, Rachel, appreciated me, unlike you. He was ... is clever, too. I taught him to read, do you know that? He was reading at three.' She stopped, felt at her neck. 'You were slow to read. Had to work hard at everything, you did, Rachel. Didn't possess the natural ability.' She took an noisy breath. 'Boys are so much easier to teach.'

But she'd hit on a raw spot and knew it, as she always knew it, drumming into my insecurities as only Margaret could.

'Did you regret having me?' I said tightly, the breath from my lungs trapped. 'That I was a girl? Were you envious, envious that I had a boy? Is that what this is all about? What it's been about all my life?'

'Are you asking me if you were a mistake? I will be truthful: one of us has to be. The answer is yes, you were. From the moment you were born, you were a mistake. Did it have anything to do with you being a girl? No. It did not. It was you. You were all wrong.' The smile that was absent for most of my childhood played around her thinning lips. 'Your father has tried his best with you.' She found my eyes. 'It was as difficult for him as it was for me.'

'You really are unbelievable.'

She had confirmed what I'd always known about her. But Dad? She knew what she was doing. I was attempting to not believe her about him, but the seed was sown. The roots would become embedded. Already, I felt them growing and spreading.

I carried on, 'And Joe, what about Joe?'

'Joe was a product of you. You made him dislike me.'

'That's not true.'

'Oh, it is. I loved Joe, very much. You see? Your selfishness. You think about only how you feel. Not how I feel, your father, even Liam.'

I waited a few seconds. 'And Hemmings?'

'What about him?'

'Don't you feel at all guilty?'

Because the boy you and Dad nurtured, I wanted to say, grew up to be your grandchild's killer.

'Why would I? It was you and Liam who weren't there for Joe. It wasn't my fault what Hemmings did. Yes, he came to see me that day, but it was a one off. I've had as much to do with him as you have, as a grown man.' She paused a moment. 'And Alan tells me that you may well be splitting from Liam.' She watched me. 'Which I'm not surprised about.' She paced the kitchen. 'Do you still see Jonathan Waters?'

I ignored the mention of Jonathan. 'I can't believe this. I really can't.' I leant against the wall. 'I should have moved away from this area years ago.'

'I was surprised you didn't, considering your lack of respect for me.'

'You know why, because of Dad. That's the only reason.'

She made a sound deep in her throat; a clicking noise that instantly made me question her. That's what she was doing – again – placing in my mind the question of my dad's love for me.

I withered. His love was the only thing I had left. And in my parents' house and inside the hurricane of my mind an understanding fell together. My dad had managed to make me feel that the bad relationship with my mother was my fault. I think I knew he loved me, but understood now that what he'd done, he'd done subconsciously – to keep the peace with Margaret.

'Look,' she said, the tight cords in her neck slackening. 'Our family has gone through a terrible time. This may come as a surprise to you, but I miss Joe. I didn't see much of him but he was my grandson, and I did love him. Your father is devastated. We have to find some peace between us. Don't you think that would be a good idea?'

'Did you love Michael Hemmings?' I don't know where my question came from.

She answered without hesitation and with less anger. 'I felt sorry for him. Bridget had no time for him, and neither did Sam.' She looked at me. 'Michael loved me … when he was young, of course he did. I looked after him, taught him … But after I had you, I didn't see much of him, seeing as we had very little to do with Bridget and Sam, apart from at Christmas and such like.' She stopped. 'You know that, don't you?'

'All I know is that you are not as a mother should be.' I picked up my bag. 'I'm going now, I shouldn't have come.' I couldn't stand the smell of the cooking any longer. 'I am going back to work, and I do intend to tell Tom about you and Hemmings.'

'Not as a mother should be? Look towards yourself, young lady. And Tom Gillespie? Tell him what you like.' She stared at me. 'It was your fault that Joe ran off. Yours and Liam's.' She walked towards the front door and opened it for me. 'If I were you I don't know how I'd live with myself.'

I walked quickly down the driveway, got in the car and turned on the ignition. Hardly able to control the clutch with my leg shaking so much, I drove around the corner, out of sight, stopped the engine and leant forwards on the steering wheel.

Grieving for Joe; for a childhood that had never existed; for a mother I'd never had; a father who was frayed and flawed and not who I'd wanted him to be, who I'd believed him to be.

For my son who I had let down so profoundly.

The loneliness and hollowness wrapped around like a net. The only thing giving me comfort was the joy of having had Joe, remembering Joe. But this was a blessing that came with a price, because, as I settled into the memories involving my son, the snatched recollections from my past poked at the greasy veneer of my sanity.

# CHAPTER TEN

I'd been sitting in the car for longer than I'd realised, ignoring a call on my mobile from Dad, wanting, I guessed, to see how it had gone with Margaret. Eventually, I sent him a text saying that everything had gone fine. I knew Margaret wouldn't discuss the details of our get-together. It would all remain a secret, undiscussed, as everything that was important seemed to do within our family.

Throughout my life I'd separated my dad emotionally from Margaret. I touched the scar that continued to burn after my earlier encounter with her. I'd allowed my dad's version of the 'accidents' to become truth because I'd had no wish for him not to love me. I wanted to make things easy for him, as children do with someone they love, someone they wish to please. But after Joe's murder, detaching my dad from my mother had become increasingly difficult; our relationship had changed – subtly – but it had. Knowing that my parents had effectively fostered Michael Hemmings had remoulded my thoughts. Memories that had seemed hard-wired began to unravel and re-form.

My mother had no love for me but she'd had love for Michael Hemmings, and yet in Joe's picture of Hemmings and Margaret there had been fear on his face, anger on Margaret's.

I finally started the engine and made my way home to Liam.

—

Autumn had begun early. A wet and grey summer had passed me by, merging imperceptibly into the next season. Earlier than normal the fruits were forming on the Judas tree. The September leaves were already starting to fall, gathering on the kids' play matting beneath Joe's Christmas present.

The blinds were closed in Liam's den, but I knew he was in there. I sat on Joe's swing, shivered without my coat and waited to feel a sense of my son.

I swung gently for a while when, suddenly, I heard the creaking of metal, felt a jolt and nearly fell from the swing. I held onto the chain holding the seat and looked up. One of the rings securing the chain had broken with my weight. As I stood, Liam opened the door of his den.

'I didn't know you were back.'

'Just.'

'Gillespie called while you were out.'

I knew he would have; he'd tried me on my mobile, too.

'I'll call him back later.'

'You're planning to go back to work, aren't you?'

'It doesn't matter what I'm planning, Liam. You're not interested.'

'Where've you been?' he asked.

'To see Margaret.'

'I don't want to hear about it. She looked after the mad bastard who killed our son, and said nothing.' He watched me. 'I want nothing to do with her, or your dad. Ever again.'

'Or me, that's what you mean, isn't it? Where are your balls, Liam? Why are you still here?'

'Where are my balls? Have you told Gillespie about Margaret and Alan looking after Hemmings as a child?'

'No, I haven't.'

His shoulders suddenly fell. 'You have one weird family, Rachel. And I'm finding it difficult to cope.'

I watched my husband, a man I had once loved, and felt only revulsion.

But I couldn't deny that he had good reason to feel like he did.

It was time to find out the truth about at least one thing.

I pulled at the sleeve of his shirt. 'You were having an affair before Joe went missing, weren't you? Admit it.'

As I spoke, a deep purple fruit dropped from the Judas tree. Liam placed his foot over it, flattening it.

'Yes, I was, Rachel.' I wondered why he no longer felt the need to deny it. 'And I'm sorry. More sorry than you'll ever know.' His eyes moved away from mine and focused on the squashed fruit. 'Everything has gone bad, hasn't it?'

'You made it go bad … before Joe.'

'You're a difficult woman to live with.'

'You chose me.' I leant against the frame of the swing. 'Do I know her?'

He faltered only for a second. 'No, no you don't.'

'You're a bastard.'

'And you are self-centred and self-righteous. And like your mother … cold.'

'So who could blame you, eh?'

I turned and walked back up the garden.

Liam would have to go. There was no way I was leaving Joe.

—

Later, I went around to Tom Gillespie's home. Luckily Rosie and their youngest, the only one left at home, were out overnight; lucky, because seeing Tom's wife with their daughter would only make me feel more desolate than I already did about my relationship with my own mother, and that day I couldn't have born it.

Tom opened the door and took me straight through to his study. Untidy and full of used coffee cups, it was a place I always felt at home. I plonked myself down on the two-seater sofa that sat underneath the window.

'How's Rosie, and Charlotte? Your other ducklings?' I asked.

'All well here, Rachel. It's you I worry about. You and Liam. What's going on?'

'Our marriage is over. He's finally admitted to an affair.'

'I'm so sorry.'

'Don't be.'

'Are you still thinking about coming back to work?'

'Will you have me?'

'Love to have you back.' He paused. 'But perhaps not on the high-profile stuff to start with…'

'You mean the paedo ops, homicides?'

'Not immediately, and you'll have to go through some retraining and preliminary psych testing.'

I smiled. 'Oh, good.'

'I do worry about you. Start off with the easy stuff … fraud…'

'Does that mean I'll be working with Morley and Mulhern?'

'Yes, I'm afraid so.'

They were the least of my problems. 'I need to talk to you about something.'

He poured himself a whisky. 'Go on.'

'A few months before Joe ... died, he spent the day with Margaret. My dad was supposed to be there, but he wasn't.'

'Was that a problem? Your dad not being there, I mean, when Joe was?'

'Sort of ... yes.'

'Go on.' He took a sip of whisky and coughed.

'Well, that day, Michael Hemmings came down from Chester to visit Margaret.' I looked at him. 'While Joe was there.'

'Why did he visit Margaret?'

'I went to see her earlier today –'

He interrupted. 'How long have you known this?'

'Since soon after the trial.'

'And you said nothing?'

'Come on, Tom, you know as well as me that there would be no point. It wouldn't affect anything.'

'Like you kept Joe's state of mind from me. You don't half make my job fucking difficult.'

'I'm telling you now.' I watched him. 'In case you want to change your mind about having me back.'

'We only ever questioned Margaret and Alan as a cursory gesture. Should I be revisiting this? Is there more you're not telling me?'

Was there more? No, there was not. But I went on to tell Tom about Margaret and Alan looking after Hemmings as a child, before I was born.

He rolled his eyes to the ceiling. 'Fuck, the press would have had a field day.' He poured another whisky. I'll go and see Margaret unofficially. I've already booked you in for the psych tests. Nine o'clock next Monday.'

'Thank you, Tom.'

'Will you be OK with your mother ... after my visit?'

'I don't think I'll be seeing her again in the near future,

not by choice, anyway.'

He put his arm around my shoulder. 'I always knew it was a poor relationship, but didn't think it would come to this.'

'Truth is, Tom, I'm glad it's come to this.'

'Whisky?'

'Please.'

That night I drank whisky and slept on the Gillespies' comfortable cream sofa. It crossed my mind to call Jonathan but I thought of Michelle and didn't.

The next day Tom, unofficially, went to see my parents.

Tom, again unofficially, reprimanded both of them for not telling either him or my barrister about Hemmings' visit when Joe spent the day with Margaret, or about having brought Hemmings up in his early childhood.

Tom was happy with Margaret's explanation of events. Yes, she had looked after him as a child. Yes, he did visit occasionally as a teenager. She told him she had been a surrogate mother until he was seven, and later, occasionally, a teacher.

When Tom narrated the meeting to me, sitting on the patio of my house, I only nodded. I thought of the black and purple room, and tried to work out why I felt such unease about my mother's connection with Michael Hemmings. I had to put it down as one of the many demons from my awful childhood.

I needed to go back to work.

# CHAPTER ELEVEN

*Three Years Later*
*September 2004*

As usual I'd slept badly and the traffic was light so I arrived early at the station.

I was still working in the fraud squad, where I'd been for the past three years. Tom had recently approved a move to murder but I'd turned it down. Give me another twelve months, I'd said. I was still struggling emotionally and often found myself in Joe's bedroom as the sun came up, lying underneath the TARDIS cover fully clothed, waking with swollen eyes. Sometimes on those mornings, I smelt the toffee popcorn, I saw the petrol blue, but it wasn't real, as Joe wasn't anymore.

'You're in early, boss,' DS Mulhern said. He was in early, too. He didn't wait for my reply and carried on, 'You need to get...'

'A life?'

He had the good grace to redden. 'Sorry.'

'Is that what everyone thinks? Perhaps they're right.'

He shrugged his shoulders.

DS Fred Mulhern didn't like me. His best mate in the station, DC William Morley, was about to be pulled into the Detective Chief Superintendent's office – Tom's office. Tom had kept the lid on Morley for as long as he could, as had I, but it had always been destined to go higher.

DS Mulhern, along with others at the station, thought that Morley's misdemeanours should be buried, even though everyone knew that was an impossibility. I was well aware that comparisons with 'unethical' behaviour were being made with one of my long-gone cases, before Joe was born, when evidence was found in a flat on the outskirts of Birmingham: evidence later found to have been 'put' there. The whole station thought it had been me who'd planted it. It wasn't, but I knew who had: a criminal I'd known since what felt like the beginning of my career, whose profligacy in selling fake ID via the internet was legendary. Colin Masson was known as 'Razor' and I'd had a good relationship with him over the years. Colin had planted the evidence, hoping to get the guy who owned the flat rapped.

The owner of the flat was a paedophile and child trafficker. To a certain extent, my role had been to protect Colin Masson. Colin had a valid grudge against the paedophile. The flat owner/paedo had hacked into Razor's account, using it for the distribution of paedophilic images and, we suspected, to traffic children from eastern European countries. Of course, I aided and abetted the evidence plant by knowing and saying nothing. Tom suspected, but he'd protected me; both of us protecting Colin. Colin had done us a favour; we'd been trying to nail the pervert for two years. But it didn't stop the rumours about me, which re-emerged later after the Asian Bride case.

The paedo got ten years. I'd been pleased; everyone was pleased. Colin still sent me Christmas cards. He was due in the station today: fake ID again.

Colin Masson/Razor must have been making a fortune;

the short sentences he did in prison were worth it, I could see that. Although I liked Colin, he was pushing it, and pushing me. If he'd picked another avenue in life I suspected he would have been very successful.

Mulhern threw his jacket over his chair and plonked himself down.

'Colin's due in at nine,' I said.

'He's early – must be keen,' he smiled slyly. 'He's already in the waiting room, ready to go, waiting for you. Made himself all cosy. A uniform's ready to sit in on the interview.' He flicked on his computer. 'Off to prison again, you think?'

I was unsure if he was being sarcastic. Razor hadn't done as much time as he should have. For years he'd stayed with driving licences, sometimes the odd birth certificate, bogus utility bills: he'd never been in the big league. But he had ventured forth, and was now roving into passports. The call we'd taken was from a disgruntled buyer. And it was Mulhern who was on that job. The buyer, a Mr Backhurst, we conjectured from the small amount of information we had, was buying fake passports for young girls coming in from east Africa. When Mulhern and his team had collated more information, we planned on inviting Backhurst in 'for a chat'.

We knew there was a possibility that several of the girls whose fake passports Backhurst had complained about were working in illegal brothels in west London, and probably earmarked for transit to the States – that was why the fakes were needed. Backhurst had been stupid, arrogant or high on drugs when he made the call to dob in Razor and his less than worthy fakes.

I picked up my papers and shuffled them into a neat pile. 'I shouldn't be long with Masson, then we can go over the stuff we have on Backhurst.' I looked up. 'Can you get Alwyn to take Masson into the interview room, please?'

'OK, boss,' Mulhern said. He stopped at my desk. 'I'm going to get tea, you want one?'

'Coffee, please, two sugars.' Mulhern knew I hated tea. He was making a point. About what, I could only guess. 'Bring it in to me.'

He rolled his eyes thinking I couldn't see him. At work I saw everything. It was in my home life that I seemed to be blinkered. Coldness ran through me. I shook myself and made my way to interview room one.

—

Razor sat at the small oblong table; the duty sergeant, Alwyn, who I'd been working alongside for the past three years, was already there. He'd applied for promotion and would sit his exams soon. I hoped he'd be successful. Alwyn was one member of my team I got on well with. And he was excellent at his job.

'Ready, Guv,' Alwyn said. 'I'll get the tape going.' The sergeant set everything up.

I looked at Razor. He was ageing gracefully; he had attractive grey at his temples and the light lines on his face told me he laughed more than he worried. His face reminded me of an older Jonathan. I'd kept in touch with Jonathan sporadically but, as much as possible, I'd cut my connections with everyone, except Charlotte and my dad, although I'd begun to dread my meetings with him. I wanted no attachments and concentrated on my work.

Razor looked up. 'Bloody hell, DI Dune, you're not looking too good.' He unclasped manicured hands and placed them on the table. 'The extra weight doesn't suit you.'

I knew he spoke the truth. I had put on weight around my hips and, to my horror, I thought I was starting to look like my mother.

'I always look forwards to your directness, Colin.'

'I was so sorry to hear about your son, Rachel,' he said quietly.

'I know you were.'

'Fucking bastard, Michael Hemmings.' The look of pity passed and his eyes glittered. 'Won't take you long to shift that weight. My wife did the no-carb diet, worked a treat.'

I heard Alwyn chuckle.

I smiled. 'You should really give up your job, Colin.'

He grinned, 'I keep picking the wrong punters.' He seemed to study me. 'Thing is about my job, I get to hear about a lot of things.'

I was taking out papers from my file. I sat down opposite him. 'Like what?'

'Like what's happening in Littleworth.'

The fine hairs all over my body rose. The dark web was informative, as well as dangerous. I didn't reply immediately. Razor looked over towards Alwyn, who seemed to have missed the mention of Littleworth.

'Sergeant,' I said jovially. 'Before we start, do you mind getting a coffee for our guest? And get one for yourself, too.'

'No prob, Guv.'

I knew Alwyn was a caffeine addict and would be gagging. He left eagerly.

Razor grinned.

'Go on,' I said.

'Michael Hemmings has grassed, it seems. Young kids being brought in to the hospital, groomed for sex over years with some "selected" patients. Hemmings pulled the lid off. Strong rumours now that he's on the fast-track to his first tribunal review.' He watched me. 'Could well be in a less secure step-down unit within a year, I hear.'

'How concrete's your info?'

'Very.'

'I can't intervene, Colin. This investigation, with you, I mean. Not this time. You do know that, don't you?'

'I do. After this I'm giving it up. I'm hoping six months max in prison. Then I get a proper job.'

'Your CV's not looking too good,' I said, smiling.

'You'd be surprised. In the computer world I'm highly employable.'

'I bet you are.'

'You must have gone through hell.'

'Yes.'

'Be so easy to get to Hemmings in a step-down unit.'

'It would.'

'If he didn't know you.'

I looked through my paperwork. 'I can't get you out of this, Razor – Colin – but I appreciate your thoughts.' I paused. 'I really do.'

He looked towards the door, looking for Alwyn, pulled out a scrap of paper and a pen, wrote something down and gave it to me. 'This is my email that you lot don't know about.'

I slipped it in my jacket pocket. And then Alwyn came back with the coffees at the same time as Mulhern appeared with mine. Mulhern grunted and Alwyn smiled knowingly. He knew the score between Mulhern and me.

'Thanks Mulhern, much appreciated,' I said.

Alwyn gave a coffee to Razor. I put mine on the desk and leaned forwards, ready to switch the tape on. 'Right, shall we start?'

Mulhern's face was thunderous. He glanced at Razor, who winked at him. Mulhern stormed from the interview room.

'On a power trip that one, eh? Doesn't like you, Rachel,' Razor said.

'I can't please all the people all the time,' I said. 'Let's get on.'

Alwyn switched on the tape recorder. 'You do not have to say anything. But it may harm your defence if you do not mention when questioned something which you later rely on in court. Anything you do say may be given in evidence.'

We carried out the interview with no further interruptions. The plan that had been like ether in my consciousness for over four years began to form. And I could do nothing about it.

The number on the dice was clear.

—

Backhurst came into the station later. It was a difficult interview. In the end, we didn't have enough to arrest him: more evidence was needed and would take weeks to investigate and collate. Mulhern was doubly pissed off and, in all fairness, so was I. To make matters worse (for Mulhern, anyway) Backhurst also backtracked and refused to implicate Razor in the fake ID. I could only guess that he'd had second thoughts about how it would look in the wider criminal community to grass up another. Razor had admitted nothing incriminating in his interview. I knew he wouldn't; he was clever, but more than that, he knew the system inside out. So we were unable to arrest Razor, either, although I knew that Backhurst would soon be nailed, but not by me. I felt a lot of regret regarding Backhurst.

By the time the week had ended I'd handed in my resignation to Tom.

# CHAPTER TWELVE

*Three months later*
*Just before Christmas 2004*

I sat down at the kitchen table, feeling sweat drip down my back, aching in my calf muscles, a drumming pain in my shinbone. There was something about exercising: feeling the agony of pushing your body to the limits, your pulse rate rage above a hundred and forty. It was the only time my mind was truly empty and, for a few moments, I was able to forget Joe.

I checked my watch. Ten miles in just over an hour. It wasn't good enough; I needed to get down to an hour.

Over a few months I'd transformed my body. Now it was lean, toned, fit. And very strong. My resting heart rate was down to forty-nine. Getting into shape had become an obsession. I'd taken up karate again, for the first time since my mid-twenties, and had moved from brown to black belt easily. I could bring down anyone, of any size, without a knife or a gun – I was utterly self-sufficient. My teacher said I was lethal; that was the same day he asked me out on a date. I wondered if he knew who I was, if he remembered the newspaper coverage. I didn't think he did, but he knew I was single.

Liam and I had gone through a quiet, but not amicable, divorce six months after I'd gone back to work. It was Liam who'd moved out. This was the way it had to be; I wanted be in the house with my memories of Joe. My son and I would be irrevocably linked, in this life and the next.

I sensed strongly that Joe was always near to me, but that he wasn't sympathetic to my plan. Was it Joe's reticence I thought I felt, or my own?

Liam had moved to a house very near to where Charlotte lived. It had a garden and he'd built a den at the bottom of it before moving in. He'd also taken up Buddhism, and we had less and less contact as we had increasingly little to say to each other.

But yesterday evening had brought us together again.

Tom Gillespie had been to see Liam, not me – he was still pissed off with me for resigning – to tell him the news that would soon break from Littleworth, news of which I was already aware. It was all as Razor had described: there had been 'visits' by young children to the institution. Brought in with adult visitors, the children had been left alone with convicted paedophiles and murderers within the hospital walls. It had been going on for years.

Michael Hemmings was instrumental in bringing much of the information to the attention of the hospital authorities. He had helped with the internal investigation that had been on-going for the previous six months. As Razor had told me after our official interview at the station, Michael Hemmings had testified at the internal hearing. The hospital's management, undoubtedly with the help of the Home Office, had managed to keep it out of the press.

Liam informed me on the phone that Jonathan was looking into the allegations. I remembered I'd had a message on my answering machine from Jonathan around six weeks before. I'd deleted it as soon as I heard his voice, just as I'd regretfully ignored the other messages over the past three years. I'd wanted to see Jonathan and to talk to him, but resisted.

Jonathan had said it was something important, but I'd thought that it would be about my not contacting him or about my resignation. The message had probably been about Hemmings and his imminent review, the first steps towards a tribunal meeting.

The last message he left had said, 'When you're ready, call me. I'll wait as long as it takes.'

One psychiatric nurse at Littleworth had been cautioned and they were still investigating a contracted psychiatrist. Michael Hemmings had earned serious brownie points for his whistleblowing. Hemmings had proven that the treatment was working, proving, said the director of Littleworth, that we may have internal security problems but the ultimate aim of the institution, to rehabilitate and give hope to the mentally disabled within our society, is indeed, working and effective.

Liam had already contacted Sean Skerrit, to see whether we should appeal against the review of Hemmings' case. Sean told Liam that any appeal would, in all likelihood, fail. Everything was too far down the line. Hemmings is responding well to treatment, Sean had said. I was sick of hearing that statement.

I left a voicemail on my karate teacher's mobile, saying I'd be missing the class. I texted Jonathan. He texted me back within an hour, saying he'd drive up from London first thing in the morning.

That night, as I lay alone in the queen-size bed my mind cracked open a little, and I pushed hard mentally at the wall I'd constructed, allowing myself in. And watched from afar as if I were someone else.

If I did that I'd found I could look, only tentatively, but it was a start.

It was a wet Sunday and Rachel's Dad was coaching the local football team. Rachel was at Sunday school. She liked going. It got her out the house when her dad wasn't around. Even at seven, she found being on her own with her mother at home wasn't that much fun. Margaret dropped Rachel off, saying she'd pick her up in two hours. Rachel had felt unwell before going, but ignored the discomfort from her stomach so that she could still attend. She suffered with regular cramps.

As soon as Rachel sat down on a small chair next to the other children, she squirmed with the pain in her upper gut. Mr Roberts, the teacher, saw straight away. They waited a while to see if the pain would go away, but it didn't. Mr Roberts left the class in the charge of his sixteen-year-old daughter, and took Rachel to his car to drive her home himself. When they got to the house, Rachel saw her mum's car in the drive and the door was unlocked. Rachel thanked Mr Roberts for bringing her home; he was keen to return to his class and happy to leave her. Rachel didn't shout for her mother. Her stomach hurt. Her mum wasn't in the lounge. She went upstairs, knowing she'd find her in the bedroom. The door was closed. Normally, she would have shouted or knocked to let her mum know she was coming in. Their relationship was like that. Only open doors with her dad. Her mum liked her privacy.

But Rachel opened the door.

My window was open and a strong wind from outside blew the lamp off the windowsill, pulling me away from the child, Rachel. The hot sweat that covered my body quickly became too cool, and I shook.

But young Rachel, opening my mother's bedroom

door, was still with me. And they were merging with thoughts of Joe, of him when he came home from Melanie's to find Liam's car in the drive, but no one answering the door, leaving him shut outside. The same as what had happened to me – my mother's car had been there, too. She had been at home, but had not opened the door. And no one had opened the door to Joe. Why didn't you go to the den, Joe?

I sat up in bed.

The painting that I'd kept away from Liam lay in my bedside drawer. I studied it in the full moonlight, as I had done periodically over the last few years.

'What did you see, Joe? What did you hear?' I asked the darkness. A strong aroma. Then it vanished.

# CHAPTER THIRTEEN

'Hemmings has been very helpful. He's not stupid.'

Jonathan sat cross-legged on my lounge carpet. It was as if I'd only seen him yesterday; the hallmark of a good friend. 'Have you any idea what happens to a grass in those places?' he carried on.

I nodded. I did. Although I suspected it wouldn't happen to Hemmings, because yes, he was clever; as Margaret had pointed out.

'But nothing has happened to him, he hasn't even been moved to an isolation area. What have you found out? I know you're investigating this. I bet Harry Broomsgrove wants an exclusive?'

Jonathan's smile was wan. He picked carpet fluff from his trousers, nervously raked his hair and put the collection of fluff in the waste bin. 'We can't report on this, just yet. Don't ask me why; I have no idea whose pockets are being filled. It'll come out soon, though. Harry has already suggested I make a visit to Sam and Bridget ... An exclusive with Hemmings' parents, to get the interview before the story breaks properly.' He paused. 'We may not get the story first but we'll have a follow-through ready.'

'It's good of you not to request an interview with me.' I touched his hand.

'No way. I'm hesitant about your aunt and uncle, to be

honest. You don't mind?'

'No, I don't. I feel for them, really. Can't be easy.'

'Hasn't been easy for you.' He pushed a stray curl behind his ear. 'Have you seen anything of your mum and dad?'

'I see my dad reasonably regularly ...' I knew my face betrayed me.

'All well?'

'Not sure. We feel uncomfortable with each other. I think Dad misses the "doting daughter".'

'What's changed? Is it because of Joe?'

'In a way.'

'You don't want to talk about it, do you?'

'Not at the moment but, one day, I'd love your ear.'

'And your mother?'

'Don't see her.'

'At all?'

'No.'

He took a breath. 'I did a bit of research ... in prep for the Bridget and Sam article. I didn't realise Margaret had been a teacher.'

'Why would you? She gave it up years ago.'

Jonathan was doing his job. I had to be careful with Jonathan. I looked at him, the softness of his hair that shone dark in the afternoon light, the defined jaw, the kindness that was so easily expressed in his face, his keen eye for motivation, for a change in emotion, or character.

'I don't intend on putting anything in the article about Margaret looking after Hemmings when he was a child, although Harry would wet his pants if I did.'

I sat down opposite him. 'It's good of you not to.' I wanted to tell Jonathan about my mother and the last time I'd seen her. It had been three years, but her words were as piercing as the reverberant noise from clinking crystal wine glasses, still ringing on inside my head. 'I'm sorry I haven't been in touch,' I said instead. And I was.

'It's OK, I understand.' He didn't understand; how could he? I didn't, really.

He carried on, 'I thought the job was going well ... from what I've heard. Your resignation came from nowhere.'

'Have you spoken to Tom?'

'A short conversation.' He smiled. 'He doesn't do journalists.'

'He's protecting me.'

'So?'

'So?' I repeated.

'Why?'

'I need a break. I plan on having a short holiday.'

'And then?'

'I don't know...'

He surveyed me. 'You look ...' His voice trailed off. 'What's going on, Rachel? You can't spend the rest of your life getting obsessively fit.'

'We all deal with things in different ways.' I caught his eye. 'How are you and Michelle?'

'We're divorced.' His tone was flat.

'I didn't know.'

'I tried to call, over a year ago now.'

'I'm sorry I've been a crap friend.'

'It was always on the cards with Michelle and I. But I thought you and Liam would survive this. I really did.'

I shrugged my shoulders. 'Did you? He finally admitted to an affair.'

'Twat.'

I laughed out loud. 'He is a bit.'

'Did he reveal who with?'

'Someone I don't know.'

111

Jonathan looked away. 'So, this is it then? You, running, and mindless keep-fit classes?'

'Yes, that's me.'

'And you're going to sit back and allow Hemmings to be sent, probably in the not too distant future, to a step-down unit? Because I think that could happen.'

'It's out of my hands now. I'll accept what will happen. As you've said, I need to get on with my life.'

He stood up and walked towards the window. 'The Hemmings thing – you should speak to your barrister.'

'Liam did.'

'You can't be alone, Rachel, not all the time. And finishing work, is that such a good thing? Just take a long holiday, Gillespie'll understand. Why don't you come to London, stay in a hotel, I'll take you out.'

I glanced at him. 'You asking me on a date?'

He reddened. 'Come on…'

'Only teasing.' He fiddled with his watch strap. 'Stop it, Jonathan,' I laughed.

'Sorry. Nerves.'

'I'll come to London soon; that would be good.' I was good at telling untruths, according to my dad. But I found it difficult to lie to Jonathan. My heart ached and I wondered how Michelle could have let him go.

'You should.' He looked at his watch. 'I have to go.'

I saw him out, returned to the kitchen and sat down. There was nothing Jonathan could have told me about what was happening in Littleworth: I knew everything. I'd met with Razor four days after our interview at the station, a day after I'd resigned, and he'd been a mine of information. We agreed that was to be our last meeting; from then on I'd use the secure email address only. A ripple of anxiety had woven through me at Razor's astuteness. A convicted criminal understood me better than I understood myself. Razor's information had encouraged me to make my own subtle investigations into Hemmings and Littleworth, and moved me forwards.

Joe visited me the evening of the day I'd met with Razor, trying to encourage me to stop pursuing my revenge on his murderer. Was it Joe, or was it the core of my old self that I heard? I'd tried to grasp the popcorn-laden air, but Joe had already disappeared.

# CHAPTER FOURTEEN

Jonathan left Rachel's feeling oddly perplexed. Something wasn't right with her. He knew she wouldn't come to London, sensing she was distancing herself, and not just from him but from everyone. Was he despondent because he thought she wasn't interested in him? No, that wasn't the reason. His ego wasn't that big.

No, something was wrong. He'd seen the same expression, the same body language a long time ago. When Rachel had shown what she was capable of; when she'd managed effectively to nail Sorojini Jain's husband.

His interest in Rachel was not professional.

He thought of her long limbs, the softness of her expressions, the quirky way she played with her hair. The strength of her resolve in all things, even if sometimes misdirected. These were the things he loved.

No, his interest was not at all professional.

He unlocked the door of his lonely flat in Wandsworth. He'd got back from Rachel's two hours before, deciding on stopping off at the local pub rather than returning straight away to an empty home.

The Christmas lights he'd admired on his way back through London were still imprinted on his mind and, casting his eyes across his own space, he decided he should at least put up some holly sometime soon. He couldn't get used to living alone with its tidiness and the absence of Michelle's stuff littering the space as it had in their Edwardian terrace in Fulham.

He hadn't been totally honest with Rachel about Margaret Hemmings, and didn't feel good about it. Margaret hadn't left her profession strictly to pursue having a family. By all accounts she'd been pushed. Although he'd have to put the Margaret Hemmings findings on hold – Harry was impatient for the Sam and Bridget article.

When he'd interviewed Bridget and Sam after Joe had gone missing, he hadn't been firing on all cylinders. It had been a mistake to cover Joe's case. Although he'd only met Joe a handful of times, he liked the boy and had been too emotionally connected to do a good job.

Bridget and Sam had been cagey that day, Bridget in particular. He'd sniffed something but hadn't pursued it, having been interrupted by a call telling him that Joe's body had been found, which was a fact he already knew. He could have given Harry Broomsgrove a brilliant scoop before it became official about Joe's body. Harry would have turned a blind eye to his 'source' of police information, but he'd stopped himself.

He was good – no, better than good – at computer and phone hacking and in the past hadn't been troubled by using the information. He didn't do celebrity stuff; he only searched for information that he truly believed the public had a right to know. He had a love-hate relationship with his abilities; he wasn't a hundred per cent comfortable doing it, but many other journalists were doing the same thing and he had to keep up. He eyed up the awards that were framed and mounted on the living-room wall, proud he'd achieved those with old-fashioned journalism.

When he'd got into the police computer network the day Joe's body was found, he'd done it for himself with no intention of using any of the information in a story. Would he have done so if he hadn't known Rachel and Joe? Probably, he admitted. Harry could have had the headline for the next morning's paper. It had been in the following morning's instead, with no detail, only that Joe's body had been located and identified.

Knowing before anyone else who'd found Joe's body, he'd managed to get the first interview with Maisie Matthews, a seventy-one-year-old who had been retrieving her dog's ball from the undergrowth in a park on the edges of Sutton Coldfield.

She had screamed, but the park was isolated and no one heard. It was the dog, a mongrel, Jed, who went off to find another walker further down the path. Thankfully Maisie recovered quickly; she had a strong heart – in more ways than one – and he'd managed to speak to her that evening after Tom Gillespie's officers had left her home.

An hour after leaving Maisie, Jonathan checked the police computer systems again and, again, knew before anyone else that Michael Hemmings had turned himself in.

He sat down on his uncomfortable office chair and stared at the whiteboard. The name Miriam Saunders, a visitor to Littleworth who had made the initial complaints that eventually led to the internal hearing and Michael Hemmings' whistleblowing, stared back at him. He'd made a good contact with her. She trusted him. He had a lot of research to do for Littleworth and not that much time – Harry's deadlines were piling up, as were his bills.

His interview with Sam and Bridget was tomorrow at 11 a.m.

Before he'd left to see Rachel, Miriam had called, telling him about a rumour that Michael Hemmings had received a letter in Littleworth. The letter had 'destabilised' him by all accounts. Miriam had found this out on a visit to her brother.

Jonathan hadn't mentioned his investigations into Littleworth to Rachel but he was aware she knew about them, as her comment about Harry had indicated. He would share more with her when he understood more, because he was worried about her; there was something swirling around in her head. He saw it, like he'd done long ago during the Asian bride case. To the astonishment of all those involved in the case the husband had been allowed free from court with a suspended sentence, but he found himself back at the police station under charges of downloading child pornography and paying for sex with minors. He'd been nailed for that – and it had all been down to Rachel. There had been rumours about how she'd obtained the information, with William Morley being one of the 'accusers', although they had died down eventually.

Rachel had been determined to get the husband. One way or another.

His eyes moved back to the whiteboard and Miriam's name. She'd also told Jonathan another nugget: that Hemmings was having a sexual relationship with one of the nurses on his ward, a Toby Abbs. The corruption at Littleworth was big, and with it he could make not only money but, more importantly, a name for himself.

In his last meet-up with Michelle, which had gone well (they really were turning into good friends), she'd been a mine of information. Information that had helped him in both his phone call to Doctor Patterson, and his initial investigations into Littleworth. He'd mentioned Rachel to her too. Michelle had articulated what he himself didn't, even to himself. That he liked Rachel too much. Michelle knew these things, she was perceptive and honest, no nonsense. Her job suited her perfectly, she was a psychiatric nurse.

Jonathan was desperate to sleep but knew he'd be awake at three if he succumbed to the fatigue that was washing over him. His insomnia – or was it more his predilection to wake early – had been with him since he could remember. The psychiatrist he'd signed up with in his late teens, a few years before he got his first job with Harry, traced it back to his troubled childhood.

He looked towards the bedroom and the lonely double bed. He opened the door of the airing cupboard and pulled out the spare duvet and pillow. Foreseeing a restless night he made his bed on the sofa. He fell asleep thinking about Rachel.

Putting on new chinos, Jonathan made his way to the kitchen where the 'Sam and Bridget' assignment folder was still sitting on the table.

Making fresh but weak coffee – he'd nearly run out again – and finding a croissant, he sat at the table trying to arrange his thoughts. He'd been pissed off that Harry expected the Sam and Bridget piece so quickly but during the night, as his mind flipped over, he began to see it as an opportunity. He might find a clump of something new about the Dune/Hemmings family. He flicked through the slim folder. Nothing new in there, not really. Notes indicating that Bridget didn't visit her son in the psychiatric hospital, but Sam did sporadically. He stuffed the rest of the stale croissant in his mouth.

He checked his watch, rotated the strap around so the blue face sat exactly in the middle of his wrist. Time to leave.

# CHAPTER FIFTEEN

Arriving earlier than he'd anticipated, he switched the engine off and tried to relax in the uncomfortable car seat.

Harry had said Sam agreed fully to this meeting, although he hadn't mentioned Bridget's approval. Harry Broomsgrove's omissions were as telling as his admissions. Jonathan looked up at their mock-Tudor home. He was halfway up the path when the front door opened.

If it were possible, Bridget Hemmings had grown even fatter, and her hair was pulled too severely from her face. The unease he'd felt in his last interview with Bridget came back, more profoundly than ever.

'Hello, Jonathan.' She looked at her watch. 'On time.'

'Always on time, Mrs Hemmings.' He was about to shake her hand, but she kept both arms folded tightly below heavy and pendulous breasts. 'Nice to see you again.'

'Good to see you too, Jonathan. Come in. Sam's here, in the kitchen. You know the way? Go straight through.'

The kitchen was homely, a few token Christmas trimmings dotted around. He'd guess that Christmas wasn't a good time of the year in the Hemmings' household. Sam sat at the table, hollow cheeks enclosed in reddened hands. While Bridget had grown fatter since their son's incarceration, Sam had become thinner and frailer.

He looked up. 'Hello, Jonathan.'

'Hi, Sam. You remember me?'

'Course I do. You were good to us the day you brought us home. We appreciated that. Your boss wants to do a piece on us? Fine with me, but not sure about Bridget.' He glanced at his wife. 'Not sure, are you, love?'

'It might be good for Michael …' Jonathan said. 'It'd put a good public spin on his forthcoming tribunal if you could give me some positive stuff about him … you know, as a child?'

Bridget grunted.

'Thank you for agreeing to see me,' Jonathan said to Bridget.

She grunted again.

Sam peered at the book lying on the table. Jonathan took a quick look: *Icing a Cake Properly*. That was Sam and Bridget's business. The bakery business. A lot of early mornings. And why Michael had been farmed out in the early years to Margaret Hemmings.

'You both got on with Rachel, she tells me. Perhaps we can start there. How do you feel about an impending tribunal review for your son, and with how Rachel and Liam … and Margaret and Alan might feel about it?'

Sam spoke first. 'I've always liked Rachel, although she can come across as a bit cold sometimes, but she's not, and these days I wouldn't blame her.' He paused, rubbing the image of a particularly ornate cake on the front of the book. 'Of course, we don't see Rachel that much.' He looked up at Bridget. She touched an earring and then pulled her jumper across her over-ample stomach. Jonathan's old Scottish great-aunt would have called Bridget an apple. A very big apple.

'Do you need me here?' Bridget said. 'I've got things to do. I'm sure Sam can help with your article. I don't visit Michael: it's too much for me.' She was already slipping on her coat.

'Do you write to him?' Jonathan asked.

She looked towards Sam and reddened. Jonathan noticed the dampness of the fabric underneath her armpits.

Sam looked towards his wife, and Jonathan saw a loving sympathy cross his face. 'Bridget can't read or write. Not properly.'

Bridget placed a hand on her husband's shoulder. 'Mind if I leave?' she said, her face falling into an ill-hidden anxiousness.

'Not if you need to go, Mrs Hemmings,' Jonathan replied. He gave her what he thought was his most engaging smile.

He watched as she adjusted her bra underneath the coat and cardigan and looked away. There was definitely something about Bridget that was making him feel uneasy. Something he couldn't pinpoint, but he knew it went back to that first meeting when she'd seemed almost unconcerned about Joe's disappearance.

He glanced at a derelict-looking Sam. His appearance must have taken years to reach this stage, and the root of his ruin was his son, Jonathan guessed.

He carried on. 'Can I just ask you one question before you leave, Mrs Hemmings?'

'Be quick.' Pointedly, she looked at her watch and he was close enough to whiff her body odour.

'Can I ask why you don't visit Michael?'

'I leave that to Sam.' Her face became drawn, the lines deeper.

Not looking at Bridget, Sam said, 'It's been difficult for Bridget ... hasn't it, love?'

'I really need to go,' she glanced at Sam. 'Someone

has to keep our business going.'

Jonathan watched her. She was desperate to get away, and the same question he'd wanted to answer years before formed in his mind again. Did Bridget know something about her son that she'd never admitted? He'd always felt she hadn't told the truth about not knowing her son had come down from Chester prior to the week he abducted Joe. It had only been a hunch, though, and nothing had come up at the trial.

The claustrophobic kitchen was quiet. Bridget left without expanding on why she didn't visit Michael.

'Do you and Bridget get on with Margaret?' Jonathan asked Sam.

'We were never bosom buddies, the three of us, but we're OK.'

'But you like Rachel?'

'We've both always liked Rachel.'

'Are they very different – mother and daughter – would you say?'

'I'd say.'

Sam crossed his thin arms. 'I know about Margaret looking after Michael when he was young, Sam. You and Bridget owe her a lot, wouldn't you say?'

'We probably do. It's Bridget who has the biggest problem with Margaret, although I was never in love with her either. Strange woman, but my brother – Alan – was besotted from the moment he met her. Unhealthy, really.' He looked at Jonathan. 'I always thought.'

'But you allowed her to look after your only son?'

'Not a lot of choice back then. Times have changed with childcare, Jonathan. Bridget and I, we both had to work. Margaret offered. We took the opportunity. Why not?'

Still staring at his book, Sam continued, 'I don't want

to talk about Margaret, and that's not why you're here. What do you need to know for your article?'

Jonathan took out his folder and began asking the questions whose answers would fill a good 1500-word article about what it was like to be the parents of a murderer. A murderer who might shortly be released to a less secure step-down unit.

Bridget didn't return before Jonathan left. And again, as he'd felt five years ago, he left the Hemmings' household knowing there was something he hadn't quite got to the bottom of.

# CHAPTER SIXTEEN

*Littleworth High Security Psychiatric Hospital,*
*Merseyside*

Michael Hemmings was enjoying his moment of notoriety within Littleworth. There had been talk about isolating him from the other patients, but it hadn't happened. Hemmings stood at six foot and, while being inside, he'd managed to keep up his fitness. Fourteen stone of hard muscle. There was no one in Littleworth who could overpower him physically. He was safe.

Whistleblowing had come easy; he'd nothing to lose. Nothing at all. Everything to gain. And he'd nailed David Juniper into the bargain. Juniper had been carted off to another secure hospital in the south somewhere, that none of the patients at Littleworth had any desire to go to. Juniper deserved it, the weird, fat, paedo shit. Michael Hemmings didn't consider himself a paedophile, and had convinced himself he wasn't one.

Michael was good at convincing himself about a lot of things.

He figured if he couldn't remember doing it then he wasn't guilty. And he couldn't remember. But he'd admitted to it, they said.

The kids' visits had revolted him. The system revolted him. The establishment revolted him. They were all weird fuckers, the lot of them. He thought about his psych, Doc Patterson; Patterson revolted him less than the others. The few moments of clarity he sometimes enjoyed, and had been enjoying today, suddenly, quickly, fell around him. And the headache came. And the colours. The fucking colours and auras.

Spotting his designated nurse making his way over, Hemmings smiled. Toby Abbs always had a greenish aura, the colour of a highly creative person, apparently. This turned Hemmings' smile into a grin. Poor Toby. Totally in the wrong job, just as he'd been totally married to the wrong person, of the wrong sex, totally denying his preference for dicks.

Hemmings knew Abbs was obsessed with him, loving him, when Hemmings made Abbs come like a hosepipe in the cupboard where the clean bedding was kept, hating Hemmings when he ignored him, or made fun of him. It was too easy to take the piss out of Toby.

Toby Abbs was indeed green. Naïve and oddly innocent. However, Hemmings felt something for the young runt. Was it what Doc Patterson would call compassion? He knew about Toby's private life, Toby shared everything with him. Everything. Abbs had told him that his ex-wife had called him a loser and a freak. Hemmings wasn't surprised – the stupid twat had told her about him, told her he was in love with Hemmings.

She'd left him soon afterwards, taking their two kids with her. Now living in Australia, she'd threatened to go to the director with what she knew if Abbs contested her demands to have sole custody of their children. Did Michael feel sorry for him? A bit.

Littleworth's director had been on Toby's back constantly since Michael had blown the whistle. Toby had been in a foul mood for weeks. He was withering,

Hemmings could see it. Needed some cheering up did Toby, and he knew just what'd do the trick. A good, full-on blowjob. Make Toby forget his woes.

Hemmings looked towards the end of the ward. It was Tuesday and mail day. Toby and dim 'Windy' Miller were sorting through the prisoners' correspondence with the ward clerk. None of the staff took any notice of what the others were doing. It was a feature of the institution: a closed place with rules that didn't apply to the outside. A world disconnected from reality – until recently. And that was all due to him.

Hemmings had presence. He had charisma. He now had power. He liked that.

Toby Abbs was opening an envelope with venom. Hemmings watched and Toby looked up, making eye contact. Toby slipped the envelope surreptitiously towards the edge of the table and under his jacket. Windy didn't notice a thing.

Hemmings heard Abbs say, as he picked up a handful of envelopes, 'I'm going to sit somewhere quiet to go through these.'

Windy grunted, 'Well, don't be long – we've got the psych appointments soon.'

Toby Abbs nodded and made his way to an empty office outside the ward.

Hemmings waited. Patiently.

Toby returned to the ward fifteen minutes later and made his way towards him, glancing around once to look at the laundry cupboard at the side of the ward. Hemmings saw Toby's boner from thirty feet. He could also see the brown aura that surrounded his own body. The unsettled aura, the distracting one. The one that came just before the grey, and grey preceded the most dangerous colour of all. White.

He'd come to recognise the meanings of these colours since seeing Doc Patterson. He couldn't believe a trained person such as the Doc believed in that garbage. Auras, colours. Patterson explained to him about them; how they could indicate when he might begin to feel angry, unsettled, and to know when the dark thoughts would come.

Hemmings didn't have dark thoughts all the time. Sometimes his mind was clear and empty. And this emptiness always accompanied stretches of time when he had no inclination to hurt people, have sex or attempt to harm himself. At those times he thought of his mother, when he was young, before the meningitis, before he saw the colours. Today though, the brown was dark, deep and muddy.

The old Doc had been exploring a different route recently. Patterson was asking probing questions, prodding into his mind, digging into the day they said he'd killed Joe. Patterson was interested in his relationship with his mum, and Sam, his fucking Dad.

Thinking of being moved from Littleworth, Hemmings' mind capsized again. It should have made him feel good, but for some reason it didn't. He wasn't entirely sure he wanted to move. He wasn't certain how he felt.

And an image floated through his brain of what it would be like to have your throat cut.

Would the breathing stop straight away?

Or would it take a while?

Or your dick sliced through.

How had Joe felt?

He'd tried to ask him, but he was already dead. He remembered that, trying to ask – both things.

Hemmings kept an eye on Toby, knowing the nurse

wouldn't approach straight away.

'Hemmings, time for your session soon,' Windy shouted from the end of the ward.

Toby Abbs. Five five, slightly built and skinny. The physique of a young adolescent. Black, greasy hair and still with a face full of puss-engorged spots. Giving Toby what he was desperate for wasn't an inconvenience for Hemmings, because, deep down, in a place that had long ago atrophied he liked Toby; perhaps even loved him a little. David Juniper had given Toby a hard time, and it was another reason he was elated to have grassed Juniper up. He felt almost paternal to the young nurse. Juniper had been a fat bastard with a bald head and a cock as thick as an overgrown cucumber. He hated fat cocks. Almost as much as he hated cunts. He'd kept Juniper sweet for long enough to entrap and then expose him. It had been a satisfying experience and Toby loved him even more because of it.

His mind filled with brown. David Juniper – Dirty Dave – was a sick bastard. But now he was gone. Gone. Gone. Gone.

Hemmings stared at the ceiling. 'What can I do for you, Toby?' He tore his eyes away from the ceiling, resting them somewhere along his forehead. He didn't like eyes, even Toby's.

Toby pulled the letter from his pocket. 'If Windy'd got hold of this,' Toby said, 'it'd be with Patterson by now.'

Hemmings reached to take the letter.

Toby held it firm. 'What do I get in return?'

'Come on, does there always have to be a barter, Toby? Let me have a look.' Hemmings pulled on his ear and then, suggestively, placed the tip of his thumb in his mouth and sucked.

Toby gave him the letter.

Hemmings slumped back on the bed. 'You've read it, haven't you?'

Toby shook his head.

'You fucking have.'

'OK, I have. It's nice that you're getting letters. You don't get much mail.' He looked at Hemmings. 'The writer's a bit religious, then? Talks about God a lot.'

Hemmings lay flat on his bed, arms at right angles to his body, the letter held upwards. 'Not religious.' It was a front, the religious stuff. He could read in between the lines. He could see the promise. The promise that had been dangled in front of him for years.

Toby shrugged his shoulders. 'Whatever you say. You're the boss.'

Hemmings tossed Toby a look. 'Yeah, right.' He jumped up with the stealth of a cat.

'Do you like it?' Abbs asked. 'The letter?'

Hemmings bit the end of his thumb. 'Yeah, I like it.' Did he like it? He wasn't fucking sure. But he'd love a visit. He would.

Abbs looked at his watch, he was impatient. 'We don't have that long before you see Patterson.'

He stared at the laundry cupboard door and at Toby's expectant face. Hemmings started making his way towards the cupboard, nodding and grinning at the other patients who littered the ward. Fucking lobotomised, most of them.

Drugged, sad and bewildered humanity stared back at him.

Toby waited a few minutes before following him into the large cupboard. Before he got started on Toby, the young nurse asked again about the letter.

'One day, Toby, I might tell you.' For the first time in

two years Hemmings kissed Toby full on the lips.

Afterwards he told Toby Abbs that he really didn't think he'd killed Joe.

# CHAPTER SEVENTEEN

At the same time Michael Hemmings was finishing up in the laundry cupboard with Toby Abbs, Doctor Thomas Patterson was trying to terminate his session with his penultimate patient of the day.

He opened the blinds of the small cramped office, indicating the session was over. It was always difficult to get rid of this particular patient because he liked to talk, and today he was in a more irrepressible mood than ever. 'Garrulous' was the word Patterson scribbled in his notepad. Patterson wasn't getting very far with him: the drugs weren't touching his psychotic behaviour. The patient was already on the highest dose he'd prescribed to anyone. Perhaps it was his bulk. Twenty-five stone of lard.

Patterson glanced at the patient, who was still talking and making strange and pointless free-associative comments from the last line of questioning. 'Time out now.'

'Sorry, Doc, did I go?'

'You did, but it's fine.' Patterson smiled tightly.

'What you smiling at, Doc? You laughing at me?' The patient lumbered out from his chair, suddenly his soft and open features pinched and hard.

'No, I'm smiling because it's been a good session.'

A little flattery always did the trick with this one. Simple and easy. For a simple and easy mind. Patterson

135

had no idea what IQ his patient had been born with, but it was safe to say that many volitional drops on the head by his father forty years before had had some impact on his current IQ of sixty.

Patterson looked at his watch. 'Well, you have a nice afternoon.'

'I will, Doc.'

Patterson watched as he shambled out the door. He was incredibly clumsy, too.

Michael Hemmings next.

Patterson thought about David Juniper and furrowed an already deeply lined brow. The internal enquiry had unearthed a shocking laxity in their security system. It had also moved forwards the time frame for Hemmings' first tribunal review. There was still a lot of work to do with Hemmings, and he felt he was getting close; the tribunal would mess up his work. Had already messed it up.

Hemmings' case wasn't all that it appeared. The psychiatrist inside him wanted Hemmings to stay at Littleworth so that he could unravel the mystery that seemed to have been completely missed. Sometimes that is what he wanted, on the days he was not tired. Today Doctor Patterson was feeling very fatigued.

Anyway, Patterson was now on a time limit. The director had given him a few weeks to get his notes up to date and perform a proper handover to Doctor Cohen. Thinking of Cohen, Patterson smirked to himself.

Getting up, he used the phone attached to the wall to call Montford ward. One of the male clerks answered.

'Is Mr Abbs available?'

The line crunched. 'He's not around at the moment, shall I find him?'

'Yes, tell him to send Hemmings to me as soon as possible.'

Patterson heard more crunching.

'Doctor Patterson, sorry, was sorting something out. Hemmings is on his way,' Abbs said.

Abbs sounded as if he'd just run a marathon, 'Busy?' Patterson asked.

Abbs gasped. 'You know how it is.'

Patterson didn't really know how it was; he left the institution most afternoons to lecture at the university, although since the enquiry, he'd stopped the university lectures, too worn out to think about them let alone give one. 'I'd like to see you too, come down now.'

'Now?'

'Yes, now.'

'OK, give me ten.'

'Now, Abbs.'

Abbs mumbled a yes and put the phone down.

Patterson had been away on a sabbatical when the young and vastly under-qualified Abbs was appointed. It wasn't that he didn't like the nurse; he had no feelings one way or the other, although he suspected Toby Abbs wasn't the brightest uniform in this enclosed institution. The director was more than worried about staff from Littleworth talking to the press. Patterson could imagine Abbs being a loose cannon.

He knew of at least one journalist who'd got a sniff of what was happening. Jonathan Waters. He'd called Patterson a month ago. Patterson hadn't called back, obviously. He was already aware that the lid would be kept on the stink until later in the year; until the director had spun his rhetoric. Part of that rhetoric would include Hemmings, and what a good job Littleworth was doing in treating him. Hemmings was to be their mascot. It would be Patterson who would be taking the flak for the scandal.

A gentle knock on the door.

'Come in,' Patterson said.

Toby Abbs looked worried. 'Is there a problem, Doctor? Hemmings is waiting outside already.'

'No, but I wanted to have a quick chat about Michael … your favourite patient.'

Abbs coloured. 'What do you mean?'

'You're quite close to him?'

'We get along fine, sir.'

'I have a question for you, Abbs.'

'Fire away, sir.'

'It may seem like an odd question.'

Abbs waited.

'Do you believe Hemmings had absolutely nothing to do with the children coming into the institution?'

'He had nothing to do with it, sir. Kids really aren't his thing.'

Patterson rubbed his chin. He had come to that conclusion too, although he conjectured as to how Abbs had.

'What makes you say that?' Patterson asked patiently. 'You are aware of why he's in here?'

He floundered. 'Just stuff he says.'

'To you?'

'Not particularly, in general.'

Patterson's eyes were drawn to Abb's crotch. 'By the way, your fly's open.'

Abbs turned the colour of an overripe tomato. 'Nipped to the loo – '

'The visitor sessions will be resumed soon. Ensure all the visitors and inmates are supervised properly. This is a high-security hospital. A psychiatric institution.' He peered at Abbs. 'We don't want any more Miriam Saunders do we?'

'No, sir.'

'Good. How is the new gazebo coming along?'

Abbs appeared confused with the change in questioning. 'It's finished. The fresh air'll be good for the patients.'

Patterson didn't want to point out that no amount of fresh air would aid the sick and sad minds of the inmates within those walls. 'Ensure someone accompanies these medicinal trips to the gazebo.'

'Yes, sir.'

'Send Hemmings in.'

Abbs left.

Patterson pulled Hemmings' notes from underneath the pile. A very different creature from his last case. Very different. Two other psychs, including Dr Cohen, had been brought in since the internal investigations to assess Hemmings. Patterson had known then that his career was on the edge of extinction. The director would ensure it. This did not unduly bother him. He was ready to go. He was so tired. But he would have liked to get to the bottom of the Hemmings case, he really would.

A metallic taste emerged in his mouth whenever he reviewed Hemmings' notes and progress. For a long time he'd had an idea of something, something he hadn't put his finger on yet. He'd experienced the metal-taste phenomenon since he'd been a graduate, and it always signified a hidden truth in a case history.

He looked up as Michael Hemmings entered the office and sat down confidently in the chair by the window. He seemed bulkier than the last time he'd seen him. Long, firm legs casually splayed in front of him. His chest, free of hair, Patterson could see from the open V of his T-shirt, was solid. His blond hair was styled differently from their last meeting, too.

Patterson couldn't put his finger on what was different about the hair.

'Wrong chair, Michael.' Patterson nodded to the chair placed on the opposite side of his desk.

Hemmings made no attempt to move. 'I like it here, by the window.'

Patterson could not be bothered to argue. 'How's it going, Michael?'

'Fine.'

'A lot's been happening. You're aware that you've been earmarked to attend a tribunal soon?'

'You going to lose your job, Doc?'

'We are not here to talk about me.' Patterson looked at his watch.

'You on a time limit, Doc? Looking at your watch won't make time go any quicker.' Hemmings grinned. 'I've tried it. Fire away, Doc.'

'Since our last session,' he rustled through his notes, 'have you had any more incidences of "colours"?'

'The auras?'

'Yes, the auras.'

'As it happens, Doc, I have one with me today.'

'What colour?'

'Dark fucking brown.'

'And you feel the emotion that goes with this colour?'

'Distracting. Yes, I feel that.'

'And are you trying to deal with it?' Patterson looked up at Hemmings. 'Have you had any more suicidal thoughts recently?'

Hemmings wiped his mouth in an exaggerated movement. 'Well, Abbs helps me ... get rid of the colours,' he grinned, 'the suicidal thoughts.'

'Abbs?'

'Yes, you've just seen him, haven't you? Maybe he

140

told you how he calms me?'

'No, you weren't on our agenda, Michael. As much as that pains you.'

Patterson watched Hemmings' thumb move towards his mouth.

'I'd like to talk about your father, Sam, today, Michael.'

'And my mother?'

'Perhaps.'

'She left me, my mother…'

Bridget Hemmings didn't visit her son; it was only Sam Hemmings who travelled north to Littleworth. 'I'm sure she will visit you,' Patterson said.

Hemmings' legs shot forwards from the chair; the lean muscles of his thighs tensed. 'She sends me letters.'

Patterson scribbled in his notes, 'delusions of correspondence?' He wasn't aware of any letters from Bridget Hemmings, only sporadic ones from the father, Sam, and a few wacko ones from sad women looking for a boyfriend who happened to be a child murderer. He made a note to talk to Abbs again.

Patterson studied Michael Hemmings and felt drained. Today was not a good day.

'What does she say in the letters?' he asked finally.

'She says sorry.'

'What is your mother sorry for?'

Hemmings' face was blank. As though in a trance. 'That I'm in here. That it is a good thing, though, that I'm better off here.' Hemmings looked up. 'I don't think she wants me to leave. Doesn't want a tribunal.'

'Well, she might be right. It isn't the best thing. Do you have the letter, Michael? Could I see it?' All letters should be censored. He really needed to have a word with Abbs.

141

Hemmings smiled obtusely. 'There's no letter. I'm making it up. Having a laugh.'

Patterson decided to let it go. 'What colour are you seeing now, Michael?'

'White.'

Patterson looked up from his notes at his patient. White. The death colour. Hemmings did seem to be confused today. 'I think we'll leave this for today, Michael.'

Hemmings' finger had been in the edge of his mouth for the whole time. He now took it out. 'OK, Doc, you're the boss.' He grinned at Patterson. 'You can go and find your young pussy now.'

How could Hemmings know about Leanne? 'I'll see you in a week?'

'No problem, I'm going nowhere.' Hemmings left the room.

Patterson checked when his next appointment with the director was. Papers fell on the floor and he was angry at his own disorganisation. Then he found it. A week. He needed to make an up-to-date report on Hemmings. Would he mention his thoughts? That over the last four years the 'aura therapy' was indicating to him that there might well have been someone else at the scene of Joe Dune's murder. And what Abbs had said – about the children – Hemmings not being interested in them. Although Hemmings had never denied interfering with Joe Dune while the boy had been at the squat, and although he questioned Abbs' intelligence, he did conjecture if perhaps the nurse might be right. There were things that Hemmings was still holding close to his chest.

Patterson had studied the court case in detail over the years he'd been treating Hemmings and was beginning to slowly draw his own conclusions which were compounded by the 'letter' today, whether it existed or not. Although he had no firm evidence. Psychiatry was a protracted business; he needed another two years.

He sat back in the chair, stopping himself from putting his feet up on the desk – a habit he abhorred. He'd managed to stitch together a working hypothesis of Hemmings' relationship with Bridget and the rest of the family. It would make for a wonderful thesis one day – for someone else. He was well past all that now.

He checked the time. Maybe he would go home before going to see Leanne.

He thought about Michael Hemmings' white aura as he filed his notes in the battered cabinet. He would put all the data in the computer system tomorrow.

He called Montford ward again, asking Abbs to return to his office. Abbs was knocking at his door within five minutes.

'Something wrong, sir?' Abbs asked.

'Has Hemmings received any letters recently?'

Abbs reddened. 'No, sir. Why?'

'He told me today he received one from his mother.'

'His mother ... that's what he said?'

'He told me afterwards he'd made it up. Ask Windy to check the mail, and let me know if anything comes in. Anything at all.'

Abbs seemed to relax. 'Will do, sir.'

Hemmings watched as Toby hurried down the ward.

'You tell Patterson about the letter?' Abbs asked meekly.

'No, course I didn't,' he replied easily. He didn't think he had; he had already forgotten. He rubbed Toby's groin, in full view of anyone that might be watching. Hemmings knew Toby was simultaneously shit scared that someone would see, or that Windy was nosing, and aroused to the point of explosion that someone could see.

They returned to the cupboard.

# CHAPTER EIGHTEEN

*December 23rd 2004*

I'd been dreading Christmas for months. It was the worst time of the year, worse than the anniversary of finding Joe's body, and each year the feeling of dread only intensified. Each year I thought of the swing, of Joe's happiness that Christmas morning, of mine and Liam's joy at seeing it. All the remembrances intensified what I had lost, what I would never be able to recover.

Charlotte was standing on her doorstep waiting when the taxi dropped me outside her house. As I lugged my small suitcase along the pavement, she rushed towards me. I'd hardly seen her since my divorce.

'Rachel!'

'Charl!' She pulled her short black faux-fur jacket tight around her slim midriff. 'Dressed for the weather as usual, I see,' I laughed.

She hugged me. 'Let me help you with the case.' She tried to pick it up. 'Bloody hell, what you got in here? Come on, Jacob's got mulled wine on the go.' She peered at me, 'You've lost weight.'

'Maybe, but losing those "mother-like" hips can only be a good thing.'

I felt her hand in the small of my back, she rubbed the space soothingly.

'Lost weight but very muscular, training obsessively, are you?' Her expression was a mixture of worry and disapproval. I don't think Charlotte had exercised once in her whole life. It was her nervous energy that kept her trim.

'Will share my secrets later.'

'How you doing?' she asked, more seriously.

Belatedly, I realised my reference to 'mother', and the few moments of not thinking about Joe ended. 'You know.'

'Come on, let's get inside.'

Jacob handed me a tumbler of spicy, warm liquid that sparkled under the festive lighting. 'Got to go, Aunt Rach, important party to attend.' He ruffled my head and I knew that, even after nearly five years, he still didn't know what to say.

'Have a good time,' Charlotte shouted towards the closing door. She plonked herself down in front of the fire.

'Christmas tree looks wonderful,' I said. 'Thanks for inviting me. Jacob looks too handsome.'

'He is, isn't he?' A mild guilt hovered on her features. 'What's Liam doing for Christmas?'

I got the impression that my friend might know what Liam was doing. 'Going off to some obscure meditative place in Thailand. I'll try not to spoil your Christmas, Charl.'

'Don't be bloody ridiculous. I've invited all the clan and Jacob will be around until New Year. He's taking a long break. His last project finished and then he went straight into some voice coaching, only just finished that.'

'After a coveted role, is he?'

'His agent has an eye on a "big script" that's

in circulation. The director and producer are looking for the supporting male actor. The agent wants to put Jacob forwards for the part.'

'And?'

'And, the director has an obsession with accents and authenticity. The role is an American from Ohio. The director is determined to find an actor indigenous to Ohio, Jacob's agent is thinking differently. This could put him on the Hollywood map good and proper. So Jacob did the voice coaching in London, some obscure little place in Soho. It's a school for method acting as well. I think he learnt more about that, too, but it was mainly the voice coaching he went for. Says it's the best thing he's done. Loved it.' Charlotte nudged a bauble into place on her perfectly chaotic tree. 'Said there were a few non-actors there, business people, wanting to change the way they speak. He just liked being in London, to be honest.'

I stood to stretch my legs. 'So, they'd take on anyone? I mean, not just actors?'

'Yep, as long as you pay. Luckily, Jacob's agent stumped up.'

'What's the name of the school?'

'Cambri School of Voice Coaching and Acting. Why? Are you interested? Thinking of taking up acting? You enjoyed it at uni. Might be a good idea – a little hobby.' She filled my glass, smiling. 'Why on earth did you resign? You need to work. Perhaps going back to the police wasn't such a great idea, but you need to do something.' She looked uncomfortable. 'I mean, what do you do all day? Every day. It's not healthy.' She paused, and gave my bare legs an admiring glance. 'I can see you're spending a lot of time working out. You're as lean as a fillet steak.'

'I took up karate again, too.'

'No!'

'I have. It's good for me.'

'Why've you been avoiding me, Rachel?'

'I haven't seen much of anyone.'

'Liam still worries about you.'

'No he doesn't.' Charlotte had obviously seen more of Liam than I had. 'He was having an affair before Joe went missing but that isn't the reason we've divorced.' She nodded and I thought she understood.

I took off the heavy cardigan I was wearing, revealing my chocolate-brown Lurex dress. I'd made an effort for Christmas. It was sleeveless and short.

'Jesus girl, look at your arms. Last time I saw biceps like that was when I threw the javelin for my school. Not mine, I might add, but the girl who annually beat me at the county championships.'

'Being fit helps the mind,' I said.

She scrutinised me closely. 'It should do, yes.' The sudden seriousness of her expression faded as fast as it had appeared. 'And your hips … gone.'

I had the height and build of Margaret. Largish hips, thick thighs and a flat chest. My shape didn't bother me but looking like my mother always had.

'Not quite. At least I will look less like Margaret,' I said lightly.

'Carry on like this, and you'll look nothing like her. Anyway, you are nothing like her.' She flicked back her long fringe. Charlotte always flicked her fringe when about to change the subject. 'Have you seen Tom Gillespie?'

'Not recently, he's annoyed with me for resigning. It was Liam he called about Hemmings and Littleworth, not me.' I'd filled Charlotte in on the details of Littleworth in an earlier phone call.

'Yes, I kn...'

'You know?'

She looked towards the exquisite parquet flooring. 'I spoke to Liam before he went away...'

'I don't mind, you know, Charlotte, you keeping in touch with Liam. He was your friend, too.'

She coloured and I put it down to the wine, the heat of the room.

She smiled indulgently. 'So maybe this New Year, you should decide what you're going to do with the rest of your life?'

Perhaps I should tell her. Tell her everything, but of course I couldn't.

'Don't worry,' I said, 'I know what I'm doing.' And I did.

'You have to live, girl. Have you seen Jonathan Waters recently?'

I'd been staring at the fire, watching yellow flames leap around the grand fireplace, marvelling at their randomness. I looked up. 'I have, a few weeks ago. He came over to talk about what's happening at Littleworth. I think he plans on writing something about it. He was about to go and interview Sam and Bridget.'

'An exclusive on the parents of the murderer who's about to be let out?' She looked at me. 'Sorry...'

'It's OK.'

'You know Jonathan has the "hots" for you?'

'He was married, Charl. And that's a very old-fashioned term. Erase it from your vocabulary,' I laughed.

She grinned. 'He isn't now, though. And hasn't been for a while.'

'He does not have the "hots" for me.' But I knew that the kind and gentle Jonathan did. I'd always suspected. It was another reason to keep away from him. I needed to

149

stay away, if only because he was a journalist. A journalist with an interest and understanding of me. And that was the last thing I needed.

Charlotte's face dropped into anxiousness. 'They won't really let Hemmings out, will they?'

'They might, at some point in the future, allow him to go to a step-down unit. It's complicated, but when public opinion has died down, he could quietly be placed in a less secure unit, and theoretically allowed out, under supervision … yes.'

She pulled at her fringe and changed the subject. 'Have you seen your mother, or other members of your illustrious family, recently? Sorry to bring all that up, but I wondered.' She grinned. 'Get all that stuff out of the way.'

'I see my dad. Try to avoid my mother, though … you know.' I'd never told Charlotte about my last visit to see Margaret, and the last conversation I'd had with her. I'd told no one. I hadn't told her about Hemmings being looked after by my mother, either.

'So. What are your plans?'

'I'm going away for a while. A short break, as I told Tom I would be doing.'

'You could have the house in Venice Beach, you know.'

'Thanks, but I'm going somewhere where no one knows where to find me, just for a while.'

'You'll tell me?'

I hesitated. 'I'll give you a PO Box number.'

'How long for?'

'That I'll be away? Just a few weeks.'

'Can I call you?'

'No, I want no phone, no computer.' I watched her. 'You'll have the PO Box, but don't tell anyone, not my

150

dad, no one. OK? Promise?'

'Promise. Come on, girl.' The mulled wine was depleted and we'd begun on the vodka. 'Let's get pissed.'

'It doesn't mix well with the pills.'

'Then stop taking them. Find another way of dealing with this. It's time.'

Charlotte was right. Soon it would be time.

# CHAPTER NINETEEN

*Seven weeks later*
*Mid-February 2005*

As usual, Jonathan was awake. He lifted his head from the pillow and peered at green luminescent numbers. Five. His head flopped back down and he allowed his mind to free-fall.

It was in the early hours when Jonathan scraped through his past. Every morning he tried not to but every morning he failed. His thought processes always took the same path. Beginning with the day the kindly neighbour, who often looked after him when his parents went somewhere without him, came into his bedroom with a lady police officer, to tell him that his mum and dad were never coming home.

The pain dulled over the years but did not leave. Jonathan never got over the cruel loss, and his life never fulfilled the promise hoped for by his doting parents.

He did not dislike the great-aunt and uncle who subsequently took care of him, he just felt little for them. When he eventually moved out, life was supposed to get better. It didn't, not for a while, not until he applied for the job on Harry's newspaper. It got better still when he met Michelle. He realised now that although he'd always fancied the pants off her, it was her grief and vulnerability that he really went for. He wanted to look after her as he himself had never been looked after.

Was that why he'd fallen for Rachel? Because she was in need? No. He'd fallen for her years before, before Michelle, before Joe's murder, when she was strong, confident and happy; but he'd never been able to say a thing. And now he couldn't stop thinking about her and her 'holiday'. She was still away and he'd heard nothing.

He'd lived by his instincts since he'd been orphaned and they had only grown stronger over the years. It was what made him a good journalist. He knew something wasn't right with Rachel. He felt it. She'd never got back to him about coming to London. OK, so his pride was hurt, but it was more than that.

Half an hour later, after too much coffee and not enough food, Jonathan was firmly ensconced in his study dialling Charlotte Gayle's telephone number.

Gayle didn't seem too fazed when she opened the door soon after Jonathan had pulled on the antiquated bell. Late thirties, and in great shape, a sarong wrapped stylishly around her lithe, compact, body, Jonathan remembered Rachel talking about her best friend: bohemian, innately kind, unsuspicious.

'All the things I'm not,' she had said. 'That's why she likes me, I'm sure – I challenge her. She has more in common with Liam.'

'Jonathan ... long time. How are you?' Charlotte opened the door wider, offering hospitality. 'Come in.'

They were soon sitting outside on her overplanted patio, the winter sun invisible behind heavy clouds. Jonathan felt the beginnings of a spring that was still a while away, not due to the temperature, it couldn't be more than eight degrees, but because of the tranquil

Mediterranean-style garden he found himself in. The terrace was full of bright ceramics, wind chimes and burnt-down candles that signified many evenings spent outside. It was welcoming and he did feel very at ease.

She crossed one slim leg over the other. 'What can I do for you? I take it this isn't a social visit?' She leant forwards. 'You're not here to ask about Jacob? I don't talk about my son. Ever.'

Jonathan sat down in a pretty but uncomfortable chair. 'No, I'm not here to talk about Jacob, although I hear he's been offered a very prestigious part. So, although I don't want to talk about him, give him my congratulations.' He noticed her clear and smooth skin. No wrinkles at all and no sign of surgery. He saw where Jacob got his looks. They both had skin that a camera loved, a translucency that reflected the light, contours that translated well in a photograph.

'Have you seen Rachel recently?' he asked.

'At Christmas.' She watched him. 'And you, have you seen her?' She wavered, her smile dimmed. 'You're not writing anything about Rachel, are you?'

'No, I'm not. This isn't work, and I can't believe you'd even think that.' Jonathan fixed his stare on her. 'I'm a bit concerned about her.'

'Are you? I'm not. She's on holiday.' Her face softened. 'I'm sorry she didn't let you know … I know you have a soft spot for her.'

'It's not about me having any spot for her. She's my friend, as she's yours, and she's been "gone" for over a month. Nearly two.'

'Look, Jonathan, she's fine.' She stood and wiped the table with a multi-coloured cloth. 'I know you're looking into what's happening at Littleworth. Are you sure you're not here for that? Finding out everything you can, because

I can assure you, there's nothing I can tell you.'

'I'm worried about her.'

She smiled again, showing even white teeth. 'Rachel's very independent, as you know. She spent Christmas here, she's OK. I like to think it was good for her, this is a nice spot.'

'It is.' And it was. 'Did she tell you where she was going? Tell you anything?'

'No, she didn't say.'

'But she told you she'd only be gone for a couple of weeks? That's what she told me.'

'She's a big girl.'

'Did she mention anything else, her plans ... anything?'

'She seemed more together, doing things for herself. She's taken up karate again. We spoke about a course that Jacob did recently in London – some voice-coaching – to get the part he wanted. Rachel seemed very interested to get the details of the school. They teach method acting, too. Maybe she'll put herself on a course there? She loved acting at university. So, you see, she is improving, forming some outside interests.'

'What's the name of the school?' he asked.

'Cambri. The Cambri School of Voice Coaching and Acting.'

He nodded, storing the information. 'You've known her for a long time.'

'Uni. Best friends since. She stayed with my family a lot in the holidays. Margaret, you know? She wanted to get away from her.' Her gaze moved towards the Bonsai tree that sat on the table. 'But I think the problem she has with her mother has got worse after what happened. I'm not surprised, though. She never really talks about Margaret. But that's families for you, isn't it?'

156

'Indeed it is,' he said. 'Do you know Liam well?'

Charlotte's expression changed. 'Quite well. He's my best friend's husband. He and Rachel have been good to me.'

'Ex-husband. Have you spoken with him recently?'

Charlotte hesitated. 'I saw him soon after Christmas, when Rachel left.'

'And neither of you know where she's gone?'

'No, I've told you.'

'Can you, or Liam, contact her?'

She looked Jonathan directly in the face. 'No.'

He sighed. 'Is Liam concerned?'

Again, he sensed hesitation. 'A little, but … he has his own problems.'

'Has he shared those problems with you?' he asked, seeing a tinge of redness on her high cheekbones and being unable to decide if it was anger or embarrassment.

'A little. Look, I can't help you.' She watched him. 'She mentioned Marek Gorski a couple of times. Maybe she plans to go and visit him in Poland; I know he had a nice place in Warsaw.'

Jonathan leant back in the uncomfortable chair. Marek. He could imagine Rachel seeking out Marek's company. A silent and solid bloke; he felt a gentle movement of air waft around his face.

'I really don't know where she is, nor does Liam,' she carried on. 'But she's OK.'

Jonathan moved his chair backwards a fraction. Was he overreacting? His answer to himself was swift no.

Charlotte smiled. 'Maybe you should go and see Alan: he might know more.'

'Maybe I should. Listen, thanks for your time.' Jonathan extracted himself from the chair. 'And thanks for talking to me. If you remember anything else give me a buzz.' He handed her his card.

'I'm off to LA tomorrow, but will do.'

Jonathan left.

He remembered seeing a nice pub on the corner of the park. He really fancied a pint, and a think.

Jonathan's bitter sat in front of him, centred perfectly on the beer mat, untouched. He'd plucked his notebook from inside his bag, half full of the information about Margaret Hemmings. He'd been in touch with Barry Haslop, who'd promised to investigate Margaret Hemmings for him. That had been a while ago, and he hadn't yet got back. As he himself often did, Barry needed a prod, but all in good time. He glanced at his mobile that perched on the wooden bench. He looked at the telephone number printed neatly on the notepad's unlined page.

Give it go, he said to himself. He pushed the relevant numbers and waited.

'Hi, is that Alan Hemmings?'

Rachel's dad agreed to meet with him later that day at a pub near his home.

He picked up his pencil and wrote down an ordered list of his thoughts, neatly underlining the ones he thought most salient with his new highlighter pen. Seeing Alan. Calling Marek Gorski. Chasing up info on Margaret.

# CHAPTER TWENTY

Alan Hemmings was sitting in the corner of the pub, staring into the open log fire and sipping an orange juice when Jonathan walked in. Alan was a tall man, with a lantern jaw; naturally slim, but even from the doorway Jonathan could see how much weight he'd lost, almost as much as Sam.

Alan looked up and smiled flatly. Jonathan held out his hand, which Alan shook in that fatigued way he recognised as a sign of depression or defeat. He thought of Michelle, of Rachel, and of Liam's forlorn posture at the trial. The ramifications of the loss of a child travelled deep and, like a stubborn stain, would never leave. They might fade with time, but the damage from working to get rid of the mark would remain visible forever.

'Hi Jonathan, nice to meet you again.' He looked at his watch. 'Can only stay an hour – Margaret doesn't know I've nipped out.'

Jonathan studied Rachel's dad, remembering his last meeting with him; on the day of the sentencing, with Margaret at Rachel's house. Christ, that had been painful. Though enlightening. Now he knew a little about Margaret Hemmings, he was surprised she'd revealed her skeleton while he'd been in the room, and hadn't insisted that he leave before talking. Margaret had been on a mission to get the visit out of the way, although he doubted she would have revealed about Hemmings without Alan's pushing. He guessed it was rare for Alan to go against his wife's wishes.

'It's good of you to meet me,' Jonathan said.

Alan seemed to study Jonathan. 'Rachel likes you.' He paused. 'A lot, I think.'

'The feeling's mutual. We go back a fair way.'

'It's nice to get out the house.' Alan paused again. 'If you know what I mean?'

'You not working?'

'Finally retired. Should have done years ago.'

'Enjoying it?' Jonathan thought not.

'It's a new thing, only decided just before Christmas.'

'You need a hobby.'

'I do.' He rubbed thin, chiffony hands together as if he were attempting to get rid of something. 'Get out from underneath Margaret's feet.' He put his juice on the table, his hand shaking a little, and the liquid flowed over the edge. 'I didn't tell Margaret I was meeting you. Are you here to ask about Michael? I know about the tribunal review, his whistleblowing. Rachel told me last time I saw her. Are you after a story? About us? Michael?' He faltered. 'Rachel said you wouldn't bother us … or her. But you're here?'

'Why did you agree to come if that's what you thought?'

'Because I know Rachel trusts you.'

'When was the last time you saw her?'

'Just before Christmas, after she resigned her job.'

'Were you surprised she resigned?'

'I was, yes. I knew she was enjoying being back.' He paused, trying to stop rubbing his hands, and placed them underneath his thighs. 'As much as she can enjoy anything.'

'I guess she told you she was going away: no phone, no computer.'

'Yes, she did tell me.'

'She's still away. It was seven weeks ago. Have you heard from her?'

'No, I haven't, but...'

'What?'

Alan shuffled forwards in his chair, skinny knees falling outwards. 'Unsure if she will call me ... to be honest.'

'You two are close. Why wouldn't she get in touch with you?'

'We've drifted.' He stopped talking, his eyes moving towards the flames of the fire.

Jonathan sensed the reason Alan had agreed to meet him was to talk. Even if it was to a journalist. He wondered if Alan Hemmings had any friends. He wondered what his life was like with Margaret. Jonathan didn't like to imagine being married to Margaret. In fact, the thought even flashed through his mind that having no parents might be a good thing.

That wasn't true, though. He had been only seven when his mum and dad had been killed, but still he softened into an unbearable melancholy at the smell of lily of the valley and the sound of Match of the Day, both reminding him of childhood, home and his parents. Their deaths had changed his destiny. He knew that as surely as he knew that Rachel was in trouble. Their sudden deaths had sensitised him to the world and to other people. It's what set him apart from most journalists. Harry had told him that one night a few months after he'd joined the paper. Jonathan had a stronger than average sense of people's lives, their motivations, and he was able to translate his understanding concisely and entertainingly into rounded articles.

'Since Joe, things have been difficult between you and Rachel?' he said. 'Why, Alan?'

'You were there. The Michael thing. I wanted to tell Rachel years ago but Margaret didn't want me to, so I didn't.'

'You didn't want to upset Margaret?'

'No.' He watched Jonathan, the rims of his eyes red, his jaw hanging in desolation. 'I never wanted to upset Margaret, at the expense of my daughter's happiness, often. I regret that now, but it's too late.'

'It's never too late.'

Alan seemed not to hear. 'She didn't want to marry me. No idea why she did. I was so grateful. I adored her. So clever. So together. Not like me.' He took a sharp intake of breath. 'I was child number one of the family. The first born…'

Jonathan shrugged a question.

'Number three died in a river accident. Left Sam and I. Sam was the middle brother, and not the one who'd been at the river and failed to save our younger brother.' He seemed to choke. 'That was me.'

Jonathan was unsure how to answer and felt as if Alan didn't need a response. He only needed to make a confession. 'What do you mean, Alan?' he said gently. '"At the expense of my daughter's happiness?"'

'Margaret was never a great mother to Rachel. I knew she missed Michael. Truth was, we thought we couldn't have a child, and by the time she got pregnant with Rachel, I don't think she wanted one. I knew that she missed having an older boy around. I stuck up too much for Margaret, I did. With too many things, too many things I didn't question. I didn't want her to leave me. Did as much as I could to make Rachel's life nice but she knew, Rachel knew. God knows what I've done.'

'What did Rachel know?'

'That Margaret sometimes did things in the heat of the moment.'

'Like what?'

'It doesn't matter.' He looked at his watch. 'I have to go.'

'You haven't finished your drink. Did Margaret ever hurt Rachel?'

Alan sank back into the chair, crossed his legs, his arms. Completely defensive body language. 'Not purposely, never deliberately.'

'Does Margaret have a temper?'

'She does, always has.'

'And what about Joe? How was she with Joe?'

'Rachel would only allow Joe to stay if I was around and, as you picked up, I wasn't around the day Michael came to visit.' He looked at Jonathan. 'I shouldn't have gone into work that day. I let Rachel down.'

Many things were becoming clearer to Jonathan. 'Rachel needs you more now than ever before.'

'Do you know where she is?' Alan asked.

'No, that's why I'm here. No one else seems to be worried about her.' He paused. 'Including you.'

'I'd like to talk to her.'

'I'd like to know where she is.'

Alan lumbered up. 'Do you have any ideas about where she might be?'

'A few.'

'Call me when you know something.' Alan Hemmings seemed sure that Jonathan would find her.

'I will definitely do that, Alan.' Jonathan looked up and met his eyes.

'I do need to go. Margaret will be wondering where I am.'

Alan Hemmings looked completely defeated.

'I'll find her. And Alan, you and Rachel should try and talk. It'll help both of you.'

'Yes, I will, and it would.' He hesitated and peered at Jonathan. 'When you find her, tell her I'm sorry.' And then the older man stumbled towards the door to return to his wife.

Jonathan stared at Alan's half-empty glass. He took it to the bar and placed it on the counter, watching as the sediment of the drink finally settled.

'Thanks, mate,' the barman said. 'Can I get you anything?'

'A pint please,' Jonathan said, 'and a packet of cheese and onion if you have them.'

He sat down heavily on the barstool.

The barman put the pint and the crisps in front of him. 'Looks like you could do with something stronger, mate.'

Jonathan smiled thinly. 'Later, maybe.'

He thought about Margaret, Alan, Bridget and Sam. He needed to chase up the ferreting on Margaret Hemmings.

He also needed some time off work.

# CHAPTER TWENTY-ONE

Harry Broomsgrove, Jonathan's boss, mentor, sometimes tormentor and best friend, summoned Jonathan as soon as he'd aimed his jacket towards his worn office chair. Jonathan's designer scruffy denim caught the edge perfectly. Marie, who sat two spaces away, clapped. She clapped every time. Broomsgrove scuttled quickly back to his office.

'Better not keep him waiting, the beast's in a foul mood,' Marie said.

'Worse than usual?'

'Much worse.'

Jonathan clicked on his computer, checked his emails and then walked nonchalantly through the main office area, speeding up when he knew Maria could no longer see him.

He stood outside Harry's door, took a breath, knocked and entered. The room was stuffy, smelling of stale garlic and cheap aftershave. Jonathan clocked the bottle still sitting on Harry's desk. The window was closed. He'd never seen it open, nor had he ever known Harry to flick on the air con.

'Ah, Jonathan. Got your request for annual leave. Four weeks? That's not annual leave, that's resigning.'

'I never take all my leave. I need some time out – I've been working like a dog since Christmas.'

165

'I know you don't and I'm sure you have.' He gave Jonathan that look: the look that said stop fucking with me. 'And why do you want time off?'

'Personal stuff.'

'Not got anything to do with Rachel Dune, has it?'

God knows where Harry got his information. Jonathan didn't answer.

Harry carried on, 'Got a call from Tom Gillespie. Said you'd been asking questions and he wasn't happy.' He shuffled in his chair. 'Leave it, unless there's a story. The Littleworth story was a storm in a teacup, legislation from the Home Office wrapping it up so tightly it went unnoticed; but that's not your fault, or mine. You did a good job on the Sam and Bridget interview.'

'You didn't publish it,' Jonathan said petulantly.

'No point. The big cover-up of Littleworth made it a bit of a damp squib, though the corruption thing should have blown by now, but it hasn't, and we can't touch it. You know the score.'

'There's still a story. Give me some time to get it. That's all I ask.'

'There'd better be a story somewhere, about someone, Jonathan.' Harry's voice softened.

'There will be.' He thought about Toby Abbs and Doctor Patterson; there was more than enough story there for Harry.

—

As Jonathan stepped out onto the grimy Farringdon Road pavement he felt a sense of freedom. Now he could find out where Rachel had gone. After speaking to Alan Hemmings, he'd called Liam who said he hadn't spoken to Rachel since before Christmas. Far from worried about his ex-wife 'disappearing', he seemed almost relieved.

He crossed the street. It was lunchtime and, despite the

cold and rain, people were out in droves. He'd made an appointment to see Rachel's old colleague and enemy, William Morley, at his flat in Lambeth, where he'd moved after 'retiring'.

He'd called Morley late in the day to arrange the meeting, and Morley had found it hard to hide the slur of his words; it was clear he was already on his way to being completely sloshed. Jonathan had made sure that the meeting took place earlier than the phone call.

He approached a line of Georgian houses, now conversions. Morley lived in the basement flat. He had to walk past the kitchen window to get to the front door. The basement was littered and in disrepair – a bit like Morley.

Before he had time to knock, Morley answered the door.

'On time, you bugger.'

'Is that bad?' Jonathan watched him gulp down something from a mug which didn't look like tea.

'Come in. Haven't got long. Taking my granddaughter out later.'

Jonathan could smell the whisky. 'Would take it easy with that then, if I were you.'

'You trying to piss me off before we've started? Come in. I've got exactly half an hour.'

Jonathan followed Morley through the tiny hallway to the kitchen. He was a tall man. His crumpled trousers hung from emaciated hips. His grey hair was too long but he possessed a full head of it. The skin on his face was leathered; the lines on his expansive forehead deep and numerous, criss-crossing at the centre of his brow.

The kitchen was surprisingly neat. Morley poured hot water over a teabag, squashed the bag against the side of the mug and added milk. He shoved it into Jonathan's hands. Jonathan didn't bother telling him that he took sugar, three in fact. He took a sip. It tasted shit.

'So you want me to tell you something about Rachel Dune, you said on the phone?' He eyed Jonathan up. 'You know her better than me, Waters. There was gossip all over the place during the Asian-bride case. What do you want to know?'

Jonathan ignored the inference. 'You worked alongside her for quite a few years.'

'Yeah, and if it weren't for Rachel Dune, the bitch, I'd still be working.'

'She tried to keep you in the force. It was your fault that you got the heave. You were the one taking bribes –'

'Fuck you, Waters. Everyone's at it.' Morley snorted. 'She was as dodgy as me. We all knew she bent the rules to get the Asian fucker who poured acid on his wife's face. And, before that, the stuff that went down with Colin Masson. She got away with all of it. Unbelievable.'

'I don't know anything about any of that,' Jonathan lied.

'Don't want to know, more like? She's hard and cold is Rachel Dune. Look, I have two grandchildren. I love kids. What happened to Joe was fucking terrible. And I wouldn't want that to happen to my worst enemy. Why have you come to see me? What do you want to know?'

'You worked with her, and, despite your … dislike for her, you probably knew her better than many people, in a way.'

'Have you spoken to her husband? Because I'm thinking you're here because she's gone. Liam'll know where she is.'

'I don't think he does. Anyway, he's not her husband any more…'

'You pleased about that then, Waters? That why you want to find her?' He grinned. 'Still getting hard-ons for Rachel Dune?'

'I'm not here to talk about me.'

'I know they're divorced.' Morley sat down heavily on a flimsy kitchen stool. 'Too burdened with grief they were, too burdened to help each other. It's tragic. Fucking life's tragic, though, isn't it?'

'Profound for you, Morley. Must be the whisky.'

'You know about Michael Hemmings and the planned trib reviews at Littleworth, don't you?'

'Course,' Jonathan replied quietly.

'That'll really piss Rachel Dune off. But you already know that, don't you, that's why you're interested.' Morley, forgetting or not caring, pulled out the whisky bottle from a cupboard and refilled his mug. 'I'll tell you what I think you want to know. I worked with Rachel Dune for years. She's harder than any of the blokes I worked alongside. Cool, intelligent and focused. Basically, unforgiving.' He paused. 'And these days, probably unbalanced.'

'Tell me more.'

'She's a dark horse. Joe's death sent her towards an edge that she's lived close to all of her life. Tell you what, though, if I were the bastard who killed her son, I'd be watching my back.'

Despite Morley's obvious vitriol towards Rachel, he understood her personality and Jonathan took him seriously. Unbalanced? Perhaps, but she was also just, fair and empathetic with those who'd been dealt a rough hand in life. Jonathan listened but could not agree.

Morley carried on talking about Rachel, begrudgingly admitting she was a superb detective, cutting no slack. It was this that had led Morley towards the disciplinary hearing, and his voluntary early retirement. He blamed Rachel.

169

'I've got to go, Waters. He gulped the whisky down in one. 'But I'm telling you, Rachel Dune has not gone away to find peace.'

—

Using the walk to the nearest Tube station to think, Jonathan tried to imagine himself in Rachel's shoes. Since Joe's death she'd immersed herself in work, she'd divorced Liam, and she was, it seemed, alienating herself from everyone, including her dad. Even Charlotte saw little of her. And Rachel was avoiding *him*, too. He knew she was, and his pride had been hurt. Now it was healing with the thought that there was a reason. Her anger that Hemmings had been sent to a psych hospital instead of a mainstream prison, where he would have had the shit kicked out of him, had never left her. And that anger and sense of injustice – now the possibility loomed that Hemmings might be released from there – was pushing her somewhere. Hemmings was only a few steps away from a type of freedom. A freedom that Joe would never have.

Jonathan now had a strong idea of what she might be doing.

He had been there and spoken to her soon after Joe's body was found. He'd seen her grief and then watched as it had turned into anger aimed at Michael Hemmings. The worm of emotion running through Rachel Dune burrowed deep, into her depths. Jonathan saw it. And it was seeing this which drove him.

The night he'd fallen in love with her was still clear and bright. It was before he'd met Michelle, but Rachel was married, so he'd kept his feelings buried. But now she wasn't and neither was he. They had gone to the pub after a long day with Sorojani Jain, and it had been the only time he'd seen Rachel slightly inebriated. But rather than

170

tipsiness leading to revelations about her life, it had been him who'd spilled his gut. He told Rachel everything about his childhood: his loneliness and isolation in his great-aunt and uncle's home in Scotland.

Rachel had listened, saying little. Not until they shared an illicit cigarette much later did she tell him about herself. It hadn't seemed that bad to Jonathan, but it was clear the relationship with her mother was not good. Now he was starting to suspect that her childhood had been much worse than his.

She had gone into no more detail about her past. Stubbing out the cigarette, she'd laughed and he remembered clearly what she'd said.

'Might be me though, eh, Jonathan? Maybe I'm just a bad daughter, a bad member of the family. My dad thinks that, I know he does. Anyway, we're all alone, aren't we, really?'

'No, we're not,' he'd replied. 'I'd always be there for you, Rachel.'

She got out her mobile and tapped it. 'Tell you what, when I'm in need, I'll get in touch with you, and you me. Deal?'

'Deal,' he took out another cigarette. 'Promise you will?'

'Promise.'

She had texted him once since that time. The day after she went with Liam to identify Joe's body.

I might as well be dead. Nothing matters anymore.

Her words had stayed with him. He needed to make a call to Marek Gorski in Poland. He had a hunch the Pole might know something; that, as Charlotte had suggested, Rachel might have gone to see him, or might have confided something to the solid, reliable and discreet surgeon.

—

Jonathan looked at the clock in his study. Four o'clock. 3 p.m. in Warsaw. He picked up the landline and punched in the numbers. It had been a long time since he'd spoken Polish. He'd spent six months there during the early 1990s investigating the strengthening rumours that the then President, Lech Wałęsa, had been a police informant during his time with Solidarity. He'd picked up the basics of the language easily.

'Dobry wieczór.'

'Hello,' he said falteringly. He was rusty.

'Jedna chwila, prosze.'

The line crackled, and then was silent. He walked towards the study window, thinking whoever had picked up the phone had put it down again. Jonathan tapped his foot. Patience wasn't something for which he was known.

'Good evening, may I help you?' The new voice was young and female, and spoke in unbroken English.

'Yes, thank you. My Polish is adequate…'

'I am sure it is. We have many people calling from the States and the UK. My English is good. How may I help you?' she repeated.

'My name is Jonathan Waters,' he said. 'I'd like to speak to Doctor Gorski if he's available. He knows me.' Again the line was silent. 'Hello – please – I'll only take a moment of his time.' More rustling down the line from Warsaw.

'Jonathan? This is a pleasant surprise.'

'Hi, Marek.' Now that he'd got hold of Marek he realised that he didn't quite know what to say. 'I wanted to ask you about Rachel.'

A movement of the phone in Poland again. 'How can I help you, Jonathan?'

'I'm trying to locate Rachel.'

'Rachel Dune? Why on earth are you calling me?'

Jonathan cleared his throat. 'She's gone missing…'

'Missing? She's gone on holiday.'

'So you have spoken to her recently?'

Jonathan heard a sigh.

'She emailed me,' Marek said. 'I haven't seen Rachel since I left for Poland. I know she's been having a bad time; it was a terrible thing that happened to Joe. I'm sorry but I can't help you.' Jonathan heard Marek's deep breaths from a thousand miles away. 'Jonathan, leave her alone.'

Marek knew something.

'Do you know where she is?'

'Maybe you should speak with Liam, or Charlotte?'

'I have. They think what you think.'

'It was a horrendous thing that happened. You know this. Leave her alone. Let her find peace.'

'Someone must know where she is. You were close to her.'

'You were close to her, too. Look, I have no idea where she is, and to be perfectly honest I don't understand why you think I would know.' Jonathan heard hesitance in his otherwise confident voice. 'She was a colleague and a friend. A strong lady.'

'A devastated lady, I'd say,' Jonathan replied quietly.

'As I have said, I am not in contact with Rachel.'

'Are you aware that Joe's murderer is earmarked for his first tribunal review? That there's a high possibility that he may be sent to a step-down unit?'

'I know nothing about that. Why would I? I do not question the law and legislation of your country. It is not my place. Look, Rachel has obviously gone somewhere to find tranquillity. It's the sensible thing to do. Any mother would do the same in her position.'

'Come on, you know as well as me she's not that type of woman. The type to look for tranquillity. Anyway, why not before? Why now?' Jonathan thought he knew why and now suspected Marek did, too.

'Perhaps she isn't who she once was – events like this change people.'

'I'm worried for her.'

'I have to go. I have patients I need to check on. I can't help you. I do not know why you are calling me. Goodbye, Jonathan.'

Marek put the phone down.

Something was very wrong. Fuck. Maybe he was reading things that weren't on the page. Maybe he was desperate. Jonathan felt desperate. Perhaps Marek was right and Rachel had gone somewhere to be peaceful. But then, Jonathan saw her eyes looking at him the last time they'd met and he felt himself filling with dread. He understood her. Jonathan paced again towards the small window and peered out.

Rachel was not relaxing in some unknown destination.

He thought of her during the trial: her blonde hair greasy, and tied into an uncharacteristic and untidy ponytail with a rubber band. Sleepless nights etched onto her once fine, smooth features. He'd asked the question the newspaper readers would want him to ask; and then immediately regretted it. How do you feel about the sentence, Rachel? It was an inane question. The worst question he'd ever asked.

She'd looked at him, her prominent chin jutting out, her shoulders slumped and sunken. He's practically got away with it, hasn't he?

# CHAPTER TWENTY-TWO

Jonathan retained a fondness for old-fashioned paper notes. He pulled out all the files he had on Joe's case, the small amount of info he had on Margaret Hemmings, and his investigations into Littleworth, while at the same time scanning the notes on his whiteboard.

He got to work on the computer. He needed to find out the names of all Marek's staff, plus those of the patients who'd checked into his clinic over the past three months. Marek's system was easy to access. He went into the clinic's appointment diary: no Rachel Dune. Nothing. He sat back in the chair.

Of course, it wouldn't be that easy.

Marek was smart; he wouldn't put in Rachel's real name. He studied the diary entries in more detail, starting again at the beginning of the previous December. Two letters caught his attention on 8th January. He worked quickly; his eyes didn't leave the screen; his fingers moving over the keyboard like a spider. M.A. An acronym? Jonathan guessed it meant something.

Rachel had stayed with Charlotte over Christmas, and he'd emailed around then asking again if she wanted to meet up in London soon after the festive season. She'd replied with a very polite but firm no. She'd also told him she was going away for a while; a week or so, she'd said. He checked his inbox. That was 28th December.

Jonathan went on to verify who worked at Marek's clinic. He had three full-time nurses: Malina Król, Cecylia Piotrowski and Irina Nowicki. There was one receptionist and the occasional med student, often from London. He opened a drawer, pulling out the screen-cloth, and absentmindedly cleaned the computer. Then he went on to find the histories of the clinic's employees, their addresses, ages, backgrounds. He might need the information, and subconsciously thanked fate for giving him the chance to learn some Polish all those years ago.

The pulse in his neck throbbed; the adrenaline began to flow, endorphins exploding through his body. He loved his job. His real job: finding out, investigating.

He clicked on and eventually found what he was looking for. The clinic's itemised phone bill; he looked as far back as last October. No calls registered from Rachel's home phone to the clinic or vice versa, but one call from the clinic to Charlotte's Birmingham number ... on the 28th December. Rachel had spoken with Marek. He looked at the diary once more, but again could find no sign of Rachel. The initials M.A. kept jumping out at him. He spent an hour getting back into Marek's personal diary. Marek was online, and live now, but Jonathan found nothing, only, and he smiled, a note by Marek that he, Jonathan, had called.

Then he stopped. At the top of Marek's personal diary was a name. Amanda McCarthy. Was this Marek's girlfriend? Was the M.A., perhaps Amanda McCarthy the other way around? He didn't know, but he stored the possibility in his mind. Best place – no one could hack that – not easily, anyway.

Jonathan clicked on another window and studied the list of patients booked in over the period just after Christmas. None had the initials M.A. or A.M. And none were British. There were four Polish names, three Indian, one Russian and, in the same column, just an asterisk and 'U.S.'. Another acronym, thought Jonathan. Fuck knows what that meant. He attempted to think laterally in the small amount of Polish he knew, which obviously wasn't enough. Think, Jonathan, think. All the info's here, you've just got to find it. Harry had taught him a lot, but the most important thing he'd ever taught Jonathan was that if you looked hard enough, there was clue to every puzzle somewhere. Harry should have been a copper, not an editor, and Jonathan smiled to himself at the thought.

He studied the files and data well into the night, then had a shower and tried to go to sleep. He couldn't, and, after an hour, got out of bed and started to compose some emails. He sent off a few phrases to a Polish correspondent friend to translate, to which he replied quickly and helpfully. It wasn't only Jonathan who couldn't sleep. He was notching up drinks owed.

His mind still too active, he decided to use the time to follow up on his Margaret Hemmings' investigations, something he'd planned to put on hold. He was on a roll.

Fortuitously and in the middle of the night (were all journos night-owls?) an email came in from Barry Haslop who'd been digging into Margaret's past, and looking into the school at which Margaret Hemmings had taught. The email struck the journalist in Jonathan as interesting, but to Rachel's friend, Jonathan, as sinister. He was absorbed for twenty minutes.

In the mid-1950s, Margaret had been a primary school teacher at a private boys' school. She had resigned her job under much speculation in 1955. The official line was that she left to have her own children.

Several years after she left the school, the complaints began to trickle in. Perhaps the more open-minded 1960s

177

made it easier for the boys to speak out. It began with a boy who was picked up for shoplifting. He was from a stable, affluent family. His parents sent him to see a child psychologist and that was when the first allegation came to light. It was followed by several more. The accusations were that Margaret Hemmings had been interfering with the boys in her care, responsible for both sexual and physical abuse. One boy claimed that she had trapped his ankle in a classroom door after he had threatened to tell the headmaster what she had done to him. It had been a 'severe compound fracture of the distal tibia', the medical notes indicated.

The school was expensive and exclusive, with a reputation to maintain. The claims were hushed up. God knows how they managed that, Jonathan ruminated, but of course he knew how. At that time, there was still a widespread unease about questioning the establishment or authority. Children's stories were not taken seriously – or not seriously enough, to risk destroying the reputation of valued institutions: as true for a school as for the church or government.

Even the parents were reluctant to pursue anything. Sometimes the parents didn't believe what their children said had happened to them, or didn't want to believe. That they had chosen a school and paid massive fees for the privilege of sending their child there, only to find out that the young English teacher was interfering with their investment, didn't sit easily with them.

Rachel had been born in 1963, and Alan Hemmings turned a blind eye regarding the rumours about his wife. Jonathan was unsure if he felt pity for Alan Hemmings or anger towards him. Probably a little of both.

He studied the email and attachments again. In all likelihood Margaret Hemmings was a paedophile, and, as with many paedophiles, her nearest and dearest suspected nothing.

Had something happened between Margaret and Michael Hemmings? Surely Hemmings would have said something? Someone would have known. Bridget? Sam? Was that what he hadn't found out from the couple?

And what about Rachel? He was certain nothing had happened to Rachel. Maybe Margaret had sought help, and that's why Rachel hadn't been on the receiving end of Margaret Hemmings' perversions.

Jonathan moved back to the computer he used for his more clandestine investigations. He spent twenty minutes getting back into Marek's system. There must be something. He looked again through the clinic diaries. The M.A. hit him again. Back to Marek's personal diary. Amanda McCarthy stared out at him. And then he saw it.

'R to go to Malina's', he thought it said, but didn't trust his Polish. He pulled out his Polish dictionary. To go. Yes, he was right.

He clicked out of there and went back into the information on his staff that Marek kept in a separate file. Malina Król. Jonathan sat back in his chair; he didn't want to have to go to Poland but, if he was going to do this properly, he must. And not to see Marek, but to visit his nurse, Malina.

—

Malina Król's parents, Maria and Stanislaw, lived on Dluga Street in a very smart part of Gdańsk. Jonathan clambered from the taxi. He knew that when Malina was on leave from Marek's clinic she lived with her parents, who looked after her seven-year-old son, Kacper.

A few linear clouds hung motionless in the sky; the wind that had blown at Warsaw's Chopin airport had died down. Jonathan spotted an ornate bench and sat down, retrieving notes from his computer satchel.

Jonathan looked along the opulent row of houses across the street for number eighty-six. Many of the buildings housed shops or restaurants on the lower level, and all were painted in different colours: happy pinks, pastel greens, sky blues. The tops of the buildings were prettily gabled. He rose from the bench and walked. As he neared the property the houses lost the restaurants, the shops, and became regular homes.

Eighty-six sat at the south end of Dluga, in its full historical glory. But the buzzer was modern. Jonathan pressed it and waited a few minutes. No answer. He pressed it again. Still no answer.

'Moge pomac?'

He turned quickly. A woman stood with a boy who must be her son. She had dark brown, glossy hair, which fell over her shoulders like a silk curtain, and violet-coloured eyes. The boy was nearly as tall as his mother, like a male replica, and just as striking. Both wore slim-fitting trousers that showed off their long, toned limbs. It had to be Malina.

'Dzien dobry Czy mowisz po angielsk?' he asked hesitantly.

'I do, but not well. You looking for my parents? They away, be back in few days.'

'Are you Malina?'

She nodded uncertainly.

'Actually, it was you I was looking for.'

Malina said something to the boy, who smiled at Jonathan before running up the two steps that separated them, pulling a key from his pocket and letting himself into the elegant house.

'Nice-looking boy you have,' Jonathan said.

She smiled politely but suspiciously. 'Thank you.'

Jonathan felt some awkwardness. Maybe that was the wrong thing to say regarding the boy. She had no idea who he was. He pulled his journalist's ID from his wallet, together with his passport. 'I'd like to talk to you about your job in Warsaw.'

The semi-smile she'd worn up until this point dropped from her face. 'Is there problem?'

The boy appeared again and said something to his mother; Jonathan roughly translated it as something about not wanting to stay in the house. She smiled at him indulgently and he remained by her side.

Jonathan grinned at the boy. 'No, no, there's no problem with anything,' he said. 'I'd like to ask you a few questions. Would it be OK if I came in? It won't take long.'

She took on the appearance of a scared rabbit, placed her arm around her son's shoulders. She scanned the street, pulling at the curtain of hair. 'Come, Kacper comes with us, we go across street, sit on the bench and talk?' she said.

'You sure?' he asked.

'Ten minutes, OK?'

Jonathan wasn't certain why she'd agreed. He didn't want her to feel uncomfortable. The woman standing facing him now, with hesitance and slight confusion etched on her face, reminded him of Rachel, reminding him why he had flown a thousand miles to be here.

The three of them sat on the bench.

'Why you here?' she asked quietly.

Jonathan looked at the boy and raised an eyebrow.

'No secrets between my son and I.'

'How well do you know Doctor Gorski?'

'I've known him long time. Was my lecturer at medical school; before Kacper.'

'You were a med undergraduate.' It wasn't a question; he knew a fair bit about Malina.

'Yes, Doctor Gorski was our anatomy lecturer. Then I left to have Kacper, and Doctor Gorski gave me job in clinic so I could save up to finish medical training.' She seemed to have gained some confidence. 'What do you want?' She peered at him.

'Malina. Is it OK if I call you Malina?'

She nodded.

Jonathan continued. 'Five years ago a little boy went missing in the UK. He was around the same age that Kacper is now. He was missing for nearly a week before they found both the man who had taken him – and the boy's body.'

Malina's violet eyes widened, but the rest of her face remained expressionless. 'What does this have to do with me?' She looked anxiously at Kacper, who was listening to every word. 'What the little boy's name?'

'Joe.'

'Carry on,' she said.

'The mother of the boy disappeared at the beginning of this year.' Jonathan wondered now what else to reveal. 'She was friendly with Doctor Gorski…'

'What you saying?'

Jonathan turned to face her. 'The boy, it's nothing to do with Gorski – we know he's a good man.'

'Then what?'

Jonathan had found the photo of Rachel in his rucksack. 'Do you recognise this lady?'

'Is this mother … of Joe?'

'Yes, it is, have you seen her before?'

Malina sat back on the bench. 'Why do you want know? You have to tell me.'

Jonathan had moved from the bench and was now

sitting on the cool stone of the street, facing Malina. Kacper stayed next to her. 'I think she wants to find the man who killed her son. And that would not be good.'

'My God...'

'Are you talking about lady who stayed with us? Amanda?' Kacper interjected. His English was good.

'Cichy!' Malina said sharply. Be quiet.

'Has this lady been to your clinic, Malina?' Jonathan caught Kacper's eye. The boy hadn't seen the photo.

'I think understand what you are saying and asking, but I can say nothing.' She peered at him. 'I am sorry I cannot help you.' She sighed. 'Marek such good man ... helping me get back to medical school. He cares for both Kacper and me.'

'She returned to England after leaving the clinic?' Jonathan probed.

Malina looked uncomfortable, a little flustered and finally angry. 'I cannot help.' She rose. 'Have to get back.' She eyed the front of her pretty home anxiously.

'Of course, Malina. I'm sorry for bothering you,' Jonathan said.

She moved to cross the busy street, pulling Kacper by the sleeve. 'I hope everything turns out OK for your friend.' She seemed to falter, about to say something, but turned away.

The wind whipped up again, and her dark hair covered her face; Kacper looked towards his mother, appearing both anxious and curious. As Malina looked first at him, then at her son, Jonathan couldn't make out her expression.

He was certain Malina had met Rachel, that Rachel had been a patient at the clinic, and that Rachel had been to the pretty house of Malina's parents.

As he walked away, heading towards the salty smell of

the sea that enclosed Gdańsk, he knew his journey had not been in vain.

The temperature had increased a few degrees and he took off his overcoat. Finally, he found a café, sat down and took out his laptop, looking at the files he'd downloaded.

Jonathan recollected Marek's quirky notetaking at the London hospital. U.S. still eluded him, but he'd work it out.

If Rachel was A.M., Amanda McCarthy, and if Jonathan's suspicions about her motives for coming to Poland were correct, and if Marek had helped Rachel knowingly, then Marek was culpable. However, Jonathan still wasn't a hundred per cent certain that Rachel had been here, or indeed been a patient at Marek's clinic, that she was indeed Amanda McCarthy. He needed more proof. As much evidence as possible. His intuition was telling him that Rachel had been here and had undergone some sort of surgery to change the way she looked. And if that were the case, if he was right, Rachel didn't intend on ever returning to her life.

As he sipped at his double espresso and looked at the scenery around him he thought about Rachel. Her long skirts, her ribboned hair, as she'd taken to wearing it after leaving the force and having Joe. They'd laughed about the ribbons. He'd been aware that she missed her job but was surprised at how easily she'd embraced motherhood. Always smart and coiffured in her employment, she seemed to turn into the opposite after giving it up. He'd asked her who the 'real Rachel' was. She'd replied quickly, 'the one you see in front of you'. At heart, she was a home girl. The sadness she'd taken with her from her own childhood, the lack of love between her and her mother had been channelled into becoming the perfect parent herself.

He imagined her in the foreignness of Gdańsk, driven here by such negative feelings. He wanted to take her back to a life in which she could be happy. He wanted to help her to face her grief and come to terms with the loss of Joe. He wanted her to wear ribbons again. He wanted to find her, and help her. He wanted to be able to love her.

Later that evening, Jonathan was sitting in an economy seat on his way back to London. The plane was between Berlin and Hamburg, the location displayed on the screen in front of him, and he tried not to check the alignment of the plane's wing on his left side obsessively. (He hated flying.) After his second beer, his mind left the puzzle of Rachel and moved towards his own life.

He closed his eyes. The policewoman telling him that Mum and Dad had been in a car crash … and wouldn't be coming back. It was a bit of a problem for the authorities, as he had no living grandparents. Mum and Dad had only one brother between them, and he had very selfishly, Jonathan had thought throughout his teens, died young. So he spent a lonely childhood with very nice but very old people, in a place far from his birthplace, the most boring place on earth: Campbeltown in Scotland. At fourteen, his great-aunt and uncle had sent him to boarding school. He'd been ecstatic, and couldn't wait to leave. But it turned out the school was worse than living in Scotland. He was shy and unconfident, and had developed a stutter.

He took a deep breath and then another swig of beer. The plane hit some mild turbulence and he took out a beta-blocker from his inside pocket. Only for when he was desperate. He thought about school, the bullying, head down the toilet on a frequent basis.

Opening another beer, he attempted to extricate

himself from the past; he didn't like to loiter in that place for long, but today he was finding it difficult to leave.

His mind flipped back to Rachel. Jonathan didn't care what happened to Michael Hemmings. But he cared about the effect he was having on a woman who was not as in control as she thought she was. If he was right that she was desperate enough to put herself through surgery, it wasn't a huge leap to conclude that she had a plan, and that the plan could be just as extreme, and would involve Hemmings. Whatever she intended to do, it seemed likely it was dangerous, probably illegal. He had to find her.

Eventually, he finally fell asleep only waking when the plane's wheels dropped from its underbelly ready to touch down.

Jonathan held the arm rests tight, staring hard at the seat in front of him.

# CHAPTER TWENTY-THREE

The next morning Jonathan slept in until seven. He'd called Sam and Bridget from Poland but had got no answer. It was time to talk to the couple again, Bridget in particular. He also needed to see Detective Chief Inspector Tom Gillespie, something he wasn't looking forwards to after the last phone call to him asking about Rachel, when he'd been sent off with the proverbial flea in his ear.

He made a pot of coffee and moved into his study. With blurry eyes he peered at his whiteboard, the names, the links he'd made using a red marker. The tale unfolding in front of him; slipping into place. Rachel's mother had the capacity for violence as well as sexual abuse. But Rachel had never mentioned brutality in the household, always drawing her mother as controlled and distant.

Had Rachel come out of her childhood unscathed? If he was right, her actions recently, he thought as he lined up paper neatly on his desk, would suggest otherwise.

He sat down in front of the computer he used for his more 'unethical' work. It was ready to go, with state-of-the-art software installed. It took him over an hour to get into Doctor Patterson's files on Michael Hemmings, which had been recently updated, he was happy to find. There were notes about Bridget Hemmings, questioning if she knew more than she'd ever admitted at the trial. A brief mention of Toby Abbs: that he'd reported to Patterson that Michael Hemmings had said he didn't kill Joe. In red, 'first time Hemmings has said this, to anyone'. Obviously, Patterson was on to something that should be looked into. After his visit to see Sam and Bridget, Jonathan planned to drive north and drop in on Doctor Patterson and Toby Abbs.

He swivelled around in his chair and picked up his mobile, pressing Sam Hemmings' name.

'Sam?'

'Speaking. Who is this?'

'Jonathan Waters.'

'What do you want?' Sam asked, his voice quiet.

'Are you all right?'

'Not really.'

'What are you doing now?' Jonathan asked.

'Nothing.'

'Is Bridget home?'

'She is.'

'Can I come and see you both?' Jonathan asked.

'I like you, Jonathan. Even though you're a reporter. I liked you then … and I like you now. There's something I want to show you.'

'What?' Sam didn't sound well. His voice was thin, hollow. 'Give me a few hours to get there. Traffic'll be heavy on a Friday … Is that OK? Hang on in there, Sam.'

He couldn't really explain why he'd said that. Hang on with what? But he felt a heaviness, a darkness, around him.

'I'm not going anywhere.' Sam hung up.

Jonathan's old Jeep was parked half a mile away from his flat. Bloody London parking. As he started the engine he wondered what it would be like to live outside the city, in a house, with a garage. A garden. A child. He shook his head, trying to erase thoughts about his own life.

We are all made up of snippets from our past and the glimpses we see of our future.

A line from his psychiatrist that resonated more now than it had when he was eighteen.

—

Bridget answered the door, looking unkempt and upset, her hair today hanging limply around her face.

'Hi Bridget. Sam told you I was coming?'

'Yes, he did. He had to go to the bakery, he'll be back soon. Come in.' She stepped back to let him in.

This was his chance to ask Bridget a few things before Sam's return. Maybe, just maybe, she might say more without her husband being around.

He followed her through to the kitchen. 'Is everything all right, Bridget?'

'As good as it can be.'

'I thought you and Sam'd be in celebratory spirits with Michael in line for a move?' He smiled what he knew was a great journalist-type smile. 'Will you visit him there?' Of course, they both knew that what he was really asking was why she didn't visit Michael.

She sniffed loudly. 'We're not having a good day, Sam and I.' She pushed past him, moving towards the kitchen table, and Jonathan smelt her; a mixture of overpowering perfume, mild body odour and fear. Sitting on the table was a set of knives and an old-fashioned sharpener. The knives of a cook. Although he supposed that Sam was a baker, it was nearly the same thing. Bridget continued, 'Sam's been sharpening his knives.'

'I can see that.' He picked up the biggest blade. 'Impressive.'

'His pride and joy.' She sat down heavily on a chair.

'Why've you come?' She faltered. 'Has Sam told you…?'

'Told me what?' he answered quickly.

'Nothing –'

The blackness he'd felt on the phone pleated through him again.

'I'm trying to get in touch with Rachel,' he said.

'Sam said you'd been asking about her relationship with Margaret, last time you were here. Alan told Sam Rachel had gone away for a few weeks, on holiday.'

'Can you tell me about Margaret, your relationship with her?'

'Why should I talk to you? You've been nice to us, I know that … but Sam's already given you the info for the article that was never published.' She appeared to have gathered herself.

'And I appreciate that. Why don't you visit your son, Bridget?'

'He's not bothered about me. It's only Margaret he was ever bothered about.'

'What makes you say that?'

'Things he said … before … this happened. Joe…'

'What did he say?'

'That Margaret had promised him that one day they'd be together again, like when he was a kid. Michael used to go and see Margaret long after she stopped looking after him.'

'When did he go to see Margaret?'

'When he was a teenager, after Margaret'd had Rachel. I knew he used to go and see her.' Her eyes fell towards the floor. 'I knew. Could always smell the bloody lavender on his clothes.' She remained staring at the floor. 'Then, I told myself that Michael spending a bit of time with Margaret would keep him on the straight and narrow, that she'd have some influence on him. Always a problem, was our Michael.' She looked up at Jonathan. 'I think he still went to see her occasionally in recent years, when he could. I don't know, but I suspect he did.'

'He told you that she promised him "they'd be together". That's an odd phrase,' he waited, 'don't you think?'

'She's an odd woman. She has some sort of hold over him, like she has over Alan.' She floundered, then became ardent. 'I know I've been a shit mum, but I'm not as bad as Margaret was with Rachel.'

'What do you mean by that?'

'It was obvious Margaret couldn't stand her. I felt sorry for her, Rachel. Always have.' She watched him. Tears filled her eyes.

'What's happened, Bridget? I feel as if something's happened.'

'Nothing's happened.' She looked at the clock. 'Sam'll be back soon. Walked off his anger.'

'I thought you said he'd gone to the bakery?'

'He's pissed off with me, gone for a walk.'

'I'm sorry.'

She studied him. 'The tribunal review, Michael going to a step-down unit, has stirred things up.'

'What things?'

'Everything.' She slumped onto a chair. 'You'll never know.'

'Try me.'

'Too late.'

'About Michael?'

A noise from the front door. 'He's back,' she said quietly.

Sam walked into the kitchen looking as dishevelled as his wife. 'Jonathan, you got here earlier than I'd expected.' He looked at Bridget in a less loving way than

191

the last time Jonathan had been here. 'Can you give us some time?'

Bridget observed her husband with anxiety. Jonathan had assumed it was Bridget who wore the trousers in the house. From the few interactions he'd had with the couple, he'd got the impression that in normal circumstances they rubbed along nicely. The tension in the house today was tangible.

She pulled a coat from the hook on the back of the door. Sam stood next to the table, picked up a knife and began sharpening it.

'I'm off, then.' She was already halfway across the kitchen.

'Perhaps catch you later?' Jonathan said.

She didn't reply, and left.

Sam set down the knife, but carried on touching its handle in an agitated way. 'We've had a bit of an argument.'

'I can see that. Sam ... I've been doing some investigating ... into Littleworth, and into Margaret.'

Sam opened a drawer and pulled out an envelope from its depths. 'It's not his fault he's bad ... our Michael. He was always a bit odd, since the meningitis, and he might have been capable of doing something to Joe...'

Jonathan eyed the letter.

'This is from Michael.' Sam held the knife in one hand, the envelope in the other, and didn't look at Jonathan.

A kernel of foreboding passed over him. He sighed, feeling as if he was moving in decreasing circular movements. Like water down the plughole.

Sam looked up, tears seeping from his small, tired eyes. 'I love Bridget...'

'What's happened with Bridget? What've you argued

192

about?' He felt that whatever the argument had been about, that it'd been serious.

'I can't talk about it.' Sam faltered and began sharpening a knife again.

Jonathan patted his shoulder; he'd wait for Sam's revelation. 'Can I read the letter?'

Sam handed Jonathan the envelope. 'I haven't been to see him for a while.'

Jonathan opened it.

*Dear Dad,*

*I know you don't want to hear from me. I know that, because you haven't been to see me for so long. You remember I told you about the colours, Dad, well they've been getting worse. They're going to let me out, into a less secure unit and I'm worried.*

*Mum's been to see me. She says she doesn't want anything to do with me. That I have to leave her alone. I think she wants me to kill myself, Dad. She said that would be a good outcome, make everything better, right. And while she was here, I thought about Joe. I know I did bad things to him, but I didn't kill him. I know I didn't. Then my mum told me I did. And I don't believe her.*

*But I might kill someone, I might kill myself. Dad, can you help me?*

*I need some help.*

*Love, Michael.*

'Fuck.' Jonathan placed the letter on the table. 'So Bridget does visit Michael?'

'She doesn't, and never has done. He means Margaret. How does that happen? Shouldn't we have been told?

Michael's talking suicide…'

'Maybe he's making all this up, Sam. Michael is unbalanced.'

'Something was always amiss about Michael and Margaret. I should have done something; Bridget and I both should have.'

'What do you mean?'

'I don't know what I mean. But I'm worried about our Michael. That place isn't looking after him properly. I should have been told if Margaret had visited.'

'You don't know if it was Margaret. It seems unlikely. Michael's mixed up. He's probably making this up.'

He thought about what Bridget had told him about Margaret, and what he himself now knew. Perhaps Michael wasn't making it up.

'Do you think Michael killed Joe?'

Sam hung his head. 'I don't know.'

Jonathan couldn't see his eyes.

The water swirled and swirled on the periphery of the plughole.

He knew he'd get nothing more from Sam. Years as a journalist told him when the well was dry.

As Jonathan got back in his car, he felt his internal antenna buzzing as if short-circuiting. He also saw Bridget's face in the window of Bridget and Sam's neighbour's house.

She looked absolutely terrified.

The smothering anxiety he'd felt watching Sam sharpen his knife returned and intensified, and Jonathan shivered in the early evening sun.

# CHAPTER TWENTY-FOUR

*Two months earlier*
*Beginning January 2005*

I'd been in the library every day, all day, for three days. It was an ugly 1970s building both inside and out, although I was oblivious to the décor as I trawled through microfiches while drinking diabolical vending-machine coffee.

Today was the beginning of day four, and today I decided who I was going to be, although I'd actually been sure enough a week before, when the big envelope from America arrived. For the past three days I'd been doing more research. Because it was now time.

She had died of a heroin overdose fifteen months before. She'd lived in Ohio with her three children, who were seven, ten and seventeen.

I found an article about her in the *New York Times*, published a few months after her death, by a journalist who was investigating the growing incidence of letter writing from females of 'low socio-economic status' to death-row prisoners. She was thirty-six years old when she died. Slightly younger than me, but looking at her photos, that wasn't an issue. Heroin ages the over-thirty woman quicker than any tragedy, I knew; I'd seen enough of them. She had been writing letters to a killer on death row for a few years prior to her own death. The killer's 'outside' best friend had supplied the fatal overdose of heroin to her. The letters she had exchanged with the executed killer and 'lover' were retrieved from the Chillicothe Correctional Institution, Ohio, where he had spent most of his sentence before being shipped to the Southern Ohio Correctional Facility in Lucasville. In Lucasville, after too many stays of execution, he finally (thank God, in my opinion) met his death with Old Sparky.

Before he died, and, of course, knowing he would, he'd returned all the woman's letters to her and, when she passed away, the letters went to her eldest daughter. I intended them to become a template for my own.

A week after my bank transfer hit the eldest daughter's account, the letters landed on my doormat. The money I sent for both the letters and for a little background on her would, I hoped, help all her children. The abstract innocence of her daughter, coming through so strongly in the letter she sent me made me feel guilty; but guilt was my constant companion. The underlying disquiet I felt at what I was doing brought an instant coolness to my body.

The letters to her death-row boyfriend were, on the one hand, revealing, and on the other, left me with questions, but studying them allowed me to find some essence of her. And it was through these long and badly spelt correspondences I learned how a woman like this would think, and what drove her to seek the love/friendship of a man with no hope of seeing American daylight again. A man who had systematically battered his wife and three young daughters to death, and then burnt all four bodies in a bonfire on his back lawn.

Uninterested neighbours had thought he had been barbecuing pork. For three days.

It was hard to comprehend why she'd befriended such a man; but she had, and I had to pretend to do the same thing, so it was imperative to discover how she would behave, her likes and dislikes. The woman I was to become had to be different from me. Very different.

For my next round of research, I made my way to the psychology section of the library. Like any self-respecting officer who had been promoted to DI as early as I had, I'd devoured every morsel of information on the criminal mind. Today, my intense concentration was not to understand the mind of a killer, but of a twice-married, divorced and widowed Ohio mother, who had been lonely and isolated in a world that had long ago abandoned her.

I sat back in the uncomfortable library chair, and, closing my heavy eyelids, a firm outline of how I would play this woman emerged. In two concentrated hours I'd imbibed the literature on women who befriended and sometimes even married convicted killers. In one famous case during the late 1980s, an adoring fan had been allowed 'intimate' time with a convicted death-row prisoner, giving birth nine months later, three months after his execution.

I picked up another book, *Families and Abuse*, which made for interesting reading, written by an American psychiatrist who, for thirty years, had specialised in interviewing prisoners on death row. Most were men who abused and murdered children, but a handful of women were included in the case studies. I saw something within the personalities of the women described that made me sit upright and think of Margaret.

I squeezed my eyes shut and a picture of her strode through my tired mind; I allowed a few more bricks from my mental wall to be removed. The closer I was getting towards realising my plan, of seeking out Hemmings and killing him, the more often Joe would visit, but his visits made me hesitant in my goal. And the more I remembered my son and our life together, the way he nibbled at muffins and Doritos during every Disney film, how we would play for hours on the zipwire at the park, how he would get bored with me in the school holidays and go and find Liam in the den, the more the memories would return. Memories I'd pushed away for so long. What came back were things I'd buried because I'd known my dad wouldn't want me to remember them, some of them he hadn't even known about.

—

Mr Roberts had dropped Rachel off from Sunday school and, despite the cramps in her stomach, her mind still jingled with the lovely songs Mr Roberts got them all to sing.

She had opened her mother's bedroom door.

The first thing she noticed was Michael. He was twelve. Small for his age, but with the trademark gangly legs and, even then, a tight, muscular body. His legs hung over Rachel's mum's bedroom chair. He sat on her lap. The white starched blouse she had been wearing when she'd dropped Rachel off at Sunday school was unbuttoned; not only at the neck, which in itself was unusual, but all the way down. That is what hit Rachel. Her mum with her blouse undone. Rachel saw the crêpey, white skin of her sagging, tiny breast and a large, purple nipple protruding from the left side of the open blouse. This was a shock. Rachel never saw her mum without clothes. The other nipple was firmly lodged in Michael's mouth. Michael had not heard her. Her mother's eyes were closed. Rachel stood for what seemed like long minutes, trying to work out what was happening. Her tummy was very sore. She could feel it moving under her jumper. They still didn't know she was there. Then a spasm overwhelmed her and she moaned quietly. And her mum opened her eyes. Rachel was right in front of her. Margaret started. Michael stopped, taking his mouth away and revealing an engorged aubergine nipple. Margaret jumped up. Michael fell to the floor; a subdued terror, mixed with devotion in his eyes, all the time watching Margaret. He didn't seem to see Rachel.

'What have I done wrong?' he asked. She had quickly buttoned up her blouse, right to the top.

'What are you doing home, Rachel?' 'I'm not well, Mr Roberts brought me' ... 'Michael, wait for me downstairs,' Margaret said to him.

'You don't want the other today, Aunt Margaret?' he asked, confused.

Margaret become cross. 'No, Michael, go downstairs and get yourself a glass of milk.'

The library seemed unbearably hot and I stumbled out to find air.

# CHAPTER TWENTY-FIVE

Because of Razor it didn't take me long to organise another identity; it was shockingly easy. But he'd promised that after this he was giving it all up for his two kids.

Razor trusted me. It was a trust between criminals, as he probably surmised I was soon to become one. There exists a strange respect within the underworld for ex-detectives who wander to the other side. Razor was supremely indignant at what had happened to my family and I.

The internet café was busy. The computer I was working on needed retiring, so I'd asked the girl on duty, Veronica, who wore an outrageous fuchsia-coloured jacket that seemed out of place in the greyness of the café, if I could be first in line to use another when it came free. She saw my impatience, saw that I was well dressed, saw I should have a computer at home and perhaps questioned what I was doing there. It wasn't that unusual, computers break down all the time; but my nerves waterlogged my usual logical thoughts. Veronica probably thought nothing.

I'd already given up my computer and mobile phone. They were safely locked away. I wanted to become familiar with not having the devices as a crutch, with being non-contactable. I was alone, in every conceivable way –and that was the way it had to be.

'Hey, missis, it'll be a while before another terminal comes free,' Veronica said. 'Come with me, you can use the spare one in the back office.'

I followed Veronica, with her pink jacket and her efficiency. She reminded me of myself in another time, in the job that I had lived for. Before Joe.

'You can have the room and the computer for as long as you like.' She glanced at her watch. 'Well, until three, that's the end of my shift.'

'That's great, thank you,' I said. This room had no ventilation and was stiflingly hot. I took off my jacket. Veronica took a step back and wavered. God, I hope she wasn't about to get friendly; ask me what I was doing. She didn't strike me as that type.

'No probs.' She studied me. 'Do I recognise you?'

'No, I don't think so. I haven't been in here before.' Maybe she recognised me from photographs in the papers from the trial, although that was a long time ago now.

'You look familiar.'

'No, you don't know me.'

She shrugged her shoulders. 'You work out?'

Her question threw me. 'A bit.'

'A lot, I'd say. My other job is personal training.'

I studied her in more detail. I could see that. Muscular but not skinny. 'Good to have more than one string to your bow,' I said, wondering how long she wanted to chat.

'You're in fabulous shape, I have to say.'

I felt a little uncomfortable. She saw it.

'I'm not a dyke or anything. I just love a good body, on a man or a woman.'

'I know what you mean.' And I did know what she meant. I'd always admired women who were toned and fit. I had been before Joe; I'd let myself go afterwards, as Razor had noticed. Two stone heavier, and all around the hips – just like Margaret.

'So, you planning on entering competitions then?' she smiled. 'There's a big trend now for older contestants in these things.'

I laughed too loud. 'Don't think so.'

'Doing it for self-esteem?'

'Sort of.'

'Sure I don't know you?'

'Absolutely sure. I'm new to the area.'

'Well, good luck with the training, you know where I am if ever you need a trainer, but looks like you're doing fine by yourself.' She turned around, theatrically and athletically, and left me alone.

I began my work on the computer, more research, more emails.

The time was getting near. News seeping out from Littleworth told me it was soon.

An email popped into my inbox, but not from Razor. I peered at the screen. The new email was from Marek Gorski. I'd messaged him two days before, asking a favour that I knew was too much. I expected a definitive no.

*Hi Rachel,*

*In reply to your request, I hesitate in saying yes, but would rather it was me than anyone else. Let me know a timeframe when you have one.*

*Also, sorry to hear about you and Liam.*

*M*

I pressed the delete button and, as I did so, another email appeared. I squinted at the computer screen. Razor. I pulled the damp fabric of my blouse away from my chest. He said a week. I emailed back saying I needed everything within three days. The reply didn't come through straight away. I sat and waited.

Finally Razor replied. My new ID would be delivered to me, at the address I'd given him – a PO Box at Birmingham's main post office – within seventy-two hours.

I stared at the screen, imagining Razor at his. We'd spoken about other areas of the dark web in our last physical meeting. I tapped my foot rhythmically on the cheap plastic tiles. I emailed him back asking for web addresses. Within ten minutes he'd sent them: six dark websites that would lead any paying punter towards an innocent child. Good man. He would give all this up.

And I created another email address. Totally untraceable. Razor had taught me that.

I composed an anonymous email to Tom Gillespie, to his private account, guessing few people knew that address. To send it now wouldn't be a good idea; half of me wanted to be reckless, but I had to be careful. I put the email in my draft folder. I would come back to it later.

After all this, I intended to do something to address the problem of the dark web – the children, that was – if I survived.

I felt Joe's presence again, and wasn't sure if this meant he approved or not, but I convinced myself he did and attempted to ignore the painful hunger that sat deep inside me, inhabited me. Owned me.

# CHAPTER TWENTY-SIX

As soon as Jonathan had left Sam and Bridget's he made his way north. From some subtle investigations he knew Doctor Patterson was at home, not at work, on 'gardening leave' for a while, and that Toby Abbs had a few days off.

Toby Abbs' flat was on the third floor. It had taken Jonathan some time to find it. The council-flat complex was a maze. Why did planners not plan? And, annoyingly, some of the numbers were missing from the doors. Either ripped off by vandals or taken off by owners who didn't want to be found.

Jonathan could hear Toby Abbs' television from outside the door. It took Abbs a while to open his door and, when he did, the groans of male ecstasy were loud.

'Toby Abbs?' Jonathan asked over the groans coming from the TV.

'Just a sec, wait there.' Toby ran back inside and the noise stopped. 'What do you want?' he asked on his return, slightly out of breath.

'My name's Jonathan Waters. I'm a journalist. May we have a chat?'

'I don't think so ...' Toby Abbs looked shit-scared. His trousers were unbuttoned, Jonathan noticed. Toby tried to close the door.

'Not so quick, Toby.' Jonathan wedged his foot at the

door's bottom edge. 'I know about you and Michael Hemmings.'

Jonathan watched with amusement as Toby attempted to gather himself. Jonathan let go of the door.

'As it happens I have a bit of free time … What's this about?' Abbs said.

Jonathan was already standing in the cramped hallway. 'It's about your job and your relationship with Michael Hemmings.'

Abbs capitulated easily and led him through the small flat. Jonathan was certain he could see Abbs' heart sprinting through his cheap cotton shirt. Toby Abbs was the type of guy who would toe the line.

He sat down on the only chair in Abbs' small kitchen. 'I'll be direct, if you don't mind. I've spoken with your ex-wife in Australia. She told me why she left you, about your "relationship" with Michael Hemmings. I know about the children who visited Littleworth. You must be glad she's in Oz … your ex-wife.' He hadn't spoken directly to Amy Abbs, but she had been very forthcoming in emails.

'You can't prove anything,' Abbs said, waiting for his answer.

Jonathan took his time.

'This is … off the record, Toby. No newspapers involved. But I need some answers.'

'About what? You know about Hemmings and I. What else do you want to know?'

'I'd like to know if Hemmings is receiving letters.'

'From whom?'

'Anyone.'

'Occasionally from his dad. A few loony letters. The usual.' Abbs squirmed, without enough time to think. 'He's had a letter from his aunt,' he blurted out.

'His aunt? Margaret Hemmings?'

'Yep. First one from her. Something weird going on in that family.' Toby studied Jonathan. 'You know what Hemmings did, don't you? Cut his…'

'Yes, I know that.'

Abbs took a quick step back, anticipating his anger. Jonathan did want to hit him.

'You sure the letter wasn't from his mother, Bridget?' Jonathan wanted to be sure.

'No, deffo no. He's never had one from her.'

'Did you read the letter?'

'Yes, all letters are censored.'

'This one wasn't though, I take it?'

'I didn't make it official, no. A man needs some privacy.'

'You mean Hemmings needs some privacy … with you?'

'I didn't show it to the Doc.'

'Patterson?'

Abbs nodded.

'What did it say in the letter?'

'Why should I tell you?'

'The hospital director, your boss, finding out about your relationship with Hemmings?'

He rubbed his head as if trying to get rid of a headache. He'd have a big one after this visit, Jonathan predicted.

'She talked a lot about God and forgiveness. She made it plain that there was a secret between them, and I got the feeling she was keen to keep it a secret. She suggested…' Abbs faltered. 'She suggested that it wasn't a good idea for him to go to a step-down unit, that he'd be better off in "the safe place, Littleworth".'

'And?'

207

'And that was about it.'

'What did you think when you read the letter?'

'I thought it was fucking weird.'

Jonathan got up. 'Might be wise to remember that in the future.' He rubbed his chin. 'You know, Toby, Hemmings isn't your boyfriend.'

'Michael cares for me, I care for him.' Abbs fiddled with the top button of his shirt. 'He's not as bad as people think he is.'

'I find that a bit difficult to believe. If I were you, I'd be careful.'

Abbs shrugged. 'Is that it?'

'Yep, thanks for your time.'

'And can I be expecting to hear from you again?'

'I would imagine so. I'll make my own way out.'

Toby wriggled from one foot to the other. 'Mr Waters, there's something else.'

Jonathan turned a little. 'What?'

Toby hesitated a fraction. 'If I tell you, you'll go easy and keep me out of any story you plan to write? And not talk to the director?'

'I'll think about it, yes.'

'Margaret Hemmings came to see Michael at Littleworth, after the letter.'

'You're shitting me?'

Hemmings had been telling the truth in his letter to Sam.

'No. They went out to the garden, to the new gazebo. I don't know what they talked about, so don't ask me. That's what kicked off the problem with Patterson. He didn't log her visit, something he should have mentioned.'

'Did it cross your mind that a visit from the grandmother of Hemmings' victim, a seven-year-old boy, is a very unlikely one?'

'I'm not paid to think that much. That's Doc Patterson's job, and one he's not been doing so well.'

'So how was Hemmings after her visit?'

'Bit screwed up.'

'Thanks for the information, Toby. I have your mobile and your landline number. I hope if I call you in the future you'll be willing to help me again? And that you'll find time to let me know if anything interesting happens at Littleworth?'

'I'll think about it,' Toby said, with confidence.

'More than think about, OK? Remember, your relationship with Hemmings, newspaper articles, the director … and your job.'

Jonathan waited until he'd reached his car and sat down before he allowed himself to relax. He wasn't a 'tough-guy', not at all. That had been a hard one to pull off, but worth it. He wondered what Patterson could tell him, if he was home, if he would speak to him.

But more than anything, Jonathan wondered what the fuck was going on between Margaret and Michael Hemmings.

——

Doctor Thomas Patterson was sitting outside in his garden. He couldn't seem to do anything useful; his usual energy dissipated. Even the compulsion to visit Leanne had left him. His quiet suspension from the hospital by the NHS Trust had surprised him, but not unduly. Nothing, really, disturbed him too much.

It had been Margaret Hemmings' visit that had tipped the scales, on the back of the internal hearing that was already underway, gathering pace, and soon to explode. A different type of person would be giving themselves a hard time about this, but not Patterson; he knew more than the bureaucrats at the top, or the inept workers at the bottom. Patterson never saw himself as being wrong. Never.

He was aware that he hadn't defended himself as well as he could. But why should he? He felt himself beyond reproach, even as that reproach tugged at the coat tails of his career. The director had quickly, and obscenely, Patterson ruminated, installed Doctor Julian Cohen. A team player, the director had said in his email. Patterson disliked team players.

With clear self-assurance, Patterson divorced himself from thoughts of another professional who would be far less effective in understanding the human mind than him, and instead gave thought to Margaret Hemmings' visit.

He remembered that 'Windy' Miller had mentioned her visit to him, asking for his 'OK'. He had been distracted that day with demands from both Leanne and the principal of the university, and hadn't properly listened. So Margaret Hemmings had visited. Michael Hemmings had complained, even though – Abbs had later told him – Hemmings had been looking forwards to the visit. The whole thing had escalated. Very disproportionately, thought Patterson.

He stared at the old oak that sat a few metres from the edge of his patio. Michael Hemmings was complicated, as was his family situation, and Joe Dune's death was in itself more complicated than it had been given credit for. His mind wandered towards the women in Hemmings' life. Bridget and Margaret, the boy's mother, Rachel. Hemmings definitely had a problem with her, and had done so for years.

Patterson's only hope was the private 'off the record' meeting he was having with the director imminently. The director would allow him to explain his argument. But

Patterson trod on muddy ground; his reputation was in tatters at Littleworth. He was aware that any postulations he had formed about Hemmings would be ignored.

Thomas Patterson was taking a sip of iced tea when a voice made him spill it down his clean work shirt. When he had dressed that morning, he'd forgotten he wasn't going into Littleworth.

'Really sorry – the side gate was open. No answer to the bell, and the car was here...'

Patterson looked at the man standing at a polite distance, waiting to be invited onto his turf. Literally. Despite his overall predicament, he managed a smile at his own joke. The handsome man took it as a sign to come forth. Patterson decided the man wasn't an axe murderer.

'I take it you're not selling anything?' Patterson said.

'No sir, I'm not. Jonathan Waters.'

Patterson stopped rubbing the iced-tea stain. 'Ah, the journalist I wouldn't speak to on the phone? What makes you think I will talk to you now?'

'A hope.'

Patterson could see no reason why he shouldn't ask the charismatic and well-spoken man to sit down and join him for an iced tea. He had nothing else planned that day. And on the phone, despite Jonathan Waters being a journalist, Patterson had liked the sound of him.

'Take a seat, Jonathan.'

'I hear that you've been asked to stay at home?'

'For a time, yes,' Patterson replied easily.

'Big scandal, the kids. Lucky for Michael Hemmings though.'

Patterson pulled the wet shirt from his skin. 'It'll be public knowledge soon enough, and you want your article, I take it?'

Waters nodded. 'I would, but I know I won't get it

here first, that's the way it will be. I'm here on more personal business.' The reporter moved closer. 'Could you tell me anything about Margaret Hemmings, Joe Dune's grandmother? And why she visited Michael Hemmings?'

'What makes you think I will tell you anything?'

'Nothing to lose?' Jonathan replied, saying it kindly.

'She visited. That's all I know. I haven't been into work recently, so I know very little.' How did this man know about the visit? Nothing was sacred these days.

'And what do you think about that? Margaret Hemmings going to visit the murderer of her grandson?'

'I think nothing about it. Odd, yes, but now, it's not my place to think.'

'The director at Littleworth is keen to allow Hemmings to go to the step-down unit. They wouldn't want any hiccups with visits from the grandmother of the victim. Is that why they're trying to keep it quiet, along with everything else they're attempting to hush up and cover over?'

'The whole Hemmings scenario, as it's worked its way out, is being used to promote rehabilitation at Littleworth and show its success,' Patterson replied. 'The last thing they want is me, or Margaret Hemmings, messing it up for them.'

'What are your thoughts on Michael's relationship with Margaret Hemmings?'

'I have no thoughts.' Patterson wondered how many crumbs he'd throw to the reporter. 'I think much of Hemmings' life was – is – shaped by the females within it.'

'Are you aware that Margaret Hemmings looked after Michael when he was young?'

Patterson nodded. 'I guessed a little. We were moving

forwards with that, before all this happened.'

'What do you really think, Dr Patterson?'

'My thoughts are still forming.'

Jonathan found Patterson's eyes. 'Were you aware of the visits from young children to the unit?'

'It was all authorised.' Patterson wriggled in his seat, the wetness on his shirt forgotten. He avoided eye contact with the journalist.

'A pretty fucked-up system, isn't it?'

'I can't keep my eye on everything.'

'You should keep your eye on *something*.' Waters sighed loudly. 'Seems to me you've had no idea what's been going on in the place where you hold such a position of responsibility.'

'What is it you want, Mr Waters?' Finally, Patterson felt a hint of antipathy towards this confident man.

'Do you think Michael Hemmings is capable of murder?'

'He already has,' Patterson felt a smirk spreading across his face, 'committed murder, that's why he's in there.' Touché, you young whippersnapper.

'I mean another murder, Doctor.'

'I think Michael Hemmings is capable of many unsavoury actions, but not premeditated murder.' Despite not spending enough time on his work these days, something had been brewing inside Patterson's brain for months, and had been piqued by Toby Abbs' remark, the bogus letter mentioned by Michael Hemmings from his mother, and the subsequent visit from Margaret Hemmings. He had ensured he'd made a note of his thoughts in his personal digital files. By talking to the reporter he was more than aware that he was effectively stirring up the pot, which he admitted, he quite fancied doing. Nothing to lose. He carried on, 'I'm not entirely sure if Hemmings was solely responsible for Joe Dune's murder.'

'What exactly are you getting at?'

'I'm really not sure yet. And to be perfectly honest, I don't have any desire to share any of this with either you or my superiors. They'll work it out eventually, but then it may well be too late. Let the system stew in its own incompetence. Too stupid, some of these people. Anyway, anything I say now won't be listened to.'

'I'll listen.'

'And you will submit an article to your newspaper? I don't think so.'

'I'm a friend of Rachel Dune's. This is all personal, nothing to do with my newspaper. From what I can see of "the system", although I think you've been negligent, you're just a symptom of the real problem within what is a mental health rehabilitation system that beggars belief.'

'I don't know what you're really looking for, Mr Waters, but I suggest you look at Margaret Hemmings and Michael's parents if you want a story.'

'Thank you, Doctor. I'm sorry about what's happened to you.'

'My fault, Mr Waters, my fault. Boredom and routine is a terrible thing, it makes the best of us sit back and not take note.'

'I won't be able to let the "Littleworth" story go, but I'll try to be fair with you.'

Doctor Patterson got up and shook Jonathan's hand. 'And I think you will. Life can be disappointing sometimes, even for the best of us.' His mind tripped back to when he was a young and keen psychology student. 'Good luck, Mr Waters.'

Waters nodded and made his way out of the side gate.

Patterson went inside to change his shirt.

—

Jonathan jumped in his car, swigged back the dregs of cold coffee and headed home.

# CHAPTER TWENTY-SEVEN

*Mid-January 2005*
*Warsaw, Poland*

Something held my eyelids down.

I took a laboured breath through a parched mouth and the air ripped at my throat. As my brain hauled itself from unconsciousness, like tyres inflating, my muscles came to life, too.

What had I done?

Remembering where I was, who I was, and why I was here, I stopped myself from tearing at the light dressing that covered my eyes. My life flashed through a drugged mind, as I imagined it would do at the point of death.

And then Joe's image emerged inside my darkness. Had Joe's short life replayed in front of him before his death? This thought caught me, taking away more of the oxygen that my lungs craved. Joe.

Unable to see, my other senses were heightened. The nurses spoke in Polish and I understood nothing.

What had I done? Joe, what have I done?

The nurses giggled. I tried to talk, to interrupt their conversation, let them know I was there, awake, but no sound came from my mouth. My throat itched. I needed a drink.

I needed my son.

The thought of iced water made me try harder to form a voice. Finally, I croaked. 'Please, please may I have a drink?'

I heard the door open.

'Ona budzi!' A nurse shouted.

'Malina! English please. I've told you. English, please.'

It was Marek Gorski. He coughed, clearing his throat.

'Doctor, I think she's awake,' Malina said in English.

'She should be awake now. The anaesthetic was mild,' he said gently.

I heard him moving towards my bed; his shoes squeaked on the lino floor. He was a big man; not fat, but tall and heavily set. When I'd first met him, before I fell pregnant with Joe, I'd thought he looked nothing like a doctor, a cosmetic surgeon, at all. Thinking of my first meeting with Marek, of Sorojini Jain, about my life, brought my thoughts in a full circle back to Joe. I read somewhere that a human life moved in seven-year cycles. The image of Joe imprinted behind the bandage was vivid, brilliant; his blue eyes like small pools of ocean, his hair the colour of thick, golden honey. I squeezed my eyes shut beneath the gauze.

Seven-year cycles.

There was a light touch on my hand and I smelt a waft of aftershave.

'How are you feeling?' Marek asked.

'A little rough,' I said, feeling the cool touch of his finger on my arm.

'You'll be fine. In a few days you'll feel completely normal. This is all routine stuff.'

Again, Marek's touch, and it calmed me, yet I heard mild exasperation in his voice. Was he was already regretting his agreement? But I heard warmth in that voice, too. When I'd asked him to be my surgeon, he had asked very few questions, sensing I would go elsewhere if he said no. 'I want to know as little as possible, Rachel,' he'd said. I had only to remind him once that now Rachel wasn't my name.

I tried to move further up the bed and failed. I was too weak. My fists clenched; it was a misguided rage and I knew it.

'I'll be fine. Please can I have some water?' It was difficult to talk. I'd never realised just how wide a mouth has to open to form coherent words.

'Water? Of course ... water,' he said, as he scraped the chair back.

More movement; another trail of aftershave, then Marek placed a cold glass in my hand, pressing my fingers against its contours with his own.

'Try to relax.' His hand remained touching mine for a moment longer. 'There's a straw. You'll find it difficult to sip.' Then I felt him gently taking away the dressing from my eyes, but I kept them closed.

I sucked the liquid, ice cold and heaven to my parched mouth, and immediately it loosened my vocal cords. The thought of heaven brought Joe back. I wanted my beautiful son to be there, but he was not. He was still waiting.

Already my throat felt better, but a smile never made it to my lips. I said nothing.

'Get some rest,' Marek continued.

I heard the sadness in his voice. 'I will,' I said.

The squeak of lino told me he was moving away.

'And, ladies, please converse in English while in this room, even if talking about personal matters ... which, of course, you shouldn't be.'

'We will,' I heard Malina say. Malina was the nurse

219

I'd met when I'd first arrived at the clinic. I liked her, and so did Marek.

The door closed with an industrial, fire-door click.

'Now is time for soup.' I felt a warm, soft hand on my arm and a lighter scent. Malina.

'I'm really not hungry,' I managed to croak.

'No matter, you need to eat. I lose job if do not.' She was silent for a moment, but then carried on. 'My little boy, Kacper, no eat after Dr Gorski fixed his ears ... I told him, you won't feel better unless eat. It took me three days to get food inside him. Please do not take three days.' She rubbed my arm and moved my feet back under the blanket, and then, efficiently, tucked it securely under the mattress. 'Too tall for bed.'

How old was her boy? Why did she have to mention her son? Malina had no idea, and why should she? I was a single, middle-aged, childless woman, whom Malina saw as a rich westerner, spending thousands on improving her looks. She must despise me. However, her tone was jovial and reassuring.

'Six feet,' I said, opening my mouth so Malina could feed me soup.

'Good girl,' the nurse said, her Polish accent somehow soporific.

My head lolled to one side and I smelt her sweet breath. Malina said something in Polish; I had no idea what, but it sounded lyrical. I felt myself falling into semi-consciousness, allowing only the most sublime of thoughts to pass through my mind. I imagined a strong wind blowing unwanted images away, as they might do to billowing grey clouds on a winter's day – revealing the crisp blue of a morning sky. But, as always, it was an impossible task. Exhausted acceptance slithered in. There was no escaping. Against my will the image, as always, appeared.

A tall man with long, muscular limbs. A bald head. Perhaps the hair had left its follicular home in protest, not wanting to belong to such a soul as Michael Hemmings. His face came into focus and then fragmented, and he became unrecognisable.

# CHAPTER TWENTY-EIGHT

*March 2005*
*London*

Amanda McCarthy stepped off the plane at Heathrow and stood motionless. Her new British passport, together with the new photo, sat nestled in her pocket. Another passport – American – was sewn into the lining of her case.

The courier had delivered them to Malina's home.

Thinking about both the fake passports and the drugs Marek had allowed her to bring, Amanda McCarthy surprised herself at how little she sweated passing through customs.

I'd left the clinic in Warsaw in early February, leaving for Gdańsk. Malina's parents had given me a room, and friendship, while I recovered from the surgery. I returned briefly to Warsaw and the clinic before leaving for England.

I'd thought that being in the same home as Malina's son would be bad for my mental wellbeing, but it had been fine; I enjoyed his company as much as her parents'. Kacper spoke good English. Joe only visited me once, the first night I spent in Malina's parents' home. Kacper had come up to my room with a sandwich and a drink and sat on the chair. I was perched on the bed. The smell of toffee popcorn was strong and I'd felt Joe's calmness. He'd not visited me in the clinic and I knew he didn't agree with my plan, but I kept telling him, 'It's all right, Joe.'

A man with a protruding stomach bumped into me, muttering something I couldn't quite catch. I hitched the flight bag higher on my shoulder and began moving along with the other passengers.

I'd booked a taxi to take me straight into London from the airport. Expertly, the cabbie swung my one large suitcase into the boot and then got in the car. I was already in the back.

'How long will it take?' I said.

'Pretty lady like you,' he glanced in his rear-view mirror appreciatively, 'no more than thirty-five minutes this early in the morning.'

I gazed back at him in the mirror and caught sight of my hair and the top part of my face, startled at the reflection that looked back. Marek had done an amazing job. I didn't recognise myself. Gone was my long, light brown, sometimes-blonde hair. In its place was a short, symmetrically cut, very dark brown hairstyle. Once grey eyes were now hazelnut, courtesy of contact lenses. The rest of my face seemed more alien. Marek had given me a brow lift to alter the look of my eyes, and implanted silicone into thin cheeks to bulk up my face. He'd assured me it was all reversible; I didn't tell him it didn't matter.

I shuffled sideways in the seat and away from my reflection, feeling the soreness in my thighs. I'd insisted he took away the remaining bulk from my hips. Now I looked nothing like Margaret, and nothing like the silhouette of Rachel, and this pleased me.

'Traffic's light today, don't know why – we're nearly there,' the cab driver said, his affability annoying and his chatter even more so. I saw him looking at me, probably thinking what a grumpy cow I was.

'Yes, it's a tough job being a cabbie,' I replied.

He grinned widely, pleased I'd taken notice.

The cab took me into the heart of the West End. I'd rented a room above a row of shops in Greek Street, above a Chinese herbalist. I'd fretted on the plane that this was Jonathan's turf, and allowed myself a grim smile: an American phrase, for a soon-to-be American woman.

Soho was teeming with people; the chances of my bumping into Jonathan were remote. I checked myself again in the mirror. Anyway, he'd never recognise me. Thinking of Jonathan brought a hard lump to my throat.

I peered upwards from the car window. My new home – for a while.

'That's forty quid, lovely lady.'

I found a crisp, new fifty and handed it over. I thought of my dwindling bank account; I wanted the change but didn't wait.

'Thank you, pretty woman.' The cab driver looked happy that I hadn't waited for the change and even retrieved my case, placing it on the pavement. I waited for more questions from him, because now I felt inexplicably lonely and his chatter would be welcome. I'd never really liked London: too big, too sprawling, too impersonal, sterile. Jonathan had always disagreed; he loved the city's anonymity.

Again, I looked up towards the building and fought the unsettling disorientation that engulfed me. The elation I'd felt on the plane – at being so near to where I wanted to be – slid away like the euphoria of landing a new job that you need but don't particularly want. A void descended, like an imaginary net flung over both me and my life.

I was still standing on the pavement and hadn't moved a limb. Taking a deep breath, I hauled the case towards the door and pressed the glinting intercom.

An oriental-sounding female voice answered immediately. 'Hello?'

'Hello, this is Amanda McCarthy.'

The intercom made an even louder sound and the door opened.

A tiny Chinese woman scuttled towards me. Her skin was smooth like polished steel, but I knew she was older than me.

'You are early, but that fine. I have to open shop soon.' She gave a half-smile, and I suspected that was all she ever gave.

'I can wait, if I need to?'

'No, room ready.' She took me in, staring upwards; I was a good foot taller than her. 'More than a room, as we discussed on phone. It was bad line, not normally that bad from the UK.' Her look was a question.

I'd called her from Poland. 'I'm sure it will be more than adequate.'

She nodded and turned delicately, beckoning me to follow her towards the stairs. She gesticulated at my case. 'You stronger than me. You carry?'

I nodded, holding my breath as much as I was able. The smell wasn't good; I recognised it as boiling Chinese herbs. Once, long ago, in another life it seemed now, I'd taken Joe to see a Chinese herbalist. He was always getting sore throats. Western medicine could do nothing, but the Chinese herbs had worked wonders. The Chinese doctor told me Joe's neck and throat were his weak points, we all had one, he said. 'A mental and physical fragility, always better to know which ones we are born with. This knowledge enables us to cope better with the periphery elements.' Liam had poo-pooed him. But, from that day, with any ailment Joe or I had, I went to see the herbalist. I never told Liam; it was easier not to. It surprised me that he'd taken to Buddhism so readily. It didn't sit well with his life-long belief in what he always insisted on calling 'conventional western medicine' – as if the fancy title made it infallible.

Throat. It was impossible to shut out memories of the day Joe's body was found. How he had died, and what had been done to my beautiful Joe afterwards. His neck, his throat. Over the years I'd done a good job of blotting it out; and not because I couldn't tolerate the thought, which I couldn't, but more because I sensed that it was something on which Joe didn't want me to dwell.

The Chinese woman waited, watching me. The suitcase clattered onto the wooden floor of her hallway; my breaths increased in speed but the air going into my lungs reduced; and I followed the suitcase to the ground.

'You OK, lady?' I had no breath to reply. 'Don't want ill people here,' she eyed me from the stairs as if contemplating whether to give me sympathy or a swift exit speech. Her face softened, as if she'd changed her mind and then offered me her hand. I took it and felt something so strong, and so unnerving. It came from her. It was calming too, the awareness I felt around her. Like a comforting, soft aura.

'Thank you,' I managed to whisper.

She tapped her forehead. 'Ill in mind, a little. Leave suitcase, I bring later.'

I followed her up the stairs. She showed me my new home as if nothing had happened.

As I had followed the Chinese woman through the small hallway, I sensed him. He was here, with me. I didn't question why, only glad that he was. And, in a strange way, it felt as if the Chinese woman had some effect on Joe coming.

Belatedly, she introduced herself as Lanfen Xú, owner

of the building. The shop was called Xú. She opened the door and stepped in, I followed. Sweeping her arms around the room she awaited my response.

'It looks good,' I said. 'Perfect,' I added.

It wasn't perfect. It was small and the smell from downstairs was stronger in the enclosed space. I suspected my room was above the kitchen where Mrs Xú cooked up her concoctions. But the aroma brought me closer to Joe.

'No separate bedroom, but bed folds into wall,' she indicated towards the bed, which wasn't folded into the wall.

Mrs Xú carried on. 'Separate kitchen, small but clean, separate bathroom, with shower. No bath.' She looked towards me, 'I explain that on phone?'

'It's fine … perfect.'

'Well, let you settle. If you need any information about anything, I do not mind you knocking on door. Alone now. Husband died few years ago. Live in room downstairs.'

'I'm sorry about your husband.'

'No matter. He left me well provided, left me with shop.'

I studied her; a tiny, almost frail woman but I knew this was deceptive.

'That's good … Well, thank you,' I said.

She nodded and left me with my loneliness. I watched as she walked down the short space of corridor towards the stairs and I saw Mrs Xú's isolation, too.

I closed the door and walked towards the window that faced onto the ugly backs of London buildings. I pulled up the blinds: the dust too visible in the late morning glare. Fine particles rushed by my eyes with the last of the draft from the closing door. I waited for it to settle. Belatedly, I sneezed three times and went to the bathroom to find toilet paper to wipe my nose. The holder was empty. I delved inside my bag looking for Kleenex, and eventually found some. Sitting down on the bed I began to clear out my bag, but there was absolutely nothing in there of consequence to indicate my life. Everything was in a safe-deposit box – out of the way and untouchable. All buried, although tucked away in the bottom of my bag was the large file, full of Amanda McCarthy's correspondence. I had a part of someone else's life but not my own.

I sat back on the uncomfortable bed and threw the bag to one side. It didn't matter. What were photos? Nothing. Only reminders of what had been snatched from me and, by my own choice, given up.

Tom Gillespie was always telling me: we make our own choices, Rachel. And then we have to live with the choice until we see fit to change our mind. And free will is what defines humanity.

I had chosen to do this. I rose and pulled the blinds closed. The room was quiet. The mild smell of damp and boiled herbs had disappeared, or was it that I had just become accustomed to it? I stood motionless and looked at nothing, and then the clear smell of Joe filled my nostrils. Of mildly perfumed soap, a hint of toffee popcorn. I smelt him as strongly as I felt my heart beating inside my chest.

'Joe, are you here?' I said, aiming the question towards the heavier smell near the door of the bathroom. There was no reply. For a moment the aroma became more powerful and then it disappeared. I felt wetness on my cheeks. He'd left, if ever he'd been there at all, but I spoke into the room: 'I love you, Joe.'

In the bathroom I stood in front of the square, smudged mirror and looked hard at the reflection, trying not to think about Joe's questioning of my plan, my questioning.

'It's for the best,' I said to him inside my head, and then out loud into the small space of the bathroom.

I was talking to myself, answering my own reluctance.

Tracing my index finger down my left cheek, I felt the plumpness. The right side felt different. Probably because I was left-handed, something else I would have to address. I could leave nothing to chance. The pads of my fingers rested on my cheeks; I stared into the mirror. Marek had done as little as possible but achieved a lot. He was a genius. I scraped hair back from my forehead. Nothing of Rachel remained, not even the scald scar on my left hand. Marek had even fixed that.

I was a different person on the outside and felt something changing on the inside, too. Standing tall, my face disappeared above the mirror. Marek could change many things, but my height was non-negotiable. At six foot, I was tall for my generation – another defining feature. I'd studied ballet as a child, and only given it up when Margaret told me my lessons were a waste of time and money. That I was selfish to expect them and selfish not to give them up easily. She had burnt my ballet gear in the garden while I was at Sunday school. I'd loved ballet and now the legacy of an upright posture made me appear even taller. I knew I could take off a few inches in height just by rounding my shoulders. With appropriate coaching it would be no problem.

I let my hair fall back into its perfect bob and absentmindedly wiped the greasy mirror with the sleeve of my blouse. I returned to the room, finding the brochure.

*Cambri School of Voice Coaching and Acting*
*London*

Cambri had accepted my deposit for the course without too many questions, and luckily I didn't have to mention Jacob to get my place.

My introductory class at the 'bijou' school was in two days.

Two days. I could sightsee. Find a gym.

Or, I could disappear into the pleasure of prescription painkillers. The plastic container lay at the bottom of my bag. I pulled it out and stared at the innocuous-looking holder. I took a deep breath and once again walked into the bathroom with Charlotte's words inside my head, 'Find another way of dealing with this, it's time.'

I emptied the contents into the toilet, flushed and put the lid down, turned and sat on the flimsy cover. I was still sitting there when the intercom rang.

It could only be Mrs Xú. I thought about ignoring the sound. It rang again. I couldn't. I opened the door and looked down into her dark eyes, noticing the unhealthy circles surrounding them. Maybe she didn't sleep much either. I looked closer. Yes, I saw the pain in Mrs Xú's eyes too. Pain was everywhere and I felt a huge compassion for this woman I did not know. For the first time in five years my empathy was stronger than my hatred for someone I did know. Although only a moment. A piercing, unselfish moment. We all suffer; we all struggle; we all attempt to live. We should do so together, not hurting and wounding each other. That was Liam's line from one of his Buddhist meetings. I'd wanted to kill him.

'You have call.' I turned and glanced towards the phone that sat on a rickety, cheap table by the door. She saw me looking. 'Not working – last tenant not pay bill, be connected tomorrow. The call come through to me.' I still hadn't spoken. 'You can take in my room … He on

231

phone now, holding. I told him could call back … said he hold.' She watched me. 'Not English.' She had brought up my suitcase and placed it inside my door.

'Thank you, Mrs Xú.' I pointed to the case. 'Do you mind me taking the call?'

'Not have mobile?'

'No, I don't.'

Unlike many people, Mrs Xú accepted easily my 'mobileless' state. I liked Mrs Xú. I felt she saw into the centre of me; that centre still holding Joe.

It could only be Marek. I was beginning to wish I hadn't told him my destination, and not because I didn't trust him, but because I didn't want him to be at all implicated. Although he already was, and the ripple of guilt threatened to turn into a wave. Shamelessly, I'd used Marek's friendship to persuade him to carry out the surgery.

His call had to be about something important.

Mrs Xú's living space was only fractionally bigger than my own, but, unlike my space, my landlady's was bright. Light streamed in from the living room, which faced onto the busy London street.

I picked up the phone.

'Hello?' I looked towards Mrs Xú and waited. She didn't move. In an exaggerated movement I put my hand over the phone. 'I won't be long,' I said. It took her too long to move towards the bright light of the sitting room and out of earshot. 'Hello,' I said again into the phone.

'Rachel?'

'Amanda, Doctor Gorski.'

'Amanda,' he emphasised the syllables, 'Marek – Amanda. We're not in the clinic now.'

'Is everything all right?' I said.

'Yes, but I think you should know, I've had a phone

call. A while ago now. I wasn't going to tell you, but thought I should.'

'Who?'

'Jonathan Waters.'

'Jonathan? What did he say?'

'He wanted to know about you.'

'Does he know anything?'

'No, I don't think so. Says he's worried about you. He wants to know where you are.'

Jonathan, why are you doing this?

'Is there any way he can get to speak with your nurses?'

'They won't talk, I hope, but I hate to ask people to lie.'

'He must know something.'

'Sniffing. You know Jonathan.' Marek was quiet for a long moment. 'Give this up, Rach ... Amanda.'

Yes, I did know Jonathan. He didn't give up.

'Give what up? I'm only a woman trying to rebuild her life, and a part of that reconstruction is changing the way I look. That's all I'm doing, Marek.'

'I shouldn't have agreed ... Let it go.'

'Stop worrying, Marek ...' I paused. 'I'm sorry...'

'It's all right. But you have to stop punishing yourself.'

'I know. Soon ... You didn't say anything ... did you?'

'No, of course not. And I won't contact you again, unless I need to.'

'OK.'

'How are you?' he asked.

'I'm fine.'

'Are you still taking the painkillers?'

'Only when I need them, don't worry.' I thought about the toilet.

'Take care.'

'I will, Marek. You too.'

I put the phone down. Why had Jonathan called? What did he know? I'd done a good job in covering my tracks. A positive leftover from being in the force. Then I thought of Marek's words, sniffing. Jonathan knew nothing. He was following a hunch.

Unfortunately, Jonathan's hunches tended to be spot on.

But a warmth whisked over me: that Jonathan cared enough to bother.

# CHAPTER TWENTY-NINE

I had too much time to think, and still two days before my course began. I did contemplate finding a gym. There had been no way I'd been able to keep up my fitness routine during my time in Poland. I'd managed some short runs at Malina's parents', but after less than a mile my thighs hurt and the swelling started. Marek told me over the phone that I was stupid, and he was right, so eventually I took to going for long walks; my legs could cope with that. Did I wish I hadn't taken it all so far? Sometimes I did. Then I thought of Hemmings, of Joe, and there was no question.

After school, Kacper had often joined me on my walks, and they were an unexpected joy. I guzzled the tales about his classes, and holidays with his grandparents and Malina to the seaside resorts of Poland. He regaled vivid second hand stories of his great-grandparents from the time of Hitler's occupation; of his great-grandmother who'd survived Auschwitz. Kacper was young and too wise for his age. Did he remind me of Joe? No, he didn't, he was so different. Joe had never been that wise, seemingly acquiring his wisdom in death, inside his ghost, inside me.

Feeling as if my life was being vacuumed away, I sat down heavily on the bed. Often I would move from the elation that taking control gave me, to despair that what I was doing was so very wrong. I wanted Joe to be able to go to the final destination, sensing he was unable to travel there until everything was resolved. And this resolution I saw only in the death of Michael Hemmings. That's what I felt and saw. And my feeling and seeing were so knitted together with memories of my son I became one with him.

My new spiritual awareness did make me smile, and was eons away from the pragmatic Rachel of the West Midlands police force. But the efficiency that had made me a good officer was also the trait that enabled me to block out Joe's unhappiness at my plan, his whispering of something I could never quite catch, never quite understand.

Was it Joe's reluctance, or my own?

I rose from the bed, exhausted with half-formed thoughts. I decided to go to the library and properly read the letters Amanda had sent to her 'lover'. I'd been putting it off; it was too sad reliving Amanda's life. But soon I would have to write my letter – Amanda's letter to Michael Hemmings.

As I padded down the dark hallway towards the front door, smelling the pungent herbs, I caught sight of Mrs Xú.

'Mrs McCarthy … you ok?' she asked.

'Of course, why wouldn't I be?'

She seemed to look into my very core and touched my hand with her own, her skin silk-like, and a shiver passed over me as she pressed her fingers lightly onto the new 'Gorski-perfect' skin on my left hand, then upwards towards my wrist.

'You are sad.'

The chill that ran up and down my spine rocked me. I was very sad, and wanted to tell her but pulled away instead. This was ridiculous. She knew nothing about me. I thought back to our visits to the Chinese doctor, who'd been more than he'd seemed; I'd known it, and I sensed a very young Joe had too. The Chinese man knew a long time before the conventional doctors what was wrong with Joe. The herbalist possessed more than just a gift for prescribing herbs.

As did Mrs Xú.

'Something very not right and you not listening.'

I took a deep breath. Thinking I knew what she was saying, thinking I knew everything but knowing that if I did I wouldn't be here. My life would have been so very different if I'd known everything.

I smiled towards her, humouring her, this woman whom I didn't know but liked. And the smell of a tree's boiling roots overwhelmed me.

She said, 'Sometimes I see, and feel, too much.'

'I have to go,' I said, feeling breathless and confused. Quickly I put a foot outside the door and, as I stepped onto the pavement, a young girl hit me on the arm as she whizzed by on skates. Everything consuming me. Everything hurting and aching.

'Watch where you're fucking going,' the girl shouted. I looked at Mrs Xú's window above the shop doorway. I felt her silence, even outside. Felt her hesitance as strongly as I sometimes felt Joe's and my own.

I could not confide in anyone.

Making my way towards the nearest bus stop for King's Cross and the library, I side-stepped mid-morning tourists, avoiding the shop windows that reflected back Marek's work. I didn't want to see what I'd done. I put my head down, hunching my shoulders forwards, now concentrating on the task ahead: writing a letter to Hemmings.

After finishing in the library I planned go to an internet café nearby. Razor had been doing some more work for me. This time regarding Margaret.

At the library I found an empty table and sat down, retrieving Amanda's letters and writing paper from my bag.

I'd arranged for a mailing service in the States to forwards the letter from 'Amanda' to Littleworth, so it would bear an American postmark. I was leaving absolutely nothing to chance. What I'd managed to find out about the 'inner workings' of Littleworth, and Michael Hemmings' part there reminded me of the cleverness buried underneath his thick coat of pseudo-insanity.

Uneasiness enveloped me at each reading of Amanda's letters. I read them again now, listening to the laboured breathing of the old man who was sitting next to me. The desolation of Amanda's life still shocked me. In the library, and with a clear image of where Amanda came from and who she was, I wrote my letter. Amanda's pain and mine meshed together. By feeling hers so intensely, I managed to convince myself that what I was doing was right, but felt like a voyeur and a betrayer of trust. Silently, hunched up on the plush new library seat, I asked Amanda to forgive me and wondered if I could ever forgive myself. Three times I crumpled the letter in a sweaty hand.

The old man turned his head at the sound of crumpling paper. 'Is it a love letter?' he asked.

I shook my head, but smiled. I didn't mind his inquisitiveness.

Finally I finished the letter, padded out with many of the incidents that Amanda had conveyed to Stephen Passaro, the murderer she'd befriended on death row. Only the thought of Hemmings stopped me from screwing up the paper again. Hotness rose in my cheeks and the pain in my thighs, and my heart, swamped me.

Outside, I reeled at how busy London was, my head still filled with sheep sheds in Ohio, cattle prods and young children living in absolute terror of a man who should, if there was any justice, never have been born.

Leaning against the wall of the library building I asked myself: could I face the unsavoury truths that might be waiting for me in an email about Margaret?

The internet café was full. I waited in a torn fake leather chair for a terminal to become free, preparing myself for what I might find out about Margaret. I allowed my head to rest on a grimy wall and closed my eyes, revisiting my childhood. Back to the day I'd found Michael in Margaret's bedroom. This time I didn't see from afar, as someone else: today I remembered as Rachel again.

My dad had finally returned home and still my mother had said nothing. I had followed her around the house, wanting to ask what had happened and why Michael had been sitting on her knee with her nipple in his mouth. The fear I felt for my mother had receded with my intense curiosity.

I remember her cooking lunch; everything perfectly ordered in her kitchen. Pots gleaming and the familiar smell of roasting chicken, mixed with her lavender scent. My parents ate and I don't think my dad saw anything was wrong. I couldn't eat as my stomach was still cramping periodically. (Later, we found out it was a spastic colon.) The tension in the house seemed to be prolonging the attack. My dad read the newspaper after finishing his homemade apple pie. I drank some water. He got up and asked me if I wanted to go for a walk. I would normally. I shook my head, rubbing my stomach. He patted the top of my shoulder, telling me to rest, and off he went.

Despite my cramps, I picked up the tea towel and dried up.

'Why was Michael here ... why was he doing that?' I blurted after the second plate.

'You didn't see anything. Michael wasn't here.'

'He was, Mum. Why was he doing that? I don't think Mr Roberts would let Mrs Roberts do that with Wayne.' Wayne was Mr and Mrs Roberts's nephew.

And she turned, looking at me, not looking like my mother, not looking like anyone's mother. All I remembered now was the feeling of emptiness.

'If you mention this to anyone, Rachel, I will slit you in two.' She held up the sharp knife she was washing. The suds falling like fairies from the blade.

It would be years before I mentioned the incident again.

I felt warmth enter the café. I tried to lift my head because I smelt sweet toffee.

'Joe, Joe...'

A light kiss on my cheek but I was unable to move, as if paralysed.

Finally I opened my eyes, feeling a prod on my arm. A woman chewing gum indicated a terminal was free. I nodded a thank you, which she ignored as she carried on filing her nails.

I sat down ignoring the pain in my thighs, a memory of the scar on my hand where the skin was now smooth and pale.

I logged on and, after a few seconds, my email account popped up. A message from Razor. He'd been busy. I hadn't told him who Margaret Hemmings was, but he knew. Of course he knew, and was probably intrigued. I sensed his ingenuity as much as I'd done the numerous times I'd interviewed him at the station.

I clicked.

His words lay in front of me. Did they shock, were they a surprise? A long time afterwards I'd admit to myself that although shocking, the words weren't surprising.

Before me, before she looked after Michael, my mother had been an English teacher at a private boys' school. She had left her post very quickly, amid rumours that she had been asked to resign. Knowing my mother, I knew immediately that she would have only left if there was a compelling reason to do so. The compelling reason was substantiated rumours that she was having inappropriate liaisons with the boys in her care.

I thought back to when I started my career in the police. How Michael Hemmings had been checked out, a given considering his conviction history. Tom wouldn't have been keen to promote me too quickly if I had a past he had to worry about. Neither of us suspected my mother would be a problem. I wondered now: had he ever checked out Margaret? If he had, he'd obviously found nothing. Margaret had fallen from Tom's, and the force's, radar.

Razor had done an excellent job in his digging.

Feeling too hot, I took off my jumper. I pushed the chair back and stood, stretching legs that felt like dehydrated twigs. I shielded the screen from anyone that might be looking. Shame gathered around me like laden clouds before a sea-storm. Humiliation that she was my mother; angry discomfort that it was only now that I was allowing myself to dredge up memories so deeply buried – by me, and my dad.

Michael Hemmings was a monster, but my own

mother had carved his character.

I felt my eyes redden. The girl with the gum and the dirty nails was sitting at the next terminal. She glanced at me quickly, and away just as quickly. I was on my own, doing what I knew was right, in the world I occupied hour after hour, day after day, year after year. What I was doing was the only outcome.

All I needed now was to hone Amanda, be Amanda, and I would be ready.

# CHAPTER THIRTY

By the time I returned to Mrs Xú's the sun was already losing its daytime lustre. Her shop was closed for business and I wondered if she'd opened up at all. I let myself in through the residential door and made my way up the darkly carpeted stairs. Turning left towards my room at the top of the staircase, I saw a whisper of light fall from the open door. My pulse quickened as I moved nearer. I threw my handbag and jacket on the floor ready for confrontation, anticipating a burglar, a madman off the streets of London.

I nudged the door with the tip of my finger. A sound came from the direction of the bathroom, and I steadied my pulse with long breaths and moved towards the direction of the noise. The bathroom door was half open; I pushed it further with a shoeless foot and entered.

An ebony black cat slithered between my legs, out of the bathroom and ran from my room. Exactly three minutes later I began to sneeze. I was allergic to cats, a fact that had made Joe, who loved them, sad. I now realised why my nose had been constantly running since coming to Mrs Xú's.

I wedged open the bathroom door, hoping that whatever cats gave off to make me sneeze would eventually disappear.

Suddenly I had an overwhelming desire to talk to

someone. I made my way back downstairs to find Mrs Xú and knocked on her door. No answer. The door next to her rooms opened directly into the shop, and was open. The shop was closed but Mrs Xú was busy. Smells permeated the small space. The cat sat on the wooden table where she worked. Mrs Xú chopped and cut. Several jars of powdered something sat on the table, and a few more were lined up on the floor. The cat moved its head, looking up to watch me, as did Mrs Xú.

'Don't like people here when working.' She said it not unkindly but forcefully. The cat meowed, jumped from the table and slunk itself around its mistresses ankles. Mrs Xú stopped chopping, took a deep breath and sighed. 'But do not mind you being here.'

And that was when I saw the grief, in its complete unprocessed form, the sadness I'd seen when I'd first met her.

'I do not know what you doing but should stop.' She bent down and stroked the cat. 'I had son. Gen was name. Was in South Tower.'

South tower, what was she talking about?

Then it hit me. 9/11.

'You're American?' I asked.

'No,' she watched me closely.

'What happened … to your son?'

'The day of disaster was his birthday. My husband gone to New York to be with him. Thirtieth, very important birthday. Husband went office to see Gen, early morning … on ninety-sixth floor, have look Gen's new place of work … Was new job.'

'And your husband was there … with your son?'

'He was.'

Instinctively I moved closer and put my arm around a tiny shoulder.

'I know grief,' she said. 'Hatred ...' she watched me. 'Desolation. No matter what do, problem always there.'

'You don't know anything about me.'

'Know too much, always known too much. Knew bad thing going to happen to Gen, knew from day was born, but could do nothing. That is not way of nature, could not interfere.' She leant against the table.

Fatigue folded over me. 'Mrs Xú, I'm so sorry about your husband and son, I truly am. I understand ...' I tried to find the right phrase. 'I understand your gift, but with all respect you know nothing about me.'

I thought she would question me but didn't. Did she hope that she could help me by sharing her own heartache? Her story was no less sad than my own. She slumped onto a stool and I saw Mrs Xú move to another place inside her mind; and I could see it; a familiar place that I understood.

For what seemed like an eternity we were silent. Then she rose from the stool and reached underneath the table, pulling out a jar of herbs. 'Boil these up ... I think know how,' her expressionless face broke into a smile, 'make you less sensitive to Mr Cat.'

I took them. 'Thank you.'

# CHAPTER THIRTY-ONE

It was an easy ten minute walk to Cambri and, as at Mrs Xú's, it was difficult to identify the correct door. The school wouldn't have been found by accident. After asking several unhelpful people, I walked into a delicatessen that I knew was in the right vicinity. A massive man who was serving a tiny old lady – '6oz of ham, 4oz of camembert, 4 pickled eggs ...' she was saying – looked up and grinned.

'I'm looking for Cambri, any idea where it is?'

'Here, sort of, next door, darlin'. Just press the big silver button on the door outside.' He looked at the 1930s Bakelite clock that hung in pride of place on the back wall of the old-fashioned counter, above shelves of cheeses and hams. 'Nearly ten, Stanley should be here now. He's not normally late, but it's Monday. Has to get over from Ealing. Godforsaken suburb.'

'George, there's absolutely nothing wrong with Ealing.'

I turned at the very English voice as the old lady nudged past me, scurrying from the shop.

'Ah, Stanley, there you are. This lady's hoping to get in,' George said.

Stanley was tall, matching my own height, but stocky. He wore an old-style tweed jacket that was too small for him. He had a mop of wild grey hair. He reminded me of Albert Einstein.

'Mrs McCarthy?'

'Amanda...'

'Nice to meet you, Amanda. Stanley Fishel.'

'Stan, mate, this is a shop, not your office,' George said good-naturedly.

Stanley took my elbow. 'Everyone here calls me Stanley, not Stan, only George can get away with it.' His eyes crinkled into a laugh. I wanted to tell him his happiness was infectious. I'd only just met him but already felt some part of me smiling in a way it hadn't done for five years. 'We are out of here.' Stanley winked at George.

'Really good to meet you, Stan ... ley,' I said as we moved outside.

He pressed the relevant numbers on the combination lock and opened the door next to George's shop. 'The others will already be here, I'm late, sorry.' He kicked at the bright-red door, pushing it open wider, and allowed me to go through first.

I was curious to see inside the school, wondering how it could operate from such small premises. Thinking about Jacob, I smiled. Unpretentious Jacob would have loved this.

Stanley was speaking. 'Come through to the office, I'll just need to get some details. Then classes begin. One-to-one voice coaching in the afternoon.' He looked up from his notebook that he'd pulled from a very battered briefcase. 'There's not much information in here. You kept it brief.'

He watched me carefully, and I was conscious of his conclusions. He probably guessed I wasn't an actor.

'I'm researching a book that I plan to write, part of it about voice coaching.'

He nodded, not fully reassured. 'People come here for

more reasons than just to learn how to speak differently. We have an acting school running from here, too, specialising in method acting. Only small, the acting part of the school, but well respected.' He paused. 'You might be interested in doing some taster sessions? They're competitively priced.'

'I might, I'll see how it goes. I'm not here very long.'

'No.' He smiled, his face creasing into kindness. 'Now, we don't have many rules, but the one that cannot be broken is attendance. We expect full commitment. By the time you finish the course, you will be able to speak in any accent you wish, or need.' He looked at me questioningly, then grinned. 'And hopefully be able to write your book.'

I smiled. 'Good. That's all I ask.'

As he turned I noticed his grey hair was held in a ponytail. 'I'll show you the communal room, where you can get tea and coffee, socialise,' he said, taking my arm and whisking me down a long corridor. The place was much bigger than I'd anticipated. 'Grab a coffee, or tea, make yourself at home,' he said.

'I hate tea.' I paused. 'Stanley, I want to be able to do an American accent, will that be do-able?'

'America's a big place – lots of accents – where?'

'Maybe somewhere like Ohio. Maybe I could be a waitress from a diner?'

'Ohio? That's very specific. A waitress? Like the generic ones in every Hollywood movie? Repressed, abused female characters,' he rolled his eyes upwards towards a mushroom-painted ceiling. 'I'm thinking Julia Roberts … *Pretty Woman*.' He peered into my face, took in my height. 'More than a passing resemblance.'

'That's just because I'm tall. No, I don't want to be Julia Roberts in *Pretty Woman*. And I think you're thinking of her in *Sleeping with the Enemy*. And I think that was Iowa.'

'Maybe. You're right though, very unrealistic in *Pretty Woman*, never met a prostitute like that.' I couldn't imagine Stanley meeting any prostitutes. 'But it was a wonderful role for Julia.'

I wanted to ask if he'd met her.

'I want to speak like the prostitute you think she should have been,' I said. 'A real one, with a sad and dysfunctional past, a woman who's sold out, given up.' I wanted to add, the type who sells her body, or mind, to murderers.

Stanley poured me coffee. 'Sugar?'

'Three please.'

'Definitely not Ms Roberts,' he said, scooping three sugars into a white mug. He handed it to me. 'Interesting. I think you're very interesting, Amanda, if you don't mind me saying.'

I grinned. 'I don't.'

'To be someone else and do it realistically, you have to be in possession of that character. Like creating a character in a novel, you have to know that character. You look from the outside in, and the inside out. You know all those subconscious thoughts – the ones we repress and pack down like newly laid tarmac? Well, those you have to have access to. To play someone else well you not only have to be inside their head, but outside too. See what the outside world sees.' He waited. 'And the voice is important.'

Every night and every day that I thought of Joe, I also thought about the person who'd killed him. To get close to that person, apart from being inside Amanda's head I needed to be inside the perpetrator's too. Tom Gillespie had taught this technique well. To be inside the perp's mind. And also inside the thoughts of the victim. To know both will always give you the edge in any murder enquiry. People are consistent, they act with an alarming sameness, and by understanding the consistencies of both the killer and the victim, you were halfway to solving the crime and the motivation for that crime.

I looked past Stanley and upwards at the ceiling, noticing the cracks that had been repaired with Polyfilla, and then painted. Like people's personalities: cracks skilfully covered, but always apparent if you looked hard enough. How hard did I have to look for Margaret's? It had seemed impossible to look, for years, impossible. But now I was able to peer inside the vault of my mind, it was opening.

The cracks in Margaret's personality were huge. An abyss.

Squeezing my eyes shut; I thought of Joe, the victim. I knew exactly how Joe would have been, how he would have reacted, even what he would have said. But Joe didn't have enough information about the person who had ripped away his life, and that was my fault. I imagined the killer, knowing what a strong position he'd been in. How opportune it had all been. How unlucky I had been. My Joe, with no luck at all. I found my eyes following one particularly large crevice that travelled from the ceiling's edge, like slashed skin from a sharp knife, down the wall.

'So, Amanda McCarthy, our task should be an easy one?' Stanley interrupted my thoughts.

I nodded. 'So what happens now?'

'Now you begin your first class.'

'Great.'

The course was ten days long. As well as honing my accent it would give me a little more time to assimilate my new face and body, before confronting Hemmings for the first time.

It was my body that seemed to be giving me the biggest problem. If I avoided mirrors, the face I could easily ignore. Marek had taken some fat away from my naturally rounded hips, making me appear more angular. Like my height, curvaceous hips were memorable. I'd always been flat chested; he'd given me a D cup. Bigger than he'd wanted to go. However, I needed something very different from Rachel. A positive consequence of Marek's work was that now I definitely looked less like the woman whose genes I'd inherited. My hand skimmed over my left breast and I smiled; it was taking me longer to get used to the large chest than it was to become familiar with a new name.

—

The sun was disappearing below London's murky skyline by the time I left Cambri. I decided I needed to walk and not return straight away to Mrs Xú's. After only one day in the school, I realised that if I was to become who I needed to become and achieve my aim, my compulsion towards isolation was not a good thing. I needed some human interaction.

I pounded the pavement toward Regent's Park, and my head cleared. From just a few hours of tuition I'd learnt a lot, and not only about voice and accent but a little about acting, too. And I needed to learn, because by the time Amanda visited Michael Hemmings there would be no turning back.

The cacophony of city noise thumped inside my head and I thought of the monster that was locked away in a mental institution, of the day Tom Gillespie walked into my kitchen that housed a fridge with a picture of three falling suns stuck on the side.

Three falling suns. Three people. A Trinity. Essence,

substance and nature: Mr Roberts, my old Sunday school teacher had explained. The three of us in our family were distinct and yet one, but now that was not so. Now we were broken. Now it felt as if Liam and I were nothing.

I looked up and saw I was nearly at Regent's Park. I waited for the traffic to stop at the red light. I was about to move, then felt a rush of air and seconds later a mild collision. My bag had been ripped from my arm. Trained reflexes returned and I scanned the street. Without thinking I sprinted down the road, my eyes never leaving the boy, my handbag held firmly in his hands. Even through the adrenaline, I noticed the looks of surprise from the people I elbowed out of the way; people unaccustomed to the sight of the victim running after the thief. The boy turned the corner and I changed gear, pounding after him. The larger bust slowed me down, but I could still see him and closed the gap fast. Making one last exaggerated effort – and feeling the effects of the liposuction on my thighs – I made a finish-line sprint. As energy flowed like heat from my own body, the thief's wavered.

I grabbed him by his sweat-laden shirt. 'You should do some training, get fit for your chosen profession.' No older than seventeen I guessed.

'Let … fucking go of me!' He shouted in my ear and punched ineffectively into my still fragile jawline.

'You fucking thief! Who do you think you are?' I shouted, not recognising my own voice.

He swung around, forcing himself free from my grip and striking me in the face again. By now, onlookers had stopped but still did nothing. I gathered myself and felt at a bloody nose. It might be broken and, pointlessly, I worried about the time Marek had spent on it.

I looked at the boy; he seemed as surprised as me at

the punch he'd executed. I could see a glimmer of an apology in his eyes and, momentarily, I softened. Then anger took over.

I hesitated only for a second before kicking him in the groin. He doubled over. I could have left it then, picked up my bag and left, but I did not. I jabbed his trunk hard with the flat of my foot and he rolled onto the ground, moaning. To protect his face he placed his arm at a peculiar angle. Bringing up my foot, I planned to push his arm down hard into the pavement knowing it would likely dislocate his shoulder. I held my foot in position. Time slowed, but anticipating my wrath he screeched, and the noise reminded me of a visit long ago to a French slaughterhouse. Of the pig as its throat was slit horizontally.

I took my foot away and allowed him to get up. I glanced around the street; still no one had ventured close to the incident.

He stared at me as if I was a lunatic.

'You mad fucker!'

People moved closer, but no one intervened.

'I'm sorry …' I said to the young thief.

'Mad fucking bitch.' And he ran down the street.

What was I thinking? It was just a stolen handbag. Thank God I'd come to my senses and let him go.

I returned to Mrs Xú's and an overwhelming desire to sleep overtook me. After checking that my nose wasn't in fact broken, and applying ice for ten minutes, I slid into bed hungry and thirsty. I slept for fifteen hours.

The next morning I woke up groggy. I got up and showered. Luckily there was no bruise on my face, just puffiness.

I was standing outside the deli at eight-thirty with a

Styrofoam cup in my hand, 'Tea' written hastily on its side, courtesy of George.

Stanley looked at me. 'A bad night?'

I smiled dimly and nodded.

'I thought you said you didn't like tea?' he said, as I followed him inside.

'I don't.'

But Amanda had done, her daughter had told me.

# CHAPTER THIRTY-TWO

I'd completed the first six days at Cambri and was loving every minute.

Being an intensive, concentrated course there was no time to make small talk and this suited me fine. It was Friday and we were wrapping up for the day. I was particularly exhausted; my one-to-one with Stanley had taken everything from me. Getting inside the head of the numerous characters he invented was like running a marathon. Although it had been only in the last hour that I'd allowed myself to 'go'. That is how Stanley described it – 'going': when you became the character, wiping out anything that might pertain to the real you. And if Stanley saw anything creeping in that might be a part of the 'real' you, he ranted a lot in a take-off of his own Jewishness, but always with a fat smile on his face. I adored Stanley.

'Not bad, not bad at all. You were nearly there – only saw a little of who you might be,' Stanley said. 'It's not just the voice, there's a certain amount of acting too. Stay here a little longer and we could go into the method…'

'I can't stay any longer, Stanley.' I sat on the floor facing him. 'And you don't know me, so how can you see anything that's not the character, but that is me?' I said.

'Years of practice, my dear girl.' He surveyed me with a teacher's passion. 'You have to leave yourself behind. Final.'

'What if I can't find her again?'

'Of course you'll find her.' He scrutinised me. 'My girl, I think you should join the Friday-night exodus.'

'I don't drink these days. I'm not very sociable. Anyway, I need an early night.'

'Then act and sound sociable. It'll do you good. You look as if you could do with a good night out,' the perceptive teacher said.

Stanley definitely looked like Einstein when he won the Nobel Prize.

'Do you fancy a drink?' I asked.

I had no idea what to order from the five-page cocktail menu.

'Do you like cream?' Stanley asked.

'Hate cream.'

'Cranberry juice?'

'Nope.'

'Mint?'

'Mint? Why, we ordering lamb cocktails?' I said, smiling.

Stanley touched my arm and shouted into the noise of the bar, towards a bartender. 'Two mojitos!'

'Yamas!' Stanley said as the bartender put the drinks in front of us.

'Yes, cheers,' I said, taking a sip. 'Nice.'

We chatted about inconsequential stuff, drank more cocktails, but then Stanley's face took on a serious expression.

'So, Amanda.' He lowered his voice so much I had difficulty hearing him in the increasing loudness of the bar; a Mexican guitarist had just begun to play. His tone told me he was going to ask something I'd rather not answer. 'Why are you really here?'

Part of my brain warned my mouth to be careful, but the mojitos were taking their toll and I could feel my vigilance departing. Stanley was curious. I asked myself if it mattered. Yes, it could. In the near future I knew it could matter. The bar was now humming with Friday night chatter. I scanned the stools filled with people and tried to gain the attention of the overworked barman. My line of vision was drawn to the end of the bar, towards the stool that stood alone from the others.

And I saw the petrol blue, Joe sitting in a crowded bar in London, looking uncomfortable. I don't think he wanted to be there. I rose unsteadily, falling forwards, then the colour faded, and so did Joe. It was the alcohol. It wasn't Joe. Joe was dead. I tried to clear my mind, override the white rum swishing through my veins.

I took a breath. 'Joe…'

'Joe?' Stanley said quietly. 'Who's Joe?'

'Joe's dead,' I said.

'Amanda, are you all right?'

What was I saying, what was I doing? 'I'm sorry, I'm drunk. Ignore me.'

'Maybe we should eat something?'

I waited for him to ask about Joe again, but the lovely Stanley did not and I gathered my brain. 'The book I'm writing … I'm doing some research on repressed and abused women. American women who feel the need to befriend characters on death row.'

'Ah …' He didn't pursue Joe. 'Some research into the character while writing your book, like a docu-drama? I thought you were writing about accents? But I'm impressed, whatever you're writing about.' He crossed his arms. 'So, a character like Julia Roberts in *Sleeping with the Enemy*?'

I gulped down another mojito. 'It was definitely Iowa

in *Sleeping with the Enemy* ... I think,' I said smiling.

'Yes, indeed,' Stanley said.

I wished I hadn't mentioned researching books, and death row. Or Joe. Stanley was switched on, he was inquisitive, and he was more than curious about me.

Two hours later Stanley was standing on Mrs Xú's step, holding me steady with one arm. I knew I was drunk. It was the same feeling I'd had many times with Charlotte, in faraway days. But this was much worse, I realised. I'd eaten nothing and felt sick. The step was moving in an alarming fashion and, no matter how much I tried, it was impossible to focus. I attempted to peer at him. I needed to vomit.

'I feel a bit ill.' I tried to centre my eyes on the middle Stanley. I began to giggle, almost hysterically, forcing away the sick feeling.

'Amanda, are you all right, I mean ... really all right?'

At that moment Mrs Xú opened the door in a black kimono.

'I think time for you to go home,' she said to Stanley, her face stone-like and not intimidated by Stanley at all. I think she thought he was my beau. Stanley was nearly old enough to be my father. My father. Dad. And I was brought back to reality.

Mrs Xú's demeanour made me feel like a daughter coming home from an illicit date. Despite her acerbity she gave me a feeling of something that I'd missed out on while growing up. In my drunkenness a part of me wanted Mrs Xú to know everything, as I'd wanted to tell Stanley more in the bar earlier. These strangers had drawn more from the depths of me than anyone had been able to do for the last five years.

I hadn't acknowledged how alone I truly was.

Charlotte wanted to be there for me, but I'd been unable to reach out to my best friend. And I had felt during the last time we'd spoken that even Charlotte held something back, some knowledge that she didn't share. This feeling of withdrawal on her part caused me to be more cautious towards my friend.

I planned to take my revenge, and then disappear forever and I now regretted giving Charlotte a PO Box number. It had been a mistake.

Stanley looked at me. 'You're OK, aren't you?' Then he took in the formidable four-foot-eleven Mrs Xú, whose steady gaze had captured him.

'I'm fine, Stanley, thank you,' I said. 'Go home, it's late.'

'See you Monday. He touched his forehead as he turned to Mrs Xú. If he'd been wearing a hat I was sure he would have tipped it briefly.

The sick feeling returned with a vengeance. 'I have to go ...' I looked at Mrs Xú. 'I need to get to the bathroom.'

She moved sideways; a faint and amused smile on her face as she allowed me to pass.

# CHAPTER THIRTY-THREE

With all physical feeling numbed, I entered my room with a sense of unusual serenity.

Mrs Xú had given me a tea that I'd drunk downstairs sitting on the stool where she made her potions. The nausea had died down and soberness settled. Had she known I would come home drunk, and prepared it earlier? I wouldn't have been surprised. She had left me alone drinking the tea and I'd felt its effects quickly.

I now sipped at a pint of water and pulled from my bag the envelope that I'd picked from my PO Box earlier in the day. It was from Amanda's daughter, Mary Lou. I'd had a quick look inside; it was a long letter and I'd noticed that the spelling and grammar were both much better than in her mum's correspondence to Stephen Passaro.

Mary Lou wanted to tell me more about her mum, and again I felt guilty. I'd told her the same thing I'd told Stanley, that I was researching a book. Mary Lou wanted to help me.

As I leant sideways to put the glass on the side table, the toffee popcorn came and the envelope slid downwards. But the internal voice of my son trailed away as quickly as it came. Joe was becoming weaker, yet the hunger I hadn't felt for weeks returned. Mrs Xú had felt him too, I was sure of it. Or did I just like to think that?

Had Mrs Xú seen her own son after his death?

I needed to release Joe. And for that I had to kill Hemmings. There was no other way.

Picking up the envelope again, I pulled out the paper and began to read about the woman I was becoming.

*Dear Rachel,*

*I haven't met you, but knowing you have read Mom's letters and something about her, I hope you now have a better understanding, and that you are able to write a book that will help others to not travel the same path as my mom.*

*I met a good man, fell in love, and we moved away from Toledo. He was good enough to not only take me on, but also my brother and sister. I have to look after them; I want to take care of them, especially Noah.*

*Mom worked at Yum Yums until Stephen Passaro's execution in 2003. She seemed to go downhill after that. Too many drugs. She had always been a cannabis user, but soon graduated to heroin.*

*Mom's life was tragic. She married young, had three children before she was thirty. She managed to get away from her first husband, our father, because of his early death. Then she hooked up with a local farmer, and married him quickly. I am the eldest and I remember it well, their marriage.*

*He was known as a man with a temper, and strange ideas. He died at the farm. A heart attack – there was local gossip that maybe he had died of something else … but nothing was proven. The police let go of their enquiries. The farm was repossessed, and we were all made homeless. That was when she started working at Yum Yums, and began writing to Passaro, then visiting him. He was a monster. I didn't understand what my mom was doing.*

*Amanda was a good mom. She tried to be a good mom. What happened with her second husband, the rumours about him ... she protected her children as well as she could. She tried to protect Noah.*

*There is something wrong with our society, Rachel. What happened to Mom in her childhood, first marriage, then her second ... her actions in seeking out this criminal – murderer – came from everything she had ever known, the society that surrounded her.*

*Recently I went back to the farm where it happened, where my stepfather died. I went back with my husband. He took me; he knew I had to have one last look. Our correspondences seemed to rake it all up, but I'm grateful for that, Rachel, because I needed to go and see, I needed to show and tell my husband, before I put it behind me forever.*

*Since its repossession it still stands unlived in. I was told that a few families have been to look at it, but no real interest. Men see too much work. The women feel too much pain. Buildings hold memories, too. It isn't a place anyone would wish to bring up a family. The truth is, it's a small community and word gets around quickly.*

*Stephen Passaro had told his friend all about Mom, what my stepfather had done to her, the same friend who supplied Amanda with the heroin, and then he must have told someone else. That someone wrote something that eventually you read, Rachel. Why you contacted me.*

*My husband and I drove to the farm, and we went inside to look. I had to; no matter what memories it brought back, the horror and terror of living there.*

*Adjacent to the house were the sheds where the sheep had been kept. I thought about what Mom had written to*

*Passaro – about my stepfather – a man who had abused her and threatened to do the same to her children, and what he had done to Noah, and what she had done to my stepfather. Did I agree with her action? The stink was crushing inside the shed, of animal faeces that had never been cleared properly.*

*It was common but hushed knowledge locally what Mom did ... when she found him. What wasn't common knowledge is why she did it. I like to think she would never have done what she did, but for Noah.*

*The night before Mom killed my stepfather, she had to take Noah to the hospital. My stepfather did what he had threatened, using the rod, and it was Noah he chose, the week before. A dirty rod, one covered in sheep excrement. It took a week for the infection to take hold.*

*That was why Mom killed my stepfather – because of what he did to Noah. My stepfather had a small heart attack, he couldn't move, she used the rod, finished the job of the heart attack. I don't agree with what she did, but I understand why she did it.*

*Why did Mom befriend another monster? I think it is a pattern. She found Passaro because she thought he would understand her, she thought she would understand him. We do strange and unexplainable things in our confusion.*

*I want you to understand my mom, Rachel, so you are able to write about her, and others like her, with empathy.*

*The money you have sent me I have used to put towards my college education. Something Mom always wanted for me.*

*Good luck with the book, and remember to send me a copy when it is finished. I'd like that.*

*Godspeed,*
*Sincerely,*
*Mary Lou.*

I read it through twice. I knew what Amanda had done but this letter explained the grotesqueness with love. I put the paper on my lap. Would I have done the same? The answer came quickly. Yes. No doubt.

Joe's image moved through my mind, and inside my head I moved towards the opening of the shed in Toledo to find fresh air. I took a deep breath and the taste in the back of my throat was not the acrid smell of excrement but the warm taste of toffee.

'Joe,' I mouthed.

Amanda had done what I intended to do. She had taken revenge on the man who had abused her son. Thank God, Noah had survived. He was living happily with his big sister. Some endings were happy. Mine couldn't be. Was that why Joe came? Because he didn't want me to join him?

It was though, the only thing I did want.

A cusp of sunshine fell across my face and, despite Mrs Xú's tea, the thumping at my temple became stronger with movement. The hangover was nothing compared to chronic insomnia though, and, in the after-glow of proper sleep, despite the headache, tranquillity visited me for a few moments.

I stared at the ceiling, imagining Amanda and the place where she had been so unhappy, where Mary Lou had been so unhappy. In my mind's eye I viewed the farm where Amanda and her children had spent a miserable three years of their lives. The letters to her 'lover' on death row were graphic – as mine had been to Hemmings. I had wanted to visit the diner she had worked in, walk the streets she'd walked. Feel her life. I was indebted to Mary Lou for giving me this insight. I could not visit Ohio, not before seeing Hemmings, and this was something that brought on an inexplicable sadness, if only because it was highly likely I would be unable to go afterwards.

Because then I might be with Joe. I hoped so. What was there that I wanted to live for? This question hovered over me like a late summer dragonfly. I missed Joe so much, every fibre of him, his touch, the timbre of his voice. My depression, because I knew that's what it was, had been intensified by my isolation from Dad, compacted with the burgeoning memories of my childhood, the new knowledge of Margaret and of my dad's complicity.

I swept misgivings aside. I had to move on with my plan. I continued to bury the flashes of understanding of my own childhood because, still, I didn't want to see.

To see would hinder me, slow me. Make me less able.

I was nearly ready for Littleworth, and Michael Hemmings. And I could allow nothing to stop me.

# CHAPTER THIRTY-FOUR

*Littleworth*

Michael Hemmings never thought he'd admit it to himself, but he was missing Doc Patterson. For years he'd taken the piss out of the old bastard and his 'aura' theory. But the truth was it did help him. He'd learnt to predict when the white was about to come, the aura that to Michael Hemmings signified chaos along with the desire to hurt himself and others.

He hadn't wanted to hurt Joe, though. He hadn't. When he'd seen him on the field talking to the stuck-up cunt, Summers, he'd wanted to help the boy, even though he was Rachel-fucking-Dune's son. He knew his mum couldn't stand Joe, she'd told him, and this had made him feel something alien. Doc Patterson would have called it compassion. Had he felt compassion for Joe?

Inside him, there existed a place that was long forgotten, a place that seemed to be like the sliding skin of someone else, a separate entity. He'd liked Joe. He'd shown Joe Dune, that day at his mum's house, a part of him few people would ever see.

Joe had seen it because Joe had watched him paint the picture.

Had he told Joe what his mother made him do? He couldn't remember, that was the thing, he couldn't fucking remember anything. Doc Patterson had only mentioned it once, about what he'd done to Joe's body.

Even in court he couldn't remember. Couldn't remember. The white had been so strong the day Joe died. His mum had been in a very bad mood, telling him she didn't want to see him anymore. She was his mum, how could she say that? The white had become dazzling then, like a fucking solar flare, the ones he'd seen on TV. Doc Patterson had said that was why he killed Joe. Had he told the Doc about his mum? Had he told him the other thing? He couldn't remember; the fucking drugs he was forced to take stopped his mind working properly.

Hemmings' mood and thoughts dipped and flowed.

A solar flare … He could have been a scientist. He could have been anything he'd wanted to be; he was good at drawing, too. The only teacher he'd liked at primary school had told him he was gifted. His dad had laughed. Too loud. He fucking hated Sam.

Joe had told him he wanted to be an astronomer and move around the universe like Doctor Who. To Hemmings that was like a scientist, so that had pissed him off because he'd been jealous. And his mother, telling him he had to stop calling her, going to see her. Yes, he'd been fucking angry, because he knew that Joe would always see her. Is that why he killed Joe?

He couldn't remember killing him.

And now he was attending his next tribunal review. He knew they didn't have much choice about the outcome; the director's position would be fucked if he couldn't pull off making Hemmings look like a fucking excellent example of their rehab.

He slid off his bed, thumb in his mouth. It had been Patterson who'd helped him the most; he wished now he hadn't made the Doc's life so difficult by agreeing to his mum's visit. He knew that Toby had done everything he could to keep her visit away from the Doc. Toby was trying to help him, and he appreciated that. But maybe it hadn't been the best thing.

Talking to Toby sometimes encouraged him to think of Joe and the time leading up to the day he couldn't remember. That day had ended so badly, and not how he'd predicted, when he picked the boy up on the field. He'd felt something for Joe. A foreign feeling when Joe had told him why he'd run away from home, and Michael Hemmings' fragmented mind went back in time to the trial. To Liam and Rachel. The smug-looking perfect fucking couple. Not.

He knew that Rachel didn't know; this gave a little comfort because he hated Rachel Dune. It also brought the yellow. Cascading through the ward. Patterson had taught him about the yellow aura.

It was the aura that signified he was gaining some enlightenment.

Lost in his thoughts Hemmings didn't notice that Toby was standing by his bed, a letter in his hand.

'For you, Michael,' Toby said. He seemed subdued.

Hemmings looked at the postmark. It looked interesting. America, Ohio.

He opened the letter. It began simply and normally enough. She lived in Ohio, the US of A, had been married twice, and both husbands had given her what for, but it was the second one – a man who inherited his parents' farm in the depths of Ohio State – where her story started to get interesting. He continued to read.

The second husband had a thing about the electric rods that he used to stun his sheep. On a bad day for the writer of the letter, the husband, instead of using household implements to insert into her ass or cunt would use the rod. The husband didn't ever turn on the electric. What the husband did was to threaten to do the same to her three kids, and turn it on, if she left him or told anyone what turned him on. As things worked out, the husband had a heart attack one day while using the rod on his sheep. The writer found him, not quite dead, and promptly put the rod up his ass and finished him off by switching it on.

He carried on reading. The husband had left the writer with massive debts; the farm was repossessed by the mortgage company. She and her three kids were left homeless. She was, she informed Hemmings, now living in a trailer park. She found his story in an old newspaper that a lone, unexpected tourist had left behind in the diner she was working in. The diner was called Yum Yums. There was more, but not as interesting as the first part.

Hemmings lay flat on his bed. 'Interesting. Says I'm a man she could get on with. She understands me, Toby, what do you think to that?'

'She has good taste.'

'She does.'

'Do you like it?' Toby asked.

Hemmings bit his thumb. 'Yeah, I like it.' And he did like it; he liked the way this woman gave him details of her life. He liked that. He delved inside the envelope looking for photos. From America. Somehow this made Michael Hemmings feel extremely important. A bit fucking famous. But he found no photo.

The letter was signed Amanda McCarthy. A large scrawl, child-like. It reminded him of Joe Dune's writing, like the signature Joe'd put on the bottom of his paintings.

Michael Hemmings put the letter neatly on his bedside table and got back on the bed, flipping quickly over onto his front and trying to ignore the brown aura that seemed to be enveloping him. He was thinking about Joe again, which made him think about his mum, her visit. And

272

about Joe. Again.

He wanted to be alone to think about Amanda McCarthy. She wanted to come and visit him, and he'd like that, very much. Oh, would he like that. He looked forwards to her stories.

He drew his knees upwards, bringing himself into a crouching tiger position, then collapsed flat in the bed, delving inside the envelope, hoping to find a photo but knowing there wasn't one there.

# CHAPTER THIRTY-FIVE

'Amanda, could I have a quick word?' Stanley said as I let myself into the school with a steaming hot coffee in my hand. I'd been given the combination code. I placed the coffee on the side. He looked at the cup. 'Back on coffee?'

As part of my plan to be Amanda I'd tried to take up the habit of drinking tea, a small detail but one that could, in the future, be important, like the left-handedness. I admonished myself for buying coffee instead; it was a mistake that later I couldn't afford to make.

Stanley had noticed. So would Hemmings.

'You look terrible,' he continued.

I followed him into the office.

'What's the problem?' I asked.

'I've been doing some thinking, and it's none of my business but I am worried for you.' He watched me. 'I've been around this business all my life practically, voice coaching, acting. I can see cosmetic work with one eye closed.' He placed a hand on my arm. 'You don't strike me as the sort of person who would.'

'So I've had a nip and tuck, haven't most people over a certain age, women anyway?' I grinned, still feeling the tightness in my face (an irony that wasn't lost).

'OK, that's fine, if you don't want to talk. I apologise for asking. It's none of my business.'

'Thank you for taking an interest, but I'm fine. I'm

really enjoying the course, really am, you're a great teacher.'

'Thank you! I've organised a little play this afternoon, with some of the acting students, I thought you could join in to practise your favourite character's voice ... the washed up, white trash, no-hoper?'

'I wouldn't quite put it like that, but great, looking forwards to it.'

—

Stanley's idea was that throughout the day we acted out random vignettes of small scenes, concentrating on different character types. I wasn't an actor, that was clear, but my underlying motivation gave an edge that instilled some 'tone'. Stanley called it tone. I still wasn't sure what he meant by that, but got the impression he was pleased with my attempts. The 'vignette' of the day was the emotionally disturbed American woman: a drug addict. Too many children and not enough money.

'Ah, my girl,' Stanley said. 'You're asking all the right questions and seem to be doing so effortlessly, "Who am I?" We see you, your character. "Where am I?" Yes, at thirty years old your character is claustrophobic, deadened by her lot. "Where have I come from?" Perfectly executed, Amanda. Abuse from childhood sometimes leading to a similar pattern in the adult's behaviour. But your character doesn't intentionally neglect her children ... what does she do? She looks for excitement somewhere else. We don't know where, yet. In the last session we'll go there, that place in the character's head. But you're doing well, my girl.' He looked at his watch. 'It's getting late, time to wrap.'

Stanley walked towards me. 'What do I want? Yes. We know that. And the most important question you have to ask your character – and you – when you're within that character is, "Why do I want it?" That's the question, Amanda.' His flecked, dark eyes looked into me. 'Yes, that's the question. "Why do you want it?" Because this is your true motivation. The reason the action unfolds. The essence of what will make the audience want to continue watching, and listening. The only reason they will believe you. We humans sniff insincerity and subterfuge easily. We know when we're being duped by the acting, by the voice.' He turned and opened his arms wide. 'Call it a day. We'll have a later start tomorrow. Say eleven. Get your beauty sleep.'

Mrs Xú was cleaning the window of the shop when I returned, but I felt as if she was waiting for me. Since coming here I hadn't seen anyone visit her.

'How is everything?' she asked. Before I had time to answer she went on, 'How boyfriend?'

I laughed. 'Stanley's not my boyfriend.'

She shrugged. 'I not want see you getting into any trouble.'

'I won't get into trouble with Stanley.' I felt touched that she cared.

I thought about Jonathan. He cared, too; an ache that was nothing to do with Joe spread through my body. 'Maybe we could drink tea together soon, Mrs Xú?'

'Would like that.' She smiled, the corner of her eyes tipping upwards. It was an open and wise smile, drawing a picture of a woman with true insight.

—

I took the stairs and ran up them two at a time, swearing under my breath at the low-grade pain in my thighs.

Once in my room I picked up my notepad and pen, and opened the drawer with Amanda's letters and other correspondence inside, trying desperately to ignore the emptiness that was spreading from my gut to the whole of my body.

I wrote the next two letters to Joe's murderer. The last two. I hadn't received a reply from the first but hoped I would get one, eventually. I told him I was visiting England and looked forwards to meeting him. I found a small photo of myself pushed inside Amanda's things. Stanley had taken it only a week before; the only one I'd allowed him to take. I folded the letters and put them in separate envelopes, placing the photo in the second letter to be posted. I put these envelopes in a larger one addressed to the company in Ohio that would do the honours of posting. Then I heard a gentle tap on the door.

It was Mrs Xú.

'You ok?'

'I'm fine, Mrs Xú, fine.'

'Do not think you fine. Can see. See from moment saw you. Recognise something in you. I don't know what happening in your life ...' again, a gentle halt, 'but terrible things happen to many people.'

'Let's not talk about it,' I said.

'Have tea if you like some.'

'Maybe later?' I smiled towards her.

She nodded and walked away, disappointed.

She had been gone less than half an hour when I slipped on my shoes, wrapped a thick cardigan around my body and went out to post the envelope.

———

I spent the next few hours organising my few belongings and thinking about Mrs Xú. She'd wanted to talk and I hadn't given her the time. This saddened me. I had blocked everything out for the last five years, becoming a person I disliked. A selfish person. Liam had alluded to this trait after Joe's death and I'd been angry with him, angry because I knew he was right. It is what my dad thought too, that I was selfish, that's what he'd said, so many times. I felt as if I was living up to it.

I would go back to Cambri one more time to say goodbye to everyone. I had to do this thing and then allow Amanda to leave, and I only hoped she would. Afterwards.

—

The next day I arrived at the school early. Stanley was sitting drinking herbal tea in the small recreational room.

'I've come to say goodbye.'

'You're leaving? Still a few days to go,' he said.

'I have to leave.'

'I'm sad to hear that.' He sipped the strong-smelling liquid. 'But you'll be here all day today?'

'I leave after lunch. I can stay for the morning; that was my plan.'

'Then we'll do this morning what I'd planned for this afternoon.'

I lifted an eyebrow in question.

'The last character you played. I think we should go through that one more time. Thinking, "Why do I want it?" Go through the scene, where the abused woman kills the abuser.' He looked at me and Albert Einstein the philosopher, not the scientist, came to mind. Stanley thought I'd been abused. Did Mrs Xú think the same? I'd changed the way I looked and behaved, but could not change what was written into the fabric of my soul, and what was obvious behind my weary eyes. A memory of scalding hot water flitted through my brain.

'OK, Stanley. Let's do that.'

'Half an hour in the big room,' he said, gulping down the tea and swilling the mug in the sink. He smiled and was gone.

The persona and voice of the woman I played became a part of me that morning. I felt her pain, thought her thoughts. Grief can destroy you, or focus you…

The scene took only ten minutes; it felt like ten hours. I hardly noticed the other students.

Stanley clapped. 'Bravo, Amanda. You have it.'

―

Outside, the sky was heavy with slate clouds; it had been drizzling all day and was threatening to turn into a less benign rain. I pulled my coat collar around my neck and began making my way to Regent's Park. I wanted to think, although I'd been thinking non-stop about Joe all morning, only distracted with Stanley's piece. Joe was stuck inside my mind, in limbo. Was it me who was holding him back?

As I walked aimlessly around the park, around the still lake, the rain beginning to pour; I convinced myself that Joe could leave when I had taken my revenge on his murderer. Then he would be free.

I love you, Mum…

'And I love you Joe,' I said to the wet air surrounding me.

More than the universe, more than infinity.

―

Almost without thinking, I found myself at the post office near King's Cross where I picked up correspondence. Two letters waited for me. One from Charlotte. Small talk about Jacob, about her work (she had begun writing TV scripts and had recently found success in finding an agent for them). Then she mentioned Liam. Something she had to tell me about Liam, and I felt myself stiffen.

Coldness that was about more than about being soaked through by London rain raged through me. She didn't say what it was; she had to speak to me in person. When are you returning? She'd asked. I think it's time to come home from wherever you are. I reread the words. She believed I'd return. I would not and had no intention of doing so. That was never part of the plan.

What did she have to tell me about Liam?

The other letter was from Michael Hemmings. I pushed that into the bottom of my bag, unable deal with it now.

Leaving behind the warmth of the post office I took a step onto the pavement, deciding I didn't care what Charlotte had to say about Liam.

The rain had finally stopped and I walked back to Mrs Xú's. I planned to have tea with her at last, and tell her that soon I would be gone.

I found her sitting behind the counter but I suspected the shop door was locked.

'You come for tea, before you leave?'

How did she know? I'd said nothing, only making up my mind that morning. But I had the strongest urge to recount everything to Mrs Xú. Not only about Joe, but about my mother, Hemmings and my dad. About my life and what I didn't know, about the memories I was constantly pushing away, but which now were jamming in on me like people crowding through an inadequately sized gate. Jostling to enter.

The desire to share with Mrs Xú brimmed with an intensity that took me by surprise.

I sat on the stool next to her behind the counter.

'It's a long story,' I said finally. 'We will need a lot of tea.'

'Thought might be.' She looked at me, really looked.

'You're perceptive,' I said.

'Come with age, attempting not to become bitter. To

comprehend others is to maintain own personal compassion for world. Compassion for others, real compassion, is what saves all us.'

She unpinned her long dark hair streaked with salt and pepper, and folded both arms underneath her tiny bust.

'Tell me about your son,' I said.

The Xús had moved from Beijing thirty years before. Set up their shop, and had their son. A son who had won a scholarship to Cambridge University and gone on to work at the biggest investment bank in New York. How proud of him they'd been; how perfect was the marriage between her and her husband. How everything had been so, so perfect. Until someone hatched a premeditated plan to slaughter so many. Mrs Xú and her husband had left China to escape oppression and potential bloodshed.

'But you cannot lose your destiny. And this was ours,' she said.

I allowed her to talk and said nothing about Joe. I decided that Mrs Xú had enough to deal with without taking on board the madness of my unravelled life.

She did not pursue; she had done enough.

———

I packed away my things; it didn't take me long as I had so little. I placed everything in my suitcase and checked inside the lining for my passports. Still there. I pushed my hand further down into the corner and felt at the glossy finish of a photograph; I pulled out the picture of Joe. This should have been in the safe deposit box too, but I couldn't leave it.

I looked and the breath caught deep inside my lungs, the strange hunger surfaced, and the never-ending fatigue overcame me. Joe in bright red swimming trunks on a holiday in Spain, the year before he died. Blond hair caught flowing in a freak Spanish beach wind, a big smile. A white T-shirt, with his name emblazoned across the front. So naff, Liam had said. 'Joe's in España'.

—

As I sat on a coach at Victoria Station, ready to leave for Birmingham, I tried to gather myself and shake off the feeling that Mrs Xú, Stanley, Joe, even part of myself, had left me with, that what I was doing was wrong. I had to focus. Sitting in the cocoon of the bus I was determined to become more the person I needed to be: more like Amanda.

# CHAPTER THIRTY-SIX

I worried how safe it would be to stay in Birmingham before my journey up to Merseyside. However, it had to be safe and I saw staying there as an experiment.

No one could realise who I was. I knew from the letter Charlotte had sent me that she was in California, and the chances of bumping into Liam were infinitesimally small. As I'd locked myself away in a new identity and obsession, Liam had padlocked himself away in his new den. As the thought of confronting Hemmings moved me on, Liam's work, his art, consumed him, sucking out part of the grief that devoured both of us.

What did Charlotte have to tell me about Liam? That he had a girlfriend? Was she the same one he'd been seeing before Joe died? Whenever I thought of Liam, I thought of Joe. And whenever I thought of Joe, I thought of Liam. Like a missing piece of a jigsaw, it bothered me, nagged at me, plagued me.

Hemmings' letter lay crumpled inside my bag. I made my way to a pub near the bus station. The beer garden was half-full and, finding a seat in the shade, with a large glass of lemonade held in an unsteady hand, I read the letter and felt the bile bubble upwards from an empty stomach.

*My dear Amanda,*

*It was great to get your letter. I'm very sorry to hear that your friend died and in such a terrible way. It seems you felt a lot for him – your sympathy for a person in such a position is encouraging for me, as you would guess.*

*I read with interest your plan to visit England, and it would be great if you were able to come and see me. I have a good relationship with the nurses who take care I don't escape! They read my letters, Amanda, so I'm unable to say everything I'd like to say. But I'm sure that you visiting will only be seen as a positive experience for me, so I hope to be welcoming you soon.*

*You mention your children. How wonderful that you have them to help you through such a terrible time – his death, losing your home. And, of course, the awful treatment you received from your late husband. I look forwards to hearing about this and hope that you might come to view me as a friend and someone who you can talk to. Really talk to.*

*There are things inside me that I've never been able to tell anyone; I think though, dearest Amanda, that I might be able to tell you. One day, after we have become proper friends.*

*My best wishes for now.*

*Love, Michael.*

A roiling sensation began in the depths of my stomach, spreading through my body. The thing that hit me was the faultless handwriting and the politeness, as if he'd written the letter from an armchair in the local vicarage. The almost perfect grammar taught to him by Margaret. The use of 'love' at the end of the letter. The cloying friendliness that shone from the page. I'd always questioned his supposed insanity and what no one seemed to comprehend was his cleverness – as Margaret had gone to great pains to point out. I folded up the paper.

As I pushed it back into my bag I realised there was another letter from him in the same envelope. A hastily scribbled one, and one which robbed me of breath.

Hemmings was awaiting his second tribunal, he told me, and it was highly likely he would soon be moved to a step-down unit. Less secure than Littleworth and the beginnings of freedom. I sat forwards on the pub bench. This is what had spurred me towards Poland and Marek; to London and Stanley.

Hemmings in a less secure unit would make the success of my final aim more achievable. I had to ensure Hemmings' move worked for me.

—

I took a bus to Coventry to post the letter back to Hemmings, deciding that was where Amanda was staying. In the letter I told Hemmings the plan for my first visit, and that I was now in England. I wondered if it was enough time for him to respond, but respond he did, hinting that the relationship he had with one of the institution's nurses had made it easy for him to reply quickly. He was expecting Amanda.

After returning from Coventry I spent days perfecting everything Stanley had taught me, honing my accent. Nearly every shop worker asked me if I was on holiday, and why in Birmingham. I was even brave enough to go into my old internet café. Veronica didn't flick an eyelid. She had no idea it was me, although I did wonder if she'd have remembered Rachel, anyway.

Inside my head I spent a lot of time in Ohio, in the farmhouse with a broken door and dilapidated sheep enclosures. The smell that Mary Lou had evoked so simply in her letter would stay with me forever. It was the antithesis of the popcorn smell but both, disturbingly, brought images of Joe.

I walked around the city, and every so often caught my reflection sideways in the mirror of shop glass; watching my posture, knowing my height was unusual, and noticing the large breasts that helped with my forming stoop. As Stanley had assured me I could, I lost a good two inches as I developed a curve in my back. The pain after days of doing this was dull, aching and annoying. The weather remained unusually hot for the time of year and the heat caused my bra to rub uncomfortably on my ribcage, causing an angry rash. My breasts were too big; Marek had been right, and I smiled grimly. Added to this was the ache in my neck. As I wasn't continually staring at the chewing-gum-covered pavements, my head poked forwards at a strange and alien angle, enabling me to look only downwards at people's knees, and I found out that a stooped posture together with big breasts leads to neck pain. I went for several torturous runs. I could keep up with my pre-surgery times but everything hurt. Inside and out.

I made myself live with it. It was the least I could do for my son.

And Joe didn't come to see me.

———

At New Street train station I boarded the 8.55 to Lime Street in Liverpool. My gait was transformed. Not only did I look a few inches shorter; I also looked a few years older. Although I guessed that Michael Hemmings wouldn't care about my appearance. In the last letter he had sent he alluded to the question I knew wouldn't be far from his lips. Had any of my 'children' accompanied me

(Amanda) on my visit to England? In my reply I didn't answer that. I was still working out that line of my tale during semi-conscious moments in the bland Birmingham hotel, often becoming confused with the delineation between Amanda and Rachel.

After this, after Hemmings, I would lose Amanda but remember her for the pain she had suffered, the mental anguish she'd endured.

Just under two hours later, I arrived at Lime Street.

Two hours after that I was inside Littleworth, waiting for the hospital security guard to search me.

I chewed gum and tried not to smudge the heavy black mascara I'd applied. I'd left my dark hair greasy and managed to scrape it into a ponytail. When I'd checked the mirror in the Ladies at the station I looked like a woman with truly nothing to lose.

'I'm afraid I have to check you for weapons. Anything that might be construed as harmful. And anything else that shouldn't be in here.' The security man searched my face. 'You haven't visited before, have you?' He glanced at his computer-printed sheet. 'Amanda McCarthy. American? You're lucky your visit was okayed, I can tell you that.' He grinned and a small amount of saliva made its way down the crease on the left side of his lower lip and chin. 'Hemmings should be in a good mood today – you'll meet him for the first time at his best.'

I took the gum from my mouth and held it out towards him. 'Don't suppose you could get rid of this?'

He attempted to gather up the spit from his mouth with a loud sucking sound. 'Disgusting habit.'

I smiled. 'You think? So why's ma future boyfriend in such a good mood today?'

'Well, that's confidential, that is,' he said.

Mr Saliva was around fifty. And, apart from having a

problem controlling his oral secretions, it was also evident as he felt my crotch in the search for a hidden weapon or drugs, that he had a problem controlling most things. He was too close, and I barely stopped myself from reeling away from his alligator breath.

He watched me with both hope and scorn. I pulled at the front of my blouse, revealing a red bra. 'They're new.' I touched my left breast. 'Had them done for Michael…'

I am not Rachel.

He looked towards the door furtively. 'Hemmings won't give a fuck about your tits, love.'

I nodded, buttoning up my blouse. With the uncertainty of what I was about to face, cramps began in the pit of my stomach.

'You're free to go into the visitors' room,' he said. 'A Mr Abbs will be taking care of you from now on.' He rubbed his groin. 'I hope you get to visit again, before Hemmings's shipped off.'

I turned away, not wanting to look at his face.

I sat in the visitors' room with four others. Three women and one man. The room was too hot. The male visitor fixated on my breasts, the red bra acting like a beacon for sex, underneath the blouse I'd purposely washed with something black at the laundrette to give it a tinge of un-housewifely-like grey.

A small-framed man appeared in the doorway. Greasy hair, a slim adolescent physique. It also looked like he'd spent the previous ten minutes squeezing the spots that covered his forehead and chin. He looked around the room, and his eyes found me quickly. I wondered if this was the nurse who was helping Hemmings. My guess was yes. I knew he'd read my letters. Amanda's letters.

He looked at the male visitor. 'Here to see Gerald?' he asked.

The man nodded. 'I am, Mr Abbs.'

'You three go through, another nurse will take care of you,' he said to the man. Finally, he looked towards me. 'I take it you're Amanda McCarthy? Alone, no minors with you?'

'Yep, just little ol' me.' I stood and Abbs took me by the elbow.

'You've come at a good time as far as Hemmings is concerned.'

I nodded, waiting for the information that Mr Saliva hadn't imparted.

'What d'ya mean?' I said.

'He's had some good news. I can't say, but if he likes you he might well tell you himself.'

'That's good.'

'I'll take you through to Montford ward. You can see him there.' He looked me over. 'If I think it's OK, the two of you can take a walk in the garden, go and look at the new gazebo, Mrs McCarthy.' He seemed pleased with this.

'That'd be nice. Call me Amanda, Mr Abbs.' I tried to emphasise his authority.

'And you, Amanda, can call me Toby.'

He whisked me off. I hoped Abbs couldn't see my thundering heart underneath the cheap cotton of my greyed shirt.

I hoped Hemmings would not see my hatred.

In the ten minute walk to the other end of the institution I changed fully into the role of Amanda. I told myself that Joe's peace depended on it. After all this I would be able to let my Joe go, let myself go. Allow Joe to stop visiting me in the dead of night because I sensed he didn't want to. Joe wanted to go to a place of which I had questioned the existence, but he told me about the 'place', whispering of its peace and serenity. But also he told me in fragmented and hushed tones about the other place. A place he was not destined to go.

To allow love, is what would free him, Joe had said. Or did I say? This isn't so, Joe, I told him. Told myself. I have to do this.

Last night, my seven-year-old son kissed me on my burning cheek in the cold hotel bed, and murmured something I did not catch. I was so sure of the kiss. The rest of the night I'd tried to decipher what he'd said. But it was gone. As was Joe.

If ever he'd been there.

—

I didn't see Michael Hemmings. I scanned the ward, noting the homeliness of each bed section, the wonderful light that fell in through oblong, clean windows, but I could not see him.

Abbs saw my confusion. 'Thought you'd have seen a photo of him ... at least.'

'It was grainy.'

'Over there, at the end. Hemmings has the best spot, next to the window.'

Joe's murderer sat on the edge of his bed. Long blond hair cascading onto his shoulders. 'There?' I nodded towards him. He'd aged, looked almost a different person. Face thinner, eyes watery and sunken deep into a blank-looking face.

'Ah, I see,' Abbs said. 'Yes, he wears a wig. Changes it every so often. But always blond. You probably saw a picture of him bald. Like a baby.' He watched me. 'Hemmings is no baby, though.'

'Oh, I get it. Well, he sure looks better with hair.' The wig was a different style from the ones he'd worn in court. Lines covered his cheeks, his skin grey. But he was

292

leaner, and as his face looked older, his body appeared younger. I'd not been the only one who'd been working on their fitness.

Abbs looked at me. 'I wouldn't be getting any ideas.' His eyes strayed towards the red strap of my bra. 'You're a woman. I read your letters, Amanda. Michael's interested in your past. Feels like you could do with a friend.'

We approached the bed. Hemmings looked up nonchalantly and smiled at Amanda's forehead and in the reflection of the big window, I saw her. Back curved. Too much make-up. Large breasts. Skinny hips. The antithesis of Rachel. The antithesis of Margaret.

And then he looked me directly in the eyes.

'At last. Amanda.' He got up and held out his hand. I was sure Amanda wouldn't shake hands. I felt my left arm move. Just a flicker. Then I moved towards him, ignoring his hand, and hugged him slightly, kissing him on the cheek. He smelt of semen and cigarettes. He was taken aback but gathered himself. 'Touchy feely, are we?' He threw a look towards Abbs. 'She'll fit in well here, won't she, Toby?'

Abbs coloured, his entire face matching the cochineal red of the volatile acne. 'Maybe. Don't get carried away now, you two. You have just under an hour,' he glanced at Hemmings.

It was difficult to see who was the patient (Abbs had informed me all the inmates were patients – this is an NHS hospital, don't forget that, he'd said) and who was the carer; the line undoubtedly smudged.

I flung a curious look around the ward, taking in the other patients, and tried to hide my disgust when I saw an old man in a bed at the far end of the room openly masturbating; the man from the waiting room sitting in the chair next to him seemingly oblivious. Although it wasn't this public display that shocked me, but the viciousness of the man's handling of himself. Blood apparent on his hands, and on ruffled sheets that hid nothing.

Like the man, Abbs ignored the massacre. 'I'll be in the office if you need me, but I'm sure you won't.' He hung around for a few more seconds. Hemmings raised his eyebrow and Abbs strode back up the ward, disappearing into an office.

Hemmings was now perched on the end of his bed, legs jutted out straight. He'd put the tip of his thumb in his mouth. I rearranged my blouse.

'So, Amanda McCarthy from Ohio.'

The thumb remained and he stared at the floor. When, finally, he did lift lifeless eyes an undisclosed fear shot through me. Michael Hemmings looked straight into me. What do I want? Why do I want to do it?

'Yep, that's where I'm from,' I said shakily.

His gaze moved towards my cleavage. 'I don't want sex.'

I felt the rapid blinking of my eyes and knew if I could see my pupils they'd be fully dilated. 'I fig … figured that, not from me,' I stuttered.

'You do know what I want, don't you?'

'To tell you about my dead fucking husband, what he did to my youngest son?'

'You said he didn't touch your children?'

What had I expected? Small talk? That was not why he had agreed to see Amanda.

'Well now mister, I didn't tell ya everything.'

I'd found it impossible to write about Noah. It was a step I was unable, and unwilling, to take.

He moved forwards on the bed. 'Well, that's not very

294

nice, is it?'

A strand of hair fell over my eyes; I pushed it away. Hemmings watched my left arm move back to my side. Damn. 'Well, sir, I didn't wanna tell you everything, had to leave somethin' now, didn't I?'

Disconcertingly, he continued to make eye contact. My right eyelid began to flicker. I pressed it hard. This wasn't going well.

'As long as you don't leave too much out … Amanda.'

I couldn't stand his gaze and flung my eyes around the ward. The old man now lay stroking a flaccid, bloodied penis. The man visiting him was reading a magazine. 'Nice place here.'

'Does old Gerald over there bother you?'

'No. Seen worse.'

'Or heard of worse?'

My eyelid carried on twitching uncontrollably. 'Seen and been through worse, Michael.'

The mention of his name seemed to cause him to finally look at my forehead.

'Ah … yes, now you must tell. It's stopped raining. Shall we go into the garden, have a chat? And maybe, if you're a good girl, I might tell you about what I did.'

I wavered, bit my lip, wanting to kill him there and then. I said, 'That'd be great.' He sounded like a vicar inviting his parishioner out for a stroll to talk about the flora. I struggled. And wondered where Amanda had disappeared to.

On the walk to the gazebo she found me. Amanda would be able to cope with what Michael Hemmings contemplated telling me.

But he didn't tell me about his crime. Thank God. He listened intently as Amanda told him about her dead husband and the boyfriend from death row. He was ravenous for every detail, and Amanda delivered. In the damp and gaily painted gazebo, in the grounds of a psychiatric institution, she told him. Time went too slowly and, after what seemed like an eternity, Michael Hemmings seemed satisfied.

'That's all really fascinating, we must talk again soon.' He stopped, registering the approach of Abbs. 'You might be able to fit another visit in here.'

'Might?' The moment I felt the jubilation that he was going to confide in me was the same instant I wished he would not.

'I'm out of here soon, it seems.' Again, he looked at Abbs who was now standing in front of us. 'Isn't that right, Toby? I'm off?'

Abbs gaze was on Hemmings, and the look of entrapment in the young man's eyes both saddened and repulsed me.

'That's right. That was Michael's news, Amanda. Mr Miller'll see you off the ward. Security will check you on the way out.' He looked back at Hemmings. 'Come on, Michael.'

I watched as the two men walked away.

'You would like to see me again, wouldn't you Michael?' I shouted to their backs but they didn't hear, or ignored me.

I made my way outside the institution and the fresh, strong wind hit me with a welcome ferocity.

# CHAPTER THIRTY-SEVEN

*London*
*March 2005*

Jonathan pushed open the door of the flat with his foot. As he did so, his mobile, which he was clutching in one hand, his keys in the other, began to buzz. Harry Broomsgrove's name popped onto his screen. He let it go to voicemail. Waited for exactly the count of twenty; that was the average length of a voicemail, he'd found, then listened to the message.

Harry was enquiring if he'd had a nice holiday. Sarcastic sod. He wanted Jonathan in the office tomorrow for a 'chat'. He had another few weeks of leave; had the reptile forgotten? As he stared at the mobile it began to shake again. Again, he left it. Again, he counted to twenty. Again, it was Harry.

Need you in, assignment for you. Topical at the moment. NHS disallowing smoking in would-be mums who are receiving IVF treatment.

Christ. Jonathan tapped the return-call button. 'It's me.'

'Ah, you. Nice holiday?' Harry replied in a croaky voice.

'Can't you find someone else to do it?'

'Why, you given up your job? Didn't notice any resignation letter.'

'I still have couple of weeks left, Harry.'

Silence.

Jonathan grunted into the phone. 'So, what's this about the NHS thing?'

'I want you to do it, shouldn't take long, and then I won't bother you until after your … annual leave. Deal?'

Harry wasn't being a bastard; Jonathan knew his editor didn't have free reporters at the moment. He thought about the above-inflation pay rise Harry had given him four months before. Absentmindedly, he pulled a wipe from its holder on the hall table and cleaned the screen of his phone.

'OK.'

Harry continued. 'Whatever you're up to … will there be something for me?'

'Patience, Harry, I'll be in later.' Jonathan disconnected.

The NHS story might be helpful. He could root around the mental health system, too. There was a less secure psychiatric unit near to the hospital where the IVF was supposed to be taking place. The hospital had strong ties with the unit, dating back twenty years to when it housed its own. If he asked the right questions he might find something out about the protocol.

Jonathan paced into the kitchen and opened the fridge. Empty shelves greeted him. He'd do this thing for Harry and then check out the Cambri School of Voice Coaching and Acting. He had a hunch that Rachel's interest in the school was not a coincidence, and not just a newly revived interest in acting. And that Amanda McCarthy, the name in Marek's personal diary, was Rachel. That the 'R' going to Malina's was Rachel. Malina had told him nothing but Kacper had told him enough.

That was his plan, to Cambri, and then to see Tom

Gillespie, speak to Charlotte again. He knew she was in the States. A phone call was fine.

He'd also received, and it'd been a surprise, an email from Morley. He'd told him about a case from a long time ago, even before the Asian bride. A known paedophile had 'helped' with info on a case Rachel wasn't working on, and subsequently investigations into his activities were watered down. Rachel hadn't been happy. She waited a year, maybe more, before – rumour had it – she ensured he was implicated in a wider paedo ring that was operating in that area.

Rachel certainly had attitude, and balls. And a strong sense of taking things into her own hands. It seemed that she'd set the paedo up beautifully, ensuring that the unit investigating found more than he actually held in his mangy flat. The rumour spread that the evidence had been planted, but it was never substantiated. Gillespie managed to entomb everything, as he'd managed to do with the husband of the Asian bride. Morley had made it clear that there was no point in him making a fuss. No one cared. The guy was a paedo that was for sure. Secretly, Morley said, everyone was aware of Rachel's involvement. She'd gone to that much trouble for a family and child she had absolutely nothing to do with, need I say more? Morley had written.

Jonathan thought about calling Gillespie now, and decided against it, but did decide to call Charlotte Gayle. He checked the time difference. Five-thirty here in London, seven hours behind. It would be ten thirty in the morning on the west coast.

He dialled her mobile from his landline.

'Hi, Charlotte Gayle speaking.'

'Charlotte, it's Jonathan Waters.'

A pause. 'What can I do for you?'

'Are you in contact with Rachel?'

Another pause.

He carried on. 'I think you might be. I'm finding stuff out, stuff I can't discuss on the phone. Rachel could be in trouble and I want to help her.' He waited a second. 'And so should you.'

'Look,' she hesitated. 'I have a PO Box for her.' A rustle on the phone.

'Go on.'

'There's something that should become known ... I was going to call Tom Gillespie, but I was unsure.' The line went quiet for a few seconds. 'I told Liam to contact Gillespie, to tell him.'

'Tell him what?'

'I can't talk about this on the phone. But I'm worried about Rachel, too. I've meetings I have to stay here for, but I'll come home as soon as I can, and talk with you.

'Be easier if you told me now. Is this something about Liam?'

'We'll speak soon,' she said.

'I think she plans to kill him,' Jonathan said.

'Liam?'

'No, Michael Hemmings.'

Why did she think Liam?

'I'll be home as soon as I can, Jonathan.' She hung up.

Jonathan threw the phone on the sofa. Something was going down with the twat, Liam, and he thought he knew what it might be. He felt Rachel's pain; he felt it as if he was feeling it himself. He wanted to hold her, protect her, love her. He wanted to save her, from everything and everyone.

———

It took Jonathan a little longer than he'd anticipated to finish the NHS assignment. He wasn't sure if this was because he had absolutely no interest in the subject, or because most of his time had been spent at the psych unit a mile down the road from the hospital asking questions. The unit was closely affiliated with Broadmoor in Berkshire. The opportunity to find out more about the inner workings of the mental health system was God-given.

Jonathan had always assumed that the people who went into these institutions never came out. He was wrong. There seemed to be a whole system of which the public in general had absolutely no knowledge. Joe Public had their eyes on the headline offenders – the patients that would never see the light of day again, who would spend the rest of their lives within these institutions. Although, there had been several cases where, not that many years after trial, 'patients' who had previously been detained 'without limit of time', were later put in an institution – being diagnosed with a personality disorder, rather than a 'mental disorder' or with 'severe mental health problems' – and so viable to be considered for a tribunal review.

Those patients deemed to be cured, or on the way to recovery, were duly sent to an independent step-down psychiatric unit. Like the one near to the hospital Jonathan was investigating. It mattered not how heinous the original crime had been. If a panel of experts, including a specialist judge, decided the patient was 'treatable' and was responding to treatment, then that patient had the opportunity to present his/her case, and if that outcome was positive, he or she could be offered a place in one of these units. This could then lead to the offender having much more freedom; mixing with the public with a 'shadow' or chaperone. And, eventually, as long as they did not live or visit the area where the crime was

301

committed, the patient could, in theory, attain full freedom. Jonathan had spoken at length with psychiatrists at the independent unit, and with a few of the patients. It appeared well-run. Broadmoor seemed a world away from the chaos at Littleworth, thank Christ, he thought.

Hemmings had already attended one tribunal and was soon to sit his second. Rachel understood the implications of this, and it was the reason why, five years after the devastating and brutal murder of her son, she had 'disappeared'.

His quest to find Rachel was turning into something more. He found himself thinking about Michael Hemmings' trial – the prosecution had never pinned down his real motivation for killing Joe. The evidence was circumstantial; the conviction had relied heavily on Hemmings' confession. Now Jonathan wasn't sure what had motivated Joe's murder. His recent research implied that in high likelihood motivation existed, no matter how warped it might turn out to be.

———

It was a few more days before Jonathan had time to go to Cambri – Harry had landed him with an unexpected editorial, too. He'd called the school and spoken with a Stanley Fishel. Jonathan explained that he was writing an article about small businesses and tax evasion.

He was meeting Fishel later that afternoon.

He tapped his mobile rhythmically, thinking about the information he'd unearthed about Cambri. For the last five years, they had been doing something quite creative with their accounts. It seemed the small school was not paying all the tax that it should. He hoped he wouldn't have to use the information to elicit his own from Mr Fishel. He hoped Mr Fishel had some information.

Jonathan had done more ferreting around on the

computer, and managed to find on Marek's records a telephone number for an address near the school, registered to Langfen Xú. Rachel must have called Mrs Xú from the clinic in Warsaw. He'd conjectured that was where 'Amanda' was, or had been, staying, mainly because after more investigating, he knew Mrs Xú took in paying guests, short term stays only.

Jonathan was due at Cambri at two-thirty. It was ten and he'd just received a text from Toby Abbs, who'd informed him that an Amanda McCarthy, American from Ohio, had visited Michael Hemmings. Abbs hoped, he'd said in the text, that his help would persuade Jonathan not to say anything to the director about his relationship with Michael Hemmings.

He had spent the morning researching Amanda McCarthys in Ohio; he found two still alive, but it was the one who had died a few years previously who caught his attention. He'd seen and heard terrible stories in his career, but the American woman's tale had affected him strongly. He was sure that was the Amanda who Rachel was basing herself on.

Although the temperature was oddly high for the time of year, London was as grey as it ever was. Jonathan paid and tipped the cabbie who dropped him outside Cambri in Soho.

Stanley Fishel answered Cambri's door at exactly two-thirty. Jonathan had been waiting outside for twenty minutes, and he'd had a double espresso from the deli next door and had finished it off.

'Jonathan Waters?'

'Great you could see me,' Jonathan said, unsmiling.

Stanley shook his hand. 'Come through.'

He followed the ambling but handsome man through

to a large kitchen area. Jonathan found it difficult to nail
Fishel's age. Anything between fifty and sixty-five.

'Coffee?'

Jonathan shook his head.

'I'd like to see some ID,' Stanley said.

Jonathan pulled out his NUJ card. Stanley barely
looked at it.

'I was surprised you agreed to see me, to be honest.'

'Let us be transparent. Cambri could do without this.
We are small. This could ruin us.' Stanley allowed
himself a fey smile. 'It's only been the last few years. The
rents around here went through the roof five years ago.
We struggle.'

It was now Jonathan's turn to be transparent. He
disliked massive businesses getting away with tax
evasion, and didn't condone what Stanley was doing with
his small set-up, but that was not the reason he was here.
Although he did hope it might be a reason why Stanley
might open up.

He took in Stanley Fishel's overall appearance,
clocking that he looked like Albert Einstein. 'There might
be something else you could help me with.'

Stanley grinned. 'A complimentary course?'

Jonathan smiled. The guy had a sense of humour. 'No,
I don't need voice coaching, and I'm not cut out to be an
actor.' He watched the distinguished older man in front of
him. 'And I'm not really interested in small-time tax
evasion either.'

'Then what do you want?'

'I want to know if you've had an Amanda McCarthy
registered here as a student recently.'

'You're not her husband, are you?'

'I'm Amanda's friend. It's a long story.'

Stanley sipped from a bright yellow mug. 'She was

304

here a few weeks ago. I liked her.' He placed the mug deliberately on the table. 'She said she was researching a book.' He sighed. 'I don't think she was researching a book. Why was Amanda here?'

'Like I said, long story.' Despite small-time tax evasion, Jonathan had decided almost immediately that he liked this man.

'I've got an hour,' Stanley said.

Jonathan told Stanley the story that he knew; and the story that he thought he knew, figuring he had nothing to lose.

Stanley had perched himself on the side of the table. When Jonathan finished he whistled. 'That would make a great script.' He watched Jonathan. 'She did well here. Obviously not a professional, but she learnt quickly. She managed to master a few accents but was most keen on one in particular.'

'And that was?'

'The Ohio accent.'

'Did you get to know her?'

'I was her teacher. I knew, sensed, Amanda was, almost like two people. Distanced, disconnected.' Stanley opened a leather satchel that hung over the chair, and pulled out his mobile. 'I have a photo of her ... here. I took it one day in the school; she was a bit miffed I took it. I was going to ask her if I could use it on our website – an example of our friendly school – but never got around to asking, seeing as she seemed so opposed to having her photograph taken. I gave her a print of it, though.' Stanley stared at the image. 'Nice photo, I thought. She left before the end of the course and seemed in a hurry.' He pointed to his phone. 'But that's what she looks like now. 'What was Amanda ... Rachel like before?'

Jonathan took the phone and squinted. 'Nothing like

this.'

'Perhaps she looked more like Julia ...' he smiled gingerly.

Jonathan's brow furrowed in puzzlement, 'Julia?'

'Roberts. Only a small joke between us. I've got your mobile number. I'll forwards this to you.'

'Thanks.' Jonathan looked at his watch. 'And if I were you, I'd get a better accountant.'

'I may well do that.' He stared at Jonathan. 'Perhaps you should just let her get on with it?'

'I know what you mean, but I can't.' He smiled weakly.

Stanley only nodded and showed Jonathan back to the front entrance.

Back home, he went through Amanda McCarthy's details again. She died early 2004. Heroin overdose. Three children, now all living in Pennsylvania. Amanda was a frequent visitor to Chillicote Correctional Facility, visiting Stephen Passaro – a really lovely character – on death row for murdering his wife and three children. He was sizzled in 2003. There had been rumours that Amanda McCarthy had killed her second husband, a sheep farmer in Toledo, by inserting a cattle prod into his anus, and switching it on. Jonathan shivered, and clenched his own bottom.

He now understood the 'US' in Gorski's diary. Amanda/Rachel was American, from the US. And this was probably where Rachel/Amanda intended to disappear to once she'd achieved her aim.

Rachel had assumed Amanda's identity, including an American passport. The works.

Jonathan couldn't quite believe it.

# CHAPTER THIRTY-EIGHT

*Littleworth*

Michael Hemmings had been looking forwards to another visit from Amanda McCarthy in Littleworth, but the tribunal panel had put a stop to all visits until he was safely inside the step-down unit – The Monastery. He thought about her. And Hemmings smiled.

Amanda McCarthy. Plenty of time to get to know her again, on the outside of this fucking place. He felt restless. This feeling had worsened since his mum had been.

But she'd said she wasn't his mum. That this thing had to end once and for all. Margaret Hemmings was his mum. Hemmings knew that. He loved her. He fucking hated her. That was the way it'd always been.

But she had promised that one day they'd always be together.

When he was alone and calm he reverted back to the time when Margaret had looked after him; it didn't seem that long ago. But time for Michael Hemmings was not linear and it was this fragmentation of time that set him on edge, mercilessly playing with his mind, making him agitated. He thought back, unsure if he'd liked what he remembered. The memories were grey, sometimes brown; like his auras.

Everyone wanted something. His mum wanted

something; she wanted to be released from him; that's what she'd said, and after years of doing the thing that he hated doing for her. And after years of saying that they'd be together one day. But he was getting confused because there were some things he couldn't remember. Patterson had tried to make him remember – with the auras. Patterson was slowly bringing back the day that had put him in this place. His mum wanted him to forget that day. This place is good for you Michael, she'd said. Without me, getting on with things, no one to distract you.

She'd left him when he was young and now she wanted to leave him again, saying it was for the best. He tried to believe her. Because she was the only one he could believe. His brain flicked to someone else. The one who didn't come to see him. He fought to remember her name. Bridget. Fucking Bridget.

Today Michael Hemmings' world seemed too white. He thought about the sharp knife he kept under his mattress. He could easily end the dark colours, and today he wanted to do so. Today he wanted to die because he knew he was not a good person. And never could be.

He wanted to see his own white.

But instead of white he saw dark colours all around. He wanted to be normal. Wanted a house like the one he'd spent his early life in – a clean and tidy home. Margaret, his mother, loving him; before the fucker Rachel had been born. He wiped out Sam, and the other woman: was it Bridget? He couldn't remember. He hadn't wanted to be with Sam, or the other woman. He'd put up with a lot to stay with Margaret, stuff he hated, things he fucking hated doing. He still tasted it. Vile.

The brown enveloped him. Followed by a hint of white.

And that was the frame of mind he was in when he sat

in front of the second tribunal review.

He couldn't believe they were letting him out.

Afterwards Hemmings sought out Toby Abbs. 'I'm out of here,' he said to Abbs, his voice low.

Abbs didn't look up. 'Good.' He feigned disinterest.

'You can come and visit, Toby, they said so, said it would be good for my transition, make sure I'm settling in properly. I'll miss you.'

'I'll miss you too.' Abbs' head lifted too rapidly, too needily.

Hemmings felt slightly repulsed but it didn't last long. He would miss Toby, and not just the sex; he would miss him. If he'd known what it felt like to be vulnerable, he would have said that it was he felt at that moment. Open to attack.

'When?' Abbs carried on.

'It's all organised. I think they want to get rid of me. Leave on Friday.'

'Three days? That's unusual.'

'It is. Have you been in touch with Amanda?'

'No, but I can call her hotel to let her know.'

Hemmings sat on the edge of the desk. 'Let her know where to find me, will you?'

Abbs nodded. 'Course I will.'

# CHAPTER THIRTY-NINE

I'd received another letter from Charlotte. Its tone hinted at a festering anxiety and I knew immediately that something, or someone, had caused this worry. She desperately needed to speak to me, she said. Also, that from the States she'd spoken to Jonathan but said no more. I knew there was more.

Jonathan knew. He knew. But what I didn't know was how far down the trail he'd travelled. Perhaps I should call Marek? I decided against it. I had no wish to bother him again. Ever again.

The safest thing I could do was move to a different hotel, one in the centre of Liverpool, so that I'd be nearer to the step-down unit, where Abbs had informed me on the phone the day before, Hemmings was being moved to. The impending removal of Hemmings from Littleworth had happened obscenely quickly.

With the knowledge that Jonathan was on to something I checked into the hotel under a different name. Picking a cheap bed and breakfast, and using cash, I was able to use any name I wanted. Who would I be? On a whim I chose Julia Roberts and saw Stanley smiling.

Every instinct told me Jonathan was near to knowing about Amanda.

'You look a bit like Julia Roberts,' the young woman said to me at the less than salubrious reception desk.

'No one's mentioned that before,' I said, with a hint of amusement.

After checking in I put my bag in the room and went out to find an internet café. Having studied the regulations at The Monastery step-down clinic I knew I definitely needed new identification. They wouldn't search me but would want to see proof of who I was, and I couldn't be Amanda. It was too risky now.

This would soon be over.

I peered at the computer screen, waiting for Razor's reply. As if smelling my desperation through the ether Razor's answer came back almost immediately. My new ID would be delivered to the address I'd given him – another PO Box at the main Liverpool post office – within twenty-four hours.

Then I composed an email to Tom Gillespie's protected email address, giving him website and email addresses that Razor had given to me regarding the dark web, the trafficking of children and internet paedophilia. This time I didn't delete or store in drafts. This time I sent it.

Collecting my things, I made my way back to the B&B.

—

The room was small. Much smaller than Mrs Xú's, and the bed was even more uncomfortable. It didn't matter. All that mattered now was that accessing Hemmings would be easier. The Monastery was a modern, purpose-built unit; although Abbs had assured me it being modern and new didn't in any way mean it was any better supervised than Littleworth. He didn't quite put it like that, but it's what he meant.

I told him I'd be visiting under another name: Julia Roberts. Abbs questioned nothing, he wasn't interested.

All he was concerned about was keeping Michael Hemmings happy. And seeing Amanda kept him happy.

I'd ringed the date I was to visit Hemmings in my diary. I checked the small steak knife that I could easily hide in my sock, knowing I wouldn't be searched. The blade was serrated and sharp.

Lying down on the gaudily patterned bedspread, I pushed the one thin pillow underneath my neck and aimlessly watched the clock tick from one minute to the next. I felt myself moving towards the sleep that was often so elusive, and my mind opening up. This time the memory was more real as I allowed myself to be me, and not watch as if someone else from afar.

It was another seven years before I mentioned the 'Michael' incident to my mother. Seven years; the cycles again. We had a day off school – for teacher training – I think. A woman we knew from church was coming round with her new baby. A girl, ten months old.

We all sat in the kitchen. My mother was baking. Nothing stopped her from doing what she wanted to do. The woman was perched, uncomfortably, on a kitchen stool, holding the rounded and happy baby. She'd been in our house for over an hour, but my mother still hadn't even touched the bundle of joy. I had, cooing and stroking. I'd taken the baby into the garden, shown her the squirrels, but now we were both back in the kitchen, and its stifling closeness. The woman looked awkward. The baby began to cry, the woman said she needed feeding. She, inconspicuously, opened her top and the baby began to guzzle. My mother hadn't offered for her to go in the lounge and breastfeed and I think the woman was scared of my mother, so she didn't ask for privacy.

By now, my mother had finished making her apple pie. It was in the oven, the homely smell so incongruous with the real atmosphere. The kitchen was baking hot. My mother was now making homemade tomato sauce for spaghetti bolognese. I stood by the sink putting the tomatoes in a bowl, waiting for my mother to pour the boiling water from the kettle over them to loosen the skins. My mother made the same sauce once a week.

The woman chatted nervously, occasionally moving her baby upwards, underneath her wool sweater.

I don't know what made me say it. My mother was waiting patiently for the kettle to finish boiling the water for the tomatoes.

'How old will the baby be when you stop feeding her?' I asked the woman, still busily plucking the green stalks from the tomatoes.

'Not until she's about one, maybe eighteen months,' she replied, happy to chat.

'And then you won't feed anyone else?' I asked.

She looked confused. My mother stood tall. I sensed, rather than saw, every muscle tighten from her neck downwards, her hand still on the kettle handle.

I carried on, feeling powerful. 'So you wouldn't feed anyone else? Only your own baby?' I felt even braver. 'And not a grown boy?

The woman shifted. My left hand was still in the bowl, holding a stalk, the bowl still in the sink. The kettle steamed, whistled. I didn't see my mother quickly move the one step to the sink. I'd taken my right hand from the bowl to scratch my nose. My mother poured the boiling water over my left hand that still held the stalk. I felt as if I was silent for too long; it was the woman's screech that activated my own. A few seconds later the pain consumed me, I looked downwards at my hand, already the skin beginning to blister and loosen, like the skin of the tomatoes.

My mother stood, watching, doing nothing. The woman was holding her baby close with one arm, and even through the pain I noticed a pink and pretty nipple poking out from underneath her jumper, so different from my mother's. The woman turned on the cold water and ran it over my hand, shaking and crying.

My mother said nothing, not even sorry.

The woman called my dad, who was working locally, and he came home. The woman left, and never came back.

It was an accident, love, he'd said, but that night, one of very few, I heard Dad arguing with my mother. The incident wasn't mentioned ever again. I never told anyone what had really happened. That my mother had deliberately poured boiling water over my hand because I'd revealed the odd secret between her and her nephew.

The pressure on my forehead was light, ethereal.

I love you, Mum.

My journey was not what I'd thought it would be and, in the midst of undulating sleep, I recognised there was a reason for everything, and nothing is as random as we tell ourselves it is. Nothing.

# CHAPTER FORTY

*The Monastery, Liverpool*

I sat in a clean new waiting room, focusing on the female receptionist who had instructed me to take a seat.

Razor had ensured I had a new American driving licence and passport. Abbs still hadn't mentioned my new identity. It was obvious he was intent on maintaining Hemmings' happiness, and part of that maintenance was Hemmings seeing me – Amanda McCarthy – a woman who had tales to tell that Hemmings would relish. Sitting in the badly ventilated room I felt relief that Hemmings wanted nothing physical from me; he only wanted Amanda's horrifying stories of men who thought like him, who were as disturbed as him.

But I was here for Joe, doing this for Joe, and I tried to scrub away any image of my son with Hemmings. Joe would not want me to see, as I knew deep inside the lining of my soul, he would not want me here, doing this. I have to, Joe. I will make everything right, trust me.

The receptionist interrupted my thoughts. 'OK, I'm ready now. Would you like to write down your details in the book?'

Tearing my eyes away from the blue-carpeted floor I stood, making my way to the desk, and gave my name to the fresh-faced woman.

Uninterestedly, her eyes roamed my face. 'American?'

'Sure am.'

'Here to see Michael Hemmings?'

I nodded.

'He's only been here a few days.' She looked at some sort of itinerary. 'He's settled in nicely. We don't normally allow visitors so soon after a move, but we've spoken to his ex-nurse, Mr Abbs, and it all seems in order.' She peered at her notes again. 'Seems Michael is doing everything early, he's scheduled for his first chaperoned visit outside tomorrow.' She shuffled a few papers. 'Mr Abbs will be with him.'

'That's mighty nice,' I said.

She looked up again, 'Friend, family?'

I faltered only for a second. 'Friend.'

'We do need to see identification.'

I handed over my recent delivery. The woman hardly looked at it. I scrutinised her. Did no one do their job properly in these places? Had I done my job as a mother properly? Guilt swallowed me and the urge to pick up my cheap 'Amanda' bag and flee the modern unit was so strong I felt myself moving towards the door.

'He's in his room, but we prefer, actually we insist, meetings take place in the main lounge area.' She glanced up. 'A security person, plain clothes, will be there. Very discreet.' She looked again at her sheet. 'Mrs Roberts.'

I gathered myself, barely hearing what the woman said. 'Thank you.'

I did not leave.

'We try to make the transition as easy as possible.' She called an extension number and within three minutes a man appeared. Normal clothes, but obviously security. 'Carl, can you take Mrs Roberts through to the communal lounge? Michael's already there.'

Michael Hemmings was standing by the window as I

entered the room. The security man took a seat outside the lounge.

'Hiya, Michael,' I said, 'nice place you've got yourself here.'

'It is. It is. Like the new name, it suits you.' I won't ask why you have a new name.' He stopped looking out of the window and looked at me. Not at my forehead. Michael Hemmings looked into my eyes again. 'Slippery lady, aren't you?' He smiled slyly. 'There's something about you, Amanda. You remind me of someone.'

'Do I?'

'You're tall.'

I moved closer. 'All tall in my family. My grandmother was nearly six. Foot, I mean. I tell you, always looked weird in a county full of midgets.' He moved away from me; I was invading his personal space. I hung back. 'Mr Abbs said you'd like to see me again, I thought we got on pretty well? I thought I could talk about Stephen a little more.'

'Stephen?' He looked confused. His eyes darted around the room, distracted; eventually they settled on my forehead.

'Passaro – ma boyfriend in Lucasville Penitentiary? I thought you might want to know more about him. Might want to know the details. I have a lot more I wanna tell you.' I tried not to sound desperate, and was saved by a man coming in asking us if we wanted tea. Hemmings declined, I nodded. The man picked up the industrial teapot and poured me a cup. I nodded a yes when he pointed at the milk jug. He smiled vacantly and left.

'I don't remember Stephen,' he mumbled.

'We don't have to talk about anyone, if you don't want to.' I panicked at his disinterest. 'I thought you wanted to know about Stephen, and me? And my husband ... what

319

he did to me ... what I did to him?'

Hemmings ignored my questions and I felt I was losing him; and if I lost him I'd have to leave. I hadn't prepared properly for today, memories of boiling water and Margaret had distracted me. Warm sweat pooled underneath my armpits.

'Why are you here?' he said, looking at the floor, reminding me of a younger Michael in a purple-and-black room.

'I'm your friend.'

He sat on his haunches, rocking forwards and backwards. 'It's strange. The visit with my mum didn't go very well.' He caught my eye. 'She upset me; made me see the white. I'm gonna miss Doc Patterson. Never thought I'd miss the mad fucker. But I will. Like I miss my mum.'

He seemed different. Less in control. Had the move unsettled him? The wig he wore sat too far forwards on his head, making him appear faintly ridiculous. For the first time I admitted to myself that perhaps Hemmings was insane. Amanda seemed to be dipping in and out today and I sensed Hemmings' suspicion. Acknowledging his insanity took away a large part of my diminishing resolve.

What would Amanda say? She would question him about his mother. Amanda knew nothing about his family. I attempted to appear nonchalant. 'What's your mom's name, Michael? Always nice to have a name.'

He got up from his semi-kneeling position. I could see he was unsure what to say. 'My mum? Why do you want to know about her?'

'Well, all I know is my mom was a bad-ass. Left my three sisters and I when we were young. So my dad raised us. If you can say "raise". He drank too much and, when he drank, he found his daughters too attractive, if you know what ah mean?'

I'd caught his attention. 'He fucked his daughters? He fucked you?'

'Not ma younger sisters, but me, yeah.' I wrestled with being Amanda.

He pulled the wig further back on his skull and I pretended not to notice.

'That's bad,' he said. I waited, he watched; puzzlement crossed his face. 'My mum, she wants it to finish.' He rubbed his hands through the false hair. The wig dislodged further.

I was almost mesmerised watching him. The man who I'd spent the last five years thinking about. This man who had killed my beautiful Joe.

Yet all was not as I had wanted it to be. Something felt utterly displaced.

'What's your mom's name?' I repeated.

He now stood with his back to me, still fiddling with the wig.

Then he turned. 'Wait here.'

He disappeared from the room, and through the glass of the door I saw him saying something to the security man standing outside. The man nodded and then sat back on his chair, continuing to text on his mobile.

Ten minutes later, Hemmings returned with his guitar. It was the same one from his room that Christmas long ago. Battered and scratched. He said nothing as he sat on the chair. He began to strum. The sound that came was quite beautiful, the music appearing to calm him. After fifteen minutes, he took the guitar from his knee, placing it upright against the chair.

'Do you play?' he asked.

I did, but not as well as Hemmings. And I wasn't sure

if Amanda would. I shook my head.

'I have a cousin who I tried to teach to play guitar, a long time ago.'

I nodded and my skin became both hot and cold; I licked dry and chapped lips.

'I could teach you,' he said.

As if it was thirty years ago. 'I think I'm too old to learn.'

'I'd like to teach you.'

'Really, Michael, I'm totally unmusical.'

'Pick up the guitar.' He stood. 'Sit here and put the guitar on your lap.'

Amanda had deserted me. I was alone with Joe's murderer and was separating out. Sweat poured down the top of my spine. I tried to think of Stanley and why I was playing this part, but as I watched Hemmings everything leaked away. I picked up the guitar and sat on the chair.

'I thought you were right-handed?' he said.

'I am.'

'You picked the guitar up with your right.'

'Yeah, because I'm right-handed, Michael. What's this about?'

'It's about nothing.' He stood rocking, from right foot to left foot. Then, in an exaggerated movement, he took off the wig, revealing the baldness that had followed me through five years of nightmares. 'Even people who don't play the guitar, they always pick the guitar up with its neck, and always with the hand that isn't dominant. So you should have picked it up with your left. And you didn't. Which means you're left-handed. Not right.' He stared at me, and not at my forehead.

'I don't play the guitar. How the fuck do I know how to pick it up? I thought ya wanted to see me, not mess with me. C'mon, Michael, I was looking forwards to telling ya about Stephen, and ma dead husband...'

He stared out the window. 'Margaret.'

'Pardon?'

'That's my mother's name. She came to see me and told me she doesn't want anything to do with me anymore. She told me she isn't my mother.'

He stared at the floor. And I swam for air.

'But she is your mother?' I said finally, and played along.

'I think so. I get mixed up. I wrote to my dad.'

'Who's your father? What's his name, Michael?' I lowered my voice.

'Sam's my dad.'

'And Sam is Margaret's husband?' I was thinking quickly.

He glanced upwards. 'No. That's the thing. The thing I can't understand. It's so fucking confusing. But my mum – if I could see her again – would be able to tell me. But they've told me I can't see my mum again. But I need to see her. To talk about something. The colours would go away then.'

He had gone. As he did when I knew him as a teenager.

I attempted to stay. 'What would your mom be able to tell you?' The early afternoon sun shone on the tightened shiny skin of his skull.

'What happened the day I killed Joe.'

I was still sitting in the chair and felt my guts move backwards; the inside of my head pounded as the pulsating tide of blood pummelled through the arteries in my neck, towards my brain. I thought about Joe's visits. But it was only a dream. Joe was only a dream. I knew that.

'Joe, the boy – why you're here?'

'Joe Dune.' He watched me, smiled. 'Rachel Dune's son.'

You sick bastard.

The horror I felt at hearing Hemmings say Joe's name overrode the fear that he knew who I was. Yet did he? I felt the edge of the knife that was hidden in my sock.

'Did you know her?' I said.

'Who? Rachel? Yes, she's my cousin.' His grin was peculiarly lopsided. 'She was left-handed.' He glanced at the mug of tea the tea lady had left earlier. 'She didn't like tea.'

I picked up the mug with my right hand, and sipped.

He carried on. 'It doesn't matter.' He sat again on his haunches. 'She came to the flat I was squatting in, the place I'd taken Joe ... while Joe was there. Mum came, Margaret came. I'd wanted to see her, to tell her I missed her. All those years, like a mother. Then she turned up when Joe was there.' He stopped, watched me, then finished, slowly. 'She made me do things for her.'

Unwillingly, the picture of my mother and Michael intruded, the nipple in his mouth. I tried not to imagine what other things Michael might be alluding to, yet was not surprised at how easily I conjured up the scene.

He'd said Margaret had been at his squat. How could that be?

'Are you saying that your mother, Margaret, was there the day you ... killed the boy?'

Please forgive me, Joe.

Michael continued as if recounting something he'd no wish to remember, but doing so for my benefit.

'She was there, yes. Margaret'd always told me, "If you don't do this, Michael, I'll stop looking after you and tell your dad." I didn't want them to know, my dad, or my mum. Not really. But I did, a bit.' He fought himself and ploughed on. 'You know, Amanda, that's what's confusing me. I think I've got it wrong. Bridget's my real mum. Margaret's not my mum.' He stopped and hummed a tune for a second, then stopped. 'Is she?'

I allowed myself to relax. He'd called me Amanda. 'Hey man, you can tell me anything you want. I'm here. Some shit's happened to me, Michael, I can tell you. You can tell me anything.' He seemed placated. 'Maybe you should see the woman … Bridget.'

He held his head with both hands. 'You're not fucking listening … I can see the white. It's everywhere. It was everywhere the day I took Joe. I wasn't going to hurt him; only getting my own back on the fucker, Rachel Dune, that's all. Make her sweat. Hated her.' He grinned at my forehead. 'Only good thing that came from it all – hurting Rachel. Bridget won't come to see me, Sam doesn't give a shit. All I have is Margaret.'

Margaret had become 'Margaret' more than 'mum'. I struggled to be Amanda but tried to think like Rachel. My police training kicked in with a strength I embraced. Michael Hemmings was trying to tell me something. I wasn't sure if he was telling Amanda, or if he knew it was me, but the fragments were falling together. The sickness inside my body grew with the realisation that what I'd find, would not be as I had thought. Sitting behind the façade of Amanda I was able to disseminate what was happening.

Had Margaret been at Hemmings' squat the day Joe died?

'Do you want to tell me?' I said.

He had both arms wrapped around his head. 'Do I want to tell you? I wanted to tell Patterson. She came, that day Margaret came, she heard Joe. She went into the room where I was keeping him. I followed her into the room. I

325

thought she'd be mad with me. Thought she'd be angry that I had Joe. She wasn't that angry. She started to tell me that I shouldn't go and see her anymore. Then Joe started screaming: I'd tied a scarf around his neck and ankles, only loosely, to hold him down, he didn't like that. I was going to untie him, let him go home with his gran. Margaret told me to take him home myself, that the police were looking for him. She didn't want anyone to know she'd been to my squat, so she couldn't take him, she said. And then Joe's screaming and she was telling me she didn't want anything to do with me. I saw the brown then. Before the white. And I told her what she'd done to me – all those years ago. That she couldn't ask me to do those things and then not want me. And Joe listened from the bed, heard everything.'

'He was only seven – he wouldn't understand.'

Oh Joe, something around your neck. I'm so sorry.

Hemmings looked up.

Would Amanda know Joe's age?

'I think it's time you left.' He picked up the guitar and began to strum.

'I have to go back to the States next week,' I said, grasping to change the subject, trying to appear normal, as Amanda would appear, but inside I decomposed.

'Do you? To see Noah? You should take care of Noah, Amanda.' He began humming the tune he was strumming. It was a hymn I recognised from Sunday school. Mr Roberts had played the guitar and sang the song in which Michael Hemmings was now losing himself.

What did our Lord and saviour say,
When others wished to drive us away?
Suffer little children to come unto me,
Of such is the Kingdom of Heaven

What did He say whose spirit shed,
Hope to the living, life to the dead?
Suffer little children to come unto me,
Of such is the Kingdom of Heaven
If on His mercy we relay,
What will his words be when we die?

Hemmings looked through me, 'Suffer little children to come unto me, of such is the Kingdom of Heaven. Joe went to a better place. I want to go, too, but because of Margaret, I don't think I'll get in,' he said.

'Can I see you before I leave?' I said. Amanda said.

I hadn't used the knife, telling myself it was because there was more to learn from Michael Hemmings, and not because I was unable commit murder. I would wait for the right moment.

He snapped away from the mental place he'd been visiting. 'I have my first trip "outside" tomorrow. I'll be at the coffee shop on Paradise Street. I like that name, don't you? Three o' clock.'

I nodded. 'Be nice to see you again before I head back to the States. Will you be with anyone, an escort?'

'It will be good to see you before you go.' He appeared more lucid. 'Yes, I'll be chaperoned, but not heavily. Abbs will smooth the way. He'll be there, he knows the "chaps". There's a park nearby, you go down the alleyway next to the shop and it brings you onto a park. I'll get away and meet you there?'

'Yes, I'll see you there, Michael.'

He watched me with a faint smile. 'And you can tell me all about Stephen. His death. What he looked like when he died. I want to know what he said to you, just before. That's what I really want to know, Amanda. How he felt, knowing he was going to fry.'

A terrible sense of foreboding overshadowed my fading resolve and confidence.

—

The day Joe died was not the day I thought it had been and it was Margaret who dominated my thoughts as I made my way back to the B&B. She had been there, at the squat. She had seen Joe, and done nothing. Could I believe Michael?

It was unthinkable, but so was what she had done to Michael Hemmings.

# CHAPTER FORTY-ONE

Jonathan had been busy. Doctor Cohen's email system had been a tough one to break but he had, eventually. To his delight Cohen liked to transcribe. He detailed everything, unlike Doctor Patterson who tended to be more slapdash in his note-taking and digital filing.

According to a file created by Cohen only a week before, Patterson had, via email, told Cohen that he questioned Michael Hemmings' sole involvement in the murder of Joe Dune.

From Doctor Patterson:

*'If Hemmings murdered the boy, he should be removed to a Category-A prison ... however, if in fact he was not fully culpable, but had admitted to his guilt due to either insanity or diminished responsibility, then he should remain in an institution such as this and be given the care that a patient who is deemed mentally ill under the 1983 Mental Health Act would expect. My question would be, Doctor Cohen: was Michael Hemmings solely responsible for the death of Joe Dune?'*

Cohen's response:

*'It is too late now to become involved in this, Doctor Patterson. Any pertinent knowledge you had should have been shared. If there is something that has come to light during your sessions with this patient, it should have been documented. It wasn't. Whatever your conjectures might be, they will now remain just that. Conjectures. Any private feeling you hold regarding Michael Hemmings' level of guilt in the Joe Dune manslaughter will remain private.'*

Highlighted in red were Cohen's retrospective thoughts.

Patterson's thoughts should be investigated. High priority. When the director of Littleworth is removed, which I expect to happen within three months of Michael Hemmings' move to The Monastery, I will begin dialogue with the new director, and the Home Office.

Jonathan looked up from his computer, thinking about the inadequacy of Hemmings' defence. In the eyes of the world Hemmings was guilty; he'd admitted to killing Joe. He was diagnosed with a personality disorder, and had been sent to be rehabilitated. He placed his finger on Margaret's name, which was written in red on his whiteboard, smudging the M.

He grimaced.

—

Jonathan spent another day finding more history on Margaret Hemmings and Bridget. He didn't come up with much that he didn't already know, other than that social services had been called into Sam and Bridget's home when Michael Hemmings was around six. He had been 'messing' with boys and girls in his class at school. When the headmistress had questioned him, he'd made disturbing references to his 'mother'. It seemed Bridget had played it down, and the incident was quickly forgotten by an overstretched social services system, which probably, thought Jonathan, felt it had bigger fish to fry.

The next day he called Tom Gillespie.

The operator wouldn't put him through.

'Tell him it's about the Joe Dune case. Something I need to discuss with him.' He paused for a second. 'I know it's early, but it's important.' It was before seven; he hadn't been able to sleep.

A few clicks and finally he heard Gillespie's hoarse voice.

'Waters, what the hell d'ya want? If this's about Rachel – I've heard you've been sniffing around from Morley – I'm not talking about her. She may not work for me anymore but she's a friend.'

'Is she, Tom? You've hardly spoken to her since she resigned, as I understand.'

'Detective Chief Inspector Gillespie to you. What do you want?'

'I'll cut straight to the nub of my problem.'

'Please do. Some of us have proper work to do.'

'And would that work include investigating Margaret Hemmings?' Jonathan heard the sigh.

'What you getting at?' Gillespie replied edgily.

Jonathan had his attention. 'Hemmings admitted to killing Joe, but, as we all know, there was never any hard evidence. All circumstantial, alongside Hemmings' confession.'

'If you remember, there was evidence that Michael Hemmings mutilated Joe's dead body. You do remember that, don't you? He's been locked up for nearly five years,

331

undergoing fucking expensive rehabilitation. In all those tête-à-têtes, he's never admitted not killing Joe. What are you suggesting, Waters … that the grandmother killed her own grandson? Where did you get this? I think you're reading too many works of fiction, and probably in the columns of that newspaper you work for.'

'I've uncovered some facts about Margaret Hemmings – you need to see the notes. No, I'm not suggesting she was responsible for Joe's murder, or that Hemmings wasn't, but there's more to this case than any of us knew. I'm sure of it. I've been to see Sam and Bridget Hemmings, found out a few things. Margaret's visited him in Littleworth, Tom.' He paused. 'And I need your help.'

'You done your homework properly?'

'Can we meet later?'

The line was silent for too long. Jonathan thought he'd put the phone down.

'OK. But not at the station,' Gillespie said. 'I'll meet you at my house, tomorrow.'

'Today would be better.'

'No, I'm in the middle of something. Tomorrow, early.'

Then he began giving Jonathan his address.

Jonathan interrupted. 'I know where you live.'

—

Jonathan left his flat at 7 a.m. Nearly two hours later (the traffic was shit) Rosie Gillespie answered the door of their modest modern detached house.

Her husband had already briefed her. Jonathan saw a shiny application of coral lipstick and short greying hair that had been recently combed, noting a few static flyaway strands.

'Good morning, sorry it's a bit early.' He grinned. 'My

name's Jonathan Waters, I have an appointment to see DCI Tom Gillespie.' Jonathan couldn't imagine Tom married. He quickly scanned the entrance of their home, which was more 'homely' than he'd imagined.

Rosie held out a small, manicured hand. 'I'm an early bird. Have to be with a policeman for a husband. Anyway, it's not that early.' She smiled and looked at him. 'I remember you from the TV coverage of Michael Hemmings' trial.'

Jonathan nodded, not remembering being captured on camera. And thinking Rosie had excellent recall. 'I'm really sorry to bother you. I don't think Detective Chief Inspector Gillespie wanted to see me at the station.'

'It's no problem, Tom sometimes does this.' She led him through to a beige-coloured lounge. Tastefully kitted out. She eyed Jonathan. 'Is this about Rachel?'

Jonathan didn't know how much he should reveal. 'A little.'

'I've been worried about her. Disappearing off the face of the earth. Tom's been worried too, to be honest. Quietly.'

Rosie Gillespie carried on, 'Tea?'

'Would be great.' He perched on the end of the sofa. 'Thanks, three sugars please.' He grinned.

Jonathan heard the front door open, and, a minute later, Tom Gillespie stood in his own lounge looking completely out of place.

Rosie entered with two mugs of tea on a tray; she gave one to Jonathan, and then handed one to her husband, rubbing his arm gently after giving it to him.

Tom smiled at her and then turned towards Jonathan, his smile already gone. 'What's all this about? And try to be quick.'

Jonathan attempted to read the man's face. Did he know anything?

'I'm going to be upfront with you because we do need to be quick.' He took an extensive breath, and noticed that Rosie stayed in the room. 'Tom ...' He waited a few seconds, 'Rachel's in purgatory, literally. All this time she's blamed herself for what happened that day.'

Jonathan's eyes swept over the vanilla-coloured room, and he carried on. 'I think what Rachel's doing, the lengths she's going to ...' He hesitated. 'It seems everyone's abandoned her, and I have no wish to. She needs our help. I'm not here as a journo. This is totally off the record.'

Tom dropped himself on the armchair, his bulk sinking into it like a body in quicksand. 'Go on.' He began to chew on the nail of his thumb.

'I'm looking for Rachel.' He stared at the police detective. 'She's my friend and I want to know what's happened to her. No one seems to know. What I've found out has made it imperative that I speak with you, get you onside.' He bored into Tom's tired eyes. 'She needs help.'

Gillespie took a sip of tea. 'Tell me everything.'

Jonathan began the story: Rachel's trip to Poland, her surgery, then the school in London. The corruption within Littleworth, including the procurement of young children. He was aware that Tom probably already knew about Littleworth but not in the detail Jonathan gave, including Toby Abbs, his meeting with Patterson, Julian Cohen's emails. Tom didn't once ask him where he'd got the information. Jonathan knew he guessed.

'We need to find her, Tom.' Seeing Tom's concentration he finished with an extrapolation of what he'd uncovered about Margaret Hemmings, and his visits to see Sam and Bridget.

Rosie spoke first. 'I bumped into Rachel just before she resigned.' She glanced at her husband then got up, moving towards the fireplace. 'She wasn't herself.' She ran her finger around a photograph of two teenage boys and a younger girl that sat on the mantelpiece. Their children, presumably.

Tom stood. 'Any investigations have to be "unofficial" at this stage, to protect Rachel … I'll start the ball rolling today.' He paused for a long moment and then looked at Jonathan. 'I think Rachel has been in contact with me.'

'Recently?' Jonathan asked.

'I may well have received an email from her. It was anonymous, but I'm certain it's from Rachel.'

'About what?'

'Extremely pertinent information regarding child trafficking and pornography. Website addresses, codes, the lot. Rachel would know that I'd suspect it was her. Only a handful of people have this particular personal email address. And I've checked with my other colleagues who do have it. It has to be Rachel. She's given me information that the new op investigating paedophile rings will be very interested in receiving, particularly the stuff about a man called Backhurst.'

'Can't you trace the address?' Jonathan said.

'I wanted to ask you that question.'

'She wants you to know. She wants you to find her,' Jonathan said.

Tom smiled – sadly. 'Seems so.'

Rosie Gillespie, who'd been watching her husband intently, interjected. 'She needs you, Tom.'

'She's up in Merseyside, I'm sure of it,' Jonathan said.

'What do you suggest?' Tom asked.

'Maybe involve one of your officers, someone you can trust. I'm sure you can use your usual resources.'

Tom thought for a few seconds only. 'Brin Leatherby, I can rely on.' He was already tapping into his mobile. 'He'll be pissed off; he's on annual leave – decorating the lounge.' He smiled at his device. 'Brin. Yes, I know,' he spoke into the phone, 'this is extremely unofficial … what? No, I can't pay you extra, it's fuckin' unofficial, remember? Yes, you can have two weeks off after we've finished this. Be at mine tonight and I'll brief you. What? I'll tell you when you get here.' He looked at Jonathan. 'Done.' Tom carried on. 'Anything you've found out about Margaret Hemmings – I need everything you've got about her. And as far as the email from "Rachel" goes – we'll sort that after this.'

Jonathan took a pile of notes out of his bag, already printed and ready to go. He handed them to Tom, who asked, 'And anything about Sam?'

'I recorded what he said, yes. I'll email all my notes to you,' Jonathan said.

'Good, as I haven't yet mastered the art of hacking into private email systems.'

'I'm a good journalist. And you know it.'

'I do.' Tom picked up a battered leather briefcase and pulled out a slim file, handing it to him. 'Here's a copy of the email I think was sent from Rachel. Let me know if you can find anything out – about the information she sent me. If we can nail these bastards …' Jonathan noted an uncharacteristic tinge of embarrassment cross Tom's face. He knew Tom had tried hard, after the spotlight eased from Hemmings' trial, to nail something unsavoury on him and his more clandestine activities.

Jonathan took the printed email, together with Tom's account details.

Tom was already flicking through Jonathan's notes on Margaret Hemmings.

'Shit. I knew nothing about this. Neither did … does Rachel. However, I think it's too big an extrapolation that Margaret is implicated in Joe's murder. You know about Michael Hemmings, his past and what he was, is, capable of?' He crossed his arms over his chest. 'You becoming an amateur psychologist now, too? Thinking that Margaret somehow had an influence on Hemmings' actions?'

'There's always something more though, isn't there Tom? If you look for it?'

'I'll call you,' Tom said, 'but plan to meet in Liverpool when I've found out everything I need to find out. I need at least twelve hours, should have all the information I need by then concerning Rachel … and Margaret Hemmings' murky past.'

Jonathan sat in his old Jeep and checked his mobile. There was a missed call from Liam, and a voicemail. He listened to the message. Liam told him Marek had called, and could Jonathan come over as soon as he was able to.

He started the engine, flicked the gearstick straight into second and began driving.

Liam answered the door before he had time to press the doorbell. Liam's new house was only a mile or so from Charlotte's.

'Come in,' is all Liam said, as he stepped to one side.

Jonathan did quick recce of Liam's newish home. Bare, empty boxes still sat in the narrow hallway. Worse than his gaff.

Jonathan studied Rachel's ex. A distant man; comfortable with his own company. A loner. Many characteristics that Jonathan knew he himself didn't possess.

337

Liam had, in the past, maintained a healthy glow about him; clear skin, bright eyes, but today he looked haggard. Surely Liam had suspected something?

Jonathan had the greatest desire to punch the man in front of him.

'Drink?' Liam asked.

'No thanks,' Jonathan said. 'Gorski's called?'

Liam nodded.

Why hadn't Marek contacted him? 'You know?' Jonathan asked.

'Gorski's told me everything. I can't believe he held onto this. I'll see him in court…'

'Fuck it, Liam, this isn't about you, your fucking art, your fucking guilt, pissing about with Buddhism. This is about Rachel, not about you trying to make yourself feel better, looking after yourself.' Jonathan felt himself travel into full swing.

Liam responded with a small movement of his head.

'Did you know what she'd planned?' Jonathan continued.

'Of course I didn't. We were, are, both suffering, we deal with it, with Joe, in our own – separate – ways.'

'This is serious shit.'

'I didn't know … If I had, don't you think I would have done something about it? I haven't seen Rachel for a while …'

The bloke was clueless. Fucking clueless. Even if Jonathan hadn't loved Rachel he would still have been elated that she'd divorced him. The fucking shit.

'Why did Gorski finally tell you?'

'He's worried about her,' Liam said.

'Thank fuck someone other than me is worried about her,' Jonathan said quietly. 'Gorski's changed the way she looks, completely.'

'He told me. He's told me so I can stop her attempting to contact Hemmings.'

'It's being taken care of.'

'Tom's already called me. I know.' Liam said, his voice flat, unemotional.

He really didn't like Liam Dune.

# CHAPTER FORTY-TWO

Jonathan was aware that Tom Gillespie had used every trick in the book to track down Rachel/Amanda. Tom had also discovered another alias: Julia Roberts (this made Jonathan laugh aloud, despite the seriousness of his quest.) Tom had been slowed by the 'unofficial' nature of his enquiries, not wanting to bring too much attention to his activities. Only Brin Leatherby knew what Tom was doing; the rest of his team had no idea.

Tom had found out Hemmings planned to meet 'Julia Roberts' in a coffee shop in the centre of Liverpool that afternoon at three. Jonathan arranged to meet Tom and Leatherby outside Liverpool's town hall at two; they'd made their way separately north eastwards to the city that had spawned The Beatles.

Toby Abbs had easily admitted to Tom that Hemmings was meeting Rachel/Amanda/Julia in either the coffee shop or the nearby park. Tom had instructed Abbs to say nothing to anyone about Tom having been in touch with him.

Thinking about Stanley's photo of Amanda, Jonathan convinced himself there was no way Hemmings would guess who she was. No way. As long as they arrived in time, it was going to be all right.

Although he still felt there was something that he – and Rachel – were totally missing. What if Michael

Hemmings hadn't killed Joe? Finding this out could destroy Rachel and would be a potentially worse scenario for her in many ways, especially if her mother had, in some way, been involved. He wiped trails of cool rain from his eyes, and in the centre of the humming city he thought of her. She had planned this meticulously. Rachel was diligent and passionate in everything she did and, although he tried, he could possess no real comprehension of what Joe's murder had done to her. If Margaret was implicated – something he still didn't know – that would be when Rachel's well-constructed defence would be obliterated.

Something wasn't hanging together.

Jonathan carried on walking, and then felt his mobile vibrate in his pocket, pulling it out, he answered. 'Yes, I'll be there in five minutes – you there?' He listened for a second. 'OK, I'll arrive the same time.' Jonathan listened intently as Tom carried on talking, and then finally punched the 'end call' button on his phone and said 'shit' to a woman who was walking towards him. She pulled her beret further onto her head, giving him a dirty look.

Tom had just told him that Bridget Hemmings' body had been found at her home.

Sam had admitted to killing her.

—

It was three-thirty and the rain had stopped. Tom had texted that he and Leatherby were now waiting outside the coffee shop, and, to save time, Jonathan should meet them there instead of the town hall.

As he got closer Jonathan saw Tom and, he guessed, Leatherby, a short stocky man with no hair, standing outside.

He conjectured that Rachel had cancelled the meeting, or that she and Hemmings were somewhere else. He felt sweat trickling between his shoulder blades.

Tom's bulk was moving towards him as a skinny man appeared in the door of the café. It was Toby Abbs.

'Where's Hemmings? Rachel?' Jonathan asked Tom.

Tom's face was red and Jonathan saw he was finding it difficult to catch his breath. Leatherby grabbed hold of Abbs' arm.

Abbs yelped. 'She's just some American slag ... nothing in the rule book ...' Abbs said, his voice more bravado than his body language. Leatherby tightened his grip and Abbs squawked again.

'Where's the chaperones?' Jonathan addressed Tom. Shit, surely they hadn't let him out without anyone ... apart from Toby Abbs?

'I've told the two chaperones to stay in the shop,' Tom replied. 'Any movement from them and I'll have them both arrested, which I will anyway, one way or the other. Abbs here,' it was Gillespie's turn to grip Toby Abbs' arm, 'says that Hemmings has gone to the park.' He pointed up the adjacent alleyway. 'To play on the swings, eh, Abbs?'

'No. I've told you, he's meeting Amanda there,' Abbs said, peering at Tom. 'I haven't said anything about talking to you, Mr Gillespie.'

Tears filled the hospital worker's eyes.

Toby carried on, 'I've been accommodating ...' He directed the remark to Gillespie and Leatherby, but it was Jonathan who replied.

'I'd be careful with the "accommodating" Toby.'

'You're the reporter who came to visit me ... I remember you,' Abbs said pleadingly to Jonathan. 'Listen, tell them,' a furtive glance at Tom and Leatherby, 'tell them I helped you ...' Then Abbs seemed to compose himself. 'Michael Hemmings isn't what you think he is.'

'What you getting at, Abbs?' Tom probed.

'He's told me something about the day of Joe Dune's murder.'

Tom rolled his eyes upwards towards a charcoal sky. 'And that would be that he didn't kill Joe Dune, would it? Talk to me later, Abbs,' Tom turned, already focused on something else. 'How long have they been gone?'

'I think she was already in the park. Hemmings left about half an hour ago,' Abbs said.

'Come on,' Tom said to Jonathan and Leatherby. And speaking to Abbs, 'You go and wait with the chaperones. A couple of PCs will be here soon. Don't fucking move.'

Abbs nodded, wiping away the tears that flooded his reddened face.

Jonathan caught Tom's arm. 'Is it definitely confirmed about Sam?'

Again, Tom rolled his eyes upwards. 'Oh, yes. He confessed.'

'Motive?'

'We'll talk later. Let's get on with the task in hand. And hope to God Rachel hasn't achieved her aim. Because it's looking as if she may have the wrong person.'

# CHAPTER FORTY-THREE

I walked for hours trying to make sense of what Michael Hemmings had told me about Margaret being at the squat. Had he meant Margaret or Bridget? Was he lying about what Margaret had done to him? Surely this was just a symptom of his insanity and delusions. But it was true that Margaret had abused him; this I did know. The flashbacks I'd been experiencing were becoming stronger. If he was telling the truth about that perhaps he was also telling the truth about Margaret at the squat.

Finally I finished treading the streets, stopping at the post office to pick up any mail. I expected something from Charlotte, who now seemed my only anchor to real life. Two letters awaited me: one from Charlotte, one from Marek.

I didn't expect to come away from my meeting with Hemmings, but if I did I planned to leave the country and never return, never to be Rachel again. I should have cut away from Charlotte as I had with Liam. And I shouldn't have opened myself up to the feelings I'd always had for Jonathan; it had only complicated things. In that moment I thought of texting him, giving up on everything that I'd painstakingly planned; and I might have done if I'd had a mobile to hand.

When had I stopped loving Liam? I didn't think it was when I knew he was having an affair. I cared about that because I still loved him then. It was after Joe I shut down. During the months following Joe's funeral, and after the court case, Liam was not the person I'd thought he should be. There was something more than Joe's death that separated us, more than his having an affair. Whatever it was, it was what had drawn Liam to Buddhism.

Standing at the surprisingly clean window of the B&B, I opened Marek's letter first. Shadows from the metal security bars sliced the early spring light, which fell across the paper in thin strips.

*My dear Rachel,*

*As you have perhaps known all along, I have always understood your plan. I pretended to you, and myself, that I did not. But of course I did. I wanted to ease your pain, because I understood that pain. There is a part of you, Rachel, that mirrors a part inside myself. A need to correct things.*

*I thought about Sorojini Jain and how, when treating the poor, lovely girl, I wanted to do the same to the man who had disfigured her beautiful face. I know you felt the same. We both want retribution, it is the type of people we are. You want it for Joe; we both wanted it for the bride. We are both wrong.*

*Jonathan has worked out your plans, and I think for all the right reasons. I know he cares for you. I wanted to help you in whatever way I could, but Rachel, you can't do what you plan to do. I plan to speak with Liam, finally. It is something I should have done months ago.*

*I suspect you'll not contact me, but if you do I won't be at the clinic, I've closed it for a while. I'll be in Gdańsk.*

*Love, as always,*
*Marek*

His contact address was at the bottom of the paper. Malina's address. Marek was with her and Kacper, and this warmed me. They were together. I should never have asked him to get involved in this. I had known and understood Marek's darker borders, and it was a side to him that had tipped him into doing what I'd asked. I looked at the letter one more time and then crumpled it in cold hands.

I opened Charlotte's.

*Hi Rachel,*

*Need to speak with you. Really important.*

*Charl*

No kisses, no love. A current ran through my body.

—

It was time to prepare myself for my last meeting with Michael Hemmings. I put on the clothes I'd worn the day before, put the knife in my coat pocket and left my room.

The day was cool and sparse; fat droplets of rain were splattering the pavement. It took me half an hour to reach the place I'd highlighted on my street map. I stood across the road from the coffee shop, allowing the rain to hit my face, making me feel alive. I had no idea if I still would be at the end of this day. And I didn't care. I looked forwards to meeting my son again.

Would Hemmings already be inside, sipping an expensive latte, eating overpriced coffee shop muffins? Joe's treat every Friday after school had been the double chocolate cake from the coffee shop. We always shared it: half each. My body constricted. I'd attempted to turn grief into fury but my anger was leaving; like fading steam.

I saw Toby Abbs first: his skinny frame could have done with a few muffins. I wanted to dislike him but could not, instead feeling an unprecedented sorrow for him, and men like him, for whom the delineation of right and wrong, good and bad, became fudged. A saying of Tom Gillespie's came into my head: you should keep in mind the disunity of people's minds ... When someone does something terrible, even contemplates it, you and I, Rachel, should be aware that something worse has happened to them. I wondered what had happened to Abbs.

And Michael Hemmings. Terrible things had happened to him.

I sank back into the doorway. Should I walk away? I watched a nervous Abbs glance furtively around the full street, check his watch, and then bump into a middle-aged, well-dressed woman who was leaving. He didn't say sorry and the woman made her way through the afternoon shoppers, her umbrella shot forwards, and I could only guess at the polite profanities that fell from her bright red lips.

I waited. Ten minutes later Hemmings, wearing a blue denim shirt, together with two other men, his chaperones, I guessed, came into view. I watched them walk through the rain towards the coffee shop entrance. Today he had no wig and looked drawn, worried, and this threw me momentarily. I focused my mind on his physical presence. He was alive when Joe was not. This man had mutilated Joe and, with this memory, I gathered myself and channelled Amanda. I needed her today. I could not waver now.

Why did Michael Hemmings want Amanda here today? After all the months of planning and physical discomfort, the fear I was now feeling was fierce and unwanted. I watched him go inside and, through the window, saw Toby Abbs get up from the table where he'd been nervously sitting and shake Hemmings' hand.

I crossed the road, walked straight past the coffee shop door and found the alleyway Hemmings had told me about. I followed it to the end and saw the park with its primary-coloured swings, slides and climbing frames. The playground was empty on such a wet day. In one corner was a bright red plastic treehouse with an outline of a child on the top of the ladder that led to the inside. My heartbeat faltered.

Beginning to jog, a few moments later I was opening the heavily sprung gate with cold hands. The pad of my thumb caught on the metal and, swearing, I watched as blood squeezed from the wound. I pushed the gate open; all the time watching the figure in the treehouse entrance. My aching legs took me nearer and I recognised the figure of the child. The clothes. The questioning face. The petrol blue.

I was now standing a few metres away from the soft 'safety' surface of the kids' playground. The figure moved from the shadow of the treehouse door and seeing my son's features so clearly took away all pain from my body; all the anguish from my mind.

'Joe!'

He smiled, looking as he did on the day he'd returned from school clutching the 'sunsets' picture. The 'simmering sunsets' as Liam had called them, proud his son displayed artistic talent like him.

Joe did not move, but his image paled, only leaving the petrol blue outline of his jumper in the same way the Cheshire Cat left its grin. But I still caught his open and questioning expression, and saw him shake his head in the way he did when I was about to do something he disapproved of – pouring too much wine in a glass at the weekend, or swearing at the cars that cut me up at a particular roundabout. Because that is what children do: see a parent's faults and impatience every day, knowing you better than anyone in the world, seeing you in all situations, watching, recognising and sometimes copying. Children are your conscience. But they do not postulate and rarely pass a rigid, adult judgement. Today, as I'd felt for months, I sensed Joe's disapproval.

The gnawing feeling that I shouldn't be here would not leave me.

I wanted someone to stop me. Joe wanted someone to stop me.

'Hey, you!'

I turned, feeling my stomach lurch. There was blue. But not Joe's jumper. Denim – the colour of Hemmings' shirt.

He was alone. How had he managed to escape his chaperones? Toby Abbs must have helped him, as Hemmings knew he would. Rain slid from his shiny skull. Instinctively, I felt for the knife and when I looked up Hemmings was standing next to me.

'I saw you across the street from inside the coffee shop,' he said. His arms hung flaccidly by his sides.

'I thought I'd make my way straight to the park,' I said, recovering a little of Amanda.

'It's pissing it down. You should have come in. Had a coffee … maybe a cup of tea?'

I ignored the reference to tea. 'I saw Toby. It's nice he's visiting you. Don't your … chaperones mind?' I was trying too hard to recapture Amanda's accent. It, and she, had deserted me.

'They said it was fine. Toby knows you're here – I told him. He didn't see you cowering across the road.' He looked at me, hard. 'I see everything, though.' His scrutiny made me more anxious. 'Abbs told the chaps I'm safe. Abbs thinks we'll be talking dirty about your dead old man and your dead lover. He raked his hand across his skull, perhaps forgetting there was no wig. 'I think my new psych knows the truth, Amanda. And look,' he prodded at his chest, 'here I am. In a nice park.' He glanced around the empty playground. 'Shame there's no kids, don't you think?' My head thumped and I wanted to look to see if Joe had returned to the treehouse; Hemmings saw the fractional turn of my head. 'Is someone here? I heard you shouting, and it wasn't Noah you were calling. There'd be no point, he's in America. Who were you talking to?'

'I thought I saw a child in the treehouse.'

'No kids here.'

Now he stood close and, despite the freshness of the rain, the smell of old oaks and birches blown through the air by the strong wind, I smelt the odour of a man I wanted to see dead. I sat down on the bench, put my hand in my pocket, and felt the knife handle.

I didn't want to speak to him; I didn't want to look at him, or smell him. I wanted him to move, attack me, so I could do something. So I could hurt him and punish him for what he'd taken away from me: how he had taken away my life, as well as Joe's.

'Apparently not,' I said finally.

He watched me, still standing. 'You saw Joe, didn't you?'

I looked towards the treehouse and then sprung from the soaking wooden bench, ready to kill the man standing in front of me, but my knife was still inside my pocket.

'Joe's dead,' I murmured. I knew I could not kill him.

'Do you think you'll be able to do it?' He waited.

'Rachel?'

Hemmings hadn't moved at all. It didn't surprise me that he knew who I was. I think he'd always known. Everything about today was wrong.

Hemmings pulled his own blade out of a trouser pocket.

I'd waited too long and now there was no time to retrieve my own weapon. Hemmings moved, holding out his right arm with the knife gripped tightly in his hand.

'You'll be much more effective if you use your left hand to attack me, Rachel.'

He stood with both arms outstretched, looking like a preacher welcoming his congregation.

'Rachel, sweet Rachel, I often think of you. What have you done to yourself? This is very bad. I liked you the way you were.' His gaze dropped to my left hand. 'You thought of everything. She didn't mean to hurt you with the boiling water, she told me that. But I think she liked me much more than she liked you, Rachel. I think she regretted you. What does it feel like to be a regret?'

I wanted my son's murderer dead.

'Why, Michael? What was the point? Why did you kill Joe? Tell me, if nothing else, tell me why?'

'I don't like your hair ...' He rubbed the baldness of his head. 'Do you remember, do you remember when I had hair? All that time ago. I wonder sometimes if it was my mum, if it was her who made it go.'

Despite myself, I answered. 'What has Bridget got to do with this?'

'Bridget?'

'Who is your mother,' I said.

Slowly he looked at my face and I saw a lucidity his eyes that I'd rarely witnessed. 'Margaret,' he said.

'She's my mother, but she isn't yours, Michael.'

He was insane. But it didn't matter, sane or not, he'd taken my son – for no reason – or none that he would give. The bastard was playing games with me now.

Hemmings was talking. 'Sweet, Rachel. Do you still not remember?'

The park seemed to spin.

'My mother and you…'

'And you think I'm sick, don't you, Rachel? You poor cow. You always knew what was going on, didn't you?'

The rain had stopped and the sky was clearing. The image of Michael sucking Margaret's breast was clear in my mind, and the sense of Margaret's pleasure. I realised I was holding my breath. Knowing he could kill me, knowing I could not take a life, I felt no fear.

'Amanda's boyfriend would have loved my story,' Hemmings said.

The mention of Amanda threw me. She was gone. Hopefully to the same place as Joe was going.

He carried on, 'Mum … Margaret would lie on the bed and pull up her long skirt, she'd peel down the big pants. I said no, I screamed. She'd push my head down there and make me lick. Make me lick her cunt, sweet Rachel. At first she'd come quickly, but then it would take her longer and longer and I had to do it for longer and longer.' He stared at me. 'And you knew.'

Words came nowhere near to my lips. I did not know, not that.

'When I was very young …' he continued hoarsely.

I found my voice but even to me it sounded distant and alien. 'How old were you when this happened?'

Hemmings' face contorted. 'She threatened to cut off my cock if I told anyone. Cut it off and stuff it down my throat…'

Feeling the bile rising I had to turn away from him.

Joe.

Quickly, I pivoted a half circle and faced him. Hemmings was nearer to me, the knife held high. Liam had kept from me, for as long as possible, what had been done to Joe's body. But I knew. The same thing that Margaret had threatened to inflict on Michael if he told.

'Fuck you! Fuck you! He was a baby. My baby,' I croaked. 'Joe did nothing to you.' The thought of Joe's pain eradicated everything.

Finally I got my hand on the knife in my pocket, but Hemmings was much quicker than me. He grabbed me by the waist, wrenching me towards his body, and turned me around so I had my back to him. At the same time, violently, and with one hand only, he pulled the knife from me, throwing it out of reach, over the perimeter fence and into the kids' playground.

I couldn't move as he positioned his knife at my throat. I couldn't even struggle, but then he seemed to calm, his breaths becoming less rapid. But the knife stayed in its place.

'The last few years I've been trying to find the answer … sweet Rachel.' I felt his breath on my cheek; bitter and rotten. 'I think Patterson was nearly there. Then they moved me. Stupid thing to do to let me out. Fucking stupid.'

Tiredness swept over me. My body ached and I wanted him to get this thing over.

'I don't understand what you're saying. You murdered my son,' I said, feeling the sharp edge of metal as my throat moved.

'I didn't kill Joe. He was here, today, wasn't he? I could feel it. I saw his aura. So yellow.'

'Stop doing this. You killed my son,' I whispered, my mouth dry.

'No, I didn't. I didn't hurt him. I wasn't bad with him. I wasn't, Rachel. Not like Margaret was with me … She was there, Rachel…'

I tried so hard to think of some plan and focus my mind.

'I found him on the field,' he said. 'He told me about Liam and the woman. Naughty Liam.'

Iciness spread through my body.

'Joe liked me, despite you never letting me see him. But he remembered me, Rachel. He wanted to come back with me. We had a bit … a bit of a play. I don't think he liked it, but I told him it would be only this once and he wasn't to say anything, and it wouldn't happen again. He cried quite a lot, but I was going to let him come home to you, I was…'

Sorry, Joe … I'm so sorry.

'What about Liam?' I asked.

'Liam had a girlfriend, and you didn't know, did you? He didn't tell? He's never told you. Joe walked in on them, in Liam's den. Joe saw them fucking, Rachel. That's why Joe found me on the field.' He stopped, almost panting. 'Shall I tell you who the girlfriend is? Joe was very upset. Very…'

'Stop!' The knife jolted and I felt warm blood trickle down my neck.

'Your mate, Charlotte.' He steadied the knife. 'Fucking hell, Rachel, how bad is that?'

What felt like a large imaginary fist punched into my stomach, winding me, I flailed around for breath. Liam was in the den with Charlotte, and Joe walked in on them. Then he ran. That was why my son was dead.

He loosened his grip, lowered the knife; I was able to turn and see his face. 'Why didn't you let Joe come home?' I asked, feeling as if I was drowning.

'I told you. She was there. Mum came.' He pulled me close again and repositioned the knife.

'What do you mean? You mean Margaret came?' The murderer of my child was holding a knife to my throat, yet I questioned him like a police officer. 'What happened, Michael?' My right hand was free and I was able to touch his arm that held the knife. 'Tell me what happened with Margaret,' I asked gently.

'She came to my place. Joe was on the mattress – just the scarf around his neck and ankles, really loose. He didn't like the scarf around his neck.'

I felt his grip loosening on the weapon, his grip loosening on reality. I raised one hand towards his knife. Now I could kill him.

Michael Hemmings seemed to struggle with his words. 'She'd come to tell me to stop bothering her, to leave her alone.' He caught my eye. 'I miss her, Rachel. She was like my mother – more than she was yours. Much more. I love her, but she'd come to tell me she didn't want to see me again, after so many years of telling me we'd be together.'

'If she came, why didn't she take Joe home?' My voice was robotic, but I felt the sagging of his muscles and now it was me who had the firmer grip on Hemmings' knife.

'We argued. I told her, in front of Joe, about what I'd been doing for her, all those years...'

'Joe wouldn't understand what you were both talking about.'

'Margaret flew into one of those rages ... She was worried that Joe now knew what she'd done to me, and would tell you – tell everyone. Joe was scared. He was on the mattress. Flailing around. Margaret tied the scarf tighter so he couldn't move. He didn't like it. I told her

356

not to. Then she told me I had to take him home, and not to mention that she'd been. That she couldn't take him. It would cause too many questions. She kept telling Joe, you haven't seen me. No one was to know she'd been. I told her they had to know – that I would tell you. Joe said he would tell you…'

I said nothing. Joe was not here.

Hemmings seemed to have forgotten I was there. His grip on me had loosened completely. 'Carry on, Michael.'

'She seemed to change her mind and tried to untie Joe, but she couldn't. I don't know why. It was only a scarf. I think she was panicking. He was writhing around too much. He was scared of her, more than he was of me. I knew then that the fucking bitch didn't love anyone. Me, Joe, you. Her sad bastard husband. I'd thought I was the strange one. Even my own dad thought I was weird. I'm not as fucked up as her, though, sweet Rachel.'

I knew he was telling the truth. He'd told me he didn't kill Joe. Everything was collapsing around me. 'What happened then?'

'She found a knife in the place that was an excuse of a kitchen in the stinking squat, and went to cut the scarf … I hadn't done it tight, Rachel, I hadn't.'

Relentlessly, Hemmings carried on with his story. 'Joe was moving around so much – she cut his wrist by accident. Fuck, he looked terrified of her. I told her to stop, that I'd sort him out. Everything was getting out of control. Joe was shouting that he'd tell his mum about her. My mum doesn't like you – I know that, he said. I told her to leave, but she was mad: mad at Joe for saying you didn't like her. Then she calmed down and she told Joe he couldn't say anything about what had happened. But then I was scared, I didn't know what to do. I knew she was fucking mad at both of us, Joe and I. She left Joe lying on the mattress. Call Sam, she said. And, like I'd always done, I did as she asked. It seemed like a good idea.'

'You called Sam? Sam came?' The vortex of disbelief engulfed me. Sam.

He nodded.

'And Margaret was still there?' I imagined Joe lying there, bleeding. People he thought he could trust betraying him.

'She stayed, my dad came. He was angry with me. I tried to tell him I hadn't messed with Joe, and I hadn't, not properly. He told me the police had been in touch with him and Bridget.

'What the fuck are you doing?' Sam said to me. 'Then he asked Margaret what she was doing there.'

'Why didn't you tell Sam, or Bridget, what Margaret had done to you? Why didn't you get help?'

I don't think he registered the question. He was still holding the knife, and I bided my time as to when I would finally make a grab for it.

'Then everything went fucking mental. I was brown, all the fucking muddiest colours in the world, then the brightest … White's not a colour, though, is it?' There were tears in Michael Hemmings' eyes. 'Margaret and Sam started arguing. She told Sam to take Joe back home. You make up the story, Sam, she said. I knew my dad wouldn't want anyone to know.'

'What about Joe, Michael?'

I saw his anger rise and bubble to the surface; his grip on the knife tightened again, and again he pressed it onto my neck. I'd missed my chance.

'I'm fucking getting to that.'

I winced, 'OK.' I was going to die, but before I did I had to know what had happened.

'Margaret left.'

'She left ... She left Joe? So now it was just you and Sam. And Joe?'

'Yep. That's when everything went wrong. When I stopped remembering. I think I tried to tell Patterson. I think Cohen guessed at something. Then they sent me to the fucking Monastery, and everything's fading.' He looked at me. 'They shouldn't have let me out.'

I took a breath as though it was my last, felt the blade cutting into my skin. Joe was still tied up. What had really happened? Hemmings was an unreliable storyteller.

'I didn't know what to do. I felt ill. I wanted to let Joe go. I was ready to come clean. I didn't want to kill him. He wasn't Ruby, Rachel. I knew he wasn't an animal. I didn't want to harm him.' He swallowed and I saw his Adam's apple bob jerkily in his neck. 'The knife was on top of the cardboard box where Margaret had left it. I went into the kitchen where there was water. I was so thirsty. I stood for a long time in there, drinking the water. And then I went back into the room to release Joe. Tell my dad I'd work everything out and go to the police. And then ... that was it.'

'What, Michael? What?' I suddenly knew and ignored the acute pain as the blade pinched at more of my skin. It wouldn't be long now.

'He'd killed Joe. There on the mattress. Fucking blood everywhere. Stuffed the fucking scarf in the kid's mouth so I heard nothing.'

The world sucked inwards. My vision faltered, and I faltered. But I could not hesitate. Could not.

'He told me to get rid of the body, and say nothing about anything. The shame was too much, the shame of the world knowing, he said. And he'd killed Joe.'

'Afterwards, what happened then?'

'Sam left. Left me with his shit. I lost it. They'd both

abandoned me. My dad and Margaret, and I kept thinking of all the times Margaret had threatened to cut off my cock, stuff it in my mouth if I told anyone about her and me … how terrified I'd always been. How often I'd thought about it; how it would feel…'

'Stop!' I shouted.

He released his grip, pushing me harshly to the ground, but kept the knife and vaulted over the low perimeter fence. I got up quickly, adrenaline driving through my body. Jumping over the iron bars I followed him, ignoring the searing pain in my thighs, searing pain inside my head, not knowing what I would do. I bent forwards, picking up my knife from where it had landed and moved towards him.

He stood still and watched me. And he smiled.

A smile of perdition and acceptance.

Michael Hemmings brought his knife up, above his chest. A brief shaft of sunlight found a hole in the thick clouds and glinted from the metal.

'Don't worry, sweet Rachel. I'll do it.'

—

Michael Hemmings could not see Rachel; he couldn't see her because the whole world had turned a brilliant white and he was enveloped in its safe promise of death. This was what he wanted: all that he wanted. He would exit this world leaving no peace for the woman who had destroyed his life, because just by being born Rachel had ruined everything.

Michael didn't know what had really happened the day he did the terrible thing to Joe's body. Despite everything that was bad and sad inside his head a very small part of him made him hold out some hope to Joe's mother. He didn't know why – but he told her that Sam had killed Joe.

—

With the expertise of a slaughterhouse worker, I watched Michael Hemmings cut hard across his neck.

I imagined his blood would be black, as I'd imagined his soul. He had spoken of white in connection with death, and I knew white to be death's mystical colour. But all I saw surrounding Michael Hemmings was obsidian darkness.

Dark, ebony and all encompassing.

# CHAPTER FORTY-FOUR

It took the three men exactly four minutes to reach the park.

Tom sprinted towards the fallen body, and Jonathan watched Leatherby pull out his mobile and call for an ambulance.

Jonathan couldn't see Rachel, but as he peered towards the playground his eyes found the bright red treehouse that sat in the middle of the park. A woman was sitting in the entrance, at the top of the ladder. He did a double take: even at this distance he could see Marek's achievement. He wouldn't have recognised her if she'd been standing next to him.

He walked towards her, and slowly climbed up the ladder that was made for small children. He perched on the rung below her.

'Are you all right? Your neck's bleeding. Come down, Rachel, please.'

'It's nothing. I'm OK,' she said, putting up a hand to shield her face.

He noticed the smooth skin. Marek had even taken care of the ugly scar. He reached upwards and gently moved her hand, and Rachel allowed him to.

'I like your new look.' He looked into different but somehow familiar features. 'We've found out quite a few things recently ... apart from you having a bit of a makeover. I think I might know about most of them. I'm hoping there aren't any more surprises.'

Jonathan tried to gauge her emotional state, of which he could only imagine. 'Did Hemmings spill everything before he killed himself?'

She nodded. 'He told me Sam killed my son; that it wasn't him, and I believe him. I'm trying to still hate him, loathe him, but I can't.' She looked at Jonathan. 'I need to tell you something ... about Margaret.'

Softly, he interrupted her. 'Later, Rachel, we'll talk about this later.'

'Why did Sam kill Joe?' she said, almost to herself.

'I don't think we know the full story, but now's not the time to talk about it,' he said gently. He didn't want to tell her more than was needed, not until he himself knew exactly what was happening.

'Now is the perfect time to talk about it,' she said.

Jonathan looked towards the perimeter of the playground fence and heard the oncoming ambulances and police cars. He looked over towards Tom, who was sitting beside Hemmings' body, wondering how the detective would explain this 'off the record' assignment away.

Rachel sensed his thoughts. 'Did Tom get involved without the force?'

'Yes, but not now. Now it's official.'

'I don't care.'

'You've done nothing, Rachel. It's fine.'

'I would have killed him.'

'No, you wouldn't.'

'I wanted to text you,' she said.

He smiled at her. 'You did?'

'I did. I couldn't, no mobile. But I wanted to.' She paused. 'Do I look very different?'

'Not very.'

'You're lying.'

'Only a little.'

'I don't want you to lie to me.'

'I won't.' Jonathan rummaged in the depths of his inside jacket pocket, and pulled out a crushed packet of ten Marlboro. He took one out and offered it to her.

'No thanks.'

'Good decision, probably.'

She smiled a shattered smile. He threw the cigarette and the packet onto the ground.

'We need to get you to the hospital.'

Rachel nodded and took his hand. 'I'm so tired.'

He held hers tight.

# CHAPTER FORTY-FIVE

*The next day*

Jonathan had bumped into Liam in the entrance of the hospital talking to Tom. The three of them had discussed telling Rachel about Bridget, but all three decided against it. He'd found it difficult to even be civil with Liam Dune.

After Liam left – without seeing Rachel – Tom told Jonathan about Liam. Liam had finally come clean to Tom about the affair.

Jonathan wasn't that surprised when the mysterious woman turned out to be Charlotte Gayle, but it would be hard for Rachel when she found out.

Why the fuck had Liam come?

Jonathan made his way up to the fourth floor and Rachel's private room. He stopped to ask a nurse for room 410, made his way further down the corridor, tapped on her door and entered.

She was sitting in the chair next to the bed, a handful of coloured ribbons clasped in her hand. The type of ribbons she'd taken to wearing after she left the force, but ones she'd stopped wearing after Joe's death.

'Hi you,' she said, so quietly he could hardly hear.

He nodded towards the ribbons. 'Where did you get those?'

He smiled as widely as he could.

'Rosie, Tom's wife, brought them for me. I asked her to. I want to find to Rachel again. Joe's Rachel.'

'She's not far away,' he said.

Rachel put the ribbons on the bedside cabinet then touched her face; gesticulated towards her body.

'Do you hate the way I look?'

'No, I don't.'

'I do.'

'I know it's early days but Marek says everything's reversible.'

'He'll be kept out of this?'

'He's flying over to speak with Tom Gillespie.'

'This isn't good for Tom.'

'Tom's OK. I think he covered his bases. You don't get to his position without covering your arse. And he has.'

'Has Tom contacted Liam?' Her face fell into a deeper seriousness.

'Did you want him to?'

'Hemmings told me things…'

'And you need to talk them through, but not now.'

'He told me why Joe was on the field.'

'Do you want to tell me?'

She nodded. He thought she would cry but her eyes, now their old clear grey – she'd taken out the contacts – remained dry.

'I knew there was something with Liam.'

'Go on.'

'Joe walked in on Liam … and the woman. Joe did go to the den.' She fingered a ribbon. 'It was Charlotte, Jonathan, who was having an affair with Liam.'

'I know.' Jonathan moved closer. She shouldn't have to deal with this. He paused. 'Liam's told Tom.' He didn't mention that Liam had come to see her and been sent away. 'Tom's told me not to talk with you too much.'

'You mean not tell me everything? I think I know everything there is to know, and it's not good stuff.'

'Tell me what else Hemmings told you,' he said, deciding to ignore Tom's advice. And he listened as Rachel recounted everything that had happened at the park, and before.

When she finished, she sat higher in bed. 'Do you believe I saw Joe, that I've been seeing him from the beginning? Am I going mad?'

'Some people would say it's your imagination.' He stopped for a second, thinking about his next words. 'Your grief, and a heightened state of consciousness because of that grief. You want Joe to have peace, Rachel.'

Jonathan took a deep breath. 'Perhaps it was your subconscious that saw and smelt Joe.'

She nodded, happy with his answer.

'And Margaret?' The fine contours of her new face collapsed. 'She was at Michael's squat. She saw Joe. She left him there, Jonathan. She said nothing.'

'I'm not sure about Margaret yet. Tom has all the information. He's investigating. But from what I've found out, it seems possible that she abused Michael during his childhood.' He glanced at her. 'I'm so sorry.'

'I knew about it. Deep down, I knew. This is all my fault...'

A nurse knocked on the door; she smiled at them both.

'Scran's up, I'm going to have to ask you to leave,' she looked towards Jonathan. Her Liverpudlian accent was strong; he only just made out her meaning.

'I have to go, but I'll be back soon and we can talk,' he said. 'And try and eat some scran.' He smiled.

Jonathan had thought she would ask more about Sam

and Margaret. It appeared she was handling it all well. Too well. He knew she was still in shock; and sitting in the safety of the hospital she'd bleached her mind of what had happened. He knew how this worked. He'd done the same thing when his parents had been killed.

He thought of the extremes Rachel had gone to, to avenge the appalling murder of her son, and what could have been the outcome of her quest.

Kissing her on the cheek he left, closing the door gently behind him. He walked into the clear air of the late afternoon.

He needed to speak to Sam, who was being held in police custody.

# CHAPTER FORTY-SIX

Jonathan got back to his flat in London just before midnight, having debriefed Tom via a mobile call about what Rachel had told him. They'd arranged to meet the next day in Birmingham. Tom had promised Jonathan could speak with Sam – off the record.

He made his way to his study and sat down heavily on a chair. He pulled out a wipe from the sachet and cleaned the keyboard. He couldn't get his head around Sam killing Joe: what was his motive? He hadn't discussed it with Rachel; that would come later, when both he and Tom knew more.

And Bridget? Where did she fit into all this? What had driven Sam to kill his wife? If Sam had killed Joe, perhaps Bridget had found out and threatened to expose him. Is that what they had been arguing about prior to his last visit? Why Bridget had looked so terrified? Or possibly, was it Bridget who had gone to the squat and killed Joe? But again: why?

He stood and threw the screwed-up wipe onto the floor. He walked to the bathroom, brushed his teeth and fell into bed, exhausted.

Jonathan arrived at the West Midlands police station just after ten.

Tom was waiting in the reception area. 'On time.

Good. Follow me, a spare interview room awaits.'

He said nothing, following the detective. The room was small and smelt strongly of damp. He wished he hadn't eaten breakfast.

Tom pulled a chair out for him. 'Sit.'

He did as he was told.

'How did Sam kill Bridget?'

'From behind, with a very sharp carving knife. Her throat was cut as she peeled the potatoes for tea. Very nicely done, the pathologist says.'

An image of Sam sharpening his knives poked in Jonathan's mind. 'Shit.' He stared at Tom, 'And why?'

'He's said nothing about why he killed her. It might be better if you spoke to him.' The policeman gave him a rare smile. 'I'd appreciate it. We're still formally questioning him, but he's not opening up.'

'I knew something wasn't adding up. After talking with Sam recently, something niggled me. But I can't believe Sam killed Joe ... I know that Bridget's murder confirms he could have but...'

'It may have been Sam who killed Joe and we have to bear that in mind. Obviously, he's capable of murder ... as you say. But I agree; I'm not convinced. But if he did ... maybe Bridget knew it was Sam, maybe he admitted it to her then realised he'd have to kill her.' He sighed. 'Or was it Bridget? We have to keep an open mind. I don't know, as I don't know why Hemmings never said anything before to clear himself, if indeed it was Sam or Bridget who killed Joe.' Tom leaned forwards, holding his hands above both knees. He didn't seem himself. 'The whole thing is a fucking nightmare.'

'It is,' Jonathan said. 'What's happening with Margaret Hemmings?'

'We've already brought her in for questioning. If what

Hemmings said to Rachel was true then Margaret Hemmings is a possible suspect, too.'

Jonathan saw the dampness on Tom's temples and felt sorry for him.

Tom pulled out a piece of neatly folded A4 paper from his pocket. 'Hemmings wrote this before meeting Rachel. It's a suicide note.'

Jonathan reached for the letter.

Tom held onto it. 'Later.'

Jonathan nodded. 'Can I see Sam, now?'

'He asked to see you.'

'Did he? I like Sam,' Jonathan said. 'No idea what that says about me.'

'Yes, he's been no trouble.'

Jonathan grinned. 'That's good.'

——

When Jonathan and Tom entered the interrogation room they found Sam sitting on the floor, knees curled up towards his chest. A grey haired and frazzled-looking man sat at the desk. Tom had informed him it was Sam's solicitor. Grey Man made no great effort to acknowledge Jonathan, only nodding towards Tom.

'Hello, Sam.'

'Hullo, Jonathan.'

'So what's going up?'

Sam looked puzzled.

'How're you feeling?' Jonathan said.

'I didn't kill Joe.'

Jonathan wavered and looked towards Tom. 'Can I have some time alone with Sam?'

'Twenty minutes,' Tom said.

'I don't think so,' the grey solicitor answered. 'Who is this?'

'He's my friend,' Sam said. 'Aren't you, Jonathan?'

'I am,' Jonathan said.

'I advise against it,' Grey Man said to Sam.

Tom intervened. 'It'll be fine, Mr Bright. Jonathan knows what he's doing. He wants to help Sam.'

Jonathan peered at Mr Bright, the grey man. Funny what makes you smile.

'It's all right, Mr Bright,' Sam said. 'You can leave.'

Grey Man nodded disagreeably. 'Ensure this is documented, DCI Gillespie.'

Grey Man left and, three minutes later, so did Tom Gillespie.

Jonathan looked again at Sam. 'Talk to me.'

'Have you seen Michael?'

Sam hadn't yet been told about his son's suicide, only that Michael had told the police that it had been Sam who murdered Joe.

'No, I haven't. Michael said you killed Joe, Sam. Did you?'

His face screwed up; he became unrecognisable. His expression a bland mask. 'No.'

'Who killed Joe?' Jonathan waited.

'I always knew something wasn't right. I let my son down.'

'Who was it Sam? Who killed Joe?' Jonathan took a long breath. 'Was it Bridget?'

'I'm not sure, not sure of anything.' Still looking downwards at the tiled floor. 'I wasn't there. I didn't go to see Michael.'

'Did Bridget go?' Jonathan asked. Had it been Bridget who was at the squat, and not Margaret?

'Michael called Bridget the day Joe died. I thought he was calling from Chester. It was only just before your last visit that she told me he'd called from the squat in Sutton Coldfield … and that Joe had been there. He called and

374

told her that he had Joe at the squat. She didn't go, she said, just told him to let Joe go. Said she heard Joe over the phone. I can't believe she kept it to herself.'

'Why didn't she say anything, all this time?' That was the mystery he'd picked up every time he'd encountered the couple since in 2000. It made sense now.

'She was protecting Michael, she said,' Sam continued. 'Then Joe's body was found and she could say nothing.' He looked at Jonathan. 'She told me all this the last time you came to see us, just before you turned up.'

'Why did you kill her, Sam?'

'I couldn't believe that she knew, and said nothing. I've loved Bridget all my life and I couldn't believe that she knew Michael was keeping Joe at the squat.'

'Why didn't you tell me about Bridget knowing about Joe – the day I saw you? I could have helped you, stopped you from doing this. You'll go to prison, Sam. This is premeditated murder.' He sighed. 'You thought about it, planned it.'

Sam said nothing.

'Why did … does Michael say it was you who killed Joe?'

'He's confused. He really thought he did kill Joe, and then convinced himself it was me.' He wrung his hands together. 'Bridget told me she thought someone else was in the squat with him. Just before I killed her, she told me that.'

'Who?'

'She thought she heard Margaret's voice in the background. That's what tipped me over, when I used my knife. Fucking Margaret.'

'And Bridget never said a thing before? All these years?'

'Not a thing.'

'Sam, what exactly happened the day Joe was killed?'

Sam now sat upright. 'Michael'd called Bridget and I in a state. As I've already told you, I thought he was calling from Chester; I refused to go but Bridget wanted to, I forbade her. She must have called him back after I'd gone to the bakery.'

Jonathan nodded. 'Did Michael ever mention to you about Margaret being there?'

'Never. Despite our Michael's problems, Jonathan, I never believed he could kill.'

'So who do you think did kill Joe?' Jonathan was pleading, wanting to know the full truth.

Sam looked hard at him. 'I have my suspicions ... since Bridget came clean with me.' He slumped forwards. 'Christ, this is all such a mess. My family – a bloody mess.'

He paused briefly, trying to calm himself. 'Michael confessed to Joe's murder and no one questioned that too closely.' He looked up, his eyes moist. 'Tell Rachel I'm sorry, Jonathan.'

'Who do you think killed Joe?' Jonathan persisted.

'You work it out,' Sam said resignedly.

Jonathan touched the broken man's shoulder. 'I'll keep in touch, Sam.' He knew he would get no more.

And he left the room, his heart heavier than he'd thought possible.

Jonathan found Tom waiting for him. He looked around for Sam's solicitor.

'He's having a crap, I think,' Tom grinned. 'Did Sam open up?'

'Can I see Hemmings' suicide essay?'

Tom pulled it from his pocket. 'Here.'

Jonathan unfolded the A4 paper and read.

*Moving to The Monastery stirred me up, made me remember, and made me think. As I write this letter, I feel almost normal, with no colours, no auras. I feel peaceful.*

*I am meeting Amanda today, but I know Amanda is Rachel. I don't like Rachel. I do prefer Amanda. I'm not sure if I will tell Rachel the truth, only because the truth comes and goes. And I'm uncertain if the truth will be there when I see her. So I'm telling the truth now, while I can.*

*I didn't kill Joe. I know Bridget is my mother; I know that today. Margaret wants nothing else to do with me, she didn't even back then. I admitted to killing Joe – it was easy, as everyone thought I'd done it anyway. Over the last five years I've become more and more confused until I really thought I'd killed Joe. I began thinking it was my dad who had done it, but it wasn't my dad, he wasn't even there. He didn't know I had Joe.*

*Bridget never came to visit me at Littleworth but she knew I had Joe, as did Margaret, because Margaret was there.*

*Sometimes I convinced myself it was me who had killed Joe. In the end it doesn't matter. Joe's dead, and I'm sorry. And sorry what I did to him afterwards.*

*My mum and dad both abandoned me, years ago – like owners would abandon a mangy dog.*

*It was Margaret who killed Joe.*

*Anyway, when this note is read it will, finally, be over.*

*Michael Hemmings.*

Tom leant against the wall of the corridor. 'What did Sam tell you? I hope something because I'm breaking all the rules here. I should have stayed in the room with you.'

'He denies killing Joe and I believe him. But this note tells us everything we need to know.' Jonathan sat on his haunches, his energy gone. 'Rachel will never get over this. Liam in the den, Charlotte Gayle, her own mother...' He glanced at Tom. 'What's Margaret said? Anything?'

'She certainly has. She's admitted the murder of Joe Dune. I wanted you to speak to Sam, to find out what had really happened. I can't fucking believe it.'

'Margaret's motive?' Jonathan wasn't surprised.

'That Joe knew about her and Hemmings. Over the time he had Joe, Hemmings told the boy everything. Told a seven-year-old everything he himself had been through with Margaret. Margaret lost that infamous temper when she realised Joe knew. So she killed him. Last night at the hospital, Rachel told me about an incident from her childhood when Margaret poured boiling water over her hand, because Rachel questioned her about the weird relationship between her and Michael.'

'Jesus ... and Joe's body, afterwards ... Margaret?'

'No, I think not. She denies that. She left Hemmings with the body, left Hemmings with the need to admit to killing Joe and to protect her. What happened to Joe afterwards,' he coughed, 'that was Hemmings.'

Jonathan looked up at Tom who seemed smaller, less menacing. 'This isn't going to look good for your investigation, is it?'

'No. It isn't.' He bent forwards, as if trying to find energy. 'Rachel will never forgive me for this.' He rubbed his eyes. 'I don't think I'll ever forgive myself.'

'She will, and you will,' Jonathan said. 'Rachel will need as much support as possible. She's gone to extraordinary lengths to get the man she thought killed her son. She finds out it wasn't Michael. He tells her it was Sam ... Now we have to tell her the truth, although I think, deep down, she already suspects.'

'You or me, to tell Rachel?' Tom said.

'If it's OK with you, me?'

Tom nodded.

'Don't you think someone should tell Sam that Michael's dead?' Jonathan asked.

'Rachel's dad is already here, in the waiting room. Came in with Margaret. We thought we'd leave it for him.' He shot a tired glance towards Jonathan. 'Poor sod.'

Jonathan shook his head. Poor Rachel. He needed to speak to her.

Saying his goodbyes to Tom Gillespie, he made his way back to Liverpool and the hospital. Back to Rachel.

# CHAPTER FORTY-SEVEN

Rachel was alone when Jonathan poked his head through the crack in the door.

She was sitting up on a crisply made bed, knees tucked in tightly, wearing jeans that appeared too large, and a baggy jumper. A petrol blue ribbon was woven into her darkened hair, just one, but it was a start. Although her face was different, he saw the real Rachel. She rocked forwards and backwards, gently. No smile on her face, yet she appeared serene.

She was listening to an iPod, which explained the rocking. Pulling out her earphones, she looked up. 'Hi Jonathan. I thought you'd gone back to London.'

'I did. I've come back.'

'I'm glad.'

The smile she gave him was all he needed. He sat on the big chair next to her bed, watching as she stretched out her legs. 'I don't want to bother you too much.'

'You don't bother me.'

'I have some news and I think you should know it,' he said. 'I've spoken to Tom and he agrees I should tell you sooner rather than later.'

Her face fell. 'Go on.' She seemed to brace herself, drawing her knees up towards her stomach; she leant forwards, curling into a ball.

'I've been to see Sam, this morning. He says he didn't kill Joe.'

She shook her head. 'No, as fucked up as everything is, I can't believe that Sam was responsible for Joe's death. But why did Hemmings lie? Even before he died, the bastard was playing with me. Since Joe's murder I had been convincing myself that Hemmings was sane, that he knew exactly what he was doing, but I was wrong.' She looked towards him, held his gaze. 'There's more, isn't there? Margaret?'

'Christ, Rachel, I'm so sorry.' He didn't think he could do this but he had to, he loved her. Had always loved her. She looked so different, but the essence of her shone through everything Marek had done.

'I know Michael was telling the truth about what my mother had done to him,' she said. 'I know because I remember things. Now I believe Michael didn't kill Joe, despite everything.' Her voice fell to a whisper and she seemed to shrink in front of him.

'Rachel ...' He moved closer, wanting to erase the misery of the truth. He touched her cheek, a familiar expression on an unfamiliar face swallowed up her features. 'The day you met Hemmings ... Sam killed Bridget.'

He watched her breathing rate increase but she said nothing. He carried on. 'He killed her because she admitted to knowing that Joe was at Hemmings' squat. She knew Margaret was there, too.' He waited a few moments. 'It was Margaret, Rachel.'

He waited for a response. None came. She hadn't moved; she seemed to have stopped breathing. He continued, 'Michael left a suicide note – he planned his death. In the note he clarifies everything.' He touched her knee. 'Are you OK?' Such a stupid question. 'Margaret's been taken in. She's with Tom. She's admitted to Joe's murder.'

She searched his face. 'Why did Michael lie, and for so long?' She wrapped her arms around herself. 'Why did he say it was Sam?' She avoided any mention of Margaret.

'Protecting Margaret? Why did he say it was Sam? I don't know, fuck, I really don't know.'

Jonathan wondered if she'd ever make sense of any of this. Christ, he was finding it difficult. He moved closer. He'd do everything he could to help and support her. He knew he could; and hoped he'd handle the situation better than with Michelle. He couldn't fail twice.

'My dad ... our life, everything, just a mask of nothingness. Liam and Charlotte, too ...' She found his eyes. 'Why? Her own grandson. Joe's body ... Jonathan.' Suddenly she sprang up as if she was unable to bear with herself.

'Don't think ... Joe wouldn't want you to think.'

'No ...' She paced the small room. 'I thought it was Joe trying to tell me, but it was *myself* trying to tell me. Why wouldn't I see?'

Jonathan said nothing because there was nothing he could say.

'So Margaret's at the station?' she continued.

He nodded. 'They've only just started questioning her. Tom's given this one to Leatherby.'

'That's good. Tom's too close.' She sat back down on the bed. 'Why did Bridget keep this to herself?'

'I think she said nothing at first, and then as time went on felt it had only got more impossible to speak out. I suspect that she had thoughts about what was going on between Michael and Margaret, retrospectively, after things she said to me. I suppose when she realised Margaret was at the squat ... she thought Joe would be OK. I'm sure that's what Bridget thought. She was scared to tell the truth at the time, at the trial, and time went by ... and she didn't say anything. Although I'm certain Bridget had no idea it was Margaret ... but now we'll never know.'

'Killing Bridget was extreme. Sam wasn't like that. It was always Bridget who was the impetuous one. I don't understand.'

'He snapped. Something went. Poor Sam. But to a judge and jury Bridget's murder will be seen as premeditated.'

'Jonathan, I feel empty, void of anything I should be feeling. I'm not Rachel anymore.'

'You'll always be Rachel to me.'

She touched his hand. 'Thank you for looking for me.'

'I love you, Rachel, I always have.'

'I know.'

'Is that OK?'

'Very much OK.'

'I want to carry on looking after you.'

'I need some time.'

'I know. Just hold the thought in the back of your head, though.'

'It's Joe I think about, with her...'

'You need to rest,' he said.

'And my part in all this? Not telling Tom the truth at the beginning. Not being there for Joe. And what I've always known about my own mother.' Jonathan heard the crack in her voice. 'Why did I bury my memories? Why did I allow Joe anywhere near her? I'm trying to forgive myself, and I'm trying because I know Joe forgives me. My son forgives me, and he always has.' She took a long breath. 'And my dad, God, my dad. He's betrayed me, too, along with Liam and Margaret. More insidiously, but he has. And Joe – he betrayed Joe, too.'

'I spoke to Alan when I started looking for you. He

knows he's been wrong. He knows, Rachel.'

'It's too late now.'

'We blank out the unsavoury things about our families. Your dad loves you.'

'It's a tainted love, though. I can see that now. He was my dad. He should have protected Joe and I. And he didn't.'

He wanted to distract her from thoughts that could send her to a place from which she could not return.

'We'll talk about Alan another time.'

'I don't want to talk about him. I don't want to see him again. It's all so clear.'

'Shush.' Gently, he took her hand.

'Has Tom said anything about an email?' she said.

'He's already moved on it, I believe. It was from you?'

'I had to do something.' She caught his eye. 'I don't want to be like my dad.'

'Your dad didn't know it was this bad.'

'Didn't he, Jonathan? I'm not so sure. But the worst thing? He made me believe it was my fault, that the way she was with me was my fault. I'll never forgive him for that. Never.'

Jonathan didn't blame her.

They sat together for a long time, listening to the muffled sound of Mariah Carey coming from the discarded earphones that lay on the crumpled sheet, both feeling a fragment of serenity that had eluded each of them for too long. Both feeling the peace within the room, with each other.

# CHAPTER FORTY-EIGHT

*One week later*

I'd spent what felt like hours speaking to Tom and Leatherby. I would be expected to give evidence at the inquiry into Hemmings' suicide, but Tom assured me that no charges would be brought against me. Both Charlotte and Liam were to be taken in for questioning for perverting the course of justice. What did I feel about Liam, Charlotte, my dad, and Margaret? I closed my thoughts off; I had to, to survive those first few days.

Jonathan took me home. We stopped in a motorway café that smelled predominantly of burgers; I think it was only I who smelt the popcorn. Just a hint. It was fading, as was Joe's presence. Perhaps I'd never seen him. But what I did know was that now the truth was out, Joe was where he should be.

My kitchen was as I'd left it and was a place I thought I'd never visit again. If I survived my last meeting with Hemmings, my plan had always been to disappear forever. To America, the West Coast. I'd already primed Razor for a completely new identity, not Rachel, and not Amanda. Someone else.

But here I was. With Jonathan.

I looked towards the fridge, wanting to see Joe's

picture. The door was polished, shiny and empty. I needed Joe's sunset picture. Liam probably had it.

I'd given Jonathan the key to the safe deposit box, and asked him to bring home the things inside, including Joe's moonsets, and the painting of Margaret and Hemmings.

'Right, coffee?' Jonathan said softly, touching my smooth left hand.

'Great.'

He pulled a small holdall from beneath the kitchen table. 'From the safe deposit.'

'Have you looked?' I asked.

'At the painting of Margaret and Hemmings? I have.' He sat down slowly on the kitchen chair. 'Joe saw something even before Hemmings took him, before hearing the conversations at the squat between him and Margaret.'

I let out a long and protracted sigh. 'Joe saw but I didn't.'

Jonathan said softly. 'Joe was special.'

'Where's Joe's sunset picture? The one from the fridge. Does Liam have it? I want it. Do you know?'

Jonathan looked at his watch. 'Liam'll be here soon. Calm down, he'll have it, I'm sure.'

'I don't want to see him.' Again I sighed and, at the same time, the doorbell rang.

'That'll be Liam,' he said softly.

'You'd better answer the door,' I said, my voice sounding stronger than I felt.

He let Liam in and it seemed, at the same time, without me noticing, Jonathan left.

Left me with a man with whom I'd shared half my life, but now I didn't know. Did I blame him for Joe's death? No, I did not. It was Margaret who had killed our son.

Liam sat patiently on the edge of his chair, arms

388

folded, legs crossed, making himself as compact as possible, as though the smaller the space he took up, the less fraught I would be.

'You ought to talk to your dad soon.'

'Have you seen him?'

He rubbed his scalp hard, 'Yes. He's a mess, his wife ...' The sentence drifted away. He began another. 'His brother.' That one faded, too.

Everything I was, had been, had known, was being ripped away; and that included my dad. The raw emptiness I'd felt when I knew Joe had gone seemed to overpower me anew, like a chronic illness becoming acute again.

I had no one. All that was left was a woman in the mirror, a woman I didn't know. But I had Jonathan and a seed of something alien furrowed inside me. Jonathan made me feel safe.

'Have you seen Sam?'

'Yes, I've been to see Sam. He knew nothing, Rachel, not until Bridget told him she'd spoken to Hemmings on the phone, and he told her Joe was there, and she heard Margaret's voice.'

'There's nothing left to say,' I said, glancing down at my changed body, noticing that Liam did the same. We were strangers: he to me and me to myself. If there had been a mirror to hand, I would have looked at the reflection that told me what I had done to vent my anger, find an end to my grief, and avenge my son being taken away from me.

I laid out Joe's painting of Hemmings and Margaret on the table. Liam eyed it enquiringly.

'I never showed you this,' I said.

He studied the picture, concentrating.

'Joe knew, even before ... that day. This painting

shows he knew something, he saw something.'

Liam turned towards me. 'This isn't Joe's work.'

'It is, Liam. Joe painted it the day I left him with Margaret … and Hemmings, the same time he painted the moonsets.' I watched him. 'I kept this away from you. I didn't want to upset you, I was protecting you.' The low tone of my laugh wasn't vindictive, wasn't accusing, wasn't saying, but I don't know why.

'Joe didn't paint this,' he said emphatically.

'Then who did?'

'Michael Hemmings, I'd guess.'

I studied the picture, and I knew Liam was right.

'And the moonsets?

'No, they were Joe's – full of hope, of an understanding that darkness occurs as succinctly and routinely as the lightness of day. Joe understood there's no light without its opposite.' He sat down on the chair, his face pale, grey, still looking at Hemmings' painting. 'Hemmings was talented. This is quite amazing, the depiction of his own pain … relating it to Margaret.'

The gnawing hunger returned. 'You see that? Or do you only see it in hindsight?'

He moved to touch my hand but stopped short. 'Probably retrospectively, Rachel. If I'd seen it as you'd done, before knowing anything, I wouldn't have seen the connection.'

Liam moved away from the table. 'I have something in the car for you.'

Five minutes later he returned with a package. He handed it to me and slowly I peeled away the brown paper; I think I knew what it would be.

Joe's sunset painting, mounted beautifully.

I looked up at him. Liam had written 'Falling Suns' at the top. 'That was Joe's title, wasn't it?'

He nodded. 'Three falling suns – a seven-year-old's metaphor for the three of us.'

'He didn't tell me that.'

'We talked "painting" the day after he brought it home. You remember you'd gone out for the day to meet –'

'Charlotte,' I finished for him. This was my cue to ask him about her. Was he still seeing her? But it was irrelevant.

He nodded. 'I looked after him. Dad/son bonding. I asked him what he would give it as a title. I planned to mount it for you, as a surprise.'

I watched my first love and a profound sadness reverberated inside the core of me, like the sound of a heavy bass in a small room. With Joe's death came a change in our destinies; and neither of us had control over the paths we had taken. Liam's heading one way; mine another. In a parallel life, with Joe alive, and with no affair, Liam would have mounted Joe's falling suns long ago. The canvas would be hung, pride of place, on one of the empty kitchen walls. Liam, Joe and I would be travelling the same road.

But this was not to be. It was never meant to be, as Mrs Xú had said.

'The suns are disappearing, though, aren't they?' I said, coming back to the present, feeling sad but not as empty, not raw.

'The sun doesn't fall but emerges on the other side – Joe knew that.'

'In another hemisphere,' we said together, repeating how Joe had described his painting.

'It's us who see the suns as falling,' Liam said. 'Children possess so much more clarity.' He caught his breath, or was it a quiet sob? 'It's just our grown-up perception, like our perception of death.'

I knew Joe would not visit me again. Like his suns, he had slipped not downwards, but to an equal and opposite place I could not yet see.

Liam turned to me. 'I'm so sorry for what I did.' I watched as his eyes moistened. 'If I could give up my own life to change what happened, Rachel, I would.' Looking at Joe's sunsets he carried on, 'He was my son, too.'

Liam left soon afterwards. I wouldn't see him again until Margaret's trial.

Jonathan returned and I smiled. I was sure he'd been somewhere near outside, waiting patiently for Liam to leave.

'Would you like to be alone?' Jonathan asked.

'If you're asking do I want you to leave, no, I don't. I like you being here.'

'I like being here, too.'

'You do?'

'I do.' I was about to tell him about Hemmings' painting but didn't want to fracture the peace that weaved through the air, hanging like a pleasing aroma around us. I smiled as I watched him align the tea, coffee and sugar pots on the counter top underneath the window that faced the garden, a garden that was well into spring thanks to the mild winter. 'Stop it,' I said.

'Sorry.'

'You like some real coffee?' I asked.

He nodded and I rummaged inside the cupboard. Finally, I found an unopened packet of ground coffee.

Jonathan took it, placing it on the counter, and then pulled me towards him. I rested my chin on his shoulder and stared through the window into the garden, at the den, locked up and unused. My eyes travelled to the Judas tree,

Joe's swing, and I remembered the happiness he'd given to me, and I hoped I'd given to him.

But I had to move forwards; I wanted to feel the joy without the desolation – something I could not achieve if I'd walked away from the park a murderess. Joe knew that.

I knew that.

I felt Jonathan's warm breath on my cheek and a tiny suggestion of toffee popcorn. I saw a fleeting sliver of petrol blue near the Judas tree; Jonathan kissed me.

And finally I allowed my mind to empty and rest.

# Epilogue

Sutton Coldfield Times
3rd March 2006

## Memorial Service for Liam Dune, Local Artist and Philanthropist 1958-2006

Born in 1958, Liam Dune overcame his disadvantaged background to win a place at the Royal College of Art. After graduation he declined offers of lucrative work in America, deciding to make his career and home in the town of his birth, Sutton Coldfield. He became a respected and commercially successful artist, selling work nationally and internationally. His paintings were heavily influenced by his roots, and the area in which he lived. Liam, together with his ex-wife, had lived in Sutton Coldfield since their marriage in 1986.

After the tragic death of his son in 2000, Liam Dune embraced Buddhism, and was a member at the Buddhist Centre in Birmingham, taking an active role in helping other parents such as himself who had lost a child through violence.

After tragically taking his own life on Christmas Eve 2005, Liam left both his parents: Graham and Dulcie Dune, and his older brother, Paul Dune. They attended his memorial service held on Friday at All Saints Church in Sutton Coldfield.

His ex-wife, Rachel Waters, was represented by her

husband Jonathan Waters. Other mourners included Charlotte Gayle, a family friend, and retired police officer, Thomas Gillespie.

———

Cross-legged on the bed in our new house in Wandsworth, I read the article about Liam's memorial service. His death had shocked me, sending me back to a place from which I'd only recently begun to emerge: a dark and confused space that still stopped me from sleeping, and often eating.

It was Jonathan who'd kept me stable, realigned me in my new life, and listened to me when, finally, I was able to talk about Margaret. I looked at the bedroom clock; he would be back soon. I allowed the love to drape over me as I thought of my new husband. He'd gone out to get the Sunday papers. After months of hard work his investigative piece on the corruption within Littleworth had been published. There was talk of a major award.

I touched the image of Liam in the newspaper and then looked at the photo of Joe, Liam and I that sat on the bedside cabinet. I had not smelt toffee popcorn since the day I returned home, and Jonathan had asked me to marry him.

The pain surrounding my memories of Joe was diminishing and finally, slowly, I was able to think of my son with joy rather than grief.

Joe wasn't alone, he would be with his dad, and I wiped away the tears that had been so long in coming.

I lay back and gathered myself, then, sitting up, I leant sideways and pulled a file from underneath the bed.

Margaret Hemmings.

Its contents included notes on the trial, and on her life. It also included details of Rampton – where she was being detained.

I began reading but hastily shoved it back under the bed when I heard Jonathan return.

Another day.

# Acknowledgements

There are so many people I have to thank for their help with this book and so here goes, and I apologise if there is anyone I have left out – it is unintentional.

Paul Bacon: mental health tribunal judge and solicitor who through numerous drafts gave his time so generously and patiently to ensure the facts in this novel are as correct as they possibly can be.

My thanks to the actress, Mandana Jones, who talked to me for several hours explaining in detail about method acting.

My writer friends who, without complaint, always read what I had to send them. Laura Wilkinson has been an especially excellent beta reader and sounding board throughout my journey. Every writer needs a mate like Laura.

Essie Fox, a great writer and wonderful mentor, and the most supportive friend a new writer could possibly have.

Thank you also to David Evans – a patient beta reader, and friend. His input and help has been invaluable.

To Caroline Green and Emma Haughton for being such insightful and patient readers.

To my lovely friend Michelle Flood who never once doubted that I could write a novel. And to my mates Tracey Dolan and Joanna Wilson, whose initial encouragement started me off on this rollercoaster writing journey.

Thank you to my mum and dad who always told me I could do anything I wanted to do.

To Gillian Stern, whose discerning and constructive criticism not only helped make this novel better, but helped shape my future writing too.

To Debz Hobbs-Wyatt, who published my very first short story, and Melanie Gow who published my first article. To Emma Darwin who is so generous and unselfish in sharing her vast knowledge. To Sarah Wagstaffe who reads my stuff and listens to my moans.

Sally Spedding, who from the beginning has never wavered in her optimistic conviction that one day I would become a published novelist.

To Alex Marwood who is so giving with her time and advice.

To my friends in The Lounge, Book Frisbees, and all on Facebook – what would I do without you all?

To my agent, Ger Nichol, who is calm, delightful and unswerving in her optimism about my work.

My thanks to Rebecca Lloyd, my patient and talented editor, and to all the team at Accent Press, including Bethan James, Anne Porter and Emily Tutton.

Lastly, for Steve and Rhiannon who are without doubt the best husband and daughter an aspiring novelist could wish for. Thank you for putting up with me.

I love you both, more than the universe.

**PAUL BURSTON**

# THE BLACK PATH

Helen has been holding out for a hero all her life.

Her father was a hero – but he was murdered when she was ten. Her husband is a hero – but he's thousands of miles away, fighting a war people say will never be won.

Then one night on the troubled streets of her home town, Helen is rescued from a fight by a woman who will change her life forever. Siân is everything Helen isn't – confident, glamorous, fearless. But there's something else about her – a connection that cements their friendship and makes Helen question everything she's ever known.

And when her husband returns home, altered in a way she can't understand, she is forced to draw on an inner strength she never knew she had. As bitter truths are uncovered, Helen must finally face her fears and the one place which has haunted her since childhood – the Black Path.

# FERGUS O'CONNELL

# THE PARADISE GHETTO

In 1944 two young Dutch women, Julia and Suzanne, are deported to the German concentration camp for so-called 'privileged' Jews at Theresienstadt. As an antidote to their appalling conditions they begin to write a novel.

At first their novel is just an escape – an imaginary world into which they can withdraw and find comfort – but as their story unfolds it becomes the way they communicate their feelings to each other and, ultimately, confront their own demons.

They become convinced that the war will end when they finish their story. But it is the frenzied last year of the Final Solution. As the darkness gathers around them, they find themselves in a race not just to finish the novel but to somehow find a means of survival.

*The Paradise Ghetto* is the story of two people whose lives are drawn together in unimaginable circumstances, and a reflection on the part books play in our lives.

For more information about
**J. A. Corrigan**

and other **Accent Press** titles

please visit

**www.accentpress.co.uk**